-12,198-

013a   Oliphant, Robert

A piano for Mrs. Cimino

-12,198--

013a   Oliphant, Robert

AUTHOR

Piano for Mrs. Cimino

TITLE

DATE LOANED	BORROWER'S NAME	DATE RETURNED
9/15	L. Weiler	
10/9	A. Karlstad	
6/16	M. Hjelmstad	

A Piano for Mrs. Cimino

by Robert Oliphant

PRENTICE-HALL, INC., Englewood Cliffs, New Jersey

The author wishes to express his gratitude to Clyde Taylor and Oscar Collier for their encouragement, professional guidance, and wise counsel. For her understanding, her support, her good judgment, and her day-after-day cheerful company, the author is deeply indebted to his wife, Jane.

The author wishes to thank the following for permission to reprint material used in this book:

Little, Brown and Company for the quotation from *Human Sexual Inadequacy* by William H. Masters and Virginia E. Johnson, Boston, 1970

C. V. Mosby Co. for the quotation from *Aging and Mental Health*, ed. 2, Robert N. Butler and Myrna I. Lewis, St. Louis, 1977

The characters and institutions in this book are fictitious. No resemblance to actual persons, living or dead, is intended. Nor is any resemblance intended to any institution presently in operation or in operation at some point in the past.

Book Designer: Linda Huber
Art Director: Hal Siegel

A Piano for Mrs. Cimino
by Robert Oliphant

Address inquiries to Prentice-Hall, Inc., Englewood Cliffs, N.J. 07632
Printed in the United States of America
Prentice-Hall International, Inc., London
Prentice-Hall of Australia, Pty. Ltd., Sydney
Prentice-Hall of Canada, Ltd., Toronto
Prentice-Hall of India Private Ltd., New Delhi
Prentice-Hall of Japan, Inc., Tokyo
Prentice-Hall of Southeast Asia Pte. Ltd., Singapore
Whitehall Books Limited, Wellington, New Zealand
10 9 8 7 6 5 4 3 2 1

Library of Congress Cataloging in Publication Data

Oliphant, Robert
    A piano for Mrs. Cimino.
    I. Title.
P74.0465Pi [PS3565.L455] 813'.54 80-10776
ISBN 0-13-851568-9

For Dorothy, Stella, Homer, and Vance

Part 1

The reversible brain syndrome remains a frequently undiagnosed illness, more so in the United States than in some other countries, for example, England. The concept first began appearing in the literature in the 1930s, and in a recent study of a large municipal hospital, 13% of the patients were found to have reversible brain syndromes, while 33% exhibited mixed reversible and chronic disorders.

ROBERT N. BUTLER AND MYRNA I. LEWIS
Aging and Mental Health

Monday, March 22, 1976, 1:15 P.M.

It was not until the ambulance pulled out of her driveway that Mrs. Cimino began to scream. Perhaps it was the sudden bite of the tires into the gravel that set her off. Or it might have been the way she was strapped into the cot: supine, blanketed, unable to see anything more than a gray blur of bare trees through the rear window.

"There, there," said a voice above her. "No one's going to hurt you."

Exactly what a kidnapper would say, she thought to herself. She paused for breath. There was a sharp left turn. A slanting beam of sunlight burned its way into her right eye. Blending pain and anger, she screamed even louder, echoing the same cry of injured violation with which she had first entered the world seventy-six years before.

Noting her distress, the ambulance attendant reached over her and pulled the window shade down. Still screaming, she caught sight of a small blue anchor tattooed on his inside right forearm. It was enough to nudge her into silence for a moment, and from silence into speech.

"It's a mistake," she whimpered. "A terrible mistake."

"Mistake?" The voice over on her left was soft, casual, tinged with amusement. "You're Mrs. Esther Cimino, aren't you?"

"I think so." She closed her faded blue eyes, tightening them in order to concentrate better. "But it's still a mistake. I'm too poor to pay you any ransom."

"We don't want any ransom." The attendant, a tall, blond young man, braced himself as his partner suddenly reduced speed. "We just want to help you."

"No!" She opened her eyes, looked over at him, and shook her head violently, as though to dislodge the idea from her mind. "You don't want me. I'm too old for that."

"Too old for what?" The attendant leaned over toward her.

"Too old to be shipped off to Argentina," she moaned, just on the verge of another scream.

"Argentina?" The attendant's voice was coming from down by

3

her feet. "What's in Argentina?" She could hear faint laughter as he tightened the straps down at the foot of the cot.

"Bad men," said Mrs. Cimino. "Terrible men." She shuddered and began to sob.

"Is that so?" said the voice, mockingly serious. "Then we won't go to Argentina."

"Argentina, Argentina, Argentina." Still sobbing, she continued to mutter the name: softly, rhythmically, so that its meaning was dissolved into a sequence of pulsing syllables.

"No Argentina for us, not this trip." The voice, cheerful and brisk, was back up beside her now. "Just a short ride over to Central Hospital."

"Central Argentina?"

"Central Hospital," said the voice, "Central *Hospital!*"

"Capital?" Mrs. Cimino closed her eyes again. "The capital is Buenos Aires." She opened them and tried to turn more to her left. "But I don't want to go there. It's bad."

"It's *not* bad," said the attendant's voice, almost defensive. "It's good, good, good. It's a very good hospital."

"There are no hospitals in Argentina," said Mrs. Cimino firmly. "Only hotels."

The attendant grunted, partly from irritation, partly from a desire to avoid further meaningless talk. He bent over her and straightened the blanket again, adjusting the straps that pinned her arms down. He forced himself to smile at her.

Her face, slightly turned toward him, was full, oval, with soft white down barely visible between the small nose and generous upper lip. Below the upper lip, the oval seemed to collapse into a soft jaw, lacking the support of dentures. With the wispy gray hair on top, the face looked very much like a balloon badly shrunken and carrying a little too much weight on top of it.

No longer screaming, the face stared coldly at him, small nose wrinkled in clear distaste. The attendant could feel the body cringe at his touch. So he gave the restraining straps an extra pull. Satisfied that matters were secure, he sat back quietly and began to think dark thoughts.

Old ones! They were bad news, nearly all of them. Screamers, cursers, scratchers, spitters: They were like aged half-wild cats fighting off the animal shelter people. Most of the neighbors were happy to see them picked up and carried off.

With some dismay he noticed that the face had managed to turn itself sideways: It was looking directly at him, a knowing slyness in its faded blue eyes.

"The store," it said. "Don't you think we should stop off at the store?"

"We can do that later," said the attendant. "Right now we want to get you to the hospital as soon as we can."

"But I can't afford it." The sobs started to set in again. "I just can't afford it. I'm too poor. You know that." The faded blue eyes closed him out and the wispy-haired head turned away in disgust.

Poor! The attendant smiled grimly. It was a word that went well with his own situation: twenty-two years old, still sharing a two-bedroom apartment with his mother, and barely managing his two-hundred-dollar monthly payment on the new Dodge. Hamburgers on the job, TV dinners at home, while Ma staggered from one waitress job to another and whined about sore feet.

Jobs! They were all bad, especially this one. The security-guard hours had been worse, but the uniform had been nicer, almost like being a real policeman. And there had been more respect: You didn't have to sit back with a dumb smile on your face while mean old ladies waved their big diamond rings at you and cried, "Poor, poor!"

There was nothing poor about the neighborhood they had just left. Large, two-story stone houses set back fifty feet or more from the street. Neatly trimmed lawns, tall hedges, and gardens with freshly turned earth. Late-model Buicks and Oldsmobiles in the driveways. People in neighborhoods like that always had money to pay for round-the-clock nursing care.

And money for jewelry, like the old woman's diamond ring. He had noticed it right away: a large stone, circled with smaller chips, hanging loosely and slightly askew on its shrunken perch. Hysterical or not, the nurse should have taken it off and put it away for safekeeping. Expensive rings had a way of getting lost in big hospitals like Minneapolis Central.

Thoughtful, eyes narrowed, he looked over at her.

Mrs. Cimino was quite still, hands limp, eyes shut. She was

trying her best to blot out her careening nightmare with a child-hood dream: a dream of summers spent on her uncle's farm in up-state New York. She could feel someone hovering over her head, but her eyes remained shut as the mind behind them forced its way back to fields of buckwheat and pastured dairy cattle.

It was only when the strong fingers closed upon the defenseless flesh of her right shoulder that she opened her eyes and began to scream. Struggling against his deep, sustained pinch, she gave voice to great, gusty yowls. And she fought, going so far as to snap toothless gums at his hand and arm. Wholly engaged, caught up in the heat of battle, she took no notice of the smooth, gentle tug at the third finger of her left hand.

"There, there," went the voice above her. "There, there." Throughout the attack it continued to croon reassurance.

She tried to shake the words out of her awareness. She tried to drown them out with her screams. But the pain—sharp, insistent—urged a high-pitched whimper upon her. And after that, spasms of heavy breathing.

"There, there. Everything's going to be all right."

She paused for a great, strengthening gulp of air, leaving a big empty space, much as a baby shapes its ominous stillness before the next fierce bellow.

"But it's all right now." Farther away from her small, tensed body, the voice seemed to seize up the empty space, filling it with a slow, bland stream of words. "It won't be long, it won't be long, it won't be long."

Pain diminishing, she strained to make sense out of what she was hearing.

"Wrong?" she said. "Is something wrong at the store?"

"Everything's fine," said the voice. "I really mean it."

"Argentina?" Again she did her best to force meaning upon the small syllables that hovered on the edge of her ear.

There was another very sharp right turn: Had it not been for the straps, she would have been thrown violently against the left side of the ambulance.

"We'll be there soon," continued the voice. "Everything's going to be all right."

When the ambulance stopped, the attendant quickly unbolted the cot and waited for his partner to open up the rear door. In one swift, graceful team effort, they slid Mrs. Cimino out and wheeled

6

her into the admitting area. There two large black men in white uniforms came up and inspected their delivery, noting with approval that the false teeth had been removed as a precaution against being bitten. The black men transferred Mrs. Cimino to a waiting gurney and took her away.

Monday, March 22, 5:30 P.M.

"Mother's in the hospital again," said Harold Cimino, looking down at his wife. He had taken his brother's phone call in their oak-paneled bar, pausing only to prepare another pitcher of vermouth-misted gin. Pitcher in hand, he had come back to the sun porch.

"Another fall?" Gloria held out her glass.

"No," said Harold. He filled her glass and sat down across from her. "They're not sure what the problem is."

He took a sip from his own drink, then set it down on a black onyx coffee table standing between them like a small lake. He sat back, trying to gauge the mellowness of Gloria's mood. Ever since receiving a handsome inheritance from her father's estate, she had been filled with immense respect for her own opinions and desires. And she had always been difficult.

"But it could be serious," he continued. "Very serious."

"That's too bad," said Gloria.

"George is pretty upset," said Harold.

"What's he doing about it?" said Gloria.

"He has a new doctor working with her." Harold nodded pleasantly, feeling that he was in reasonable control of the conversation. He was a short, stocky man who kept fit playing tennis and golf. His complexion was fair, his hair light brown, and he made sixty-five thousand dollars a year as vice-president of a farm equipment company. For a forty-three-year-old man, he played a surprisingly good game of tennis, largely because of fierce concentration on the quality of his first return.

"It's about time," said Gloria. "That Dr. Petersen she was going to is older than she is."

7

"The new one is supposed to be one of the best neurologists in Minneapolis," said Harold. "He has her in Minneapolis Central."

"Neurologist?" Gloria sipped her drink and considered the matter. "Do they think it's a brain problem?"

"Dr. Mitchell thinks it might be a brain tumor that's making her confused." Harold's blue eyes were shrewd and steady under his heavy eyebrows, somewhat lighter in color than his hair. His lower jaw was square, almost heavy, going well with the thick neck and broad back packed with muscle. Most of the muscle had been laid down in his college football days, but some of it bore witness to the earnestness of his struggle against paunchiness and flab. He took pride in the fact that Gloria had never been able to goad him into violence.

"Are they going to operate?" said Gloria. She put her glass down on the black onyx table and sat back, relaxed, receptive.

"They have to do tests first," said Harold. "They'll probably know tomorrow or the day after that."

"I suppose George wants you to come up." Gloria looked out the window to her right, much as though her gaze was intended to carry a strong message of disapproval from Des Moines, Iowa, to Minneapolis, Minnesota.

"He wanted me to fly up tonight," said Harold. "But I told him I couldn't get away until tomorrow afternoon." He smiled cheerfully and drew his wife's glass over for a small refill. "I'll phone him in the morning."

"What about the executive committee meeting?"

"I'll have to miss it." Harold shrugged, still with an athlete's grace, in a manner designed to indicate complete control of the By-zantine world in which he labored.

"The East Coast people are going to be there, aren't they?"

Harold shrugged again. Gloria shook her head. She picked up her drink and began to rub the outside of the glass with her finger, as though to trace in the moisture the lineaments of some obscure moral flaw in her husband's behavior.

She was forty-one years old: slender, well-groomed. Her hair, intricately curled, had a reddish tinge to it that served to draw attention away from her pale green eyes. The body underneath her white pleated skirt and blue velour blouse had been kept in good repair with tennis, swimming, massage, and numerous special ointments. From a distance she might have passed as a stringy older sister of their two sons, Kevin and Patrick, both now safely away at college. But her face, lined and leathered by twenty years of sun, wind, and casual drinking, offered secure testimony to her age and position.

"That cataract operation was a mistake." Harold took a good pull of vermouth-misted gin and set his glass down with modest force, as though calling a sales meeting to order. "They had no business doing both eyes together." He got up and walked over to the window. "Cooped up in darkness like that, it's no wonder she fell and wrenched her back."

"What's that have to do with a brain tumor?" Gloria raised her voice a little. Some of her consonants were blurring.

"I don't know," said Harold. "I'm not a doctor." An edge was beginning to creep into his clear, professionally pleasant voice. "But I know she had no business being in that big house alone, especially in bad weather."

"That's where she wanted to be," said Gloria. "She seemed just fine to me when we went up for Christmas." She nodded her head in emphatic support of herself. "Just fine."

"She should have sold that store when Dad died." Harold stared reflectively toward the lights of the country club. "And she should have sold the house." He turned back to his wife. "I told them that, but they wouldn't listen to me."

"She didn't want to," said Gloria. "George was still married to Alice then." She contemplated her glass sadly, as though its emptiness symbolized her sister-in-law's recent misfortune. "And those three girls were in and out of Elm Street all the time."

"At least she could have sold the music store and the building," said Harold. Again he came over and filled his wife's glass halfway. "Anyone could see it was getting to be too much for her." Watching her closely, he sat down.

"But she didn't *want* to," said Gloria, her voice growing shriller as she reiterated her central theme. "And she certainly didn't want to put the proceeds into that warehouse scheme of yours."

"She was wrong," said Harold.

"Everybody has a right to be wrong," said Gloria. She raised her glass as though to toast the profundity of her statement. "Even you, dear heart."

"There's nothing wrong with wanting to have your own business," said Harold patiently. "It's a simple matter of understanding how the tax structure of this country works."

"The only thing I understand is that you never give up," said Gloria. From across the black onyx table she looked at her husband with a knowing glint in her eye. "You're still determined to have that warehouse business, even if it means using up the money I got from Father."

"It's not the money, dear." Harold shook his head firmly. "It's your lack of confidence in me." His voice was gentle, appealing, like the soft tones of an adolescent pleading for the keys to the family Lincoln.

"But I have plenty of confidence in you," said Gloria. "Loads of confidence, heaps!" She shook her head violently as though to force away the merest suggestion of any disloyalty. "Everyone says you have a good chance of becoming executive vice-president."

"I'd still be working for someone else," said Harold.

"But you would *be* somebody." Gloria looked out through the clear glass on her right, populating the deepening twilight with hosts of banners and accolades. "You might even be one of the most important men in Des Moines." The reverence in her voice blurred her *t*'s into humming *d*'s.

"Just like Daddy used to be?" Harold's shrewd blue eyes—bland, quizzical—looked straight at her.

"That's not fair," wailed Gloria. "You're mean, Harold Cimino, real lowdown mean." Still holding her drink, she rose to her feet, moving with slow dignity to the door. "My father . . ."

". . . one of the most important men in this great city," interjected Harold, as though the phrase were liturgically obligatory.

"That's not the point," said Gloria, still blurring her *t*'s. "My father liked you. He liked you a lot. And he certainly helped you a lot."

"So why doesn't his daughter trust me?" There was a faint smile on Harold's strong, square face.

"Why should I?" Overcome by the enormity of the suggestion, Gloria fell slightly sideways. It was her right hand that sought and found support from the doorpost.

"Because I'm your husband," said Harold. Again his tone was patient, as though he were an accountant translating important tax implications to a dear and loyal client. Even though the client

10

might grow irritated, it was important to retain composure and control.

"You are now," said Gloria, not without sadness. She looked away from him and out through the clear glass again. From across the valley she could see the lights of the country club.

"What's that supposed to mean?" Harold's voice was sharp, crackling. His blue eyes blazed a little.

"It means I have to be careful." Gloria looked down at the knotted muscles of her brown legs as though they might suddenly unravel and collapse. "Look at that brother of yours." With grim conviction she looked back at her husband.

"What's George have to do with it?" For Harold the focus of the discussion was becoming as blurred as his wife's speech.

"Running off with a young girl like that." Gloria took another sip of her drink as though to console herself. "Marrying her, too." She looked at Harold appraisingly. "With all that hot Italian blood, maybe it runs in the family." She gave a short laugh, amost a giggle, and relinquished the support of the doorpost long enough to wiggle an accusing finger. "Hot Italian blood!"

Harold was quiet for a moment. George's affair, divorce, and remarriage had been worse than immoral: It had been unpredictable. Solid fifty-one-year-old George! Handy George, churchgoing George! Build-a-giant-cabin-at-the-lake George! They had all thought him safely chained to his job with the state of Minnesota and to his thrifty, sensible wife. And they had all seen him as properly dutiful: to his wife, to his three daughters, to his widowed mother living nearby.

Yet George had somehow broken out and flown madly off: running amok like King Kong, dancing Greek folk dances, and marrying Lisa, a twenty-five-year-old secretary in the department of bridge maintenance. With his mother's recent flight into confusion following close behind, it was hard not to wonder whether family madness would stay in the family—like an heirloom cedar chest or a favorite diamond ring: always there, working its way silently from generation to generation like a furious little gopher drilling its way into the soft, sweet earth, there to squat and suck the green out from the fragile grass above.

"A lot of that was Alice's fault," said Harold. "If she had been a better wife, George would have been a better husband." He looked up at her, shrewd blue eyes carefully neutral.

11

"Beautiful!" said Gloria. "That's very profound." She swirled her drink and gazed thoughtfully at its small waves. "And it's true, too." With speech a little crisper, she looked directly at her husband. "Alice should have kept track of things better—especially the money."

"Who knows?" Harold shrugged the parallel away. "But I can't understand why a young girl like Lisa should be so threatening to you."

"Threatening!" Gloria shook her head incredulously. "Your brother's wife doesn't threaten me at all." Suddenly confident, she permanently relinquished support of the doorpost. "Nothing threatens me—not as long as I have something to say about what goes on around here." Gauging the distance, she looked in toward the kitchen. "I think I'd better see how Juanita's coming with dinner."

Harold forced a smile of approving affection to his face. Gloria slowly headed for the kitchen, walking very erect. There was the sound of a small thump from the dining room. But the absence of any serious clatter reassured Harold: It was clear that his wife would make it into the kitchen safely.

Even the business about the brain tumor was reassuring. Operations like that had a strong, dramatic simplicity to them: Either they were successful, or they were not. If she recovered, his mother would undoubtedly be willing to follow his earlier sage advice. If she did not pull through, the end would be swift and clean.

Harold liked clarity. Given his mother's age, he had been prepared to deal with physical illness when it came: a stroke, a heart attack, a tumor, even a long drift downward sustained by probing tools and miles of plastic tubing. Cruel as these assaults were, they came as natural gusty changes in their proper season. And they could be endured in a warm public glow of sympathy and understanding. As it had been with the husband, so it would be with the wife—or so they had all assumed.

But the present state of affairs was fuzzy: It had sneaked up on them after the double cataract operation in January. The recuperation had been slow, and her balance had been poor, and she had fallen, and they had taken her back to Presbyterian Hospital. In low spirits, slightly confused, she had been sent back to Elm Street with round-the-clock nursing care and a variety of soothing medications. Despite this help, she had begun to wing out over some strange private sea of fear and trembling: She had insisted that she was in a hotel, and she had accused the practical nurses of poisoning and theft, and the practical nurses—an admitted progression of reformed alcoholics and bumblers—had simply given up in despair.

"So you're going up there, are you?" Gloria's pale green eyes were suddenly back in the room again.

"It's a crisis situation, dear."

"You've got plenty of . . ." She paused to remember the appropriate plural form. "You've got lots of those things down here." Glass in hand, she sat down, clearly intent upon bringing matters into businesslike focus. "And you certainly can't spend all of your time running up to Minneapolis."

"When Mother recovers, we can solve that problem very easily," smiled Harold. In difficult moments he always liked to raise the prospect of having his mother come down to live with them.

"We've been through all that," said Gloria. "It wouldn't work." She shook her head mournfully. "It just wouldn't work."

"How can you be so sure?" With a half smile Harold looked directly at her.

"I'm sure," said Gloria. "She doesn't know anybody down here." She put her drink down on the black onyx table with an air of finality. "I'd have to spend all my time with her."

"But I'd be here." Harold's voice was again patient, understanding.

"Here!" Gloria gestured around her capaciously. "You're never here. With you, it's either the office, the plant, or a business trip."

"We could solve that problem too."

"What problem?"

"The problem of my long absences from our home," said Harold urbanely. "I've been thinking about it lately." His tone grew serious, reproving. "We can't have it both ways, you know."

"What are you talking about?" Suddenly suspicious, Gloria looked darkly at him.

"I mean you can't expect me to work seventy hours a week trying to become executive vice-president and also expect me to spend a lot of time around the house." Harold stretched forth his hands, looking at each of them as though a choice were clear and inevitable.

"You've never complained before," said Gloria, puzzled yet sure of her ground. "You like being a big man."

"I'm not complaining," said Harold smoothly. "You're the one who's complaining. And it's your happiness I'm thinking of."

"You are?" Gloria blinked her pale green eyes several times, as though some odd, unfamiliar bug had flow in from outside.

"It I had my own company, I would have much more control of things." His smile opened up a pleasant vista for the two of them. "So I would have much more time to spend with you."

"Damnit!" wailed Gloria. "You never give up." She shook her head and keened wordlessly. "We were talking about your mother—I know we were." She tapped on the black onyx table as though to summon the topic back. "And somehow you work your way back to that damn warehouse business of yours!" Frustrated, incredulous, she stared at him in half-respectful wonder.

Tuesday, March 23, 6:00 P.M.

"It might be better if we went out for dinner," said Mrs. Cimino. She had worked her body free of the covers.

"No," said the tall, sharp-faced nurse. "You have to stay here for a while."

"Goddamn!" said Mrs. O'Hara, peering out from behind a frieze of side-rail bars and plastic tubing. A large freckle-faced woman with iron-gray hair, she had been watching Mrs. Cimino from her bed by the door.

"Can't you take these things off me?" said Mrs. Cimino to the nurse. She gestured with her head toward the two white straps attached to her wrists. Like leashes collaring a pair of willful puppies, the straps permitted the hands to move within reasonable bounds, bringing them up short only when they ventured too far away.

"No, dear," said the nurse. "The doctor wants you to wear the posies so you won't hurt yourself." She bent over and rearranged Mrs. Cimino's smock. Twisted around as it was, it exposed her upper torso and thighs.

The thighs were not large. But they were ample enough to fit well with the rest of Mrs. Cimino's small, compact frame. Just a little over five feet, built close to the ground, she had withstood the pull of gravity well: Her calves were firm, and the flesh of her upper arms did not sag noticeably. With the exception of the bruise on her right shoulder, her skin was clear, unblotched, and unveined.

But she was fleshy. And her generous bosom posed a major problem. Unrestrained, free from the support of a bra, her two large breasts plunged heavily downward: Immediately under them there were marks of chafing.

"Goddamn!" said Mrs. O'Hara again, hearkening to the high, insistent drill of an ambulance siren pulling in below them. She looked blankly past Mrs. Cimino to the window. Displeased, she shook her head. It was the only part of her that could move, so she did not need posies on her wrists.

"The police?" said Mrs. Cimino, allowing the tall, sharp face to bend over her and crank the bed up to a sitting position.

"I don't think so," said the nurse. "Isn't that more comfortable?"

Mrs. Cimino nodded, smiling happily to herself at the thought of a possible rescue. Her left hand reached over toward the posie on her right wrist.

"Would you like some juice?"

"Yes, loose all the way." Mrs. Cimino held up her manacled wrists as far as they would go.

"Juice, *juice!*" The sharp face veered suddenly over toward her, the voice cutting through her. "Would you like some juice to drink?"

"Some juice to drink." Mrs. Cimino's faded blue eyes were speculative, careful. "Do you think it's a good idea?"

"Yes," came the reply. "With all the tests you've had, you need plently of fluids."

"Let's have some juice, then," said Mrs. Cimino. She smiled over at Mrs. O'Hara. Mrs. O'Hara's green eyes narrowed and a soft gurgle worked its way up from somewhere down in her throat.

Mrs. Cimino continued to smile at Mrs. O'Hara as the nurse left the room. A minute later the nurse was back. She had a small yellow plastic container in her hand. There was a straw sticking out of it. Mrs. Cimino took the straw between her lips. She sipped thoughtfully for a while.

"Isn't that better?"

"Yes, much better," said Mrs. Cimino. "Thank you, my dear." She sighed and let her head fall back against the pillow.

The nurse put the plastic container on a stand near Mrs. Cimino's bed, then went over to busy herself with Mrs. O'Hara.

"Goddamn!" Mrs. O'Hara was staring at the doorway with soft, green malevolence.

Mrs. Cimino followed her gaze. There were two large blurs standing in the doorway. But they were not blue blurs. So they were probably not policemen. As the blurs came closer, Mrs. Cimino saw that one was a short, stocky man with heavy eyebrows The other was taller, dark-haired, with long sideburns.

It was a shame these men were not policemen. But they seemed respectable. The tall, dark one had a familiar look to him, as though he might be running for city council. That might account for the slightly artificial smile on his somber face.

"Are you Democrats?" said Mrs. Cimino, looking sharply down at the two men by the foot of her bed.

"Not lately," said the short, stocky man with heavy eyebrows. He smiled and came up to her. "We're Ciminos."

"So am I," said Mrs. Cimino, feeling that her words were not coming out quite right. "And how long have you been staying at this hotel?"

"We're here to visit you, Mother," said the tall, dark man with sideburns. He came up to the other side of her head. Recognizing the voice, she turned toward him with great pleasure.

"Oh, Harold!" she said, faded blue eyes misting slightly. "I'm so glad you were able to come."

"George," said the tall, dark man. "I'm George." He nodded in the direction of the stroking that was being applied to her left hand. "That's Harold over there."

Mrs. Cimino turned her head and inspected the short, stocky man. He was still smiling. She turned back to her right and looked up at the tall, dark man. With his sideburns, he reminded her of Uncle Oscar.

"Can't you get them to take these things off me?" She held up her wrists in a gesture of supplication.

"I'll ask the nurse," said the tall, dark man. He looked over at Mrs. O'Hara's bed, where the nurse was now checking the intricate array of plumbing fixtures.

16

"Damn!" said Mrs. O'Hara. "Damn, damn, damn." Eyes closed, she was murmuring softly as the nurse ministered to her. The inert mound underneath the light-blue blanket offered no resistance as various pouches and bottles were replaced.

"Harold came up from Des Moines to see you," continued the tall, dark man, still looking thoughtfully at Mrs. O'Hara's bed. Tasks finished, the nurse smiled thinly at the three of them and left the room.

"All the way from Des Moines!" Mrs. Cimino glowed with pleasure and turned back again to the short, stocky man. "Oh, Harold, that's such a long trip for you."

"I wanted to see how you were coming along." The short, stocky many embraced her warmly, letting his cheek remain close against hers.

"I wish you could stay longer, Harold." She paused, then looked brightly at the two of them. "Why don't we all go downstairs for dinner? Her eyes were now alive with good humor. "My treat this time."

"They'll be bringing your dinner up here," said the tall, dark man.

Mrs. Cimino began to relax and enjoy her company. The tall one was George, and the shorter one was Harold. It had always been that way. She directed her attention back to the shorter one: He was still smiling, eyes looking straight at her.

"Harold, you're getting gray," she said. She turned back to the tall one. "Don't you think so, George?"

"Maybe a little here and there." came the reply. The tall one's voice was in motion, coming round the foot of the bed. With the short, stocky one in a chair beside her, the tall one's head appeared to grow out of the one below it, like a dark, somber helmet put on for some obscure ceremonial purpose.

"How are you feeling?" said the lower head, the one with heavy eyebrows.

"How am I feeling?" Mrs. Cimino tried to flex her still-tender back muscles. "Not bad," she smiled. She looked down at her toes and wiggled them cautiously. "No big aches or pains, as far as I can tell."

"That's good," said the upper head, the one with the long dark sideburns that reminded her of Uncle Oscar.

"Very good," said the head with heavy eyebrows.

Mrs. Cimino smiled, basking in their warm approval.

"You know me," she said, giving a little laugh. "I've never been much for aches and pains." She looked down at her compact, well-fleshed body with modest satisfaction. It still seemed to work well for her.

"So you're feeling pretty good, are you?" said the lower head, the one with the heavy eyebrows. His blue eyes seemed intent, probing.

"Everything's fine," said Mrs. Cimino. "Except for my eyes and the fact I don't hear very well."

"Glasses," said the heavy eyebrows. His voice was clipped, his manner peremptory. "They must still be at the house along with her other things."

"I'll have Karen bring them over," said the head with the sideburns.

"Glasses?" said Mrs. Cimino. She sighed. "Those new ones are such a nuisance, and so are those hearing-aid things." She stretched and sighed again. "I'd be better off if I had a new head." She gave an embarrassed little laugh.

"There's nothing wrong with the head you have," said the heavy eyebrows.

"It doesn't seem to be working very well," sighed Mrs. Cimino. Her eyes were moist.

"They have good doctors here," said the heavy eyebrows firmly. "And they're going to help you."

"Boys, boys!" Mrs. Cimino struggled to regain her poise and take charge of the meeting. "You've always been so sweet. And I've always been proud of you."

"We've been proud of you, Mother," said the heavy eyebrows.

"Very proud," said the long, dark sideburns.

"Well, boys—George, Harold—here I am." Mrs. Cimino looked over at Mrs. O'Hara and shook her head. "And I've made a lot of mistakes, no doubt about that." She looked at them as though pleading for forgiveness.

"We all make mistakes," said the heavy eyebrows.

"But it's still not right," said Mrs. Cimino. "It's my body, and I should have more say about what's going on here." She looked down at her manacled wrists and shook her head in strong disapproval.

"Everything's going to be fine," said the heavy eyebrows, voice crisp with authority.

"Do you think so?" Mrs. Cimino looked at them anxiously.

Both of the heads nodded forcefully, so she immediately brightened at the prospect of good times to come.

"Wonderful!" she said. Had it not been for the posies, she would have clapped her hands with joy. "We'll all go out to Uncle Oscar's. If Emily brings her mandolin, the three of us will sing for you."

The heads stopped their nodding, puzzlement upon them. It was the upper head, the one with sideburns, who managed the first smile.

"You always had a lovely voice, Mother." The voice was deep, reflective.

"Do you think so?" She smiled shyly. "I've never been much for singing solos, but Rose and I always did pretty well with our harmony parts."

"Uncle Oscar had a nice farm, didn't he?" said the heavy eyebrows.

"Most farms are nice." Mrs. Cimino's voice crackled with conviction. "They're a lot better than those big cities."

"Big cities?" laughed the heavy eyebrows. "What's wrong with our big cities?"

Mrs. Cimino paused, suddenly cautious. She looked over at Mrs. O'Hara, who had been quietly following the proceedings. Deciding to risk a small confidence, she beckoned the two heads closer and lowered her voice.

"Bad men," she said. "Terrible men." She lowered her voice to a whisper and looked furtively round. "No place for a young girl." Her gaze came back to her ring finger: She shook her head sadly.

"Don't worry, Mother." It was the head with sideburns, now detached from the head with heavy eyebrows. It was speaking to her from down by the foot of the bed. "Everything's going to be all right. Just you wait and see."

"Sí, sí, señor." laughed Mrs. Cimino. Her faded blue eyes remained fearful.

Her fearfulness was not assuaged by the sound of a great clatter out in the corridor, as the tall, sharp-faced nurse came up and rolled a gray metal cart in by her bed. Nor did the farewell hugs and kisses restore her spirits, as the two men blurred their way out of the room. But she tried to smile engagingly at the sharp face hovering over her.

The two men left the room quickly, followed by Mrs. O'Hara's sternly green, unwinking stare.

They walked together in silence down to the nurses station. There the tall, dark man with the long sideburns paused to address a few questions to the head nurse on duty. The short, stocky man walked over to a nearby alcove. There was a sofa in the alcove and a large plate-glass window that looked out over the city.

The short, stocky man gazed out the window, shrewd blue eyes narrowed, as though trying to pierce through the twilight and make out the shape that had crept into his mother's small gray kindly head. Sitting there, it was now twisting the mind into strange, unfamiliar directions, taking it back to far-off times and people like Uncle Oscar, Emily, and Rose. A quick attack was clearly called for.

He wiped his eyes for a moment. It was the first time he had ever seen his mother without her false teeth.

From behind him a hand came up and found a resting place on his shoulder. He turned and looked gratefully at his brother's long, somber face. The stocky man allowed himself to sigh and clear his throat a couple of times. Then he nodded, and the two of them walked over to the elevator, waiting to be boxed and carried down to the hospital lobby.

As the elevator took them down, the stocky man watched the floors unroll before him. And he wondered which of them held the operating room in which the neurosurgeon's knife would do its work, coming cleanly in to cut the alien creature out, storing it in a tiny jar somewhere for study and display.

By the time they reached the ground floor the short, stocky man had recovered his confidence. So he nodded encouragingly and stepped aside, letting his brother lead the way.

Tuesday, March 23, 9:30 P.M.

"Your father called." Alice Cimino stood in the middle of her spotless kitchen floor waiting for Karen to close the door.

"What's happening with Grandmother?" Karen closed the door, sat down at the kitchen table, and tossed her green cloth book bag on the floor beside her. Gracelessly, she allowed her shoulders to slump.

Attractive postures did not come easily to Karen: She was a plump middle-sized girl of nineteen who drudged her way through evening classes at a local junior college and a morning shift at Jack In The Box. Her hair was light chestnut, stopping just short of her shoulders, and the upward tilt of her eyebrows gave her round face a slightly puzzled look. The mouth was small and sensitive, with a tendency to tremble in moments of stress.

"Don't you think you could put that in your room?" Alice looked at the book bag with distaste.

Karen nodded and got up.

"With what I make teaching school, there's not enough here for a live-in maid." Alice watched her daughter drag the book bag out of the kitchen toward the green-carpeted stairs.

"I know that," said Karen in a low voice.

"And there's not enough time in the day for me to pick up after you," said Alice, following close behind her.

Karen groaned. She slung the book bag over her shoulder, bending wearily under the load as she went up the stairs to her room. It was the smallest of their four bedrooms: Even though Ann and Gretchen were away at college, they still retained major territorial rights.

"I don't see why you can't stand up straight." Like a well-fleshed terrier, Alice continued to snap at her daughter's heels. "The school system has interviews now for teachers, and they judge you on how you carry yourself."

"Maybe I should be taking ballet lessons like Lisa," said Karen over her shoulder.

"Ask your father about that," said Alice. "He's the one with the money."

Karen winced. She bit her lip to keep from straying further into painful ground. Her mother's bitterness over the divorce continued to color their moments together, like a large red eczema crying to be scratched.

The split had come upon them suddenly: the low-voiced phone calls, the absences from home, the knowing looks in the eyes of friends. Finally there had been the two of them alone, rattling around in an oversized house like the last two chocolates in a big box, while her father nested down in small apartment with his new wife, Lisa—twenty-five years old, tall, slender, with long dark hair and a passionate yearning to act in little theater groups.

As George's secretary, Lisa had been forced to suppress her artistic ambitions. But they had always been there, and they were now flowering under his proud encouragement. Since Alice's teaching job ruled out alimony, it seemed more than proper for Lisa to quit work immediately and spend her days sallying forth to dance lessons, voice lessons, and rehearsals with the Chekhov Club. On weekends she and George were accustomed to seek well-earned release at George's court-awarded cabin on the lake.

"What about Grandmother?" Tossing the book bag on the bed, Karen faced her mother.

"They're still doing tests," said Alice. "But your father has some things he wants you to do for him." She looked back down the stairs as though to indicate the need for additional wholesome exercise. "I made a list."

Alice believed firmly in keeping busy. She was a chunky woman of fifty, strong and capable. Of solid Norwegian stock, claiming relationship to Thorstein Veblen, she had an oddly long, fair-complexioned face with an angular, methodical jaw. Below lightly frosted brown hair and chilly blue eyes, her nose was sharply pointed, like a flagship leading the rest of the fleet into action. After tacking round, it led the two of them back to the kitchen. There Alice picked up her note pad and read from it in the clear, slightly nagging voice of an experienced home economics teacher.

"One: Your father wants you to go over to Elm Street tomorrow afternoon. You can get the key from Mrs. Washburn across the way." Alice looked suspiciously at her daughter. "Do you know which house it is?"

Karen nodded, wondering if there was ice cream in the refrigerator.

"Two: He wants you to check all the windows and doors to make sure everything's locked up."

Again Karen nodded. She decided not to open the refrigerator until her mother finished.

"Three: See if you can find her glasses, her hearing aid, and her dentures." Alice paused and ruminated for a moment. "They're probably still in her bedroom."

"Glasses, hearing aid, dentures." Karen repeated the items as though to fix them in her mind.

"It's all down here for you," said Alice impatiently, pointing to the note pad. "The important thing is to find them and take them over tomorrow evening."

"But I have a class," said Karen.

"All I did was take the message," said Alice. "If he doesn't know what your schedule is, you've both got a serious problem."

"I guess I can work it out." Karen nodded her head with cheerful resolution, much as though a customer had come in and asked for a hamburger with mayonnaise rather than Jack's Secret Sauce.

"I don't see why you should have to." Alice gritted her teeth in sudden support of her plump, unprepossessing child. "Your teen-age Bette Davis over there has plenty of time."

"Maybe," shrugged Karen. "But what do you want me to do about it?"

"Stand up for your rights!" With forceful dispatch Alice tore the list from her note pad. She handed it to her daughter with the air of a girls vice-principal delivering a diploma together with a short inspirational message.

Karen took the list and stared at it bemusedly, as though her rights—whatever they were—might somehow be discerned in her mother's firm, squarish script. She had not given her rights much thought lately. Originally she had expected to go away to college just as Ann and Gretchen were now doing—Ann taking graduate work in anthropology. But the divorce had ruled that out: It apparently made more sense for her sisters to finish their studies in Oregon and California than it did for her to begin.

And it seemed right for her to stand between her mother and father, like a shadowy screen in which each could see a faint reflection of the other and cast darts toward it. The pricks came softer now, as though the outer shell had grown harder, more protective in the last six months. But the weight was heavy, and she moved more slowly, if at all, like a turtle stranded by the ebbing tide on some bleak sandy spit while her sisters—bright, handsome, straight-backed, and brown-legged—sailed merrily out to sea in the company of various sportive, eligible young men.

"This hasn't been easy for Dad," said Karen. She opened up the freezer section of the refrigerator and took out a carton of strawberry ice cream.

"It's not easy for anyone," sniffed Alice. "Except for Miss Broadway Melody over there."

Karen remained silent, intent on scooping the ice cream out and into a bowl. Noting her mother's disapproving gaze, she limited herself to two smallish scoops.

"I know I'm just an outsider now," continued Alice, watching—eagle-eyed—for spills as Karen put the carton back and sat down at the table. "But I don't see why Lisa can't involve herself more in the problem."

Karen remained silent, spooning the strawberry ice cream into her small mouth.

"She has more free time than you have, wouldn't you say?" Intent on the matter, Alice sat down across from her daughter and pressed for a response.

"Maybe it's too far for her to drive," said Karen.

"Too far!" said Alice. "It wasn't too far when she was commuting."

"Maybe she feels uncomfortable around Grandmother," said Karen.

"Why should she feel uncomfortable?" Alice watched her daughter bolt down the last of the strawberry ice cream, get up, and take the utensils over to the sink. "She's one of the family now."

"Maybe she lacks confidence." After rinsing her things, Karen nested them neatly in the dishwasher.

"Confidence!" As though enraged by the word, Alice got up and rushed over to turn the dishwasher on. "That girl has youth, good looks, brains, and a certain amount of talent—a lot more than you'll ever have." As Karen started for the stairs, Alice followed her, still incredulous. "How on earth can you say she lacks confidence?"

"I didn't say she lacks confidence," said Karen. She turned for a moment before starting up the stairs. "I said *maybe* she lacks confidence."

"Maybe, maybe, maybe." Alice stood at the foot of the stairs, watching her daughter's plump retreating form with maternal regret. "You're too tentative, too wishy-washy." She raised her voice to school-auditorium level as Karen neared the top. "In those school interviews they expect girls to be forceful, not wishy-washy."

Desperate, Karen wheeled round and raised her own voice. "Look, Mother! How can I be anything when you're picking at me all the time?"

"That's right, dear, blame it all on me." Alice did not smile with satisfaction. But she lowered her voice enough to indicate that her objective had been met. "That's what I'm here for." Her chilly blue eyes flashed toward her daughter with the threatening impact of a landing from one of her forebear's Viking ships. "Blame it on me. Then go in your room and feel sorry for yourself."

"I am going in my room to phone my father," said Karen. She took a breath and tried to invest her high-pitched voice with as much dignity as possible. "If there's something else I can help him with, I want to know what it is."

After Karen slammed the door, Alice remained where she was for a moment. Despite the brisk abrasiveness of the scene, her face felt tight and drawn. With forceful will, she made it relax as best she could, taking deep cooling breaths the way she had learned in her Wednesday night yoga classes. Then she turned round and went through the house: It was important that everything be in place for her well-organized rush in the morning.

The house was impressive: only five years old, custom-built, with shrewdly chosen materials and thrifty use of space. George had gone back and forth with the architect, trying to save the two big oak trees on the property, hammering out plans and revisions in his clear engineer's hand until he was satisfied with every detail.

Handy with tools and plans, George had been a builder all through their marriage. First there had been the garage-conversion rumpus room for their little tract house. Then there had been the big garage in back, towering over the house itself. After that, the cabin at the lake: almost a castle of stone and timber, with boathouse, mooring dock, and sleeping capacity for twenty. George had put ten years of weekend sweat into their castle. She had been there beside him: scrubbing, sanding, painting, calculating costs, and balancing their budget on the precarious tightrope they had stretched out between two relatively modest salaries.

All this time they had continued to live in the small tract house. It seemed to grow smaller as the girls grew, thrusting their tiny bodies upward to young womanhood, all five of them sharing one bathroom. When Ann was a senior in high school, they had joyously moved into their well-deserved reward: a four-bedroom house in a lovely neighborhood.

Building, building, building—that's what people were supposed to do. And that's what she and George had done. It had been the same way with most of their friends: tight budgets, savings accounts, thrift plans, mountain and lake property that gobbled up weekends in high-pitched orgies of masonry and woodwork. Working, working: at school activities, at church groups, at home improvements, at part-time jobs and full-time jobs when the children were older. And always doing without, always looking far to the future for a vacation, a fur coat, a new refrigerator.

It was her refrigerator now—completely hers. And so was the house: an empty house, now that Ann and Gretchen were away at school. How lively it had been when they were in and out! And what fun it had been to joke with the good-looking young men coming by to court her bright, pretty, jewel-like daughters. There were no young men now, only a slow, chubby girl who kept to herself far too much.

Wednesday, March 24, 11:10 A.M.

Dr. Wolf rubbed the red blob of syrup into the left sleeve of his white coat until it was barely visible. He had been eating cherry pie and chocolate ice cream in the staff room of the hospital cafeteria. As junior member of the neurological practice of Mitchell, Golden, and Wolf, he was required to spend most of his time in Minneapolis Central Hospital.

The call over the paging system had forced him to hurry: He crammed a large forkful into his mouth and pushed the plate away with ill-disguised petulance. Under severe jet-black eyebrows his big red moon face was scowling as he took the elevator up to Mrs. Cimino's floor. When the doors opened he stepped out and took up a sternly impassive position. Out of the corner of his eye he could see two men standing in the alcove over toward his right: a short, stocky man with heavy eyebrows and a taller, darker man with long sideburns. The short, stocky man remained where he was. It was the taller man who moved toward him.

The man was not extremely tall: He stood just a little over six feet. But he had a lean, tanned outdoor look. Together with his long sideburns, his height gave him the appearance of a thoughtful western gunman: too dark to be sheriff, but pleasant and clear-eyed enough to be a trusted deputy. He had a good nose, almost

Roman, and dark curly hair, cut short but artfully combed to mask a small bald spot in the back.

The only false note was struck by the tall man's plaid jacket: It was too loud, too loosely hanging, to command quick deference. But the short, stocky man's clothes were another matter: The beautifully cut brown suit must have cost over four hundred dollars, and the collar of his white shirt was just high enough to assert a custom-made provenance. It was with a certain amount of suspicion that Dr. Wolf stared at the short, stocky man.

"Dr. Wolf?" The tall man in the plaid jacket was properly tentative.

Dr. Wolf nodded, still staring at the short, stocky man.

"I'm George Cimino. With Dr. Mitchell away, it's good of you to see us."

"Glad to do it," said Dr. Wolf. He continued to stare at the expensive brown suit. As it moved toward him, he could see that there were tiny little slimming stripes woven through it.

"This is my brother," said the tall man in the plaid jacket. "Harold Cimino." There seemed to be a quality of clear relief in his voice, as though the expensive brown suit had come to salvage matters for him.

Dr. Wolf nodded again. He shook hands with the expensively brown-suited Cimino. It was a strong handshake, almost aggressively so.

"Harold just came up from Des Moines," added the plaid jacket.

"Des Moines." Dr. Wolf uttered the name with reverence. "I have a brother-in-law there. He's a dentist."

"Does he like it?" said the expensive brown suit. The voice was crisp, almost like that of an attorney initiating an examination.

"He likes it very much," said Dr. Wolf.

"Good!" There was a quick smile. The shrewd blue eyes looked over at the plaid jacket and then returned to continue their assessment. "We were wondering what plans you had for our mother."

"She's very confused right now," said Dr. Wolf, unintimidated.

"George tells me Dr. Mitchell feels there might be some surgery involved," said the expensive brown suit.

"He said the confusion might be caused by a tumor pressing on the brain," added the tall plaid jacket.

"That's true," said Dr. Wolf. "Pressure of any kind in there could lead to symptoms like these."

"And your operation would attempt to relieve that pressure, wouldn't it?" said the expensive brown suit.

"Operations like that are always risky, but we've been having better luck lately, even with older people." Dr. Wolf looked reflectively down the corridor toward Mrs. Cimino's room.

"Is she in good enough physical shape for an operation?" said the expensive brown suit.

"I would say so," said Dr. Wolf. "But our tests haven't turned up anything that would justify going in there."

"There's no tumor?" The expensive brown suit's voice was suspicious, slightly accusing.

"No tumor, no pressure of any kind, either on the X-rays or on the printout from our brain scan."

"She had a bad fall a few weeks ago," said the expensive brown suit.

"I know that," said Dr. Wolf. "It's in her file. And we looked very hard for a hematoma, swelling of some kind."

"All of this has come on so suddenly," said the tall plaid jacket, sensing that his brother was beginning to grow intent and truculent. "Could she have had a stroke without our knowing it?"

"That's always a possibility," said Dr. Wolf. "But our spinal tap shows no sign of stroke." He shook his head regretfully.

"Are you trying to tell us that there's no physical abnormality that you can find?" The expensive brown suit moved in closer to Dr. Wolf.

"I didn't say that," said Dr. Wolf. He sighed and left the protection of the elevator, leading the two men over to the alcove. "If we didn't have our new brain-scanning system, we might be still in the dark. Dr. Mitchell and I both went over the results of that test yesterday before he had to leave town. It's very clear to us that there's been shrinkage."

"Shrinkage?" said the expensive brown suit.

"Shrinkage, atrophy, loss of brain cells," said Dr. Wolf. "It's a very natural condition for a woman of her age."

"What about the cataract operation?" The face of the expensive brown suit was tight, beginning to redden a little.

"What's the cataract operation have to do with it?" said Dr.

Wolf irritably, chafing at the subordinate role that kept him in Minneapolis while Mitchell and Golden junketed off to Hawaii.

"Our mother was in perfect shape up to that operation," said the expensive brown suit. "She was completely alert and capable. Isn't that right, George?"

The tall plaid jacket nodded. Noting his discomfort, Dr. Wolf looked kindly at him for a moment.

"If there were brain shrinkage," continued the expensive brown suit, "that would have been a gradual process, wouldn't it?"

"Most of the time it's a slow process leading to a gradual decline," conceded Dr. Wolf. "But I've seen a number of cases just like your mother's—one day perfectly fine, the next day out of it altogether. It's not an easy situation for the family to accept."

"But what about the confusion, the disorientation?" said the expensive brown suit. He was beginning to wilt a little. "Can't you be more specific for us?"

"Those are the symptoms, Mr. Cimino. The brain atrophy is the cause. What it adds up to is irreversible senile dementia."

"You're sure?" said the expensive brown suit, eyes narrowed.

"That's my diagnosis," said Dr. Wolf stiffly. "If you'd feel more comfortable with another opinion, there are a number of other neurologists, good ones, in this city and in Des Moines."

The blue eyes of the expensive brown suit blazed for a moment. He quickly lidded them with a gaze of abstract concern. For the first time in the conversation he looked over at the tall plaid jacket with an air of expectancy.

"Will she improve?" The tall plaid jacket's voice was almost a whisper.

"She may be calmer once she gets out of here, but the basic condition is something that can't be changed." Dr. Wolf started to edge toward the elevator.

"Isn't there anything that can be done?" said the tall plaid jacket, his voice stronger but still shaking.

"Very little," said Dr. Wolf. "My advice would be to start looking for a good nursing home."

"A nursing home?" The tall plaid jacket blanched and looked over at the expensive suit. The expensive brown suit walked over to the window and began to examine the Minneapolis skyline with sudden interest.

"Our social services department will be glad to help you in making plans," said Dr. Wolf. "Other than a few more routine tests, there's not much we can do for her here." He looked over toward the nurses station with a proprietary air and down the corridor that led to Mrs. Cimino's room. After lingering there his gaze moved over toward the elevator light.

"We want to thank you for everything you've done," said the tall plaid jacket. He looked over toward the expensive brown suit hopefully, but the well-draped, wrinkle-free back had been turned upon them with clear finality.

"I wish I could have given you a more positive diagnosis," said Dr. Wolf. "It's not an easy problem to deal with."

"No, it's not," said the tall plaid jacket. He sighed, not without deep weariness. "We'll just have to work something out for her."

"Good luck," said Dr. Wolf. With the elevator upon them, he made a quick dash that put his white-clad rotundity safely inside its broad protective gulp.

As the doors closed, slowly eclipsing his big red moon face, he could see the tall plaid jacket looking over toward the window. His brother, was still standing there, back turned.

Wednesday, March 24, 4:00 P.M.

"I brought your glasses over for you." Karen dangled them in front of her grandmother like a bright, shiny toy.

"Glasses?" Mrs. Cimino's bed had been raised up. She had been staring out the window when her granddaughter came in.

"Your new eyeglasses. I stopped by the house on my way over."

"Are those my glasses?" Mrs. Cimino looked suspicious. "They seemed a little big for me."

"They're the glasses Dr. Sandoval prescribed for you last month.

"I guess they're mine if you say they are." Mrs. Cimino smiled. She looked over toward Mrs. O'Hara as though seeking support. Mrs. O'Hara's eyes were closed.

Karen fitted the thick-lensed glasses over her grandmother's small nose. She smoothed the thin, wispy gray hair back. Behind the lenses the faded blue eyes seemed large and searching.

"Isn't that better?"

"Not bad," said Mrs. Cimino. "But they're heavy." She turned her head toward the window. "What are those big gray things out there?"

Karen followed her gaze. "They're buildings, Grandmother. Big tall buildings."

"Is that so?" Mrs. Cimino continued her examination for half a minute. She sighed and let her head sink back. "Well, I'm tired of them."

Karen pulled up a chair and sat there quietly, not sure of what she should say. Her grandmother seemed listless, dull—much less restive than yesterday. There were no restraints on her wrists. With her glasses on and with her face in repose, she had an air of calm wisdom, almost as though she were sitting on her front porch, a pitcher of lemonade by her side, watching the neighbors walk their small dogs up and down Elm Street.

At her father's urging, Karen had gone over to her grandmother's house before coming to the hospital. There she had searched through the bedroom until she had located the glasses, the false teeth, and the hearing aid. The hearing aid had given her the most trouble, but she had finally found it buried under a pile of papers in one of the bureau drawers. In a vague way, she felt it would help her grandmother to have all these appliances once again in place, but she was not quite sure how to handle them.

A red-haired nurse came in and began to check Mrs. O'Hara's plumbing. Mrs. O'Hara kept her eyes shut but gurgled a little. When the nurse came over to her grandmother's bed, Karen mustered up her courage.

"I brought her dentures." Karen nodded over to the window, where the dentures and hearing aid were, neatly boxed and ready for use.

"Wonderful!" The red-haired nurse bent over her grandmother. "Mrs. Cimino, Mrs. Cimino!"

"Yes, my dear?" Mrs. Cimino stirred herself.

"We have your dentures for you, your dentures." The nurse spoke loudly, articulating each syllable with force.

"My what?"

"Your dentures, Mrs. Cimino, your false teeth."

"False teeth?" Mrs. Cimino worked her lower jaw and smacked her lips. "I'd forgotten all about those things."

"Well, here they are, Mrs. Cimino, here they are." The red-haired nurse reached for the larger of the two boxes, took out the gleaming red and white object, and held it aloft. "Let's see you put them in."

"You want me to put them in?" Mrs. Cimino smiled down at Karen, as though to indicate the demand was oddly eccentric.

"They're your teeth, aren't they?"

"I guess they are if you say so." Mrs. Cimino allowed the red-haired nurse to place the dentures in her hand and guide it up to her mouth. Then she opened her mouth wide and popped the teeth into place.

"Isn't that better, Mrs. Cimino?"

"Yes, my dear, much better." Mrs. Cimino looked down at Karen and smiled broadly. With her glasses on and her dentures in place, her face suddenly reacquired some of its old authority.

"Now let's do something about that hair, Mrs. Cimino." The red-haired nurse took out a black brush and began to nudge the wispy gray halo back into a controlled framing pattern.

Mrs. Cimino nodded her head in approval. "These new hotels certainly go to a lot of trouble in taking care of a person."

"This is not a hotel, Mrs. Cimino." The red-haired nurse stopped brushing and faced her subject directly. "This is a hospital, Minneapolis Central *Hospital.*"

"I guess it is if you say it is." Mrs. Cimino smiled patiently and looked at Karen.

"It's what?" The red-haired nurse continued to press the point.

"What you said it was." Mrs. Cimino nodded her head in the same good-humored way that she had always used to calm difficult customers at the music store.

"That's right, Mrs. Cimino. It's Central Hospital, Central Hospital." The nurse paused and looked over at Karen. "Now you say it."

"Central Hospital." Mrs. Cimino uttered the name with mild wonder.

"Very good." The nurse beamed approval and went back to brushing Mrs. Cimino's hair.

Karen watched the black brush reshape the small gray creature in front of her into a reasonable semblance of the lovely elderly lady who served them all Christmas dinner a few months ago. As a clan gathering it had been less than full, less than perfect: Not wanting to go with Dad and Lisa, she had driven over by herself, feeling very much alone in the absence of her mother and two older sisters.

After dinner she had helped her grandmother with the china and silver. Aunt Gloria and Lisa had stayed in the living room, deeply engrossed in a pointed debate of the merits of Edward Albee. She had not resented the chore: Lisa was far too quick for her, and Aunt Gloria far too rasping. It had been a pleasure to watch her grandmother's small hands work with the Haviland china and sort the silver into orderly groupings.

Those hands had always been quick and dextrous: an alert extension of the clear mind above them. Karen had marveled at the way they could flicker over the keys of the big Chickering grand piano in the living room, taking them through carols and old-time songs. In recent years the piano had stayed closed, as though the music had been interred with her grandfather. Now the house itself was closed: a big, gray stone, empty thing with no one to tend it.

"Where's George?" Mrs. Cimino, her coiffure complete, looked over past Mrs. O'Hara's quiet bulk toward the doorway.

"He'll be here tomorrow, Grandmother."

"Tomorrow." Mrs. Cimino nodded brightly at the nurse, who was now beginning to smooth out the bed.

"That's right, Mrs. Cimino. Your son will be here tomorrow—Thursday." The red-haired nurse stopped for a moment and bent directly over Mrs. Cimino. "And what day is today?"

"Today? It's a nice enough day, a little chilly perhaps."

"Today is Wednesday, Mrs. Cimino, *Wednesday.*"

"Is that important?" Mrs. Cimino was taken aback by the red-haired nurse's vehemence.

"It's always important to know what day it is, Mrs. Cimino, and today is Wednesday, *Wednesday.*"

"Wednesday." Mrs. Cimino said it slowly, as though the name belonged to an old, half-forgotten friend.

"It's Wednesday," said the nurse. "And you're here in Minneapolis Central Hospital."

"I guess I am, as long as you say I am." Mrs. Cimino sank back and closed her eyes. When the nurse had finished letting the bed down, she came over to Karen.

"Keep reminding her what day it is and where she is."

"Will that do any good?" Karen had been a little upset by the nurse's loud insistence upon primitive facts.

"Oh, yes." The nurse looked at Mrs. Cimino again. "You'd be surprised at how they can come along if you keep at them. I've seen them much worse than this at St. Hild's."

"St. Hild's Hospital?"

"Not the hospital. It's a convalescent unit about forty miles north of town."

"For older people?"

"That's mostly what they have now. But they're still connected with the hospital. We spent two weeks out there as part of our training."

"Working with people who are . . . confused?" The word was the one that seemed to be most in use as a label for her grandmother's condition.

"Right." The nurse smiled confidently. "That's why you have to keep hammering in what day it is and where they are. After a while it starts to take effect and you go on from there."

The nurse went over to Mrs. O'Hara's bed and busied herself with one of the tubes. When she finished, she smiled again at Karen and left the room.

Karen watched the crisp white uniform disappear, envying the red-haired girl's command of her trade. Like herself, the girl was on the heavy side, but the effect was somehow different: Under the uniform the weight signaled strength, competence, and imperturbable good humor. She looked down at her own sturdy frame, as though seeking reassurance in its heavy lines. She could see none: She was clearly small, purposeless, and good for nothing except to smile appreciation at those who were trained and masterful. For a moment she felt like crawling into bed beside her grandmother, there to spend the night in quiet, cared-for repose.

"Karen?" Mrs. Cimino was awake and beginning to sit up.

"Yes, Grandmother."

"I think you'll like it out at Uncle Oscar's."

Karen felt suddenly empty inside, as though a roller coaster had started its downward rush without any warning. Uncle Oscar had been Great-grandmother Cora's brother. Growing up in Jamestown, New York, her grandmother had spent the summers on his farm, not too far from the Pennsylvania border.

"On his farm?"

"Yes, dear." Mrs. Cimino grew serious. "Of course there's work to be done as far as the canning goes, but we'll all be there together. I'm sure you'll enjoy it."

Karen got up from her chair and bent over her grandmother the way she had seen the red-haired nurse do.

"Grandmother, Grandmother!"

"Yes, dear." Mrs. Cimino's voice was sleepy.

"Do you know where you are?"

"Does it matter?"

"You're in Minneapolis. Minneapolis, Minnesota."

"Minneapolis." Mrs. Cimino yawned. "We get awfully bad winters here, don't we?"

"Yes, we do. But it's March now, March twenty-fourth. It's Wednesday, March twenty-fourth."

"Wednesday." Mrs. Cimino accepted the matter without protest. "Will you be coming over tomorrow?"

"I'll come over to the hospital after I get through at Jack In The Box in the morning." Karen kissed her grandmother goodbye and walked slowly out of the room.

Pausing for a moment in the doorway, she looked over at Mrs. O'Hara. The large freckled face was impassive, but the green eyes were wide open. Karen smiled. There was a soft gurgle from somewhere down inside Mrs. O'Hara. Up from the gurgle ascended a large drop of friendly spoken commerce.

"Goddamn!" said Mrs. O'Hara.

"I'll be back tomorrow morning," said Karen. She smiled again, shyly.

There was another gurgle. Then the green eyes were hooded and Karen passed safely out into the corridor.

Thursday, March 25, 11:15 A.M.

The voice from the social services department had been softly insistent. It had phoned George Cimino at work that morning and had expressed both sympathy and understanding. In return it had exacted his promise to appear in a couple of hours and discuss plans for his mother's discharge from Minneapolis Central Hospital. Since the promise had been made reluctantly, George took more time than usual in parking his car and making his way through the hospital lobby.

The lobby was elegant: deep-piled blue rugs; large, well-pillowed, upholstered chairs and sofas; fluted columns that took the eye to the high ceiling; and a number of cut-glass chandeliers. The overall impression would have been that of a first-rate metropolitan hotel, had not the left-hand wall been devoted to the display of three immensely large full-length portraits. From each portrait the unsmiling eyes of one of the hospital's founders scrutinized all those who passed by.

They were all white-haired, elderly gentlemen, comfortably posed in a natural stance of authority, as though about to address an assembly of subordinate physicians and call them to account for their feckless ways. The firm, controlled lines of each mouth still seemed about to voice recurrent themes of duty, vision, and good sense. And the rich, solid texture of each setting seemed to signal the fair reward in store for those who saw fit to order their lives accordingly.

George returned the gaze of each founding father without flinching. He had encountered the gaze before, and he had heard the themes before—many times. His own father, Frank Cimino, had always stressed the noble old-country theme of filial duty: respectfulness at table coupled with work at the music store after school and on weekends. When the war came, and the draft with it, George went into the army with mingled fear and relief.

Discharged from service, George came home and continued to help out at the store. At the same time he began to study civil engineering at the university, receiving his degree in 1951. Just as his mother's favorite theme of Good Sense had justified his use of the GI Bill, so it also seemed to justify his taking a job with the state. Frank had grumbled at his son's defection, but the grumbling had been assuaged by the store's growing prosperity and by Harold's bright promise as both student and athlete.

Two years later George married Alice, an elementary school teacher in Mankato. The girls came quickly: Ann in 1955, Gretchen in 1956, and Karen in 1957.

And with the girls came more duties: sober sacrifices of immediate satisfactions in favor of long-range goals. He had worked hard at building his home and providing his daughters with modest advantages. His wife had worked, too, always on the basis of a shared expectation that a fair reward lay somewhere waiting for them.

There was none: only a set of habits, good and bad, deeply ingrained over the years. Twenty pounds overweight, short of breath and hope, George Cimino began to see himself as tied down upon an altar of domesticity: there to await the knife and bleat his way without complaint into whatever darkness lay before him.

So he decided to break free, first of all from the soft flesh that had settled down upon him, urged there by sullenness and self-pity. With diet, with exercise, with true affection for the flatness of his stomach, he forced his wasted years of service back into the corner where they belonged. By 1974 he was again strong and trim: handsomer, more attractive than at any time in his life.

That was when he decided to break free of Alice, leaving behind a bed without joy, a morning without humor, and an evening without the slightest trace of lively movement. He did so quietly, decorously, trying his best to maintain both his marriage and his liaison with Lisa. He had not been successful. But the divorce had opened the door to a life with Lisa: a life of pleasure and excitement, a life about to be encrusted with new layers of filial duty. Nor was George surprised to find himself once again encumbered.

He had always been a good boy.

Jaw set, George forced himself to march briskly toward the elevator. The elevator took him down to the lowest level of the hospital. There, tucked in among vending machines and accounting offices, he located room 30-B, the Department of Social Services. The door was open, so he walked in and found himself staring at two dazzling rows of perfectly aligned white teeth.

The teeth belonged to Ms. Sarah Marshall, a superbly groomed young woman of twenty-five. In company with the gentle gaze of her long-lashed brown eyes, a large emerald on her left hand pulled George over to a small chair beside her desk.

"Mr. Cimino?" There was a tone of pleasurable anticipation in the soft voice, as though mutual friends had arranged for them to spend a weekend in Acapulco together.

"That's right." George took a breath and tightened his pectoral muscles. Encounters like this made all those grueling sessions at the Golden Wing Spa more than worthwhile.

"It's good of you to come over at such short notice."

"Is there a problem that's come up?"

"No problem," Mr. Cimino." The white teeth gleamed reassurance. "But Dr. Wolf has suggested that I talk to you about your mother."

"He said something about a nursing home, but we haven't had a chance to work anything out yet."

"We?"

"My brother and I. He came up the day before yesterday, but he had to get back to Des Moines."

"That's too bad." The long-lashed brown eyes looked down at some papers on the desk.

"His job keeps him very busy," added George.

"Has he made any plans?"

George shook his head. Harold's suggestions had been directed toward taking their mother back to Elm Street as a temporary measure.

"I see that you arranged for your mother's admission here." An emeralded right hand picked up a paper for the long-lashed brown eyes to inspect.

"That's right."

"That means the responsibility for your mother rests with you, doesn't it?"

George nodded. His mind began to roam through a forest of threatening arithmetical figures. Since he had signed the statement of financial responsibility, he felt very much alone in that dark, hostile place.

"At a time like this, Mr. Cimino, we often have feelings of anxiety, feelings of guilt." The long-lashed brown eyes were moist with sympathy. "Sometimes we even have feelings of anger at the aged parent."

George nodded again. He let his pectoral muscles relax and his long legs stretch out. After the stern gaze of the founding fathers it was heartening to encounter a little warm understanding.

"And sometimes it's helpful to bring those feelings out into the open, to express them, to share them with others." The soft voice paused and the long-lashed brown eyes looked down at the desk.

George sighed. He felt as though he had been offered an opportunity to break into sobs. After half a minute he cleared his throat and leaned forward. His voice was low, soft, almost intimate.

38

"I'm a little concerned about how to handle the expenses of all this."

"Naturally." The long-lashed brown eyes continued to look at the desk.

"Not that our mother doesn't have funds of her own," added George hastily.

"Do you have her power of attorney?"

"No. She's always handled everything herself."

"That's too bad." The brown eyes looked up and began to narrow thoughtfully. "Is she in a condition to sign one for you?"

"No." George shook his head. Harold had first raised the power of attorney issue after their father's death, along with the business liquidation-warehouse scheme. But their mother had resisted with vigor. And she had continued to resist each time the topic was raised.

"That's too bad."

"What do other people do in a situation like this?" George was beginning to feel more and more hemmed in by the murky numerals taking shape in his mind.

"Let's take stock for a moment, Mr. Cimino." The white teeth continued to gleam reassurance. "First of all, your mother's condition has been diagnosed by Dr. Wolf as a permanent one. Isn't that right?"

"Yes, but we're still hopeful that she might improve somehow."

"I understand that. But part of my job is to help you deal with the situation as it stands now. I know it's not easy for you."

George nodded, a bit sulkily. It was as though one of the founding fathers had taken over the soft voice and injected a sharp tone of authority into it.

"I'm sure you understand that the hospital is not equipped to offer long-term care. The cost alone would be prohibitive."

George sighed and looked helplessly around the room. His black number shapes were growing bigger and bigger.

"As well, we must consider the cost of her care once she leaves here. That will be a long-term responsibility. Do you follow me?" The long-lashed brown eyes were filled with soft concern.

George nodded.

"Even though your mother has funds of her own, the responsibility for her care rests with you until such time that you—or your brother—acquire the legal authority to act for her."

"Does that mean going to court?" The thought of judges and

lawyers added to George's panic. He could feel wolves prowling through the black forest, along with other strange, predatory beasts.

"Yes."

"Isn't that pretty complicated?"

"It can be." The white teeth reappeared as part of a wise, knowing smile. "But it's much easier if it's done when the aged parent is right here in the hospital."

"I'm not sure I understand what the hospital has to do with all this."

"It's very simple, Mr. Cimino. The court in effect convenes right here—right down the hall from this office."

"Really?" George suddenly had a vision of belted sheriffs knocking out partitions to make room for judicial chambers and robing rooms.

"It's very quiet, very informal. But it's a perfectly legal competence hearing." The long-lashed brown eyes sparkled at the notion.

"Competence? Is that like a sanity hearing?" George bristled a little. "I don't think Mother would like that."

"I understand how you feel. But with aged parents a hearing like this is often necessary. That's why Judge Schultz keeps every Monday morning free."

"Wouldn't we have to get a lawyer?"

"Not as long as the hearing is held right here in Central Hospital. Part of my job is to help you with the forms and get things moving along." The emeralded hands gestured airily around the room.

"How does a hearing like this work?" George eased back in his chair, feeling the emeralded hands were about to caress his trials away.

"To begin with, a member of the family submits a petition to the court."

A drawer was opened and a large, formidable legal document appeared on the desk in front of George. He stared at it blankly.

"The court examines the petition along with the report of the attending physician," continued the soft voice, investing each word with calm authority. "Then the court talks to the aged parent for a while and makes a decision."

"What kind of a decision?" said George, suddenly fearful that

40

his mother might be spirited away to a dark, grim, barred, fury-ridden place.

"A trustee is appointed—generally a member of the family. Once appointed, the trustee has the legal authority to act for the aged parent in financial matters."

"And all this would take place Monday?"

"Monday morning, ten o'clock. You should be there yourself, in case Judge Schultz has questions he wants to ask you about her financial affairs."

"I don't know much about how she handles things, apart from the fact that she's always dealt with Minneapolis Southern Bank." George looked at the long-lashed brown eyes humbly, fearful that they might cloud with anger at his lack of information.

"That's enough right there," said the soft voice, growing a little brisker. "I know it's not an easy decision to make, but these matters are much more easily handled at the beginning when the doctor's records are available. Later on you might run into serious difficulties."

"As you say, it's a long-term problem." George looked at the large legal document with thoughtful respect. The trustee idea seemed reasonable enough, particularly since Harold had left the problem for him to deal with. As trustee he would have authority commensurate with his responsibilities, even perhaps a modest fee as fair reward for his efforts. The grim black numerals in his mind seemed to retreat a little, like a row of overgrown bushes trimmed to manageable hedgelike size. He could even hear the joyous chirping of robins as great drops of golden sunlight began to trickle through the trees of his forest.

"Why don't you take a look at the form we use?" The graceful, emeralded hands turned the form around so that George could examine it. It was surprisingly uncomplicated: merely a simple request that Blank residing at Blank be declared by the court as mentally incompetent. Down toward the middle of the page was a request that a trustee be appointed by the court with full authority to act for Blank. At the bottom was a place for the signature of another Blank, the petitioner, together with still another Blank for the relationship of the petitioner to the first Blank.

"I'm not really asking to be appointed trustee, am I?"

"Not in so many words. What you're asking for is that the court make a decision in the best interests of your mother."

"It seems like the right thing to do," said George. The language of the request made him feel less lonely, less boxed into a remote corner, much as though he had come upon a wise old gentleman who was prepared to lead him out of the forest and back up to his cabin on the lake.

"Many times it's the only thing to do," said the soft voice with quiet certainty. "Under the law we can only keep a patient seven days against his or her will. By next week your mother could walk out of here any time she wanted to."

George filled out the petition as quickly as he could, signing his name at the bottom with a flourish. It was Lisa who had raised the gray, dismal speculation that his mother might one day take a taxicab and suddenly appear at the door of their apartment, overnight bag in hand.

"There it is," he said. "The first step."

"Good." The long-lashed brown eyes inspected the document thoroughly, making sure that the copies were in good order. "This means we'll be able to discharge your mother on Tuesday or Wednesday."

"So soon?"

"As you can see, we can't do much for her here. She needs good long-term care, someplace quiet and wholesome."

"Do you have any suggestions?"

"Many of the staff here think very highly of White Towers. It's located right here in the city, so it's more convenient for visits from the family."

"Maybe I should run over and take a look at it."

"Dr. Sorrel, their director, would insist upon an interview before putting you on their waiting list."

"Waiting list?" George's spirits fell. In place of a taxicab, he saw his own Buick pulling up to their apartment and his mother greeting Lisa with a faintly proprietary smile. The picture was not only dismal: It was explosive.

"In times like these there's always the availability factor to consider. Why don't I phone him right now and see if he has something that might fit your mother's needs?"

"I'd certainly appreciate it." George sighed but remained tense as the graceful hands made the call. It was only when the call revealed the existence of an empty private room on the fifth floor that he began to relax. With humble enthusiasm he nodded his acceptance of Dr. Sorrel's suggestion that they make their final arrangements on Monday morning, immediately after the hearing.

"That was a stroke of luck," said the soft voice, white teeth gleaming triumphantly.

"It certainly was," said George. He got up and allowed himself to stretch a little, feeling that the long-lashed brown eyes were looking him up and down. "To be frank, Ms. Marshall, I was pretty discouraged when I came in here."

"It's not an easy situation to deal with, particularly when it comes to making a decision like this." She rose and extended her hand for him to take, letting his large, powerful hand envelop her emeralds for a moment.

"You've been very kind," said George, his voice throbbing with gratitude.

"I wouldn't say that, Mr. Cimino." The soft voice gave a mildly self-deprecating laugh, as though to suggest that a weekend in Acapulco would chart boundaries of delight far more rich than those to be found among the vending machines of Minneapolis Central Hospital. "But if I can be of any further help, please feel free to phone or drop by."

George took his leave with mingled feelings of humility and giant self-respect. It was truly amazing how younger women responded to him, how they sought to open doors for him. Lisa had once characterized it as his air of strong yet vulnerable masculinity. As he walked out through the lobby he smiled knowingly up at the three founding fathers, secure in the weekend with Lisa that now stretched out before him. On Friday afternoon they would be able to drive up to the cabin, there to hike and try out the new motor in his cabin cruiser. Suddenly everything was in order, like a good-sized clearing in the forest hewn out by earnest, thoughtful, strong hands.

For a moment George considered going back and asking Ms. Marshall to come along for the trip. It would not be Acapulco, but it would be better than Minneapolis: a fire blazing in the noble stone fireplace, catching the highlights in Lisa's long dark hair and Ms. Marshall's long-lashed brown eyes. He smiled the fantasy away in favor of making an authoritative exit from the hospital parking lot.

After George's tall frame vanished from her office doorway,

Ms. Marshall picked up the petition forms and placed them in a large manila envelope. From behind the perfectly aligned white teeth a soft red tongue appeared to moisten the sealing flap. Ms. Marshall's gleaming right hand neatly addressed the manila envelope and put it to one side.

A drawer was opened. Two pieces of paper were taken out and scrutinized—not without affection—by the long-lashed brown eyes. The pieces of paper were bills: one from a garage which specialized in servicing expensive foreign cars, the other from a hairdresser which she visited twice a week.

Ms. Marshall placed the two bills in a white envelope, addressed the envelope to Dr. Sorrel at White Towers, and sealed the envelope with neat precision. Gracefully rising from her desk in one smooth, satiny movement, she picked up the large manila envelope and the smaller white envelope. She walked out of her office and down the corridor to the hospital message center. As she walked—pertly, directly—the heels of her lovely shoes went click, click, click.

Monday, March 29, 9:45 A.M.

Mrs. Cimino was sitting up in bed. Off in the distance she could see clouds: a fat, gray-fleeced flock herded along by the promise of rain. Still parched herself, she moistened her lips and thought of what it would be like to put on big rubber boots and tramp through the marshy part of the meadow. According to Uncle Oscar, a spring rain only stayed a little while before hurrying on to the next county.

Resolved to sketch the prospect out in fuller detail, she took off the heavy-lensed glasses. Reaching over, she placed them carefully on the night stand next to her hearing aid. She looked at the hearing aid with distaste: It had always been a nuisance, pulling strange buzzings and rustlings into her ken, much as though a swarm of trains and trucks had suddenly begun to grope for a new nest in a peaceful upstate valley.

Transferring her attentions to her left hand, she scowled down

44

at her wedding ring: Unaccompanied, it looked incomplete, almost alien, so she wiggled her fingers as though the action would make the engagement ring suddenly reappear.

She was not restless: The red-haired nurse had taken her down the hall for a lovely warm tub bath, and Dr. Wolf's little pills had drained some of the darkness from her spirits. As she sank back, Mrs. Cimino looked over at her room companion. Even though Mrs. O'Hara was not much of a conversationalist, it was reassuring to have those fierce green eyes guarding the room.

Mrs. O'Hara's eyes were closed, but her bed was now more noisy than before. In the night they had come and attached a new tube to her, moving up from the blue-covered mound to assault the base of the throat. Even without her hearing aid Mrs. Cimino could hear the new tube wheezing steadily away, not unlike a small child learning to whistle. Mrs. Cimino closed her own eyes and allowed herself to hum softly.

As Uncle Oscar's farm began to take clearer shape, she noted with irritation that voices had come into the room. She kept her eyes closed but the voices did not go away.

"Teeth," said a rich, low, booming voice, almost on the verge of song.

"Teeth?" The reply was higher-pitched, with more of a whine to it. It was coming from closer to her left ear.

"Teeth, man!" The soft boom was firm. "Before we do the show, those teeth have gotta go."

"You're sure?"

Mrs. Cimino let the farm dissolve and opened her eyes. Down at the foot of her bed was a gigantic black man in a short-sleeved white coat. He was pointing to a recently healed wound on the fleshy part of his left forearm.

"Before we do the scene, those teeth must go, I mean." The black man snapped his fingers for emphasis, not unlike the click of castanets.

Mrs. Cimino tightened her muscles and tried to clear her mind: If these men were determined to take her off to Argentina, there was little she could do to stop them. But there was always the chance of escape if she could catch them off guard.

She looked up at the man beside her. He was younger, skinny, with straight black hair, high cheekbones, and a St. Christopher's medal. The medal did not reassure her.

45

"Mrs. Cimino?" It was the young skinny man who seemed to be in charge of the kidnapping.

"Yes, can I help you?" Mrs. Cimino smiled artfully and used the same tone of voice that had always worked well in selling guitar strings.

"We're going to take you on a little trip," said the skinny man.

"Teeth," said the gigantic black man, showing his own in a broadly carnivorous smile.

Mrs. Cimino squinted up at the skinny man. It was not easy to make sense out of the jumble of sound flowing in toward her. A little ship would have difficulty in making the long voyage to Buenos Aires. She decided to take advantage of the uncertainty.

"I don't think that's a good idea," she said.

"But Judge Schultz wants to see you," said the skinny man. He moved in closer to her.

Another bad sign! There were lots of Germans in Argentina, some of them Nazis, with secret hiding places and strange, unspeakable rites. It was clear to Mrs. Cimino that stronger measures were called for.

"There's a policeman just outside that door, young man, so you might as well go back to where you came from."

To Mrs. Cimino's surprise the skinny man was not intimidated by her bold threat. He simply grunted and reached for her nose, holding it while she gasped for breath. With her mouth open it was an easy chore for the black man to slip her teeth out and place them on the night stand beside her glasses and hearing aid.

Since Mrs. O'Hara was asleep, it seemed manifestly inconsiderate to scream: Quiet, implacable resistance was all she could offer. It was substantial. The black man's caution had been soundly based. Mrs. Cimino was far from frail and her 125 pounds kicked and squirmed like a young wrestler in a crucial match. It took five minutes to wear her down and pin her. When they finally had her robed and strapped into a wheelchair, both men were breathing heavily.

"Teeth," said the black man. He nodded over toward the nightstand like an attorney resting his case.

"I see what you mean," said the skinny man. There was a touch of admiration in his voice as he inspected Mrs. Cimino's wrappings.

46

As they began to wheel Mrs. Cimino out the door, the red-haired nurse came in with a small plastic cup.

"My dear, my dear," said Mrs. Cimino to her. "You've always been so sweet. Why are you doing this? It's not at all nice."

"Don't worry, Mrs. Cimino. Everything's going to be all right." The red-haired nurse tried to speak with conviction as she stepped aside for the kidnappers to make their exit.

"Why does everybody keep saying that to me," wailed Mrs. Cimino. "Everything is wrong, wrong."

Before the red-haired nurse could reply, the two men wheeled Mrs. Cimino down the corridor, past the nurses station and past the visitors elevators. When they reached the freight elevator they stopped. The skinny man pressed a button and the door opened. The black man wheeled her in. The skinny man got in and pushed another button. The elevator moved slowly down, very far down, to the lowest subterranean level of Central Hospital.

The elevator door opened and they wheeled her out, turning left and taking her down to the end of a corridor lined with accounting offices and vending machines. The skinny man opened a door and the black man wheeled her into a small room. It was a storage room, lined with stacks of large oblong boxes, but it still had space enough for a couple of desks and a few folding chairs.

"I do declare this court in session," said the gigantic black man. He left Mrs. Cimino in the near corner of the room and began to unfold the chairs. Working quickly, he moved one of the desks to the center of the room and placed a chair behind it. The other desk he positioned at the far corner, directly opposite Mrs. Cimino. The two men took chairs and sat down beside their passenger, framing her like a pair of exotic saints in an early medieval triptych.

A middle-aged woman came in and examined the triptych for a moment. She was wearing dark horn-rimmed glasses perched on a large hook nose. In her right hand she carried a large black case.

"Flag," said the middle-aged woman. Her voice was gray and tired. Without pursuing the matter further she went over to the corner desk. She put the large black case on top of her desk. She opened it up, took out an electric cord and plugged it into a wall outlet. With the top of the case removed she began to click away at a bank of white buttons.

The black man got up and began to rummage in back of one of

the stacks. He pulled out a long, polelike object. Once unfurled, it turned out to be an American flag. He placed the flag to the right of the center desk and resumed his seat. The middle-aged woman stopped her clicking and looked expectantly toward the door.

A tall man wearing a plaid jacket came in. With his dark hair and long sideburns he reminded Mrs. Cimino of Uncle Oscar. He took a chair by the door and sat there, arms folded. He did not look at Mrs. Cimino.

Suddenly there was a bit of a bustle as the middle-aged lady jumped up from her chair and motioned everybody else to do likewise. A very bald man with little tufts of hair over each ear walked quickly in. He was wearing a blue suit. He was carrying a briefcase. After sitting down behind the center desk, he looked grimly around the room as the others resumed their seats.

The bald-headed man opened up his briefcase and took out two manila folders. The middle-aged lady looked expectantly at him. With her dark horn-rimmed glasses and large hook nose, she poised herself, an eagle ready to strike. When the bald-headed man began to mumble, Mrs. Cimino noticed that the eagle lady clicked out a castanet background on her white buttons. Mrs. Cimino stared over at the doorway, just behind the Uncle Oscar man. She expected to see a guitarist and dancers enter, but the door remained closed.

There was a tap on her right arm from the skinny man. He motioned with his head toward the bald-headed man up front. The bald-headed man's voice was louder now, so she leaned forward to hear him better, wishing that she had brought her hearing aid.

"Do you understand?" said the bald-headed man. The question seemed to be addressed to her.

"Understand what?"

"What this hearing is for?"

"My hearing aid has never worked right," said Mrs. Cimino.

The bald-headed man looked irritated. When he motioned for them to wheel Mrs. Cimino closer, she knew that she would have to be cautious.

"Your name is Esther Cimino, isn't it?" The bald-headed man pronounced it "see-minnow," rather than "suh-meenow."

Mrs. Cimino was silent. It was clear that the bald-headed man was having difficulty, but she repressed her natural desire to help.

"Can you tell me your name?" The bald-headed man was taking a different approach, but Mrs. Cimino was not to be tricked.

"Why are you so interested in my name?" Mrs. Cimino scowled in spite of her resolve to put on a fair face. White slavers were very tricky with names: Their victims ended up with labels like Carmelita and Passion Flower.

"Do you know what year it is?"

"No better than most of them, I would say."

At the black man's deep chuckle the eagle lady stopped her castanets and stared him quickly into silence.

"Can you tell me the name of the President?"

"Juan Perón, I think." The long silence that followed told Mrs. Cimino that she had scored an important point.

"J-U-A-N P-E-R-O-N," said the bald-headed man, spelling it out for the benefit of the eagle lady.

"Very good," said Mrs. Cimino. It was encouraging to find out that the bald-headed man could spell.

The bald-headed man nodded once more and the black man wheeled Mrs. Cimino back to her corner. Then the bald-headed man began to talk to the Uncle Oscar man about weather and shipping accommodations.

"I'd like a clearer picture of her liquid assets," said the bald-headed man.

The Uncle Oscar man got up and gave the bald-headed man a piece of paper. The paper was scrutinized, first with care and then with irritation. There was a long pause.

"I don't like the idea of liquidating a business. With proper management that store should be able to stay afloat."

The Uncle Oscar man nodded.

"So I'm going to appoint Minneapolis Southern Bank as trustee."

The Uncle Oscar man looked blank, puzzled. The scowl on his long face reminded Mrs. Cimino of a small boy playing with a chemistry set: Such boys usually sulked when the experiments didn't turn out the way they were supposed to.

"Believe me, Mr. Cimino, it's the best way to avoid family conflicts." The bald-headed man began to mumble very rapidly while the castanets rose to a crescendo. Then he rapped on the desk with a littler hammer—once, sharply.

At the sound of the rap, the black man and the skinny man wheeled Mrs. Cimino around and took her out the door. She tried to get a closer look at the Uncle Oscar man: It was clear that the proceedings had taken her name away and given it to him. She tried to weigh the virtues of Carmelita as opposed to Passion Flower, closing her eyes as the kidnappers wheeled her rapidly down the corridor toward some swampy port of embarkation.

When she finally dared to open her eyes, it gave her quite a turn to see Mrs. O'Hara's broad, freckled face propped up near her. For some reason they had called off the trip to Argentina. Always a modest person, she did not overly applaud her own handling of the business, though it was clear that passive resistance worked well.

She allowed the two men to transfer her without protest. Even when they attached the posies to her wrists, she did not object. It was a comfortable bed. With her eyes shut she lay quietly, waiting for her mind to stop spinning.

It did not. Thoughts kept jumbling over one another like wet clothes in a dryer: picture thoughts of buckwheat fields and blackberries growing on the slope against a long, zigzagging wood fence. One of those blackberries, she remembered, had turned out to be a stinging creature—a bee, probably. But she had not stopped to investigate when she felt the sharp jab dig into her arm. Her closed eyes tightened as she recalled how she had winced.

She had not dropped the blackberries: They could still be heard rattling in the pail, only a quarter full, as she ran her way homeward through the heavy sweet smell of new-mown hay. With all of them at table there had still been enough to go round, swimming in clotted cream that sang of good pasturage. To the best of her knowledge there were no blackberries in Argentina.

Monday, March 29, 10:50 A.M.

It would not be accurate to describe White Towers as a skyscraper: The building was only eleven stories high. But it effectively dominated the small apartment houses nearby. Secure, gleaming with glass and concrete, its narrow hulk was positioned well back from the roadway, thus providing a generous parking lot for the use of visitors and staff.

George Cimino pulled his Buick into the parking lot and searched for a space. He located one near the glass-doored entrance. It was a roomy space, but the length of the green van on the right forced him to go in at more of an angle than was his usual practice. After locking his car he stood there for a minute examining his handiwork: If the van pulled out it might rake his right fender like an angry fingernail on sensitive skin. Cursing softly, he unlocked the door, squeezed back in, and reparked.

His irritation at the green van fueled further the small, steady flame of resentment that had been kindled that morning. Contrary to Ms. Marshall's bland promise, Judge Schultz had blathered on about community needs and appointed Minneapolis Southern Bank as trustee in charge of his mother's financial affairs. The responsibility for getting her settled was still his, as always, but the actual power would henceforth reside in a downtown file cabinet. He felt as though he had been tricked into burglarizing a house and handing the booty over to someone else: The guilt remained with him, but the fair reward had suddenly disappeared.

George was still scowling as he walked into the White Towers lobby. To his surprise it was quite small: only a pair of light green sofas and a metal desk. Behind the desk was a large, beefy middle-aged lady with frizzy hair. She looked up from her film magazine and scowled back at him.

"I'm George Cimino."

The beefy lady looked him over with a calculating eye, as though she were weighing her chances of besting him in an arm-wrestling match.

"I have an appointment with Dr. Sorrel."

"Eleventh floor," said the beefy lady.

The two of them continued to scowl at each other. George tensed his muscles for combat, but the beefy lady smiled . . . and refused the challenge.

"Elevator," she said. "You have to take the elevator."

Her gesture turned George around. There were two elevators at the far corner of the small lobby. He started toward them.

"Take the right one," said the beefy lady, "It's faster."

The right-hand elevator turned out to be quite fast: It whooshed

George up to the eleventh floor like the rocket of an office-building express. When the doors opened he stepped out onto an electric blue carpet out of which grew a number of glass cubicles. Down past the cubicles was the anteroom for Dr. Sorrel's office. There, drenched with a view of the surrounding city, George sat down on a purple couch with chrome legs and waited for a tight-skirted secretary to usher him in.

Dr. Sorrel was a large, fleshy man with light blond hair, most of it growing from the left side in long strands which crept over his bare scalp like a small army of ivy tendrils seeking refreshment. He was not a doctor of medicine: He was a doctor of divinity from Bob Jones University. Like many clergymen, he had shrewdly shifted from marriage counseling to geriatric administration.

True to his early training, he rarely drank and never smoked. His only vice—if it could be called that—was an uncontrollable tendency to pray audibly at moments of crisis.

"How old is Mom?" Dr. Sorrel had welcomed George into a large room ringed round with certificates and letters testimonial— one from Hubert Humphrey and another from Barry Goldwater.

"Seventy-six."

"Wonderful!" said Dr. Sorrel. "And how is Mom's walking?"

"She gets around pretty well."

"No appliances to weigh her down?"

"She's really in very good health."

"Wonderful!" Dr. Sorrel continued to beam.

"But she gets confused about things."

"Of course, of course." Dr. Sorrel nodded sympathetically. "Ms. Marshall told us a little about Mom over the phone, but we're used to dealing with problems like that.

"She has a trustee now, Minneapolis Southern Bank."

"Fine!" Dr. Sorrel beamed again. "That means that nearly all of Mom's paper work will be handled by experts."

George pondered the matter. With the bank as trustee, everyone seemed to breathe more easily. In a way it gave them all greater status, greater credibility.

"Let me show you around the place, Mr. Cimino." Dr. Sorrel rose and extended a proprietary hand toward the door. "It'll give you a chance to meet some of the family."

George followed Dr. Sorrel's artfully masked scalp down past the cubicles to the elevator. Once in, to his surprise, they darted up.

"Our roof terrace," said Dr. Sorrel proudly.

George looked out from the elevator to a broad expanse of graveled asphalt. In the middle were two red umbrella tables. A small, wizened man got up from one of the tables and shuffled toward them. The journey seemed interminably long.

"Here's Jerry," boomed Dr. Sorrel. "How's it going, champ?"

The small, wizened man did not speak, but he managed to bare the few yellow teeth he had in an obviously cheerful grin.

"Take it easy, Jerry," said Dr. Sorrel as they stepped back into the elevator. Shakily, the small, wizened man executed a military salute, holding it as the doors closed shut.

"Isn't it wonderful when they hang on to their own teeth?" said Dr. Sorrel, shaking his head in admiration.

"He's certainly spry," said George.

"Our active ones all love the roof terrace. The joggers, we call them."

"Wonderful," said George, finding Dr. Sorrel's flights of warm ecstasy somewhat contagious.

"Here's our Royal Room," said Dr. Sorrel as they stepped out to view the tenth floor.

The Royal Room was a dining room running almost the length of the building. It was filled with large circular tables. Several young women wearing pink, crepelike uniforms were setting the tables with cutlery and heavy restaurant china. At the far end a woman in a white slacks suit got up from one of the tables and came toward them. Although she was smaller than the average professional football player, the yards of yellow curls woven together and piled high on her head went far to redress the difference.

"Mrs. Coughlin, our head nurse," said Dr. Sorrel, his voice softening with awe.

George braced himself for the handshake coming his way and managed to emerge unscathed from Mrs. Coughlin's hearty assault.

"Mr. Cimino's Mom is going to join our family," said Dr. Sorrel.

"Fantastic!" said Mrs. Coughlin. "And where is Mom now?"

"With our friends over in Central Hospital," said Dr. Sorrel.

"Fantastic!" said Mrs. Coughlin. "You just go back there and tell her we're waiting for her." She gestured around the room. "And we'll want to see you over here for dinner every now and then, Mr. Cimino."

George looked questioningly at Dr. Sorrel.

"The Royal Room is always open to members of the family," explained Dr. Sorrel. "All we need is a little notice and we can handle a birthday party, an anniversary, or a friendly visit."

"With wine," added Mrs. Coughlin. They all shared a soft chuckle at the prospect.

Dr. Sorrel ushered George back into the elevator and took him down to the ninth floor. There he proudly showed George through the beauty shop, the gift shop, and the snack bar.

"It's Susan, isn't it?" Dr. Sorrel's boom addressed its full force to a small gray creature in a red kimono. Startled, the creature looked up from its cup of tea and tried to puzzle out the attack upon it.

"How's my best girl doing?"

The best girl simpered weakly and returned to her tea, holding both saucer and cup together as she brought them, rattling slightly, up to her mouth.

"Isn't it wonderful to see serenity like that?" said Dr. Sorrel.

"She seems very content," said George.

"Our quiet ones love a little nook to themselves. The philosophers, we like to call them."

Dr. Sorrel took George farther down the corridor to point out various recreation rooms and therapy rooms. Most of them were empty.

"Afternoon is our busy time," explained Dr. Sorrel. "That's when the university people come over."

"Do they actually give courses here?"

"Not exactly," said Dr. Sorrel. "It's more research and things like that, but it's a lot of fun."

"Wonderful," said George. He followed Dr. Sorrel back to the elevator. The elevator took them to the fifth floor. Stepping out, George was enveloped in the swell of several thousand violins.

"Mantovani," smiled Dr. Sorrel. "Research has shown his music is the most soothing."

Most of the rooms along the corridor seemed to have closed

their doors against the music, but George managed to catch sight of a few shadowy figures lying in bed as they walked along.

"Liberty Hall," chuckled Dr. Sorrel. "Isn't it wonderful to be able to sleep in whenever you want to?"

It was hard for George to imagine his mother wanting to sleep in, but he had to admit that having the alternative was attractive.

"And here is Mom's room," said Dr. Sorrel proudly. He flicked on the lights and stood aside, like a painter unveiling a minor masterpiece for the first time.

It was far from being a tiny room: a bed, a night stand, a dresser, a writing table, an overstuffed chair, and a television set placed it squarely in the American contemporary innkeeping tradition. Off to the right was a bathroom with both shower and tub. The cupboard space was substantial.

"Color television," said Dr. Sorrel. "It's much more soothing than black and white."

"Very impressive," said George.

"Mom's room," said Dr. Sorrel. Overcome by the thought, he stood there in silence for a moment.

A short, chunky girl with heavy black eyebrows appeared at the door. She was carrying a broom.

"Miss Rehder!" Dr. Sorrel hailed her with glee. "Mr. Cimino's Mom is going to make her nest with us."

Mis Rehder nodded sullenly and disappeared from the doorway. When they came out of the room they could see her farther down the corridor. She had opened a large closet and was standing there pensively, as though she were trying to decide whether or not the broom would fit in there.

Back to the elevator and up to the eleventh floor again. There Dr. Sorrel pressed upon George a number of brochures in which photographs of Dr. Sorrel and other members of the staff appeared. He explained to George the relationship between White Towers, the Soegard Clinic, the Castle Foundation, and other service agencies: weaving a gracious web of concern that found some threads stretching back to the Department of Health, Education, and Welfare.

"Fifty dollars a day, Mr. Cimino. That's our comprehensive base rate."

"And that includes medical care?"

"Everything outside of special medications and therapies," smiled Dr. Sorrel. "Our accounting service itemizes all the little extras for you when they come up."

"I think it will work out very well," said George.

"Wonderful!" said Dr. Sorrel. "When will Mom be coming over?"

"Tuesday or Wednesday, I guess," said George.

"Tuesday will be fine," said Dr. Sorrel. "I'll phone Ms. Marshall and she'll set everything up for you."

"Will we need an ambulance?"

"Ambulance?" Dr. Sorrel laughed indulgently. "Not for a family matter like this."

"I should bring her over myself?"

"Anyone in the family will be fine once we get the paper work out of the way." Dr. Sorrel gestured deprecatingly toward the forms on his desk.

"I'll have my daughter pick her up," said Geroge. "She has a little more free time than the rest of us."

"Wonderful!" said Dr. Sorrel. "The sooner, the better."

George signed the various forms for his mother's admission. Then he said goodbye and took the fast elevator down to the lobby. Once safely past the beefy lady, he whistled his way out to the parking lot.

Suddenly he felt free: Even the loss of the trusteeship failed to sting him now. With his mother in the firm, benign hands of Dr. Sorrel, he could rest easy, secure in the knowledge that he had done his duty wisely and well, rather than turning his back upon it as Harold had done. With one quick masterful swoop he pulled the Buick out of the parking space and headed home for lunch. Lisa had promised to cut her ballet lesson short and be there waiting for him.

Despite his own professional good cheer, Dr. Sorrel had said goodbye to George with vague feelings of distress: Seeing Miss Rehder down there on the fifth floor had reminded him of an unpleasant disciplinary chore. Even though this was her first full-time job in some time, Miss Rehder's work was more disappointing than they had expected. It was the people at the state mental hospital in Mankato who had assured them that she would be perfectly adequate.

56

This last episode went far beyond mere inadequacy: It had involved locking poor Mrs. Willets in the fifth-floor broom closet for more than six hours. For the last two days he had wrestled with the problem and with his conscience. The problem had won and now commanded his immediate action.

After Mrs. Coughlin brought Miss Rehder in, Dr. Sorrel scolded her softly for a while. Then the three of them knelt down in front of the large plate-glass window that faced south, offering an almost unbroken view of the downtown skyline.

It was Mrs. Coughlin who prayed first for Miss Rehder. Then Dr. Sorrel went to work. He loosened his tie. He balanced himself firmly on his generous haunches. Arms outstretched, he turned his face heavenward as far as he could: From that source he invoked divine assistance for Miss Rehder, for Mrs. Coughlin, for the entire White Towers family, for Professor Evans and his oral history project, for the Soegard Clinic, for the Castle Foundation's experimental grants which might be in the offing.

By the time Dr. Sorrel had encompassed the entire nursing-home industry and the Board of Foreign Missions in his anguished plea for help, both Miss Rehder and Mrs. Coughlin were weeping profusely: sometimes sobbing, sometimes uttering sharp little cries of ecstatic agony. It was only then that Dr. Sorrel allowed the cadences of his rich, plummy voice to sweep them to their feet and off to a well-deserved lunch.

Tuesday, March 30, 3:10 P.M.

They had taken Mrs. O'Hara off to Argentina. Although she had not protested the matter, Mrs. Cimino was quietly indignant. Early in the morning the kidnappers had come, two of them in long white coats. After checking Mrs. O'Hara's plumbing they had declared her fit for the trip. Then they had wheeled her off, bed and all.

There was a new bed by the doorway now: empty, clean, inviolate. The gurgles and the wheezes were gone, along with the fierce green eyes that had guarded the room.

"Darn it!" said Mrs. Cimino under her breath, as though the incantation might invest her surroundings with greater safety.

The red-haired nurse came in. Mrs. Cimino stared at her suspiciously.

"How are you feeling, Mrs. Cimino?"

"Just fine, my dear." Mrs. Cimino's tone was neutral, not unfriendly.

"What about your hearing aid?" The red-haired nurse looked over at the night stand where the hearing aid lay. It was a small plastic coil designed to fit into the left ear. On the top, just above the tiny battery enclosure, was a small ridged wheel that controlled the volume.

"It's not working very well," said Mrs. Cimino.

"I'm sorry to hear that," said the red-haired nurse.

"It's always been a dreadful nuisance," smiled Mrs. Cimino.

"Why don't we try it out?" The red-haired nurse picked up the hearing aid. Gently but firmly she placed it in Mrs. Cimino's left ear. After switching the little control button on, she adjusted the volume wheel, working downward from the squeal that signaled the battery was still lively.

"I don't know," said Mrs. Cimino, as some of the street noise began to filter through. "It seems to be making funny sounds."

"The funny sounds are part of the world," said the red-haired nurse. "You have to keep track of them to know what's going on."

"Maybe we should turn it off now," said Mrs. Cimino. "I wouldn't want that battery to run down."

"If it runs down, we can get you a new battery," said the red-haired nurse.

"They're expensive," said Mrs. Cimino.

"They're essential," said the red-haired nurse. She began to brush Mrs. Cimino's hair with vigor, as though to magnify the impact of the brush on the scalp.

With her glasses positioned on her nose Mrs. Cimino was able to survey the room and even monitor the doorway effectively. As the slightly plump blur came in she brought it quickly into focus.

"Why, it's Karen," said Mrs. Cimino. "Dear little Karen."

"I've brought some things over from the house for you," said Karen. She set the suitcase down and waited for the nurse to finish.

"Doesn't that feel better?" The red-haired nurse stepped back to admire the wispy gray coiffure she had shaped.

"Feels just fine," said Mrs. Cimino. She smiled confidentially at Karen. "They keep telling me the name of this place, but I can't seem to keep it in mind."

"It's Central Hospital," said Karen.

"That's right." Mrs. Cimino glowed with recognition. "Minneapolis Central Hospital. Right downtown, aren't we?"

"Not too far from the Radisson," said the red-haired nurse.

"Yes, yes, the Radisson." Mrs. Cimino smiled. "We used to go there for dinner. A little too spiffy for me." She laughed self-consciously. "But very nice."

"I brought a nice warm robe and slippers for you." Karen gestured toward the suitcase. "Along with some other things you can use."

Mrs. Cimino looked at the suitcase without enthusiasm.

"Wouldn't you like to get bundled up and come along with me?" continued Karen.

"Do you think it's a good idea?" Mrs. Cimino asked the red-haired nurse.

"Yes, Mrs. Cimino, a very good idea."

"I suppose it is if you say so," said Mrs. Cimino. She brightened. "Are we going home?"

"Not right away," said Karen. "It's another hospital."

"Another hospital! Dear me!" Mrs. Cimino looked roguishly at the red-haired nurse. "Here it's taken me all this time to learn the name of this place." She gave a little laugh of self-dismay. "I hope I do better with the new one."

"It's a very nice place for getting your strength back," said Karen. "And you'll be closer to Dad and the rest of us."

"Oh, yes, George." Mrs. Cimino furrowed her brow for a moment. "How old is he now?"

"He's fifty-one, eight years older than Uncle Harold,"

"That old!" Mrs. Cimino shook her head in disbelief. "To think of those two boys growing old like that!" She gave a helpless little laugh. "I've never been able to keep track of all the cousins."

"Cousins!" Karen looked at her grandmother with sudden distress, as though a void had gapingly opened up under her feet. "They're brothers."

"I guess I wasn't very far off then, was I?" Mrs. Cimino added a touch of self-confidence to her smile.

"They're not only brothers. They're your two sons, George Cimino and Harold Cimino." Karen looked up appealingly at the red-haired nurse.

"That's a nice-sized family, Mrs. Cimino. Two fine grown sons and some lovely grandchildren."

"I guess it is if you say it is." Mrs. Cimino directed her attention out the window for a moment, wondering whether or not it was time for the gloomy weather to move on.

Karen opened up the suitcase and took out a clean nightgown, robe, and slippers. With the help of the red-haired nurse she got her grandmother dressed and comfortably seated in the chair beside her bed. The nurse went out and came back with a wheelchair. Mrs. Cimino rose, a bit unsteadily, and sat herself down in the wheelchair, noting with pleasure that there were no restraints and wrappings this time. Conditions like these augered well for the trip.

The red-haired nurse wheeled Mrs. Cimino past Mrs. O'Hara's empty space, out of the room, and down to the elevator. Karen followed behind her carrying the suitcase. After taking Mrs. Cimino down to the ground floor, the nurse took her out to the main entrance. There she waited with Mrs. Cimino while Karen brought the car around from the parking lot.

"Here we are," said Karen. With a festive pretense, she hopped out and came round to open the right-hand door.

"You're sure we're doing the right thing?" Mrs. Cimino looked at both of them with renewed anxiety as they helped her in.

"Yes, Grandmother." Karen's voice was brisk and firm. "Dr. Wolf feels you're well enough to leave now."

"But we're not going home, are we?"

"We're going to a place called White Towers."

"Another hospital, isn't it?"

"It's a convalescent hospital. They have a dining room and lots of interesting people to talk to. Much nicer than a regular hospital."

"This Central Hospital isn't so bad," said Mrs. Cimino, struck with a sudden fit of loyalty. She reached for the red-haired nurse's hand and gave it an affectionate squeeze. "Thank you for everything, my dear."

"Take care of yourself, Mrs. Cimino." The red-haired nurse gave her a big hug and closed the door, locking it as she did so.

"You've been awfully kind to her," said Karen.

"She's a very lovely person." The red-haired nurse looked in through the window at Mrs. Cimino, who was sitting quietly, eyes closed. "I hope it all works out for her."

"Do you think she'll get better?"

"There's a good chance. If they push her at White Towers the way they do at St. Hild's, you may see her start to bounce back in a few weeks." Solid, friendly, the red-haired nurse smiled at Karen.

"I hope so." Karen stood there awkwardly for a moment. Then she took the nurse's hand and gave it a squeeze. "Thanks again."

"Good luck," said the nurse as Karen darted around and got in the driver's seat.

As they pulled out of the hospital parking lot and into the heavy traffic, Mrs. Cimino opened her eyes and smiled at her granddaughter. She knew that Karen was a good driver. And she was reasonably sure the two of them would not end up in Argentina.

Part 2

By means of the idea of rights, men have defined
the nature of license and of tyranny. Guided by its
light, we can each of us be independent without
arrogance and obedient without servility. When a
man submits to force, that surrender debases him,
but when he accepts the recognized right of a fellow
mortal to give him orders, there is a sense in which
he rises above the giver of the commands. No man
can be great without virtue, nor any nation great
without respect for rights; one might almost say
that without it there can be no society, for what is a
combination of rational and intelligent beings held
together by force alone?

ALEXIS DE TOCQUEVILLE
Democracy in America

Thursday, April 16, 11:15 A.M.

"Another guitar?" Edward Leach looked sadly at his son-in-law and picked up a red felt-tipped pen. An assistant trust officer with Minneapolis Southern Bank, Mr. Leach always felt more secure when he was able to march figures, red and black, across ruled yellow worksheets.

He had asked Brian to come to his office regarding what Brian had airily characterized as a Career Loan: Mr. Leach had hopes that the marble austerities of the main branch might awe his son-in-law into a more responsible frame of mind. Ever since Brian and Robin, his only daughter, had moved in last year, the Leach household had become as chaotic as an estate left by an eccentric recluse. To restore order, direction, symmetry: This is why Mr. Leach had asked Brian Markle to come in.

"It's part of the staging concept for the group," said Brian, smiling brightly at his father-in-law.

"But you already have two guitars," said Mr. Leach, trying to imagine what feats of juggling might be involved.

"We need more flash," said Brian. "With a Les Paul, I could start with my straight Gibson, go to the Les Paul, go back to the Gibson, and then go to the Stratocaster." There was a faraway look in his eyes, evoking the glitter and blare of actual performance. "Then I'd move to the Les Paul again and finish up with the Stratocaster."

"Is it important to move around like that?"

"It gives us better visuals," said Brian patiently. "And that's what everyone's into these days."

Mr. Leach sighed. His son-in-law's group had not been prospering. And his wife's disposition had begun to turn shrewish. But the boy was basically likeable: a natural salesman who had wandered his way into the ranks of superannuated rock guitarists. So a little help now might stabilize matters and build confidence. Later on it might be possible to arrange a transition into a steadier line of work.

"Think of it as a capital investment," smiled Brian, brushing

65

back his long, beautifully full-bodied hair. His blue eyes were friendly, helpful, and almost overpowering the threatening lines of his piratical mustache.

"That makes sense," said Mr. Leach, pleased at finding a justification for taking out his checkbook. "How much do you need?"

"Five hundred dollars."

"That's quite a bit." Mr. Leach tried to chuckle as he wrote out the check. "But I guess good equipment is expensive."

"It sure is," said Brian. "That's why I always try to come up with as big a down payment as I can."

"Very prudent," said Mr. Leach, his voice breaking a little. Although he prided himself on being able to face uncomfortable facts, he decided not to ask the total price of the instrument. But it was clear that there was more money to be made in selling the things than in playing them.

"I try to be sensible," said Brian earnestly. "Maybe some of your ideas are beginning to rub off on me." He stretched easily and got up to leave.

"We'll make a businessman of you yet," said Mr. Leach, forcing a smile as he walked Brian to the door.

"No harm in trying . . . Grandpa." With the magnificent insouciance of an unemployed twenty-eight–year–old, Brian grinned farewell.

Mr. Leach took a deep breath and went back to his desk. Now that Robin was pregnant it was essential to keep the household running smoothly. Order and symmetry would have to wait for a while.

He looked at his calendar. George Cimino was scheduled to come in shortly. He pulled Mrs. Cimino's file over to him and began to review the situation.

On paper Mrs. Cimino's assets were substantial: The house on Elm Street, free and clear, was worth over $70,000, and the stock portfolio had a market value of nearly $100,000. The music store had turned out to include the building as well: a three-front structure with a couple of offices on the second floor. After making allowances for the mortgage, he had entered the building as a net asset of $180,000 and the store itself as an asset of $75,000. With checking accounts and savings accounts, Mrs. Cimino's present net worth came to just a little under $450,000.

Mr. Leach put his worksheet down and rubbed his eyes. They

were small eyes, not piggish but tiny, deep-set gleaming dots that took an agreeable magnification from the lenses of his dark-rimmed glasses. Now that he was in his early fifties, his forehead was beginning to invade his hairline, which by this time had been pushed back to an inch in front of his crown. From time to time wrinkles of concern appeared on this generous expanse, particularly when the expenditure of money was involved.

When George came in, Mr. Leach's forehead was unfurrowed. It was a routine conference, one in which the script had been crafted and slimmed down on the basis of long banking experience.

"Thanks for coming over, Mr. Cimino." Mr. Leach directed George's tall frame into a smallish chair. "How's your mother doing?"

"Pretty well," said George. "She's not as restless as she was."

"More alert, would you say?"

"No." George shook his head and looked awkwardly around the small office. "I don't think she recognizes any of us."

"That's a shame." Mr. Leach sat back in his chair as though leaving his custodial duties for a proper moment of shared grief.

"Dr. Sorrel says she's on a permanent philosophical plateau," said George.

"Any physical problems?"

"She seems to have trouble walking," said George. "Otherwise she's fine."

"She might live another twenty years," said Mr. Leach with a gentle smile. "Have you and your brother talked about that possibility?"

George shook his head again.

"Our responsibility to the court requires us to assume that as a minimum," continued Mr. Leach, warming to his task. "That's why we should begin to think in long-range terms."

"Are there any problems?" said George, a puzzled look on his long somber face. "Harold and I always felt she was pretty well fixed."

"She is." Mr. Leach pushed a yellow worksheet over for George's inspection.

"Gosh!" said George. "I'd no idea it was anything that high."

"If you don't spend it, it begins to add up after a while." Mr. Leach smiled affectionately at the impact of his neat phalanx of figures. "My guess would be that your mother used all the income from the building and from the music store to reduce the mortgage principal."

"Then there's no problem at all," said George, obviously relieved. "She's a wealthy woman."

"On paper it's a reasonably handsome estate," conceded Mr. Leach. "And you and your brother are the chief beneficiaries of that estate?"

"Estate?" George winced a little at the word. "You seem to be talking as though we're going through . . . probate."

"In a way we are." Mr. Leach smiled to underscore the finality of the matter. "Your mother's will is in her safety deposit box at one of our local branches. In view of Judge Schultz's ruling, that will stands as written."

"I wish she'd spent more of it on herself," said George.

"That's in the past, Mr. Cimino. It's the future we have to think about now."

"She could stay on at White Towers forever." George began to relax more and more.

"Very possibly," smiled Mr. Leach. "But you must remember that the court requires me to protect that estate for you and your brother."

"She has more than enough coming in, doesn't she?"

"This year, yes. Next year, maybe. Five years from now we might have to invade her principal." Mr. Leach shook his head sadly at the prospect of assorted Goths and Huns storming the frail citadel that Mrs. Cimino and her husband had built.

"With almost half a million dollars?"

"Half a million dollars on *paper*." Mr. Leach reached for his red felt-tipped pen. "If we were to liquidate her low-yield stocks and building, we'd have a very serious capital-gains problem."

George nodded glumly.

"And then there's inflation to think of." Mr. Leach warmed happily to his topic. "Your mother's income will remain as it is, but her expenses are certain to go up and up."

George nodded again.

"A good rule of thumb is to set aside one-third of any retirement or pension income for reinvestment. With a hedge like that you're always protected against rising costs."

"One-third!" George blanched, looking as though an unforeseen heavy snow had suddenly crushed the roof of his cabin at the lake.

"One-third is what we recommend," smiled Mr. Leach. "And we know of many men—successful men—who took early retirement on what they thought was an adequate income." The smile grew broader as he unveiled his favorite Gorgon for shocked inspection. "Now they're desperate. Too old to go back to work, and too young to collect their social security."

"But expenses go down when you retire, don't they?"

"Down?" Mr. Leach chuckled benignly. "I'd say they go *up*." He permitted himself to gesture with luxurious panache. "You can't play golf and travel seven days a week for nothing—even if you don't drink," he added primly.

"One-third." George shook his head. He was clearly whipped, clearly malleable.

"So we need to generate some more income for her," said Mr. Leach. He pulled out another yellow worksheet from the folder. "That's why I'd like to sell the Elm Street property as soon as we can."

"Sell her house?" George, obviously uncomfortable, squirmed a bit. "So soon?"

"It's standing empty, unprotected. And your mother's age would permit us to escape the tax liability."

"But how about her furniture?" said George.

"I know it's a painful thing to think about." Mr. Leach's voice floated each word out slowly, as though the mind behind them were reluctant to bring any kind of grief to the attention of a dear and treasured client. "And yet this is the time for you and your brother to decide what you want to keep in the family."

"I just don't know what we're going to do," sighed George. "My wife and I don't have much room in the apartment."

"Have you thought of buying a larger place? A house, perhaps?"

"We've thought of it," said George. "But the last year has been pretty busy for us."

"This might be a good time for a move. Now that your mother's estate is a matter of record, I'm sure we could work out an attractive loan for you." Mr. Leach gestured airily, as though a natural approach to prospective heirs was to place them firmly in his debt.

"That's very kind of you." For the first time George began to smile.

"We're working together," said Mr. Leach, nodding chummily. "So why don't you and your wife start looking around. That way you'll have a better idea of what you want to keep."

"How about my brother?"

"I'll correspond with him on the matter," said Mr. Leach. "Though it might speed things along if you talked it over with him yourself."

"I'll give him a call." George's voice was brisk, and his spirits had brightened a great deal. "I'm sure he'll be glad to know that she's going to be in good shape."

"Not quite." Mr. Leach's place face etched out deep lines of sorrow. He reached into the folder for a third yellow worksheet. "I've been taking a very hard look at these White Towers charges."

"You think they're too high?"

"It's not just the high room rate. There are extras—the medications, the special services. These things have a way of building up."

"The hospital recommended it to us," said George slowly.

"I'm not surprised that they did." Mr. Leach permitted himself a thin, knowing smile. "And I'm sure the program there is quite good." He paused to signal a tactful concern. "But my impression is that your mother is there on a basic custodial arrangement."

"She's just off in her own little world," said George sadly.

"Good, long-term custodial care." Mr. Leach nodded his approval of the notion.

"Do you think their charges are out of line?"

"I think the program is more ambitious than what she needs at this point," said Mr. Leach carefully. "And I also feel the expenses are a little high in terms of our goals for the estate."

"Do you have any suggestions?" There was hopefulness in George's voice, as though Mr. Leach's red felt-tipped pen might magically conjure up a proper locale for someone on a permanent philosophical plateau.

"Svendsen's Rest Home, about thirty miles north of here, has a very fine reputation," said Mr. Leach. "And its charges are much more reasonable than what we have here." The magical red felt-tipped pen tapped the worksheet with reassuring emphasis.

"That's quite a drive," said George. "Maybe my daughter could run up and look it over."

"I'm sure you'd be able to trust her judgment," said Mr. Leach piously. "Whenever you feel comfortable about it, I can arrange to have your mother transferred."

"I'll get Karen out there as soon as I can." George, greatly relieved, smiled at Mr. Leach. "As you say, we're working together."

"And we've certainly accomplished quite a bit this morning," said Mr. Leach with clear approval. He rose and forced his pudgy white hand into George's lean brown one. Then he accompanied his new partner out into the sea of worried traffic that heaved and moiled on the large marble floor of the central branch. It was with pleasure that he noted George's confident stride out the front door.

When Mr. Leach came back to his small office, he did not immediately put the Cimino file away. Speculatively, lips pursed, he looked through it again, making detailed notes on a fourth yellow worksheet.

The notes were pleasant to make, and even more pleasant to contemplate when finished. If Mrs. Cimino's basic expenses could be cut back to twelve hundred dollars a month, the music store could be put aside as a basic low-yield growth property. And as a growth property it would call for a new growth-oriented management: an alert young couple, possibly, with a husband who was knowledgeable about the esoterica of Gibson, Les Paul, and Stratocaster guitars.

Mr. Leach took out a fifth yellow worksheet and began to scribble rapidly.

It was a long time before Mr. Leach put his fifth worksheet away, replacing it with a small sheet of white paper. On the sheet of white paper he wrote down the address and telephone number of Cimino Music. Under the telephone number he wrote down another number, one in four figures: After careful thought he had decided to make his monthly salary offer to Brian as tempting as possible.

Monday, April 19, 10:00 A.M.

The view from the dining room of Svendsen's Rest Home was magnificent: It commanded almost the entire valley of the gently winding Manitou River. The original building had been constructed just before the turn of the century, when the big, well-cut blocks of granite had been lugged all the way up to the top of the hill by sweating Finns and Poles at the behest of a vulpine railroad vice-president. And what remained still gave the effect of a dour Northumberland castle wrenched out of its settings and transported for service in the colonies.

In 1912 the building and grounds were acquired by the Svendsen family. Old man Svendsen had farmed it for a while before distributing it among his five tall sons. Leonard, the oldest, had been given the big house.

During the lean years after 1933 Leonard had begun to take in elderly pensioners. By 1960 Leonard's son, Claude had remodeled the place and turned it into a full-fledged nursing home. The venture had prospered. So Claude built a smaller house down the road for his own family to live in. But his wife, Joan, still continued to come over and supervise the cooking. The food at Svendsen's was considered to be excellent.

Miss Carver, the head nurse, had suggested that Karen come out well before lunch, so Karen had switched shifts with one of the other girls at Jack In The Box. Her drive from Minneapolis had taken almost fifty minutes. Cramped from sitting, she had welcomed the chance to stand in the dining room for a moment, waiting until Miss Carver was free.

"Shall we go into my office for our little chat, Miss Cimino?"

Engrossed in the view, Karen turned with a slight start as Miss Carver came up to her. The head nurse was a woman just over sixty, slender, with rimless glasses and a perfectly starched white uniform. Like many women her age she wore low shoes with rubber soles, so that her walk was barely more than a soft caress of the gleaming walnut floor.

72

"I've been admiring your view," said Karen, feeling flustered and a bit uneasy at being taken by surprise.

"It is lovely, isn't it?" said Miss Carver. The words came out in a slow, resonant whisper. "Particularly in autumn, when the leaves change color." The two of them gazed out the large picture window toward the river curling through the fields below. It was a quiet prospect, almost impossibly so, much as though the green stands of corn had been placed there with the intention of muffling the sounds of the few cars and trucks passing by.

"We feel this is one of our most pleasant rooms," added Miss Carver. There was the bare curve of a faintly proprietary smile.

"It's beautifully furnished," said Karen, looking round at the tables, vases, and tall lamps. Over by the entrance were two large carved mahogany bookcases, one of them flanked by an ornate Chinese chest.

"Some of these belong to the Svendsen family," said Miss Carver. "But many of them have come to us from our residents."

"It's nice that you have the space," said Karen, trying not to falter as she looked into the steady gaze of the light blue eyes behind the rimless glasses.

"We try to *make* space," said Miss Carver, putting a slight edge to her whisper. "And we encourage each resident to bring a favorite piece or two with them for their own room." She led Karen past the Chinese chest to a small door, and through the small door to a small office. Once Karen had seated herself, still uneasy, the slow, resonant whisper began to float toward her again.

"How old is your grandmother," Miss Cimino?"

"Seventy-six," said Karen, almost hypnotized by the starched uniform. She could feel her own voice softening, slowing down.

Miss Carver did not speak immediately in reply. She seemed to ponder the number, nodding slightly as though there were magic buried somewhere under the brute arithmetical fact.

"Seventy-six years," she finally said. There was a touch of awe in her voice. "Seventy-six good, rich, full years. That's a long time, isn't it?"

"Yes," said Karen, feeling greatly humbled. "It's a very long time."

"And it's a lot more than many of us can expect to have on this earth," said Miss Carver. "Seventy-six years of health, vigor, and service to those we love." Behind the rimless glasses, the light blue eyes were deep, fathomless, looking out toward something far away.

"Grandmother was always strong," said Karen, thinking back to the years when she and her sisters had gone over to Elm Street after school.

"Strong, independent." Miss Carver's low whisper seemed to stroke each word respectfully. "That's what we'd all like to be, isn't it?"

Karen nodded.

"But there comes a time—for all of us—when we can't be strong and independent any more." The smile was gentle, as though its purpose was to soothe a frightened child at bedtime. "That's why we have places like Svendsen's."

"Don't people sometimes get their strength back and go home?" said Karen. She looked at Miss Carver appealingly, trying to coax some comforting words out of the beautifully starched white uniform. Even though the visits to White Towers had been discouraging, Karen still had hopes of someday seeing her grandmother walking briskly toward her.

"Very rarely." Miss Carver paused, her smile faintly tinged with pity. "That's hard for you to accept, isn't it?"

Karen nodded once more, feeling her thoughts had again been searched out by the light blue eyes behind their rimless glasses.

"It's always hard," continued Miss Carver. "Every family has difficulty in accepting the fact that a strong, active person might someday need care, constant care, more care than the family itself can give."

"But don't you see improvement now and then?" Karen looked over toward the small door, as though to summon up reassurance for her grandmother: presently immobile, sitting in her private room, silent in the midst of street noise from down below and Mantovani strings from the corridor outside.

"Of course we see improvement." Miss Carver's pale face lit up. "Good food is probably the best medicine we have."

"I guess the right diet might help a lot," said Karen lamely, disappointed at the lack of an ambitious therapy program.

"The right diet is a well-balanced diet," said Miss Carver. "Elderly people living by themselves tend to snack on doughnuts, sandwiches, and cookies." A frown crept over her pale face and

74

quickly vanished. "These are a lot easier to fix than a well-balanced meal."

"Cooking for yourself isn't easy," said Karen, trying to imagine her grandmother alone in the kitchen of the Elm Street house.

"Not when your sight is failing and you have trouble finding your way around," said Miss Carver grimly. "Out here our residents have good food, regular hours, fresh air, and pleasant country to walk around in." She rose and gestured toward the dining room. "Why don't we take a look at what we have?"

Miss Carver took Karen out to the dining room again. Passing through the mahogany bookcases that framed the main entrance, they went upstairs to the second floor. There, from an enclosed porch facing toward the back, they could see a doll-sized lake with ducks swimming on the far side. Not too far from the ducks a woman in a blue jacket and white skirt was walking a small group of elderly people along a brick pathway that led to one of the outbuildings.

They left the porch and walked along a corridor that traversed the east wing of the building. Without exception the doors to each bedroom were open and the beds could be seen as freshly made. Some of the beds were regulation hospital beds. Others had elaborate headboards and flowered bedspreads. There were two vacancies, both of them in small single bedrooms at the far end of the corridor.

As they came back toward the porch Karen saw an elderly white-haired lady approaching them. She stepped aside to let them pass, not unlike a small child removing herself from the ominous progress of two adult giants. Miss Carver nodded pleasantly to the elderly white-haired lady, but neither of them spoke. It was a quiet encounter.

And it was Karen's only encounter. Nearly all the residents, bundled and sweatered, had gone outside, savoring the newly arrived spring with the eagerness of those forced to watch winter through frosted glass.

After touring the west wing and the physical therapy rooms, Miss Carver took Karen back downstairs to the small office. There she took out a mimeographed sheet and explained the charges and clothing requirements, noting as well the relationship of Svendsen's to a local group practice of internists.

"What kinds of medication do you use?" said Karen hesitantly, fearful to offend, yet thinking of what her mother's dark speculations had been like after a visit to White Towers.

"We use it as little as possible," said Miss Carver firmly. "If a resident is fearful, one of the doctors may prescribe something. And sometimes we find it necessary to use restraints. But we never use the stronger drugs—Thorazine, for example."

"Thorazine?"

"You may have seen some nursing facilities where the residents sit motionless for hours at a time."

Karen nodded, picturing to herself quiet rooms at White Towers where elderly ladies and gentlemen sat listlessly watching television.

"That's a good indication they're using Thorazine," frowned Miss Carver.

"Something that makes them easy to handle?"

"Exactly." Miss Carver permitted herself a grim smile. "But that's not good care." Although the voice remained soft, a strong intensity rippled beneath it, like a cold underwater current coursing deeply.

"Are some nursing homes worse than others, then?"

"Some of them are a disgrace!" Miss Carver's intensity began to surface. "Take bed sores, for example. Bed sores are *always* a sign of poor care, and we've seen plenty of them in people who have been brought to us." The light blue eyes flashed slightly. "Three months ago we had an elderly woman come here with bed sores *all over her back*. Have you ever seen what they look like?"

Karen shook her head, sensing that Miss Carver's small burst of anger would not brook denial.

"They're dreadfully painful, they take forever to heal, and they're *completely unnecessary.*" Miss Carver paused to let the heat fill the room before cooling it with her soft voice again. "Elderly people need good care, and that means a one-to-eight ratio of working staff to residents."

"Does the ratio vary much?"

"On paper, no. It's a state requirement. But some places— profit and nonprofit—eat into that ratio with special programs and administrative staff." Her smiled returned: gentle, almost complacent. "That's why Svendsen's has stayed small and emphasized good long-term care for the residents we have."

"If my grandmother were to come here, you would see her as a permanent guest?" Karen was surprised at how well the question came out, almost as though she were comfortable with an interviewer's role.

"A permanent guest." Miss Carver took the phrase and made it her own, smiling with pleasure. "Living out her days in comfort and dignity with us." She paused, letting a faraway look come into the light blue eyes behind their rimless glasses. "And when the end comes, as it must, we prefer that it come right here, rather than in a hospital with all the tubes and pumps." She sat back and smiled kindly at Karen.

"It's a lovely place," said Karen, somehow reluctant to say the words that would irretrievably ticket her grandmother for delivery to Miss Carver's quiet domain. "But as I told you over the phone, my father and Mr. Leach will have to make the formal arrangements."

"I understand," whispered Miss Carver. "And they're fortunate in having a mature young person like you to do some of their work for them."

"I'm glad to do whatever I can." Karen reached for the mimeographed sheets and rose, taking the initiative, much to her surprise.

Softly, noiselessly, Miss Carver got up and led Karen out through the dining room again, past the mahogany bookcases to the main entrance. There they walked down a short flight of carpeted stairs and took a corridor curving round to the front of the building. Miss Carver remained standing there until Karen reached her car and pulled out of the parking area.

Although Karen had glowed a little at the implicit praise in Miss Carver's last remark, she was happy to see the beautifully starched white uniform disappear from sight in her rear-view mirror. And she was happy that she had not made a firm commitment to Miss Carver: a commitment that would in effect ratify Mr. Leach's thrifty suggestion.

Svendsen's was a lovely place, far superior to the plastic brutalities of White Towers. And yet there was something upsetting about it, something subtle, something darkly murmuring under the whispered words floating through the carpeted corridors.

"Come, relax, give up the struggle, let us take care of you at Svendsen's." This was what she had heard in Miss Carver's slow resonant whisper. A kindly invitation, but a disquieting one. An invitation that called for a complete surrender to the soft voice and to the steel will that lived beneath it. Not that the steel will would ever impose itself with violence and hurtfulness: It was impossible to imagine Miss Carver giving way to rage, just as it was impossible to imagine anything happening at Svendsen's without Miss Carver's complete knowledge and approval.

Karen tried to shrug the matter away. But the feeling remained, when she drove up to a roadside coffee shop a few miles away. It disappeared for a moment as she went inside, sat down at the counter, and gave her order to the waitress. Then it returned, bringing with it a specific detail to support her uneasiness about the gray blocks of granite brooding quietly over the stands of corn below.

It was the mahogany bookcases in the dining room. They were handsome pieces, and she had admired them along with their contents: bowls, figurines, even intricately carved ivory elephants. But there had been no books in the bookcases. Nor had she seen newspapers and magazines in her tour. It was as though Miss Carver had blotted out the rest of the world by a gentle act of will.

And the erasure had been complete, like soft successive strokes of a pencil's rubber head on bond paper, so that only the surface remained: a kindly and pleasant mist, much like a dimly remembered childhood. As in childhood, the mist was lit up every now and then with colored story-pictures. But these were always hazed over by the rhythms of daily concern and care, so that it was necessary to move slowly, led by the hand sometimes, doing as one was told docilely and without strong-voiced complaint.

When her bowl of soup came, Karen was still pondering her odd mixture of uneasiness and desire. For she had found Svendsen's to be lovely, just the kind of place she would choose for herself if ever the day came when her own mind began to burn with a fainter and fainter glow. Many times she had yearned for a blurred enchanted garden from which pain and failure would be forever banished, never to come back and thunder at a door kept firmly locked.

Monday, April 19, 1:15 P.M.

Karen's progress on the narrow, deep-rutted dirt road was unbearably slow. The cement mixer ahead of her was elephantine, impassable, its gray bowl—revolving like a whimsically dislocated carnival ride—barely visible through the dust. And behind her was

78

a dirty blue pickup truck: Through her rear-view mirror she could see the driver, a bearded young man wearing a bright yellow workman's hat. The pickup truck was impatient, snapping at her heels every time she slowed down to avoid a particularly heavy cloud of dust from the creaking bulk in front.

Unable to pull off or turn around, she glowered at her circumstances, knitting her brow and letting her lower lip protrude slightly. By rights her father should be traveling this rural stepchild of the highway department. Or the thrifty Mr. Leach. Or Lisa. Or Uncle Harold, or Aunt Gloria. A nineteen-year-old girl had no business canvassing nursing homes like a cosmetics saleswoman knocking at one door after another.

And the door to St. Hild's Convalescent Hospital had swung open and shut several times.

It had first opened up for her in the coffee shop: As she pondered the quietly implacable hopelessness of Svendsen's, she found herself thinking of Minneapolis Central and of the red-haired nurse there. The red-haired nurse had been optimistic, insistently so, dinning a sense of place and time into her grandmother's reluctant ears. And according to the red-haired nurse this was the approach used at St. Hild's.

Remembering that St. Hild's lay somewhere north of the city, she had quickly finished her soup, paid her check, and gone outside to the phone booth. The door to the phone booth had been shut, the phone booth itself occupied by two heavy-thighed young women in jeans, boots, and leather jackets. When it finally opened to explode them out, roaring away on their motorcycle, she had gone inside to search for an address and a phone number in the directory.

But the directory had been in tatters, completely useless.

She had stepped back outside to contemplate the omen. Choosing not to heed it, she had returned to the phone and dialed for information, stammering slightly as she outlined her vague request to the cool flat voice of the operator. To her surprise St. Hild's had turned out to have actual existence and to have a telephone number attached to it. Encouraged, she had dug through her purse for change and made the call. But the line had been busy.

So she had gone back outside again, relinquishing the booth to a sweaty middle-aged man in a corduroy coat. After he had made several calls she tried again, letting the phone ring persistently until a voice came on the line. The voice had told her that both Mrs. Polanski, the supervisor, and Mrs. Nash, the head nurse, were at lunch. Deciding to call again after driving home, she had gone back to her car.

She had not started the car right away. She sat there, speculatively eyeing the still-empty phone booth. Like a detective, she had the scent of the chase in her nostrils. Besides, as she glumly reminded herself, the afternoon stretched out before her like a blank piece of note paper. So it was with sudden resolution that she darted out of her car and back into the coffee shop. There she accumulated more change on the pretext of buying a pack of gum, and proceeded to place another call to the disembodied voice guarding St. Hild's.

The disembodied voice had not been unfriendly: Giggling a little, it had given her a complex maze of directions, along with an apologetic description of the construction work in progress on the south side of the building. She had followed the directions to the best of her ability, trying to keep track of turns, jogs, and landmarks. It had not been easy: After getting a school landmark confused with a church, she had almost given up. But she forced herself to stop at a small fly-ridden grocery store for reorientation.

Finding herself reasonably close to her target, she had gone on. Even then she had to retrace her steps a couple of times before finally locating the promised weather-beaten stenciled sign.

The sign had pointed her up the narrow dirt road: a road that ran parasitically along the railroad tracks for a while and then struck off up a hill toward the right. There she had fallen in behind the cement mixer, reassured when it bypassed a left fork that led to a Methodist summer camp. But the dust was distressing. Like the giggling voice, it suggested irresponsibility, an enterprise in tatters, as had been the ill-omened phone book back at the coffee shop.

Karen's distress was not removed by her first sight of St. Hild's. As she pulled into a long one-way drive, still following the cement mixer, she saw a large old red brick building topped by a faded white cupola. In front of the building was a sparse lawn with a few wicker chairs scattered aimlessly about. A small cracked concrete driveway circled its way through the lawn and up to the front entrance, ducking in and out of an arched carriage porch. There was no parking area.

She pulled off to the right and watched the blue pickup truck herd the mixer over to the other side of the building. There she could see piles of sand, lumber, and gravel brought to a focus by a pair of construction trailers. Though almost a hundred yards away, she could hear the hoarse cries of workmen urging one another on in what appeared to be a sustained demolitory attack, much as though the summer camp Methodists had sent their mercenaries to destroy the impious headquarters of some strange, eccentric religious cult.

Deciding to leave her car where it was, she got out and picked her way across the sparse lawn, taking care not to trip over the mounds and holes that pocked it. As she reached the front entrance one of the cult members—a small gray-haired lady wearing knee stockings—came out and accosted her.

"Has Mr. Anderson arrived yet?" The pinched face of the elderly fanatic had a clearly accusing look to it.

"I don't know," said Karen, fearing that her uncertainty might stamp her as a Methodist spy.

The two of them stared at each other, mourning the absent Mr. Anderson. The small elderly lady walked back inside. Karen followed her, standing awkwardly by the door while the lady marched on to confront a trim, fortyish woman dressed flamboyantly in gray slacks and bright blue blazer, not unlike a squad leader from an Elks Auxiliary drill team.

"Has Mr. Anderson come yet?" The small elderly lady was apparently not to be denied in the matter.

"No, Mrs. Anderson," said the trim, fortyish woman. "Your son won't be here until five o'clock." She bent down and shouted into the pinched face below her. "That's almost four hours from now, four . . . hours . . . from . . . now."

"Four hours from now," said Mrs. Anderson. Finding comfort in the phrase, she wandered slowly down the corridor and disappeared from sight.

"Hello," said the trim, fortyish woman, finally turning her attention toward Karen, who was still standing awkwardly in the doorway. Even though the distance between them was short, the voice was loud and accompanied by a facial gesture of more-than-ordinary explicitness. It was a broad face, fair, with clear blue eyes, capped by short blond curls.

"I'm looking for Mrs. Polanski," said Karen. "I phoned earlier today."

"The red room!" said the trim, fortyish woman. "The . . . red . . . room." With a large dramatic gesture she clapped her hand to her head, as though to cudgel it for some mysterious offense. "And here I was on my way outside!"

Karen smiled and shifted her weight from one foot to the other as she tried to puzzle out the meaning of the strange cultish cryptogram.

"I'm Mrs. Polanski," said the trim, fortyish woman. "And Nancy put the message right on my desk." She gestured toward a small office opening off the corridor on Karen's right. "How about a cup of coffee?"

"Thank you," said Karen, resolved to humor this odd person. She followed Mrs. Polanski into the cluttered office and watched two Styrofoam cups appear, to be filled with coffee from a vacuum warmer.

"Here it is," said Mrs. Polanski, triumphantly locating a piece of paper somewhere on the other side of the sugar and cream. "Miss Karen Cimino, Miss . . . Karen . . . Cimino." She sat back, lit a cigarette, and sighed heavily.

"My father has asked me to look at places that might be suitable for my grandmother," said Karen stiffly. Still under Miss Carver's spell, she kept her voice low and unhurried.

"I hope you're not looking for a rest home!" The fair face under the blonde curls dissolved into sudden, bold laughter. "This construction has thrown everything into an uproar, into . . . an . . . uproar."

"I suppose the noise is . . . upsetting," said Karen, letting her ear sort out the various hums and grindings that came through the top of the window behind Mrs. Polanski's right shoulder.

"The residents are taking it very well," said Mrs. Polanski, leaning forward with a confidential air. "It's the staff who are cracking up." She threw both hands above her head as though to hold back the ceiling from crushing the two of them. Then she collapsed and took a deep pull from her cigarette, exhaling the smoke with great and obvious gusto.

Karen's interview with Miss Carver had given her a sense of the basic information necessary. So she launched into a brief history: her grandmother's age, the cataract operation, the confusion, Dr. Wolf's diagnosis, and the trusteeship.

"Atrophy of brain cells!" Mrs. Polanski gave a couple of vigorous hoots. "Shrinkage! Alzheimer's disease!" She blew them away with a deeply generated puff of smoke. "That's what they all say."

"But it showed up on the brain scan," said Karen, not quite prepared to accept such a blithe disregard for advanced medical technology.

"Of course it showed up on the brain scan," said Mrs. Polanski. "It would show up on your brain scan, too."

Karen stared blankly at the fair face smiling at her from across the cluttered desk.

"We're all losing brain cells," continued Mrs. Polanski airily. "You, me, everybody—you . . . me . . . everybody."

"What's the cause of senile dementia, then?"

"Senile dementia? Senility?" Mrs. Polanski shook her blonde curl-capped head forcefully. "Those are just words the medical profession uses when it doesn't want to do anything. And it certainly doesn't want to do anything with people over sixty-five." She snubbed her cigarette out with finality, then lit a new one. "If your grandmother had been under that age, they would have referred her to a good psychiatrist, to . . . a . . . good . . . psychiatrist."

"Psychiatrist?" Karen tried to puzzle out the haziness creeping into what had been a clearly defined landscape. "Are you saying my grandmother's condition is a . . . psychological problem?"

"Yes!" Mrs. Polanski enunciated the word with relish. "Except for the fact that people over sixty-five aren't *supposed* to have psychological problems. So the only thing left is to lock the door and throw away the key."

"Permanently," said Karen, thinking back again to Miss Carver's soft, resonant whisper. "And that's what custodial care is, isn't it?"

"Exactly," smiled Mrs. Polanski. "But at St. Hild's we don't give custodial clare. We give rehabilitation care."

She rose and gestured expansively toward the corridor. Karen got up and followed her out. Just down from her office was a four-bed ward. Inside it Karen could see a tall elderly man sitting in a chair, reading a newspaper.

"Mr. Higgins," said Mrs. Polanski without breaking stride. "Ninety-five years old."

At the end of the corridor was a circular hall, part of it taken up by a nurses station. Behind the counter was a thirtyish woman in a white pantsuit. She was wearing dark-tinted horn-rimmed glasses that seemed to give her thin face a look of perpetual concern.

"Mrs. Nash, this is Miss Cimino," said Mrs. Polanski.

"The red room?" said Mrs. Nash, a faraway meditative look in her eye.

"I think so," said Mrs. Polanski. Leaving the cryptogram undeciphered, she whisked Karen off to the other side of the circular hall. There they looked in at the dining room, still filled with the clatter of dishes being removed from the various-sized tables. Over by the window on the right were three elderly ladies, one leaning heavily on a cane, watching the construction activity outside.

"It's the beards," said Mrs. Polanski. "Most of those young men have beards." She wheeled Karen immediately around and took her up a nearby flight of stairs. On the right-hand side of the stairs was an inclined plane with a small chair-seat at the top.

"Our elevator." Mrs. Polanski nodded, then frowned severely. "But the state inspectors don't like it. That's one of the reasons for all the furor, all . . . the . . . furor."

Once up the stairs, they went rapidly down a corridor lined with two-bed rooms. The door of each room was painted a different color, brightly echoed by the woodwork trim inside.

"For old eyes the colors are a lot better than those tiny numbers," said Mrs. Polanski, taking Karen down to the far end where a red door stood open. They went in. It was not a large room: two hospital beds, two small dressers, two night stands, two straight-backed chairs, and one closet.

"Mrs. Yeager has the far bed," said Mrs. Polanski. "So your grandmother would have the near one." She paused and looked sharply at Karen. "It's the only one we have free."

Karen nodded and Mrs. Polanski sped her back down to the circular hall. There they took a few steps down another corridor. The right-hand side was lined with small color photographs of elderly ladies and gentlemen.

"Our graduates," said Mrs. Polanski. "These are residents who have left us."

"Left?" said Karen, fearing some macabre euphemism was involved.

"Left, departed, recovered, convalesced," said Mrs. Polanski firmly. "That's why we still call it a convalescent hospital."

"Where do they go?"

"Back home." Mrs. Polanski wheeled Karen round again. "Back to their families, back . . . to . . . their . . . families."

With mounting excitement Karen followed Mrs. Polanski back to her cluttered office. There Mrs. Polanski poured out some more coffee and lit up another cigarette.

"Could you help my grandmother?" The question was not an easy one to ask. Karen was prepared to endure a cautious disclaimer or even a rebuff.

"From what you've told me, I think we might be able to bring her around." Mrs. Polanski exhaled mightily and watched the smoke float up to the ceiling. "We've certainly had them much worse—violent, suicidal, completely disoriented, climbing the walls."

"I still don't understand what brings something like this on."

"Bad luck," said Mrs. Polanski flatly. "Generally it's a response to a series of blows, one right after another."

"Like a double cataract operation followed by a fall?"

"Exactly." Mrs. Polanski sipped her coffee reflectively and savored her cigarette again. "We had a man of sixty-eight come in here last fall. In the space of only four months his wife had divorced him, his house had been sold, and his gall bladder had been removed. Pretty upsetting for anyone, wouldn't you say?"

Karen nodded.

"Two weeks after getting out of the hospital he developed a serious staph infection and had to be taken back to the hospital again. Another bad blow?"

Karen nodded again.

"When his son brought him home for the second time he was completely out of it, completely . . . out . . . of . . . it. They had to bring him here in a straightjacket under heavy sedation."

"Did he get better?"

"After two weeks with us he knew who he was and where he was. After three months he went home." Mrs. Polanski smiled at the memory. "A fine, tall man he was, too. The best dancer we had at the Christmas party."

"So it was a psychological problem?" said Karen.

"A psychological *response*," said Mrs. Polanski. "Something set in motion by a series of traumatic experiences."

"Like getting depressed?" Karen's voice was shy, tentative.

"In a way," smiled Mrs. Polanski. "When things get too much for us we get depressed, hysterical, physically sick sometimes. Or we may rob a bank. With elderly people the general pattern is to withdraw into confusion from a world they don't like and that doesn't like them." She sat back beamingly, as though the matter were easily summed up, easily manageable.

"Do you have many cases that work out successfully?"

"We don't win them all," said Mrs. Polanski ruefully. "Especially when there are serious physical problems involved. But about thirty percent actually leave here under their own power and go home."

"Thirty percent!" said Karen, thinking back to Miss Carver's air of quiet downhill certainty. "That's incredible."

"It's not easy. We have to stay on them all the time to keep them from slipping back. And in some cases they're too far gone for us to do them any good." Mrs. Polanski looked pensively at her cigarette before snubbing it out in a dark green ashtray over on the left-hand side of her desk.

Karen was silent for a moment. With only one empty bed there was a feeling of urgency in the air, some of it generated by the fast pace of their brief tour of inspection: a tour that had allowed no time for detailed scrutiny. And the place itself was bizarre: a chain-smoking director, shabby furnishings, loud construction noises outside, and an overly theatrical arrogance.

But the promise was unequivocal, the first words of hope she had heard since her talk with the red-haired nurse at Minneapolis Central. And the promise seemed to have substance to it, judging from the general talkiness of the residents. The small elderly lady in knee stockings, for example, had marched right up to Mrs. Polanski and spoken her piece, rather than shrinking quietly back.

"I'd really like to see my grandmother come here," she said, trying to make her voice sound forceful and mature. "What are your admission procedures?"

"Complicated," frowned Mrs. Polanski. "Technically we're still administered by St. Hild's in the city. I haven't even let them know about the red room yet."

"Is there some way we could work this out today?" said Karen, suddenly fearful that the red room might fall into other hands. "I'd like to give you a firm commitment."

"Maybe you should take a look at our schedule of charges," smiled Mrs. Polanski. She took out a mimeographed sheet of paper and handed it to Karen. Then she sat back and lit up another cigarette.

To Karen's surprise the basic rate was only thirty-two dollars a day, less than Svendsen's and far under the inflated bloodletting of White Towers. Exhilarated, she phoned her father at work, holding her breath until he was safely on the line. Though not enthusiastic, his approval was firm, supported in large part by the relatively low room rate. Just to be on the safe side, she went on to phone Mr. Leach at the bank and got his assurance that the transfer would be both thrifty and wise. Cheeks glowing, she heaved a sigh of relief, sat back in her chair, and smiled shyly at Mrs. Polanski.

"I've never been much good talking on the telephone," she said.

"You seem pretty enterprising to me," said Mrs. Polanski. She gestured expansively with her cigarette. "Just finding this place is quite an accomplishment, quite . . . an . . . accomplishment."

Karen nodded, thinking of the network of false starts, chance and discouragement that had finally threaded her up the narrow dirt road to her grandmother's new address.

"Monday is our regular admission day," continued Mrs. Polanski. "And we like to keep it that way, since our orientation procedure takes a full week of intensive work."

"What should we bring her?"

"Wash-and-wear things, as much as you can manage it," said Mrs. Polanski, taking out another mimeographed sheet. "The knee-length stockings are a good idea at first. Make sure she has some spending money for stamps, phone calls, and incidentals."

"She's always liked handling her own money," said Karen.

"We encourage it—even with the gamblers." Mrs. Polanski cast a disapproving glance in the general direction of the four-bed ward down the corridor.

"What time Monday?"

"Ten o'clock will get her off to a good start," smiled Mrs. Polanski. "And the red room is hers until she's in shape to go home."

Karen said goodbye and headed for her car, walking on air. If she hurried she would be able to get the admission forms signed and in the mail that afternoon. Her father's coolness had dampened her spirits a little, but it had been a good day's work: ups and downs, highs and lows, finally taking shape in a hopeful trajectory pointed far beyond the immediate horizon.

And she had been the one to find the target, light the fuse.

Her car was parked a good hundred yards away, and the one-way drive required her to round the building before heading back on the narrow dirt road. It was several minutes before she passed by the construction area, taking note of several overalled men looking collectively up at a newly forced, jagged hole in the old red brick building. Beside the men, gesturing dramatically and commanding their attention, was a small figure in a blue blazer wearing a bright yellow workman's hat.

As Karen slowed down to get a better view of Mrs. Polanski's performance, the light blue pickup truck began to pull out in front of her. With firm resolve she honked three times and speeded up. The bearded young man at the wheel of the pickup scowled at her. She did not scowl back, but chose to smile urbanely: sure of her just claim on the road and confident of her ability to maintain a proper speed ahead of him.

It was not until she reached the freeway, some twenty minutes later, that her confident good humor melted slightly, like a noble fancy put to close scrutiny by cold, able, hard, unfriendly folk.

Tuesday, April 27, 8:10 A.M.

When Mrs. Cimino came down for breakfast, the first thing she saw by the nurses station was a large sign in vivid purple letters. Curious, she adjusted her glasses and approached it, slowly spelling out what it had to tell her: "Today is Tuesday, April 27, 1976. The Next Meal is Breakfast. The Next Holiday is Mother's Day."

She shook her head, irritated at the intrusiveness of the announcement. Cautiously she continued her progress toward the clatter of plates and cutlery that filtered in through her hearing aid. She did not like the hearing aid, but a young woman in a blue smock had come bustling into her room and stuffed it in her ear.

Her room had a red door. It was small. It was too far away from the dining room. The stairs had been difficult for her. There

88

was a seedy look to the place: It reminded her of the cheap hotels she and Frank had stayed at during their last year on the road with Chief Kona Kai and his Hawaiian Serenaders.

"Mrs. Cimino! Mrs. Cimino!"

She stopped her slow journey toward breakfast. She turned around to confront the noise attacking her. It was a woman with blonde hair who had been doing the shouting. The woman was wearing a bright green blazer and beige slacks. Gaudy, but better than the sullen white creatures of the other place.

"You're shuffling." There was a stern, accusing tone to the blonde woman's voice.

"Shuffling?" Mrs. Cimino looked down at her small feet as though they had somehow been attached to her by mistake.

"Yes, you're shuffling," said the blonde woman. "Shuffling . . . shuffling . . . shuffling." Her broad, fair face seemed curiously contorted. It was now bent down, dangerously close to Mrs. Cimino's nose.

"I'm not walking very fast, if that's what you mean." Mrs. Cimino smiled up at the hovering blonde woman. "But a person my age has to be careful these days."

"That's no excuse for shuffling." The blonde woman continued to dominate Mrs. Cimino's field of vision. "What's my name?"

"I've never been very good at names," said Mrs. Cimino. She gave an embarrassed little laugh.

"We had a long talk yesterday," said the blonde woman.

"It's nice to see you again," said Mrs. Cimino, nodding pleasantly as she tried to sort things out. "You must be the manager of this hotel." She brightened at the notion and attempted to direct the conversation toward more neutral ground. "Isn't it wonderful what interesting jobs there are for young women these days?"

"This is not a hotel, Mrs. Cimino." The blonde woman seemed resolute in her refusal to engage in small talk.

"I used to be in business myself," said Mrs. Cimino, faded blue eyes clouding a little. "My late husband and I had a music store."

"This is not a hotel." The blonde woman's voice was growing impossibly loud. "This is a hospital . . . hospital . . . hospital!"

"A hospital?" Mrs. Cimino looked up at her in mild wonderment. "What on earth am I doing in a hospital?"

"This is St. Hild's Convalescent Hospital, and you're here to get better."

"That sounds like a good idea," said Mrs. Cimino. She puzzled over the premise for a moment and tried to see where it would take here. "If I get better my walking should improve."

"That's right."

"So I really should be careful about my walking right now." Mrs. Cimino smiled engagingly up at the blonde woman. "Isn't that right?"

A brief smile flickered over the blonde woman's fair face. She looked down and over at the right lapel of her green blazer. A white card was pinned there. The card had red lettering on it.

"Can you read what's on this card, Mrs. Cimino?"

"Let me see." Mrs. Cimino squinted up at the card and spelled it out. "Mrs. Po . . . lan . . . ski." She stepped back and relaxed a little. "You're Mrs. Polanski."

"Very good!" said Mrs. Polanski, as though something of moment had been achieved.

"It's nice to see you again, Mrs. Polanski." Mrs. Cimino lowered her voice, as though to share a confidence. "But I have to be careful about reading things." She reached up and tapped the right sidepiece of her thick-lensed glasses. "My eyes have been giving me a lot of trouble lately."

"That's a cop-out, Mrs. Cimino." Mrs. Polanski's voice was hard, unsympathetic.

"A what?"

"A cop-out, an excuse."

"Do you think so?" There was mild interest in Mrs. Cimino's eyes. She appeared to entertain the notion without rancor.

"I'm sure of it," said Mrs. Polanski firmly. "With your glasses on you can read anything you want."

"That's good to hear," said Mrs. Cimino cheerfully. She continued to smile at Mrs. Polanski, as though the conversation had arrived at a point where it might properly be terminated.

"How about some breakfast?" Without waiting for an answer Mrs. Polanski led Mrs. Cimino into the dining room. A young girl in a light blue smock came up.

"This is Mrs. Cimino, Wendy."

Wendy smiled and took out a small ruled notebook.

"We have you down as a member of our violet-table group," she said, gesturing over toward the window on the left. "Along with Mrs. Anderson, Mrs. Wohlsteader, and Miss Schmidt."

90

Mrs. Cimino looked around the dining room. It was not very impressive: tables without tablecloths, paper napkins, and a great deal of idle chatter, particular from some of the men in the center. On each table was a small, cheap white vase with artificial flowers in it, giving the effect of a desperate attempt to maintain gentility in a shabby, run-down boardinghouse.

"We'll see you in class later on," shouted Mrs. Polanski, hurrying back out the door to the nurses station.

Determined to maintain a pleasant façade, Mrs. Cimino followed Wendy over to the table decked out with three plastic violets. There she was introduced to her companions and given a glass of orange juice. Smiling, she sipped her juice and inspected the other elderly ladies.

Mrs. Anderson, seated directly across from her, with a good view of the window, was a small woman: thin, pinched-faced, but with the stringy endurance of someone who has spent a lifetime squeezing a subsistence out of two hundred acres. Her hair was in a bun and she was wearing a plain cotton dress. Speaking little, she kept her head moving back and forth as the conversation volleyed between the two others.

Mrs. Wohlsteader, on Mrs. Cimino's left, was a tall woman, still on the heavy side, with gold-framed glasses and gray hair. The hair, with a bluish tint to it, showed signs of proper attention, as did her carriage, for she sat very erect in her chair, much as though the admonitions of dancing teachers and gimlet-eyed relatives still rang in her ears. She was wearing a diamond ring—not a large one, but cunningly designed and set. It reminded Mrs. Cimino of her own engagement ring, bought by Frank in Erie, Pennsylvania, back in early, prosperous times.

She had treasured that ring, taken joy in it: Like a wee splinter in her finger, its loss still fretted her; and she still blushed hotly at what, according to George, had been her carelessness in letting it slip off.

On her right was a very short, squat, heavy-faced lady: Miss Schmidt. Her hair was beautifully white and thick, coiled in a large bun that certified its length and resiliency. Her rimless glasses were small, oblong, permitting the gray-green eyes behind them to peer over at moments of quizzical interest. She was dressed severely in a black skirt and plain white blouse. Over the back of her chair was a sturdy rubber-tipped cane.

"Scrambled eggs again," said Mrs. Wohlsteader. There was clear reproach in her cultivated voice as the girl wheeled a cart up to their table.

"They always have scrambled eggs on Tuesday," announced Miss Schmidt, looking over at Mrs. Cimino. She closed her statement off with a quick, toothy smile, much like a teacher of mathematics trying to find intrinsic charm in an obvious geometrical proof.

Mrs. Cimino smiled back at Miss Schmidt. The sign in the circular hall had apparently been correct: It was Tuesday. In much better humor she began to butter her toast.

"My son likes scrambled eggs," said Mrs. Anderson, a faraway look on her pinched face. "Too bad he's not here."

"Well, he's not," said Miss Schmidt. "We're here and he isn't."

Mrs. Cimino shrank back from the clear logic of the observation: She would have preferred something blander, something on the order of a pleasantry regarding young men and hearty appetites. If Mrs. Anderson had not been staring out the window, she would have smiled reassurance at her.

"And in a while even we won't be here," continued Miss Schmidt, punctuating her dismal sentence with another quickly flashed smile.

"The Good Lord will decide that in His own sweet time," said Mrs. Wohlsteader. Finding solace in her thought, she helped herself to more toast.

"He has more time than we have," said Miss Schmidt.

"It doesn't bother me," replied Mrs. Wohlsteader. "I'm leaving my body to medical science." She munched her toast, lightly buttered, with an air of proud resignation.

"Medical science!" said Miss Schmidt. "Doctors!" She took up her fork and divided her scrambled eggs into four neat sections. "All those doctors do is poke at you." She gave another quick, toothy smile of punctuation.

Mrs. Wohlsteader remained unruffled.

"Some doctors are good, some doctors are bad," she said. "I'm leaving my body to the good ones." Tall, erect, she allowed her diamond to gesture complete control of the matter. "It's all spelled out in my will."

"Lawyers!" Miss Schmidt nodded over at Mrs. Cimino as

92

though to enlist her in the forces of dark cynicism. "You can't trust them either."

"Those lawyers have to do what your will says," explained Mrs. Wohlsteader patiently. "And my will clearly states that my body is to be left to medical science." She smiled graciously back at Miss Schmidt.

At this point one of the young girls came by with more coffee. As the cups were being replenished the conversation waned, and Mrs. Cimino was able to give more sustained thought to Mrs. Wohlsteader and her curious bequest. The bequest was generously intentioned, she concluded, but Mrs. Wohlsteader was still a little too much the great lady for comfort.

The erect carriage and gracious air reminded Mrs. Cimino of her older sister, Rose. Of the three McDonald sisters, Rose had early moved into the position of family princess. When she entertained callers it was always in the parlor, and it was there in the parlor that she imperiously required her younger sisters, Esther and Emily, to serve tea. Not content with this regal demand, she had further insisted that Esther and Emily curtsey like French maids.

Still boiling at the unfairness of the arrangement and at the injustice of her father's indulgence of it, Mrs. Cimino found herself beginning to scowl at the well-intentioned Mrs. Wohlsteader.

"How do you know they'll take it?" said Miss Schmidt, looking speculatively over her rimless glasses at Mr. Wohlsteader.

"Take what?" said Mrs. Wohlsteader. She had been sipping her coffee and looking about the room, avoiding only the tables in the center. Some of the elderly gentlemen there—Mr. Stewart and Mr. Monsour, for example—had been known to pass remarks if given the appearance of encouragement.

"How do you know they'll take your body?"

"They'll take it," said Mrs. Wohlsteader. She smiled composure at her companions. "Those doctors need all the bodies they can get."

"I doubt that," said Miss Schmidt. She sipped her own coffee and winked broadly at Mrs. Cimino.

"They need bodies very much," said Mrs. Wohlsteader. "And that's a known fact."

"A fact?"

"I saw it in the newspaper last year," said Mrs. Wohlsteader, lowering her voice slightly. "That's what gave me the idea."

"Newspapers?" Miss Schmidt shook her head with obvious distress. "Most of them are notoriously unreliable." She looked grimly at Mrs. Cimino and at Mrs. Anderson. "If they need bodies at all—which I seriously doubt—they're certainly looking for *young* bodies, not old ones like yours." After her customary smile of punctuation, Miss Schmidt looked over at Mrs. Wohlsteader's large frame with thinly disguised contempt.

"That's not what the newspaper said." Mrs. Wohlsteader's aplomb was visibly shaken, but she managed to hang on.

"The newspaper didn't have to spell it all out," said Miss Schmidt. "It's a matter of simple logic, and simple logic ought to tell you that those doctors do not want your body." She emphasized her last point by tapping her spoon vigorously against the side of her cup.

It was an awkward moment.

"My son would have been a good doctor," said Mrs. Anderson. "He delivered a calf once." She turned her gaze away from the window and managed a smile for Mrs. Wohlsteader. "But he works for the county now." It was the most effective support she could muster.

"Those doctors simply do not want bodies with wrinkles all over them," said Miss Schmidt, pressing her point. "And there's no reason to pretend otherwise." She closed off her end of the conversation with a final large-toothed smile, holding it as she nodded farewell to her table companions. Struggling judiciously up from her chair, she shifted her weight over to her rubber-tipped cane. Slowly she hobbled out of the room, taking good-sized, firm, solidly placed steps.

"Everybody has wrinkles these days," said Mrs. Cimino, finally breaking the dark silence that Miss Schmidt had left behind. She had completely put aside her earlier distaste for Mrs. Wohlsteader: There was good stuff here, honest affection and concern which called for comfortable words.

"Even my son has wrinkles," said Mrs. Anderson. "He'll be fifty this year, I think." She stared out the window, her glance fixed on the trunk of a nearby oak tree.

"Peaches and cream, that's what they used to call it." Mrs. Wohlsteader mournfully contemplated the back of her left hand, the one with the diamond ring. She looked as though she were counting each liver spot.

The breakfast was clearly beginning to disintegrate: Mrs. Anderson was now humming softly to herself, and the young girls were clearing the dishes, stacking them in large metal carts with a great deal of clatter. Feeling it was appropriate to leave, Mrs. Cimino got carefully up and said goodbye.

As she walked past the tables in the center she could hear loud guffaws. Outside some kind of machine was beginning to grunt and chug, and she could even hear men shouting to one another in deep, barking, gruff voices. All in all, the place—whatever they called it—was certainly the noisiest hotel she had ever visited.

Before she started up the stairs to her room with the red door, Mrs. Cimino paused to take a couple of quiet, unhurried breaths. Carefully she looked around, taking in the nurses station and the two corridors leading off from it: The loud, forward blonde in the bright green blazer was nowhere in sight.

Reassured, Mrs. Cimino allowed her left hand to move upward and brush a few gray wisps of hair into place. The hand rested for a moment on the tip of her left ear. Burrowing quickly in, it turned the little ridged wheel down, down, down, and finally off.

The solution was appropriate, and long overdue.

Thursday, April 29, 7:40 A.M.

When Mrs. Nash, the head nurse, came up, Mrs. Cimino was still sitting on the edge of her bed. Dressed in a light blue wrapper, she was busily engaged in sorting through a number of small white envelopes. Beside her on the bed was a large black purse, half open. The bed itself had been made, as had Mrs. Yeager's bed over by the window.

Miss Martin, the nurses aide, was standing by the red door, obviously distressed at the situation. Mrs. Nash nodded to her and the two of them went in together.

"Mrs. Cimino, is something wrong?" Mrs. Nash kept her voice low, letting her words come out at clearly spaced intervals.

"I'm not sure," said Mrs. Cimino, looking thoughtfully at her purse. "But it seems to me I had another envelope here." She smiled up at Mrs. Nash. "Perhaps I need a little desk to help me organize things better when I do my accounts."

"You have a dresser," said Mrs. Nash. She took a closer look at the envelopes: Most of them were stuffed full of small note sheets. A couple of the note sheets were out on the bed. They had been covered with numerical computations, some of them circled for emphasis.

"Yes, I do," said Mrs. Cimino. "And it's a very nice dresser." She put the envelopes and loose note sheets back in her purse.

"Have you decided what you're going to wear down to breakfast?" said Mrs. Nash, moving directly to the issue at hand. She remained standing in front of Mrs. Cimino while Miss Martin moved over to the far side of the room. Miss Martin, new at St. Hild's, had just graduated from high school the preceding January, so she was quite happy at being able to assume the role of observer.

"Breakfast?" Mrs. Cimino looked cheerfully up at Mrs. Nash. "Mabye I should get dressed after breakfast." Her faded blue eyes were full of good humor. "I seem to have a lot of trouble with buttons and things like that."

"You could pick out something simple," said Mrs. Nash quietly. "Something that wouldn't give you much trouble."

"That makes good sense," nodded Mrs. Cimino. She gestured airily over toward the closet. "You girls are all so clever. Anything you decide will suit me just fine."

"But that's not what I said." Mrs. Nash's voice, though calm, was pitched slightly higher. "I asked *you* to pick something out."

"I guess my hearing's not so good either." Mrs. Cimino gave an embarrassed little laugh. "These old cars aren't so easy to start up in the morning, are they?" She turned around for a moment to smile at Miss Martin.

"You have a hearing aid," said Mrs. Nash, choosing not to acknowledge Mrs. Cimino's small pleasantry.

"Maybe I need a new one," smiled Mrs. Cimino. She turned around again to include Miss Martin in the discussion. Miss Martin smiled back but remained where she was, arms folded.

"Why don't we check the one you have?" Mrs. Nash picked up the hearing aid from the night stand by Mrs. Cimino's bed. She turned it on and rolled the little ridged wheel up until a squeal signaled that the battery was still providing power.

"Do you think it's going to work?"

"It *is* working." Mrs. Nash turned the squeal down and placed the hearing aid firmly in Mrs. Cimino's left ear. When it was well seated she turned the volume back up.

"Thank you very much," said Mrs. Cimino. She looked over at the closet again. "And what have you decided I should wear?"

"*You* must decide, Mrs. Cimino."

"Why not?" Mrs. Cimino clapped her hands in a businesslike way and got up. "If I'm going to wear it, I might as well be the one to pick it out." She walked over to the closet, rummaged through it, and emerged with a light blue pleated cotton dress, belted and with pockets on each side. Holding it up queryingly, she looked over at Miss Martin and then at Mrs. Nash.

"That's lovely," said Mrs. Nash. "Very sensible."

"I suppose I need some underthings now." Mrs. Cimino looked expectantly over at Miss Martin, but Miss Martin remained where she was.

"Your underthings and stockings are in your dresser," said Mrs. Nash.

"I suppose they are, now that you mention it." Mrs. Cimino smilingly stood her ground for a while before going over to the dresser and opening up the second drawer from the top. From it she took out slip, panties, and bra.

"Don't forget the stockings," said Mrs. Nash. Her voice was beginning to acquire a clearly discernible edge. And understandably so. Tactfully phrased though they might be, battles like these were immensely tiring. Before coming to the hospital at seven-thirty, Mrs. Nash had risen at six to get breakfast started for her husband and two children, ages seven and ten. Later on in the afternoon, around three o'clock, her feet would begin to hurt.

"Do you think the stockings are a good idea?" Mrs. Cimino furrowed her brow and looked over at Miss Martin again. "Maybe I could come back and put them on after breakfast."

"Your knee-length stockings are very easy to put on," said Mrs. Nash, clearly not amenable to compromise. In another week Mrs. Cimino would be firmly set in a self-sufficient pattern if they kept pushing her. But the pushing wasn't easy: Mild, good-humored resistance, like a wall of Jell-O, was far more difficult to deal with than outright confrontation.

"Yes, yes, of course," said Mrs. Cimino hurriedly. "I might as well put on the stockings." She paused and smiled understandingly at the two of them. "Seems like a lot of trouble to me, but you may be right."

By this time the clothes were all laid out on the bed: light blue cotton dress, slip, panties, bra, and knee-length stockings. Mrs. Cimino stepped back and inspected them with approval. She smiled expectantly at Mrs. Nash and Miss Martin, as though to indicate that her task had been completed.

"Very good," said Mrs. Nash, making no move to fulfill her end of the implicit bargain. "We'll wait outside for you while you get dressed." She nodded to Miss Martin, who left her post by Mrs. Yeager's bed and started for the door.

"Don't worry about me," said Mrs. Cimino, smiling at Miss Martin as she exited. "I'm sure I'll be able to manage very well."

"When you come out we'll walk down to breakfast with you," said Mrs. Nash, permitting herself a smile as she followed Miss Martin out the door.

The two of them walked down the corridor and stopped about halfway between the orange room and the purple room. Like the rest of the rooms, these were empty, their occupants all dressed and down in the dining room.

"Maybe I should go back and help her," said Miss Martin anxiously. "I'm afraid she's going to be very late."

"First things first, Nancy." Mrs. Nash shook her head. "If she's late they can set a place for her at one of the back tables."

"I'm sorry I had to bother you," said Miss Martin. "But she seemed so helpless."

"You did the right thing. She's not an easy one to deal with."

"She's really very sweet." Miss Martin, not without affection, looked back up the corridor.

"Yes, she is," conceded Mrs. Nash. "But there's a lot of stubborness under all that sugar."

"Do you think she understands what's going on here?"

"She understands that we're pushing her to get back in touch with things and she doesn't like it, not one bit." Mrs. Nash sighed, thinking back to her own desire to stay abed that morning. "Not that I blame her."

She walked a few steps toward Mrs. Cimino's room, partly to listen for sounds of wholesome action and partly to distract Nancy from responding to her last remark. For there had been a slight tint of heresy to her words, colored by certain reservations she had about the St. Hild's approach: an approach that was just a shade too aggressive in its insistence that the elderly remain in constant touch with the world around them.

Someone like Mrs. Cimino had surely earned the right to look at the world around her and find it wanting. Her family raised, her resources in order, why shouldn't she withdraw into a comfortably passive existence? Why shouldn't she lose track of the days? Why shouldn't she tell herself that she was in a hotel? Why shouldn't she resist a program designed to nag her away from the fantasy that had softly settled down upon her. It was *her* fantasy, after all.

Mrs. Nash herself was not averse to the pleasures of fantasy. Her husband sold used cars and spent most of his time either on the lot or cronying around town. Her children whined and sniffled their way through the impossible Minnesota winters. Her neighbors, having cast her in the role of Florence Nightingale, were forever seeking her gratis medical advice and assistance. Her house, like a demanding infant, screamed shrilly to be wiped, dusted, and nurtured. And there was no fairy godmother, no magic wand, that would transform these actualities into something better.

Except the mind itself.

So it was on this basis, in a hot bath at the end of the day, with the door securely locked, that Mrs. Nash habitually exercised the only option open to her: She transported herself to Waikiki Beach, Hawaii. Somnolent, kissed by the warm water, she conjured up a vision of herself toweled and stepping out into a luxurious hotel room just beyond her bathroom door, there to dine on mahimahi, papaya, and countless other island delicacies. Later she would go down and enjoy the dancing: well-groomed men in white dinner jackets and ladies in long flowered dresses, an orchestra with steel guitar and soft voices gently harmonizing melodies that dipped and soared like the surf whispering from out beyond the terrace.

It was a noble fancy. And it had begun to creep upon her more and more. Someday perhaps, on a warm afternoon, she would take it outside with her: She would sit in her back yard sipping a frosted glass of iced tea while the acquiescent sunshine rubbed her sallow skin to golden brown. She would sit there for a long, long time: When her actualities came to importune her she would look pleasantly up at them and say, "I didn't ring for room service. But I know the Royal Hawaiian Hotel is justly famous for anticipating the needs of its guests. Now that you're here, please being me another Mai Tai, a big one, with lots of fruit in it." And from that moment on, no matter where they took her, she would always be in the Royal Hawaiian Hotel, smiling appreciation at those who sought to serve her.

Mrs. Nash was still smiling to herself when Mrs. Cimino came out, neatly dressed and ready for her walk down to breakfast. It was Miss Martin who noticed Mrs. Cimino's bare legs.

"Where are your stockings, Mrs. Cimino?" Miss Martin looked over at Mrs. Nash, seeking approval of her firm tone of voice.

"My walking?" Mrs. Cimino smiled happily. "I really think it's getting better, except for judging distances."

"Stockings . . . stockings . . . stockings!" Mrs. Nash quickly put her smiling fancy away and gestured back toward the room with the red door. "Go back and put them on, please." There was obvious irritation in her voice.

"Now, now!" Irritated herself, Mrs. Cimino marched right up to Mrs. Nash, shoulders squared and standing quite straight, as though she were determined to stretch herself a few more inches skyward. "I'm not going to be ordered around like this." She looked at Miss Martin, faded blue eyes ablaze. "What kind of place are you running here?"

"Let's tune in, Mrs. Cimino." Mrs. Nash held her ground and spoke firmly. "This is a hospital, and you know very well it's a hospital."

"If it's a hospital, where are the doctors?" Satisfied that she had scored a telling blow, Mrs. Cimino nodded at Miss Martin, who was beginning to shrink back.

"It's a convalescent hospital, and Dr. Gonzalez comes in every Monday to check you over."

"Gonzalez?" Mrs. Cimino's small nose wrinkled in distaste. "Are we in Argentina?"

"Dr. Gonzalez is an American citizen, just like you," said Mrs. Nash. "He's a fine specialist in geriatric medicine."

"I know what that means," said Mrs. Cimino. "It means old people. And you certainly have enough of them around here." She looked up and down the corridor, as though to chastise the occupants of its variously colored rooms.

"We're a convalescent hospital for older patients—people like yourself who need special care."

"Special care?" Mrs. Cimino paused to consider the matter. "I suppose you must be a nurse of some kind."

100

"I am not a nurse of some kind, Mrs. Cimino. I am the head nurse and my name is Mrs. Nash."

"Mrs. Nash, Mrs. Nash." Mrs. Cimino tested the name for euphony and found it acceptable. "Well, Mrs. Nash, I can't see why a person in your position should get so upset over a pair of silly old stockings."

"I am not upset, Mrs. Cimino, and neither is Miss Martin here." Mrs. Nash forced a smile upon her thin concerned face to indicate complete poise and good will. "But we must insist that you wear stocking down to breakfast with the other ladies."

"The other ladies?" Mrs. Cimino furrowed her brow. "Now that you mention it, it seems to me that Mrs. Wohlsteader and the others do dress up a little." She looked down at her rounded white calves. "Bare legs aren't very attractive, are they?"

"No, they're not," said Miss Martin, feeling she should make a contribution. "Otherwise, you look very nice."

"Stockings it is, then." Mrs. Cimino cheerily led them back to her room and sat down on her bed. "Why don't you two go on ahead? I'll be down there in a jiffy."

"We'll wait here for you," said Mrs. Nash.

"Suit yourself, Mrs. Ford."

"Nash, Mrs. Cimino. The name is Nash."

"That's right, my dear. Just like the car."

At this point Miss Martin, apparently struck with a severe choking spell, left the room and walked down the corridor. There she waited until the stocking victory had been irrevocably won. When the two of them came up to her, Miss Martin smiled warmly.

"You really look very nice this morning, Mrs. Cimino."

"Do you think so?" Mrs. Cimino smiled with pleasure. "I hope it was worth all the trouble." She paused and searched for a moment. "Thank you . . . Miss Martin."

"Very good," said Mrs. Nash. "And can you tell us what day of the week it is today?"

"You have me there." Mrs. Cimino gave another one of her embarrassed little laughs. "But I remember we have a big sign downstairs that spells it out for us." She looked anxiously up at Mrs. Nash. "Is that good enough for now?"

"It'll pass for the moment," conceded Mrs. Nash.

The three of them walked to the head of the stairs. There Mrs. Nash hurried, on, so that she was well below Mrs. Cimino as the descent was made. Last month there had been a bad fall on those stairs, and Mrs. Nash was inclined toward caution in matters like these, knowing that old bones were brittle and that they sometimes gave way unexpectedly.

Holding methodically on to the banister, Mrs. Cimino came down the stairs unassisted. Once down to the circular hall, she went directly over to the large, purple-lettered sign.

"Thursday, April twenty-ninth, nineteen seventy-six." She gave a pleased little giggle. I guess that makes me Thursday's child, doesn't it?" She winked at Miss Martin and slowly made her way into the dining room.

"I think her walking is getter better," said Mrs. Nash, watching Mrs. Cimino's progress over to her table by the window.

"What a strange thing to say," said Miss Martin.

"We don't think it's so strange," said Mrs. Nash. "After you've been here a while, you'll discover that the walking is the best indication of how they're coming along."

"I meant the business about Thursday's child," said Miss Martin, a little flustered at being misinterpreted.

"Thursday's child?" Mrs. Nash was still a bit abstracted. With the stocking battle won, she had begun to speculate on the appropriateness of taking her bath immediately before dinner, rather than later in the evening.

"Mrs. Cimino said she was Thursday's child," said Miss Martin. She was still puzzled.

"I suppose she is," said Mrs. Nash slowly. Brightening, she smiled at Miss Martin. "Wednesday's child is full of woe, Thursday's child . . ." She look expectantly at the young girl beside her.

"Thursday's child . . . has far to go!" Miss Martin's brown eyes glowed with the pleasure of sudden recognition. She looked at her superior and hesitated a moment before venturing further. "Is that good enough for now?"

Mrs. Nash's thin face broke into a broad, genuine smile, partly at the parallel and partly at the overall success of the morning's action.

"It'll pass for the moment," she said. She sighed and looked down at her watch. "If you need me again, Nancy, I'll be in my office."

Miss Martin watched Mrs. Nash walk briskly up the corridor, past the nurses station to her office. Like Mrs. Polanski's office

102

it was near the main entrance, right next to the public telephone. And by virtue of its isolated position it was a place where Mrs. Nash could smoke one of her allotted five cigarettes a day.

After Mrs. Nash disappeared from view, Miss Martin looked back at the dining room: Breakfast was noisily in motion, cups clattering and voices humming. And from outside, almost drowning out the breakfast din, came the sound of the cement mixer churning away, much like a bright waltz rhythm, against which the rasping clamor of trucks and workmen played in oddly pointed, angular melodies.

The day's cacophony was already in full swing. With the warmer weather, the men had insisted on starting promptly at eight o'clock in the morning. But the residents in the dining room seemed quite unperturbed: It was as though their traffic with one another took place under a large, thick, impenetrable bell-shaped glass dome.

Wednesday, May 5, 10:10 A.M.

"Creamed peas," said Mrs. Cimino. "I think creamed peas would be very nice."

Miss Rochester nodded approvingly. Thirtyish and tall, with dark curly hair and a long Saxon nose, she was conducting the short-term memory class in a small room two doors back from the nurses station. There were five elderly ladies seated in straight-backed chairs along the wall: Mrs. Cimino, Mrs. Anderson, Mrs. Wohlsteader, Miss Schmidt, and old Mrs. Kenniston—the only resident centenarian at St. Hild's.

"What do we have so far, then?" asked Miss Rochester.

"Roast beef, new potatoes, and creamed peas," said Mrs. Cimino. She looked anxiously up at Miss Rochester. "Did I leave anything out?"

"Did she?" Miss Rochester looked queryingly at the others. Jealous of their own suggestions for the menu, they would be certain to spot any omissions. There were no objections.

"How about you, Miss Schmidt?"

"Carrots," said Miss Schmidt. "They're very nutritious." She underlined the addition with a quick smile. "That gives us roast beef, new potatoes, creamed peas, and carrots."

"Mrs. Kenniston?"

"Butter," said Mrs. Kenniston. "And I don't mean margarine." Always a strong supporter of the farm-labor bloc, she looked truculently round the room and glared down any potential opposition. "So far we have roast beef, new potatoes, creamed peas, carrots, and good wholesome creamery butter."

"Mrs. Wohlsteader?"

"Homemade bread," said Mrs. Wohlsteader. "There's nothing like homemade bread."

Mrs. Cimino smiled at Mrs. Wohlsteader. She breathed in a little more deeply, trying to catch the faint, piquant beer smell of loaves in the making. She could see them in pans, yeast-driven, swelling slowly to high estate, a winter treat devoutly to be yearned for.

Her father had been the baker: A man of strong Celtic passion, Archibald McDonald had often rushed home from the pharmacy and attacked the kitchen. As he spread out his array of battle implements, he would sneer at the weakness of store-bought provender in much the same way that his ancestors had taunted the Duke of Cumberland's men before Culloden. But the Geordies had won: After the battle they had taken his great-great-grandfather, tried him in Southwark, and sentenced him to fourteen years of bonded service on a Georgia plantation. From Georgia the first of the American line had made his way to western Pennsylvania, there to farm and make strong whiskey. Out of tribal loyalty Archibald felt obligated to drink heavily on Saturdays.

Mrs. Cimino, like her mother, had never held with the drinking, but the breadmaking had been a joy to watch: rich, fecund loaves that would last the family for more than a week. She let the smell fade away in favor of concentrating on Mrs. Wohlsteader's summary.

"Roast beef, new potoates, creamed peas, carrots, butter, and homemade bread," said Mrs. Wohlsteader.

"Mrs. Anderson?"

"Parker House rolls," said Mrs. Anderson. "My son just loves Parker House rolls."

"But Miss Rochester!" Miss Schmidt tapped lightly on the floor with her cane, underscoring her point of order. "There's no point in having Parker House rolls when you already have bread."

Mrs. Anderson looked stricken, and Mrs. Cimino quailed. Dear soul that Miss Schmidt was, she had a contentious way about her. And Mrs. Cimino's mother had been contentious, ever ready to deflate a flight of bold fancy. Of English stock, with her brother still working the family farm outside of Jamestown, Cora Johnson had married Archibald after meeting him on a visit to her uncle's place in Uniontown. It had been her father who had helped him start his own pharmacy in Jamestown. Genteel, firm, Cora had kept a clear, restrained voice of Good Sense flowing up from her end of the dinner table.

Despite the underlying warfare between Celt and Saxon, Jock and Geordie, the two of them had found basic agreement in the management of the store. They were also in clear accord regarding the roles that their three daughters were to play: Rose was the beautiful great lady, and Emily—the youngest—was the bright, talented jewel, with her lovely soprano voice and knack for learning languages. For Esther, then, the only position left was that of Loyal Helper: bearing the brunt of the load around the house and moving to the pharmacy counter after graduation from high school. It had been natural for the family to see Esther's marriage to Frank as a betrayal, as an assault upon Good Sense in the same way that Mrs. Anderson's Parker House rolls damaged the logical development of the class menu.

"Mrs. Anderson is entitled to choose what she wants, Miss Schmidt." Miss Rochester looked around at the others, appealing for implicit support. She smiled gratefully at Mrs. Cimino's enthusiastic nod.

"That gives us roast beef, new potatoes, creamed peas, carrots, homemade bread, and Parker House rolls," said Mrs. Anderson.

"Butter," said Mrs. Kenniston. "She left out the butter." Tiny, under five feet, she had a web of fine wrinkles throughout her face, much like the cracks that cry the antiquity of an heirloom china teacup. Like a longer, massive master crack, her mouth was a straight line, quietly indignant at the slip. "Our hard-working Minnesota farmers wouldn't like that."

"Roast beef, new potatoes, creamed peas, carrots, butter, homemade bread, and Parker House rolls," said Mrs. Anderson.

"Very good," said Miss Rochester. "How about some dessert, Mrs. Kenniston?"

"Mince pie," said Mrs. Kenniston. "So we have roast beef,

creamed peas, new potatoes, carrots, butter, Parker House rolls, mince pie."

"Did she leave anything out?" Miss Rochester looked around for confirmation.

"I'm afraid Mrs. Kenniston left out our homemade bread," said Mrs. Wohlsteader.

"A very natural mistake," said Miss Schmidt. "The homemade bread and Parker House rolls don't go together at all. That's why it's hard to remember both of them." Closing off her demonstration with another geometer's smile, she sat comfortably back in her chair.

"You may have a point there," conceded Miss Rochester. "But it's still a very attractive menu." She looked over at Mrs. Cimino. "Would you like to give us the menu, Mrs. Cimino?"

"Roast beef, new potatoes, creamed peas, carrots." Mrs. Cimino closed her eyes tightly in order to concentrate better. "Butter, homemade bread, Parker House rolls, and mince pie."

"Very good, ladies," said Miss Rochester. "Now let's think of some guests to invite, famous people whom we'd like to see."

"Hubert Humphrey," said Miss Schmidt. "I wouldn't mind seeing Hubert there."

"Ronald Reagan," said Mrs. Wohlsteader. "He's still very good-looking."

"Henry Kissinger," said Mrs. Cimino. She wasn't really sure who he was, but the name had a pleasant ring to it.

"Nelson Rockefeller," said Mrs. Anderson. "He seems like such a nice man."

"Who do we have so far, then?" Miss Rochester gestured magnanimously to Mrs. Anderson.

"Hubert Humphrey, Ronald Reagan, Henry Kissinger, and Nelson Rockefeller," said Mrs. Anderson.

"That's a very distinguished group," said Miss Rochester. Who would you like to add, Mrs. Kenniston?"

Mrs. Kenniston sat in her straight-backed chair, arms folded, and stared fixedly at the small blackboard behind Miss Rochester's desk.

"What's wrong, Mrs. Kenniston?" Miss Rochester's tone was slightly impatient. "Surely you can think of someone you'd like to add."

"I can, but I won't." In her high-necked black dress, with its white choker, Mrs. Kenniston looked like Queen Victoria silently reproving an abjectly repentant Prince Albert.

"Why not, Mrs. Kenniston?" Puzzled, Miss Rochester looked at the other members of the class. "We certainly have an interesting group." The other ladies nodded vigorous assent.

"Not as far as I'm concerned," said Mrs. Kenniston.

"What is it, then, that displeases you?"

"Too many Republicans!" Mrs. Kenniston looked around at her colleagues with mingled pity and disgust. "I wouldn't have most of those men in my house, much less sit with them at the table."

"We're all very sorry," said Mrs. Rochester. Looking gravely round, she evoked courteous murmurs of apology from the other ladies. As their resident centenarian, Mrs. Kenniston had been granted plenary indulgence in matters political. She had grown up under the golden spell of William Jennings Bryan and she had voted a straight Democratic ticket in every election since 1922. In meeting strangers, she invariably began the conversation with a question regarding party membership: If the stranger turned out to be a Republican, she would snort contemptuously and totter away. With her fellow residents she was more tolerant, as long as they refrained from any mention of the party of McKinley, Harding, Coolidge, and other Wall Street machinators.

She was something of a showpiece for St. Hild's: Every election would find a photograph of her in the local newspaper, indomitably posed in front of the polling booth. Since the newspaper's politics were Republican, the reporters generally wrote a story celebrating her age and citizenship rather than her party loyalty. These omissions grieved her, but she still found comfort in the hope that a future interview would reflect her position accurately.

Her position was strong and consistent: She watched the news carefully for signs of Democratic resurgence, and she went to bed each night consoling herself with dreams of sudden Republican collapse. In particular, she distrusted the Rockefellers: Their postures of public service were far more suspicious than the private venalities of the Mellons and Du Ponts of her youth.

Satisfied that her colleagues had been sufficiently reproved, Mrs. Kenniston balanced matters by adding the names of James A. Farley and William Fulbright. The nominations then moved into safer territory: Cary Grant, Helen Hayes, Prince Charles, and Fred

Astaire were added to what promised to be an impressive guest list.

"Hubert Humphrey, Ronald Reagan, Henry Kissinger, Nelson Rockefeller, James A. Farley, William Fulbright, Cary Grant, Helen Hayes, Prince Charles, and Fred Astaire," said Mrs. Cimino when her turn came.

"That's very good, Mrs. Cimino," said Miss Rochester.

Mrs. Cimino sighed with inward relief: Names were hard; it was hard to picture the faces that went with them, except for Fred Astaire. She was getting tired.

"I think we've done very well this morning," said Miss Rochester. All we have to do now is check our birthdays.

"June, fifth, nineteen hundred and three," said Mrs. Anderson.

"September third, eighteen hundred and ninety-nine," said Miss Schmidt.

"January twentieth, eighteen hundred and seventy-six," said Mrs. Kenniston, graciously acknowledging the moment of respectful awe. "During the administration of Ulysses Simpson Grant. A good general, but a disgraceful president." She looked challengingly around the room. "Not that we haven't had worse."

"How about you, Mrs. Wohlsteader?" Since she had not volunteered, Miss Rochester felt impelled to prod her a little.

"May twentieth, eighteen hundred and ninety-six." Mrs. Wohlsteader's voice was low, unenthusiastic.

"And what's today's date?" said Miss Rochester, somewhat aglow with excitement.

"May fifth, nineteen seventy-six." Mrs. Wohlsteader looked down at the bare floor as though a door might providentially open up for her.

"How old will you be on your birthday coming up?"

"I'll be eighty," said Mrs. Wohlsteader. "But I don't want a party."

"Why not?" Miss Rochester was still glowing over the prospect of imminent festivity.

"It's not worth celebrating," said Mrs. Wohlsteader. "I haven't celebrated a birthday since I was sixty."

Miss Rochester paused and looked at the others. Most of them were nodding sad concurrence. She elected to press the matter.

"You don't like being old, do you?" Miss Rochester's voice was forceful, almost tactless in its naked use of the word.

"I guess not." Mrs. Wohlsteader looked around at the others and tried to smile.

"And you don't like having to depend on other people, do you?"

Mrs. Wohlsteader shook her head.

"But we can't help growing old, Mrs. Wohlsteader." Miss Rochester looked around at the other ladies to insure their attention. "Growing old is something we have to accept as part of life."

Mrs. Cimino, equally saddened, listened to Miss Rochester lecture them about the nature of noble oak trees and other growing things. She found the lecture unpersuasive: An oak tree never had to worry about not being able to see or hear as it stood in its place—majestic, admirable—until the time came to cut it down for a useful purpose. They were more like poplars, growing too long and too top-heavy, an easy prey to sudden gusts of wind that would have left them unscathed in earlier years.

"How about your birthday, Mrs. Cimino?" Her lecture finished, Miss Rochester returned to the main topic.

"I'm not sure," said Mrs. Cimino. "My memory's been giving me a lot of trouble lately."

"That's what our class is for," said Miss Rochester. "To help your memory."

Mrs. Cimino closed her eyes and tried to see a date shining out of the blackness. There was none. She opened her eyes and looked up at Miss Rochester. The nostrils of Miss Rochester's long Saxon nose seemed large, predatory, as though they were about to sniff out some dark, unpleasant secret.

"Let's say I'm old enough to know better." Mrs. Cimino smiled equably as she made her little joke.

"I think we can be more precise," said Miss Rochester. She went over to her desk and opened up a large black loose-leaf notebook. Why don't you take a look at what our records say?"

Mrs. Cimino got awkwardly up and went over to Miss Rochester's desk. There she was, right above the strong, imperious index finger: Mrs. Esther McDonald Cimino, 4567 Elm Street, Minneapolis, Minnesota, born February 10, 1900. The date was like an address, except that she could never move away from it. Like an inseparable carapace it would forever weigh her down, growing heavier each year.

"February tenth, nineteen hundred, that's what it says." Her voice was small, dry, matter-of-fact, as though she were reading off the music store's net receipts after a bad month.

"And what's today's date?"

"It's Wednesday, May fifth, nineteen seventy-six," said Mrs. Cimino, reassured by the way the big purple letters suddenly appeared in her mind's eye. "So that makes me seventy-six years old." She gave another embarrassed little laugh. "As long as I know what year it is, I know how old I am."

"Very good," said Miss Rochester, watching the small legs slowly take their owner back to her straight-backed chair. "As long as we know where we are, we can keep track of our ages very well."

"That seems reasonable," said Miss Schmidt. As Mrs. Cimino sat down she gave her a friendly pat on the arm. "And it gives us good practice doing sums."

"It's good to keep in practice," said Miss Rochester. "And now would be a good time to practice our exercises."

The five ladies smiled at the notion. Miss Rochester's exercises represented an agreeable descent from the lofty mental plane of the class. Seated in their chairs, they solemnly followed her in various twistings and turnings. After the final twist they stamped noisily on the floor with their feet, creating a sound not unlike unruly schoolchildren suddenly dismissed for the day.

Mrs. Cimino stood by while Miss Schmidt laboriously pushed herself up with her rubber-tipped cane in solid, supportive position. She walked out the door with Miss Schmidt to the nurses station. There she said goodbye to Miss Schmidt and watched her lumber down the corridor to her first-floor room.

When Miss Schmidt had disappeared from view, Mrs. Cimino turned her attention to the stairs that stretched upward in front of her. They were steep, formidable, not without hazard to elderly folk. She sighed and made sure her glasses were firmly seated on her nose before beginning the attack. Like a wise general she worked successively from positions of strength: With a firm hold on the banister she would lift her right foot up and slide it cautiously forward until its progress was stopped by the riser. Only then, reassured, did she permit her left foot to leave the safe level surface on which it stood.

"I know it's upsetting, but it has to be done." From the right-hand seat of their Porsche 912E, Lisa gazed reflectively, eyes narrowed, at Mrs. Cimino's two-story gray stone house.

"I wish Harold were here," said George, making no move to open the door and get out. "He promised he'd come up and go through all the letters and things."

"It's been almost a month, honey." Lisa, still looking at her target, gave George's hand a reassuring squeeze. She turned toward him and smiled.

Lisa, smiling or not, was fair to look upon: long dark hair, delicate features, and a supple young body that fell naturally into a position of grace no matter where she was. She was two inches taller than Alice and fifteen pounds lighter. On occasion, George would lift her above his head and hold her there like a slim, airy creature floating high above the sullen earth.

Once back on the ground, brown eyes darting, Lisa was always in motion: She flickered from one place to another like a bad-tempered hummingbird. An only child, she had first adored and then despised her father, a peripatetic Air Force major. When he had been transferred to Texas, she had defiantly stayed in Minneapolis: She worked as a receptionist, as a cocktail waitress, and as a secretary. At present her goal was to play a leading role in one of the Chekhov Club productions.

"It's not as though they live in California." George continued to glower at the house, as though it were somehow accountable for his brother's defection. It was a squarely built structure, with a large front porch and a high-pitched slate roof. Its appearance suggested that the architect, a no-nonsense fellow, had taken out a large cube, plumped it down in a pleasant neighborhood, and proceeded to tack on the necessary porches and outbuildings. After this he had prescribed fifty years of roses and ivy to gentle all the sharp edges. The Ciminos had bought it in 1941.

The place had always been a little alien to George: He had really grown up in the small frame house around the corner from the music store. Two years after they had moved into this house he had been drafted: It had been Harold who lived there and who had enjoyed the bicycles, the camps, the free time after school, the lovely middle-class girls in light, bare-backed summer dresses. And it had been Harold who had gone away to the University of Iowa: There he had married a cheerleader with a well-to-do father, and from there he had soared on to an M.B.A. from Leland Stanford Junior University. By all rights Harold—who had moved into the biggest room and stayed there, even after George came back from the Army Engineers—should be here now, shouldering a properly giant weight of responsibility.

"Shall we?" Lisa gave his hand a final squeeze, opened the car door, and slid herself out in one swift, fluent motion. After George came around the car to her, she took his hand again. "All you have to do, honey, is make a few decisions with me." She nodded toward the front door. "Later on in the week Paula and Lurene will come over and help with the packing."

"I hope you find some things you like," said George. Two weeks before they had signed the papers for their new house. It was an expensive three-bedroom place with a superbly staged sunken living room. Since escrow was due to close on June third, Lisa had begun to frequent the higher-priced furniture stores, much to George's distress. Standing empty, their new home seemed like a voracious child clamoring to be fed costly delicacies.

"We'll see," said Lisa. Suddenly maternal, she pulled him up the long walk that led to the front door.

George unlocked the door, opened it, and stood aside while Lisa went on ahead. He followed her into the living room. They opened the curtains and let the afternoon sun touch up the room with color and depth.

Like most guitarists Frank Cimino had loved good wood. Rosewood, maple, oak, cherry, walnut, mahogany, teak: He knew their textures and how they took the knife. More than his wife, he had sought out the pieces and brought their carvings back to rich, impressive glory. Even his favorite chair—comfortable, cushioned—had carved arms that spoke of craftsmanlike affection and concern.

In his last five months Frank had spent his afternoons sitting in that chair, Esther in another chair beside him holding his hand, as though to wall out the quiet waves of pain that came upon him. When his sons had come to see him, Frank had forced a smile to crease his strong, square Milanese face. But the smile had never stayed long: He had sat there immobile, silent, holding his wife's hand, waiting for one last big wave to sweep over him and wash him out to sea.

"Very nice," said Lisa. "You can't find things like these in the shops." Her eyes lit up as she caught sight of a Chinese papier-mâché chess table from Grandfather McDonald's estate.

"Do you really want them?" George glowed a little, as though Lisa had suddenly, unexpectedly, given something of herself to him.

"We'll see," said Lisa. She directed his attention out to the hall, where a curved flight of stairs led up to the second floor. "The cedar chest is gorgeous."

"I think it comes from the Johnsons," said George. "When Great-uncle Oscar died they sent Mother that piece and some of the silver."

"Is there anything from your father's family?"

George shook his head. His father had been the fifth son of Marcello Cimino, a steelworker in Donora, Pennsylvania. With his wife, Antonia, Marcello had been brought from Italy—along with thousands of others—by Henry Clay Frick to meet Carnegie Steel's need for cheap, strong labor. After the recalcitrant Irish had demonstrated their untrustworthiness in the Homestead Strike, the mill owners had opened the tap from southern Europe and let it flow: Over a million a year had poured in, drawn by bright promises and kept docile by the ruthless work of the Camorra and other paramilitary strikebreaking groups.

The other four sons had followed their father into the mill, toasting their luncheon sandwiches on the cherry-red walls of the open-hearth furnace, the closest known approximation to Hell on this good green earth. But Frank had gone into the Navy along with his banjo: He had developed winning ways, and he had polished his musicianship. When he came out it was natural for him to become a professional musician and to stop going to mass regularly.

"How about the piano?" Lisa stepped over to the big walnut Chickering grand piano. She sat down and tried to open up the keyboard. "It's locked."

"There's a key around here somewhere," said George. He stood back and looked thoughtfully at the Chickering. It had been a surprise for his mother on her fiftieth birthday.

As a girl Esther McDonald had never been an impressive pianist. But she had always liked to play, and she could accompany singing with a measure of sympathy. With her sisters, Rose and Emily, she formed a singing trio. Even when Emily was still in high school, the McDonald Sisters had performed professionally in local supper clubs. It was in one of those supper clubs that Esther had met Frank.

Frank was at the time traveling as a steel guitarist with Chief Kona Kai and his Hawaiian Serenaders: Although Frank had never been to Hawaii, he was dark enough to create an illusion of authenticity. Like most musicians of the time, he drank a little too much, but he was a cheerful, sweet-tempered man and much livelier company than most of the local boys.

Esther had not planned on getting married, but it seemed the logical thing to do: Rose had married the son of a local banker, and Emily—with her father's blessing—was talking about going to New York and studying voice. When Frank proposed, Esther agreed—quickly. And it was with real pleasure that she said good-bye to the pharmacy.

The pleasure continued for about seven years. Chief Kona Kai's agents were active in securing engagements in theaters and first-rate hotels. As was the custom, the orchestra traveled by train, living in what struck Esther as elegant style. Even George's arrival in 1925 did not halt the respectful procession of hotels, restaurants, and spectacular vaudeville palaces where ushers wore gleaming uniforms and saluted each patron like Viennese admirals paying homage to the Emperor Franz Joseph.

By 1930 the hotels had begun to grow less luxurious, at times even approaching derelict cheapness. And in November of that year Chief Kona Kai, faced with a bleak winter, elected to abscond with the week's receipts and leave the Serenaders stranded in Minneapolis. Most of the musicians returned immediately to their native Bronx, but Esther and Frank decided to stay where they were.

Frank got a job playing banjo with a local Dixieland band. They rented an apartment. George started school. Frank began to teach banjo, guitar, and steel guitar during the day. They rented a small house. Frank began to sell guitars and other instruments at a local music store. They prospered modestly and began to think of opening up a store of their own.

In 1935 they opened Cimino Music. They did not prosper, but they survived. By 1941 they were able to buy the gray stone house. By 1951 they were able to buy the store building, expand, and float upward on a rising economy in which fretted instruments became a popular device for the expression of juvenile disaffection. The grand piano had been the first of many small luxuries: a fair reward for years of thrift and self-denial.

"Chickering," said Lisa. She got up from the bench and walked around it, stroking it with her hand. She placed herself in the curve of the harp. She struck a pose, as though she were about to sing a Gershwin song in an intimate little club. "Very nice!" Her brown eyes sparkled.

"I don't know about the Chickering," said George. "That's the one thing Harold and Gloria might want."

"If Harold and Gloria can't be bothered to come up here and help us, they have no right to object if we try to keep some of this in the family."

"I'd never thought of it that way," said George.

"But that's the way it is." Lisa broke away from the piano and skimmed around the room. "All these beautiful things have meaning to us because we know them." Her eyes shone. She crossed her hands over her hard, pointed young breasts and looked up toward the ceiling, much like a slightly dissolute postulant invoking divine assistance. "We belong to them as much as they belong to us."

"Gosh!" said George, overcome. "I never knew you felt this way."

"That's the way I feel, honey." Lisa smiled gently at him. "If we had room, I'd take it all."

"But Lisa!" George was shocked. "That doesn't seem right." He looked wildly around: at the piano, at the dining room, at the stairs that led up to the second floor and to the attic beyond that. "I thought we were just going to pick out a few family pieces."

"I know why you thought that," said Lisa. She came over and took both his hands. "You thought that because I was looking through all those expensive stores with Lurene." Still gentle, her mouth curved a little more. "Isn't that true?"

Unable to speak, George nodded his head.

"But these things are so much better, so much more stately." She dropped his hands and drew herself up, queenlike.

"What about Mr. Leach?"

"He told you to pick out what you wanted, didn't he?"

"What about Harold?" George shook his head. "He'll raise the roof if we take all these things." He looked in toward the dining room and toward his mother's glass display cupboard for the special porcelain pieces. "And what about the china and silver?"

"Let him raise the roof." Lisa tossed her head and went back to the protective embrace of the Chickering. "It'll be the first thing he's done since this whole business started." Her eyes flashed dangerously. "And remember, darling, it hasn't been easy on me either."

"I know it hasn't." George sighed deeply. "It's cut into our weekends and into some of our evenings together."

"You did what you thought was right," said Lisa. "Even though everybody else kept letting you down."

"Karen's been helpful," said George.

"Dear, dear Karen," said Lisa. "I must take her out to lunch sometime." Secure in her position, she smiled brightly. "And it's Karen, Ann, and Gretchen that I'm thinking of."

George looked blankly at her, not sure of how to interpret this incongruous burst of stepmotherly affection.

"Don't you understand?" Lisa's voice quivered a little. "In time these things will be theirs. All that we'll do will be to use them for a while."

"You may have a point there," said George.

"Trust me." Lisa smiled and moved slowly toward him, her brown eyes slightly moist with feeling. When she reached him she burrowed her head into his shoulder so that his face could do nothing else but dwell in the fragrance of her long dark hair. Raising his head a little, George could see their reflection in the large beveled mirror over the stone fireplace: What a handsome couple they were, and how his friends—even his brother—envied the vital new life he was building. There in the mirror, farther behind them, he could also see the long gray couch by the window: How exciting, how imaginative it would be to pick Lisa up and carry her over to it!

"What do you think we should do?" Out of the corner of his

116

eye George had caught sight of his father's chair. Its reproach had directed him back to housekeeping matters.

"Decide to decide." Lisa stepped back and gestured around. "If we decide to furnish the new place with what we have here, the rest is easy."

"It is?"

"Child's play," bubbled Lisa happily. "I'll come over tomorrow and tag all the furniture we need, and the girls will come over later on and help me pack the linens, bedding, silver, china, and smaller things."

"What about the pictures, the letters, the attic stuff?"

"Since there's no hurry about them, I think Harold and Gloria will be able to get up here and go through things." Lisa paused to count numbers in her head. "But it would be better if they came after June fourth."

"June fourth?"

"Moving day," said Lisa. "With Paula and Lurene to help pack, I bet it won't cost us more than three hundred dollars." She smiled again, glowing with pleasure and Good Sense. "The refrigerator alone is worth twice that."

"You're wonderful," said George.

"Yes," smiled Lisa. "Isn't it lovely?"

The decision behind him, George walked out to the porch while Lisa took her notebook and made a preliminary check of the second floor. He looked up and down the tree-lined street. Everything was quiet, as though most of the neighbors had gone away. When Lisa came out, he closed the door and made sure it was locked.

"It's a nuisance, having to drop this off by the bank." He held up the house key, oddly foreign with its large white tag. "But that's the way Leach wants it."

One of the first things Mr. Edward Leach had done—after checking the contents of Mrs. Cimino's safety deposit box—was to have the locks to the house changed.

Tuesday, May 25, 4:00 P.M.

It was a quiet time. Mrs. Cimino and Mrs. Yeager were in the room together. They were not talking.

Like neighbors living side by side for many years, the two women had early felt their way into a relationship of cautious neutrality: In the closet their clothes were separated by an empty space of almost two inches, even though it meant bunching dresses and coats together at the far ends. As the senior member of the living arrangement, Mrs. Yeager was entitled to initiate conversations. She rarely exercised this privilege, preferring to spend most of her time gazing out the window at a distant grove of pine trees.

She was a short, thin woman, almost birdlike, with sparse white hair and small brown eyes that blinked a great deal. Far from fair, her complexion had the general color and texture of wet sand. She had a chin that receded almost to the point of invisibility: Even in repose her face had a feeling of forward motion, as though she were somehow about to leap out the window.

Mrs. Cimino, purse open on the bed beside her, was doing her accounts: The spending money Karen had brought her was sensibly segregated into white envelopes for each denomination, including half dollars, quarters, dimes, nickels, and pennies. Her procedure called for the replacement of anything removed with a small sheet of paper noting the date and occasion. By now the small change envelopes bulked large with withdrawal slips, so she was forced to consolidate them, transferring their notations to a single master list. When the addition failed to come out right, she merely wrote down "to balance" and went on to the next envelope.

When she finished, Mrs. Cimino looked over at Mrs. Yeager: Her roommate was still staring out the window. Mrs. Cimino put her purse back on the bottom shelf of the night stand. She took out some writing paper from the top drawer. Miss Rochester had told her she should start writing letters. She tried to think of what it would be like to write a letter a day the way Mrs. Wohlsteader did. Shaking her head over the grandeur of the feat, she picked up her pen and began to attack the clear blue surface challenging her. When she had conquered one page, she sat back and examined what she had done.

Dearest Harold and Gloria,
    Here I am writing a letter. I'm at a place they call St. Hild's. It's out in the country. I think it's a school of some kind. We have classes

and nature walks. How is your weather? How are those dear little boys? Write me all the news.

Love, Esther

It was not a good letter. The margins weren't even and the lines slanted too much. She looked at her pen. A new one would help. She made a note on another sheet of paper: "Ask Karen to bring pen from house." She considered crumpling up the light blue page and starting over. She looked at Mrs. Yeager again, half hoping that sound advice would come sliding her way on the rays of the late afternoon sun. Mrs. Yeager was still intent on her pine trees, much as though an act of will would equip her to pierce through them and catch sight of the Methodist summer camp on the other side of the hill.

Mrs. Cimino sighed and folded her letter as neatly as she could. She rummaged through the top drawer of her night stand and located one of the envelopes Karen had addressed and stamped for her. She put the light blue page into the envelope, sealed it, and stood up. Not wishing to distract Mrs. Yeager from her thoughtful vision, Mrs. Cimino quietly went out the door and down the corridor to the stairs. Slowly, carefully, she negotiated them with success and began her walk across the hall to the mail basket.

"Why are you shuffling, Mrs. Cimino?"

"Oh, Mrs. Polanski!" Mrs. Cimino smiled graciously at the onslaught coming her way from the left. "Am I shuffling?"

"Yes, you are," said Mrs. Polanski, her fair face agleam with disapproval. "Shuffling . . . shuffling . . . shuffling."

"Is that what you call it?" Mrs. Cimino looked down at her feet as though they were somehow culpable in and of themselves.

"You don't have to shuffle," said Mrs. Polanski. "You don't have to take little baby steps, little . . . baby . . . steps." She demonstrated by making a small-paced trip to the nurses station and back. "Why do you do it?"

"Is that what I'm doing?" Mrs. Cimino gave one of her embarrassed little laughs. "I suppose it looks silly to a big girl like you, but it seems right to me."

"Right?"

"Right for me, I mean." Mrs. Cimino smiled as though to indicate that a truly democratic scheme of things allowed for substantial variations in taste and style.

"Why do you think it's right for you to shuffle?"

"That's the way I'm supposed to walk," said Mrs. Cimino stoutly.

"So you think old people are supposed to take little baby steps all the time, do you?"

"That's right, Mrs. Polanski." Mrs. Cimino bolstered her engaging smile with a flattering use of this rather vain person's name. "We old folks have to be careful." She gave another little laugh.

"There's no law that says old people have to shuffle . . . shuffle . . . shuffle." Mrs. Polanski's fair face remained sober, uncharmed.

"I'm not talking about laws, Mrs. Polanski." Mrs. Cimino replaced her gracious mien with one of serious Good Sense, much as though she were going after an overdue account at the music store. "I'm talking about being careful." Firmness was obviously called for here. "You know I've had trouble with these eyes of mine, and I'm sure you wouldn't want me to take another bad fall."

"Certainly you should be careful." Mrs. Polanski seemed to wilt a little before returning to her stubborn attack. "Especially with stairs and on the uneven ground outside." Gathering force, she gestured largely toward the nurses station. "But this is a smooth, level surface. I don't see why you can't step out a little more, as though you were going somewhere, going . . . somewhere."

"Going somewhere." Mrs. Cimino, glad to see a minor concession wrung out of this vociferous person, blandly considered the matter. "I suppose I could take bigger steps every now and then." She held her letter up like a small banner designed to lead her onward. "As a matter of fact, I was just on my way to the mail basket."

"Excellent!" Mrs. Polanski seemed monstrously enthusiastic over this small bit of news. "Those letters are very important."

"It's good to write a letter every now and then," agreed Mrs. Cimino. "As long as one doesn't overdo it." She waved farewell to Mrs. Polanski and headed for the mail basket on the far end of the counter at the nurses station. Consciously, she attempted to lengthen her pace: partly to placate the bright blue eyes behind her and partly to see if the muscles could actually be stretched a little more. To her surprise, she was able to make the journey without pain.

Mrs. Polanski watched Mrs. Cimino transact her business and go back up the stairs. Then she walked down the corridor to Mrs. Nash's office. Mrs. Nash was sitting behind her desk checking through a stack of Medicare forms.

"How's Mrs. Cimino coming along?"

"Progress," said Mrs. Nash. Not without pleasure, she pushed the Medicare forms aside and pulled out a rather thick folder from the shelf behind her. "Miss Rochester says she's been doing well in the classes."

"How about the rest of it?"

"Pretty good." Mrs. Nash opened up the folder and consulted the most recent checklist. "Makes her bed, dresses herself as long as the clothing is simple, enjoys her bath, and eats with gusto."

"Her walking's not good," said Mrs. Polanski.

"She seems to be fearful about that." Mrs. Nash dug farther down in the folder. "But she's come a long way since she was in Minneapolis Central." Mrs. Nash located another checklist and read from it. "Needs restraint, needs help in eating, needs help in going to the bathroom." She put the checklist back, closed the folder, and smiled at Mrs. Polanski. "Sounds like a completely different person, doesn't it?"

"It's the same person," said Mrs. Polanski. Thoughtful, she did not appear to share Mrs. Nash's feelings of accomplishment. "And she's very hard to read."

Mrs. Nash nodded, thinking back to some of the genteel battles of the first week.

"Very hard to know what's spinning around in there," continued Mrs. Polanski. "Has she ever opened up to anybody?"

"She likes to stay on the surface," said Mrs. Nash. "Very sweet, very pleasant, very compatible as far as the other ladies go."

"What about her family?"

"The two sons stopped by for an inspection tour right after she was admitted." Mrs. Nash looked longingly at her drawer: There were two cigarettes still left in her pack. "But they seem to have left everything up to Karen."

"We have to keep pushing about that walking, about . . . that

. . . walking." Mrs. Polanski lit up a cigarette and took a deep, or-giastic puff. "Otherwise I'm afraid she'll slip back."

"What if she has another bad fall?"

"That's a chance we have to take." Mrs. Polanski watched her smoke spiral upward as though it indicated the heights that could be climbed by the strong of spirit.

"I don't think she wants to be pushed too much," said Mrs. Nash. A little on the cautious side, she still tended to favor bed-rails. And she tended to console herself with modest achievements rather than gambling on dramatic successes.

"Who knows what she really wants?" said Mrs. Polanski. "We can't get in there and walk around looking for big neon signs to tell us what to do."

"As you say, she's hard to read," conceded Mrs. Nash. "But it's not as though she has something to go back to."

"She has her family, her two sons, her grandchildren," said Mrs. Polanski. "She has more assets, I would guess, than most of our residents."

"But they're under the control of her trustee," said Mrs. Nash. "And her sons don't want to be involved."

"We can't help that," said Mrs. Polanski. "Our job is simply to bring her along as far as we can."

"But that's part of the situation," said Mrs. Nash. "With Mrs. Wohlsteader, it's different. She'll be going back to her son's home."

"Mrs. Cimino could go back to her own home," said Mrs. Po-lanski. She snubbed out her cigarette. She lit a fresh one. She nod-ded firmly to herself as though the matter had been settled.

"By herself?"

"Mabye not," said Mrs. Polanski. "Maybe she would have to live with a companion." She blew a reasonably ambitious smoke ring. "But even that would be something worth working toward."

"That's opening the door to disappointment, isn't it?"

"I think it's the only way for her, to be pushed along as far as she can go," said Mrs. Polanski. "When she reaches that point, we'll start to deal with the rest of it."

Mrs. Nash was silent. She watched the smoke drift upward. She tried to avoid breathing in its temptation. She thought of her two cigarettes: one for after dinner, one for her bath.

"Could I have one of your cigarettes?" she said to Mrs. Polanski: It seemed a reasonable price for her implicit assent.

Mrs. Polanski pushed a cigarette up from the pack and extended it to Mrs. Nash. Mrs. Nash took the cigarette and took a light from Mrs. Polanski, breathing a deep sigh of guilty gratitude. Suddenly cheerful, her thin, concerned face grew animated.

"Miss Rochester wants to open up a small advanced class in a few weeks," said Mrs. Nash. "Maybe Mrs. Cimino will be ready for it."

"Good," said Mrs. Polanski. "We want to keep the momentum going."

"I'll tell Nancy to keep after her about the walking," said Mrs. Nash.

"Good," said Mrs. Polanski again. "Do you want another cigarette?"

"No, I'm trying to cut down," said Mrs. Nash.

"So am I," said Mrs. Polanski, gesturing boldly. "Next week I'm going to cut back to a pack and a half a day. The week after that it'll be down to just a pack. And then it's going to be cold turkey, a complete stoppage." She smiled at the wholesome prospect opened up for her.

"Good luck," said Mrs. Nash.

"Cold turkey in three weeks," said Mrs. Polanski. She got up and headed for her office across the hall.

"Good luck," said Mrs. Nash. Mrs. Polanski had tried to stop completely several times in the past two years. Her attempts, as they all knew, had not been successful. But her spirit remained undaunted.

Some spirits seem to be stronger than others. Mrs. Nash thought back to Mrs. Kenniston's pneumonia last year. Frail, wasted, at death's door, she had been given up by both doctors and staff. Even Mrs. Polanski, stopping by to see her, had been resigned to losing her just a few months short of her hundredth birthday.

Mrs. Polanski had bent over the tiny body, lying doll-like under a broad expanse of hospital sheeting. Mrs. Kenniston had struggled to say something, clutching Mrs. Polanski's arm as though the message might flow across by touch as well as by faint, barely perceptible speech. Then the words came out, whispered but unmistakably clear. "I'm not ready yet," said Mrs. Kenniston, and her grip tightened on Mrs. Polanski's arm, tightening and tightening, staying there leechlike until sturdy Mrs. Polanski had been ready to cry aloud with the pain of it.

The bruises left had remained visible for five days: black and blue clawlike marks on Mrs. Polanski's lower right forearm. She had displayed them proudly, like stigmata left by some strange unearthly visitation from a far-off ethereal realm.

Monday, June 7, 3:30 P.M.

Mrs. Cimino was a little out of breath when she got back to her room with the red door: She had hurried on ahead from the close of the nature walk, hoping to finish her letter to Alice before the afternoon mail went out. As usual she nodded pleasantly to Mrs. Yeager, who was watching the pine trees.

Briskly, firmly, Mrs. Cimino added a final paragraph to her third page. She placed the pages in an envelope, addressed it, and stamped it. As she stood up to examine herself in the mirror before going downstairs, she noticed that Mrs. Yeager was staring at her: a clear signal to speak.

"They say it's a good idea to write letters," said Mrs. Cimino, displaying her envelope as tangible proof of her cooperativeness.

"They're full of ideas, aren't they?" Mrs. Yeager's thin lips curved in a grim smile, like an ominous crack appearing suddenly at the base of an old stone building. "But they don't fool me." She leaned forward and lowered her voice. "They've never fooled me."

"Who?" Mrs. Cimino was beginning to feel uneasy.

"The vegetarians." Mrs. Yeager's voice had dropped to a whisper, forcing Mrs. Cimino to come closer. "They're thick as weeds around here." Looking out the window toward the pine trees, she shook her head. "Kellogg was the first, and then there was Post—both of them carrying on with their young girls up there in Battle Creek, Michigan."

"Where the cornflakes come from?"

"Cornflakes, oat flakes, rutabagas, turnips, soybeans—no matter what you call it, it's still pig food." Brown eyes growing moist with tears, Mrs. Yeager looked pleadingly up at Mrs. Cimino. "It's the children I'm thinking of. Little children, little babies, little boys and girls eating pig food every morning." Choking with grief, Mrs. Yeager paused to shake her head violently before going on. "When they could be eating kippers, rock cod, ham, bacon, and good Philadelphia scrapple."

"I'd never given it any thought," said Mrs. Cimino, a tone of mounting horror creeping into her own voice.

"Of course not," said Mrs. Yeager. She sniffled a little and gave Mrs. Cimino's hand a consoling pat. "You're a dear, trusting soul. That's probably why they brought you here."

"The vegetarians?" Mrs. Cimino looked down at her ring finger, trying to imagine herself in the role of victim. "Is Mrs. Polanski one of them?"

"One of the worst," said Mrs. Yeager firmly. She appeared to be regaining control of herself. "How do you think she keeps her hair so blonde?"

"A rinse, maybe? They do a lot of things these days."

"Black-eyed peas," said Mrs. Yeager. "Black-eyed peas and beer."

"It's hard to believe Mrs. Polanski would do something like that."

"She opens your mail, doesn't she?" There was almost a taunting slyness in Mrs. Yeager's low rasping voice.

"Opens my mail!" Mrs. Cimino looked down at the envelope in her hand. "I don't know whether she opens it or not."

"Of course you don't." Mrs. Yeager's brown eyes blinked rapidly in sympathy. "Like I said, you're a dear, trusting soul. Too trusting to wonder why they have a mail basket down there instead of a legitimate postal box protected by the United States Government."

She gave Mrs. Cimino's hand a few more affectionate pats before releasing it. Struck by what appeared to be a happy thought, Mrs. Yeager got up from her chair and went over to the closet. There she reached very far back, out of sight. When she returned, she was carrying a small plastic-wrapped package.

"Beef jerky," said Mrs. Yeager. "My niece brings it over for me." She opened the package, took out a strip, and separated it into two parts—not without effort. Keeping the smaller part for herself, she handed the other over to Mrs. Cimino.

"Thank you," said Mrs. Cimino. She looked down at the grainy black strip in her hand, wondering how long it had been in the closet.

"Good beef jerky," said Mrs. Yeager, after she had gnawed off a bite and begun to grind it with her teeth. "A lot better than that soybean meat loaf they give us all the time." She motioned to Mrs. Cimino, waving the remnant of her piece like a conductor's baton.

Mrs. Cimino, who had always liked celery, took a bite: The grainy black stuff resisted her weak jaws, forcing them to clamp down and release many times.

"Good meat fights back at you, doesn't it?" said Mrs. Yeager. A warm smile wreathed her dark, white-thatched face: It was clear that the moment gave her great joy.

Mrs. Cimino, her mouth full, could only nod assent.

The two elderly ladies chewed in silence for a while: Mrs. Cimino lamely; Mrs. Yeager with animation and serious delight, vicariously gourmandizing as Mrs. Cimino after earnest effort ground up the last stringy mouthful and forced it down her small throat.

"Good, good, good beef jerky," said Mrs. Yeager, smacking her thin lips over the fat sound of the phrase.

"Very good," said Mrs. Cimino. "But I must run along now and see about this letter."

"You're going to put it in *their* mail basket?"

"I don't know," said Mrs. Cimino, trying to remember if she had said anything damaging in her letter to Alice. "This one isn't very important."

"Like I said before, you're a trusting soul." The party over, Mrs. Yeager shrugged and returned to her vigil at the window.

Mrs. Cimino started toward the red door: When she reached it, she looked back at Mrs. Yeager, expecting to see her once again intent upon the pine trees. But Mrs. Yeager had suddenly wheeled round. After a moment's silence, she brought her right index finger up to her tightly closed thin lips: There was a touch of supplication in her brown eyes.

Mrs. Cimino nodded, put her finger up to her own lips, and went softly out.

Her progress down the corridor was slow, thoughtful: The envelope she held seemed to offer little defense against prying hands. She decided to ask Mrs. Polanski if there was an actual mailbox nearby, phrasing the matter in an offhand way so as not to betray

126

Mrs. Yeager's knowledge of the vegetarian conspiracy. Dear Mrs. Yeager! Dear generous, tormented soul, worrying more about those little children than her own fragile welfare! Mrs. Cimino sighed as she made her way down the stairs with extra caution.

As she headed down the first-floor corridor toward Mrs. Polanski's office, she came to a full stop just before the four-bed ward. Some of the men at St. Hild's were inclined to pass remarks, so it would be important to march past the door with obvious purpose and authority. Standing there, taking a few deep breaths, she could hear the sound of Mr. Kappelhoff's radio.

Mr. Kappelhoff was seventy-four. He was in the process of recovering from a stroke which had left his right side almost completely paralyzed. Apart from trips down to physical therapy, he spent most of his time listening to ball games on the portable radio his daughter had brought to him. Pale, a little on the portly side, he had spent most of his life as a fry cook.

The man in the bed beside him, Mr. Salves, was seventy-eight. Severely arthritic, he had recently wrenched his back in a bad fall. Short, dark, and wiry, Mr. Salves had recovered, but continued to resist efforts to get him up and about. He spent most of his time playing solitaire.

Over in the far corner was the bed belonging to Mr. Higgins. One of the oldest residents, Mr. Higgins was ninety-five years of age: tall, thin, with sparse gray hair. He had outlived all of his five children, and three of his grandchildren. Four years ago his bladder had been removed. In its place he carried a light blue pouch with tubing connected to his lower left side.

Mr. Higgins did not get around well, but he managed to occupy himself. Every morning, immediately after breakfast, he started in on the *Minneapolis Tribune,* following each story from page to page until he had read his newspaper cover to cover—including the want ads. With time out for lunch, a nap, and a couple of short walks, the project generally took him until five o'clock in the afternoon. For the Sunday edition, he got up an hour before breakfast and stretched his afternoon time out further—sometimes into the evening. He had never been a fast reader.

The fourth occupant of the ward was Mr. Bjornson, recently arrived at St. Hild's: a towering, burly man of seventy. After several bouts of major surgery, Mr. Bjornson had wasted away to less than two hundred thirty pounds, hardly enough to permit his six-foot-five frame unrestricted dominance over the local bars of New Oak, Minnesota. Concomitant with his surgery, Mr. Bjornson's spirits had turned gloomy, gruff, even a little on the angry side, it was said. With his black beard, bushy eyebrows, and broad hairy chest, he looked like a large bear slowly waking up from a drug-induced hibernation: The staff, however, was hopeful that the bear would be friendly and companionable.

As Mrs. Cimino stood there, she heard a sharp thud. Then there were slaps—two of them, flesh on flesh, followed by a woman's scream. Immediately after the scream, Mrs. Cimino saw young Miss Martin rush out of the room in tears. Close behind her was Mr. Bjornson, his giant grizzled body almost bursting the bonds of the white smock they had clothed him in.

"No electricity is going to get me!" Mr. Bjornson stopped just outside the doorway to his ward and roared again as Miss Martin fled into Mrs. Polanski's office. "Electricity! Arrgh!"

"Mr. Bjornson! Mr. Bjornson!" Mrs. Polanski had come quickly out of her office. "Mr. Bjornson!!"

"Arrgh!" A mighty arm was raised as Mrs. Polanski approached the creature.

"Don't you grunt at me, Mr. Bjornson. Don't . . . you . . . grunt . . . at . . . me. Don't . . . you . . . grunt . . . at . . . me!" In a surprisingly loud voice, almost as loud as Mr. Bjornson's, Mrs. Polanski addressed the huge man, stepping in close so that her eyes were level with the top button of Mr. Bjornson's smock.

"What's that, lady?" Puzzled, seemingly pained by Mrs. Polanski's volume, Mr. Bjornson dropped his arm and stared down at her.

"We will not have slapping," said Mrs. Polanski, firmly tilting her head back so that her blue eyes could look directly up at the glaring brown eyes and bushy black eyebrows. "We . . . will . . . not . . . have . . . slapping!"

"What are you going to do about it, lady?" There was the touch of a sneer in the deep, gruff voice. "Are you going to call the guards?"

"I am not going to call anyone, Mr. Bjornson," said Mrs. Polanski. "You are going to stop it right now, stop . . . it . . . right . . . now."

"Well, lady, I'm not going to have all that electricity getting at me." Mr. Bjornson's voice became petulant. "You can tell the warden I'm wise to his tricks."

"There's no warden here," said Mrs. Polanski. "This is a hospital. St. Hild's Convalescent Hospital . . . St. Hild's Convalescent Hospital!" She continued to reiterate the name, articulating it with utmost clarity.

"All right!" Mr. Bjornson threw up his arms in surrender. "It's St. Hild's Convalescent Hospital. What do you want me to do about it?"

"I want you to say your name for us."

"My name?" Mr. Bjornson looked puzzled again.

"Your name—Ralph Bjornson."

"I know that," said Mr. Bjornson, not without irritation.

"Then say it."

"Say what?"

"Your name."

"Ralph," said Mr. Bjornson, a slight tinge of wonder in his voice, as though he had just run into an old logging buddy.

"Ralph what?" Mrs. Polanski was inexorable.

"Ralph Bjornson. My name is Ralph Bjornson."

"Mr. Ralph Bjornson," said Mrs. Polanski with approval. "And there's no electricity going to hurt you."

"No electricity?" Mr. Bjornson paused to consider the matter.

"No electricity. You're perfectly safe here at St. Hild's."

"St. Hild's . . . what was the rest of it?"

"St. Hild's Convalescent Hospital," said Mrs. Polanski.

"St. Hild's Convalescent Hospital," said Mr. Bjornson slowly. He looked back into the ward, where Mr. Kappelhoff, Mr. Salves, and Mr. Higgins were cowering at the far end of the room. He looked out toward the main entrance. He looked up the corridor to the nurses station. Catching sight of Mrs. Cimino pressed against the wall in fear, he smiled absently at her. "It's not very big."

"We can do a big job," said Mrs. Polanski, beginning to breathe a little more easily. "Why don't we take a walk?"

"Why not?" Mr. Bjornson stretched himself tentatively, almost touching the ceiling as he did so. "That sounds like a good idea."

"Put on your bathrobe and slippers. Miss Martin and I will show you around."

"Okay."

Mr. Bjornson went back into the ward. In half a minute he returned wearing a heavy plaid bathrobe and a pair of black slippers. By that time Miss Martin had come up to Mrs. Polanski. As they came down the corridor, three abreast, Mrs. Cimino hastily retreated before their progress, dropping her letter in the mail basket and hurrying upstairs to her room.

As Mrs. Cimino came in, even more breathless than the time before, Mrs. Yeager turned her white-thatched head slowly away from the window. A thin smile creased her dark, grainy face.

"What's for dinner?" she said.

"The menu outside the dining room listed turkey and dumplings," said Mrs. Cimino, smiling cautiously.

"Turkey." Mrs. Yeager frowned. "We've had that one before." She permitted herself a sour laugh at the prospect. "Mock turkey made out of soybeans and pressed sunflower seeds." She shook her head in mournful homage to the artfulness of her adversaries. "I never said they weren't clever."

Not wishing to dispute matters, Mrs. Cimino nodded. But she had reached a conclusion on her way up from down below: Since there was no electricity trying to get at Mr. Bjornson, there were probably no vegetarians conspiring to deceive her taste buds.

"And Jell-O salad," said Mrs. Cimino. "They're having Jell-O salad." She smiled engagingly, as though to indicate a pleasant time in store for the two of them.

"It could be worse," said Mrs. Yeager, resuming her vigil at the window: a vigil apparently intended to make sure that the pine trees would not get any closer.

Wednesday, June 16, 12:10 P.M.

The rumble behind Mrs. Cimino, though familiar by now, was still ominous. As quickly as she could she sought the safety of the corridor wall. She barely made it. With a roar and a whoop Mr. Stewart's wheelchair hurtled by her and skidded into the dining room.

Mr. Stewart, an intense sandy-haired man of seventy-three,

liked to wait until the last minute before seeking lunch. From his room at the end of the corridor he would start up with a strong push and accelerate quickly down the slight slope that led to the central area, sometimes caroming off the wall like a faded red billiard ball. Only last week his left wheel had caught Miss Schmidt's cane and pulled it out from under her: He was clearly the most dangerous wheelie at St. Hild's.

"That man is a menace," said Miss Schmidt. After making sure the corridor was safe, she had come up to Mrs. Cimino.

"He certainly gets around well," said Mrs. Cimino, not without admiration.

"Too well," said Miss Schmidt. With narrowed eyes she watched Mr. Stewart take his place at one of the center tables, just across from Mr. Monsour.

Mrs. Cimino nodded. Some of the more frail wheelies were permitted auxiliary sources of power, but most of them—like Mr. Stewart and Mr. Ayledotte—sculled themselves along with masterful, self-generated, sinewy force. Technically, she knew herself to be an amblie: Her red room on the second floor had required ambulatory status. Yet she traveled with much less speed than Mr. Stewart, and her endurance was much less than Miss Schmidt's, whose cane required her to be classified as a first-floor hobblie.

"I think we can go in now," said Miss Schmidt, smiling approval at the sight of Mr. Bjornson squeezing his great bulk into a small chair just to the right of Mr. Monsour. In his red and green lumberjack shirt he towered over the others like a chastely decorated Christmas tree.

Mr. Bjornson's arrival had somewhat assuaged their climate of mild sexual innuendo: Like a large gentlemanly bear in the herd of whimsical goats, he had begun to frown restraint upon Mr. Stewart and his tendency to pass suggestive remarks. And he had also discouraged Mr. Patterson, an eighty-year-old college professor, from pinching those who wandered too close. Even Mr. Monsour, who still waxed his mustache, had given up his soft yet embarrassing mating cry of "baby, baby, baby."

It was accordingly with great poise and grace that the two ladies made their way in, walking smilingly by the gentlemen at the center table.

"Perhaps a cane would help my walking," said Mrs. Cimino as she watched Miss Schmidt deftly lower her squat frame into place.

131

"I'd advise against it," said Miss Schmidt. "It's like having a third leg to trip over." Her large teeth appeared and then retreated in her customary smile of punctuation.

"You seem to manage very well," said Mrs. Cimino.

"It's not easy," said Miss Schmidt. "That's why I have to start my day so early." She nodded in the same way that she had always used in introducing new equations to her classes. "Every bone, every joint seems to be frozen stiff."

"Is it painful?"

"Very." Miss Schmidt smiled with pleasurable reminiscence. "First I work my neck." She demonstrated with a series of widening circles. "Then the arms and hands, as I work my way down to the fingers." Pelicanlike, she flapped her elbows as though to shake a few still-remaining vital juices free. "It takes at least half an hour before I dare to try sitting up."

"You're a brave soul," said Mrs. Cimino. "I don't think I could endure it."

"I must admit that the wet weather gets me down sometimes," mused Miss Schmidt. She smiled kindly at Mrs. Cimino. "But I never seem to have trouble keeping track of the seasons."

"Good afternoon," said Mrs. Wohlsteader, coming up to the table with Mrs. Anderson in tow. "So sorry I'm late."

"I hope you didn't mind our coming on ahead," said Mrs. Cimino.

"Not at all," said Mrs. Wohlsteader. "I could have been tied up for another fifteen minutes on that pay phone." She sat down, smiled graciously at Miss Schmidt, and proceeded to shift the position of the plastic violets a little farther away from her.

"I was just telling Mrs. Cimino about my morning exercises," said Miss Schmidt.

"Exercises," said Mrs. Anderson. She brightened, almost excitedly, like a sparrow in a birdbath. "My son used to exercise with barbells." She paused, trying to splash up additional substance. "But he gave them to the Salvation Army a few years ago."

"I'm not sure that was wise," said Miss Schmidt. "When my niece and nephew closed up my little house, they gave away most of my library." She looked at the plastic violets accusingly, as though their displacement from the geometric center of the table was an offense against good order. "Some of those algebra books might have been great fun for the children to browse through."

132

"I agree," said Mrs. Wohlsteader. "It's much better to keep things in the family." She gave Miss Schmidt's heavy arm a kindly, understanding pat. "Though it's never easy to close up your home."

"No, it's not," said Miss Schmidt. She detached her gaze from the plastic violets and looked sadly down at her silverware. "But it's very hard to manage a place all by yourself."

"That's true," said Mrs. Cimino, happy that they were all on safe common ground.

As the serving cart clattered up with its small freight of Spanish omelets and cottage cheese, she tried mightily to envision her own house and the neighborhood around it. Blank at first, her mind slowly began to recall details, just as a blur of dark green dissolves into an array of clearly defined trees and bushes once the morning light starts to work its way down a hillside.

Almost as though she were standing on Flora Washburn's porch across the street, Mrs. Cimino suddenly sketched out a full picture: mailbox, gravel driveway, steps, front door with herself walking out—letters in hand, diamond ring glinting in the sunshine. It was a pleasant picture: hands under the table, she rubbed her wedding band, talismanlike, in hopes of keeping the picture in focus.

The perspective was a familiar one. Though only sixty-seven, Flora had been quite close to the Ciminos, especially after the death of old Dr. Washburn, twenty years her senior. Since Dr. Washburn, a longtime fixture in the neighborhood, had accumulated several good pieces of property, Flora had gone into real estate, advising Esther—among other things—to hold on to both the Elm Street house and the music store building.

As for her own large house, Flora had wisely elected to convert it into modest apartments, reserving the ground floor for herself and Puddles, an aged but still lively poodle. There she had spent most of her time, apart from visiting her sister in Sioux Falls, South Dakota. After Frank's death Esther and Flora became closer than ever, remaining so until Joe South moved into one of the second-floor apartments as a tenant.

Joe South, a widower, was a quiet man, a retired auditor for the Burlington Railroad. He was neat, clean, even fastidious about his clothes. He was also an excellent bridge player: an accomplishment which pleased Flora greatly; for with Joe always there as a congenial fourth, it was easy to invite friends over at least once a week for drinks and an evening of cards.

Never a bridge player, and almost ten years older than her friend, Mrs. Cimino found herself spending less and less time with Flora. And as the neighborhood gradually changed, replacing the Ochs, the Traynors, and the Zwinglis with younger couples, Mrs. Cimino spent more and more time by herself: During winter especially, when it was hard for her to get out, she would stay for days and days completely alone in the big gray stone Elm Street house.

"I guess it's still there," said Mrs. Cimino finally, breaking into their collective assault upon the Spanish omelets.

"What's that, my dear?" said Miss Schmidt.

"I meant to say that I still have my house," said Mrs. Cimino.

"You're fortunate," said Mrs. Wohlsteader, looking at her with interest.

"My sons, George and Harold, are taking care of it for me," said Mrs. Cimino, wondering if George had searched the house thoroughly in his hunt for the missing ring.

"Which one has your power of attorney?" asked Mrs. Wohlsteader.

Mrs. Cimino paused, searching through her splotched files for a moment: The power of attorney business had come up once—at Harold's insistence, but she had rejected it.

"Neither," she answered. Her voice was soft, and she had begun to flush a little.

"A joint power of attorney?" said Mrs. Wohlsteader. "That must be pretty complicated."

"My son is good at complicated things," said Mrs. Anderson. She traced a small design in her cottage cheese. "Once he had an electric train that filled up the whole attic." Enchanted by the image, she gazed out the window as though expecting a line of flatcars to hurtle by.

"My attorney's name is Michael Ryan," said Mrs. Cimino. "His son used to take trumpet lessons at the store."

"But who signs your checks for you?" said Miss Schmidt, stepping it to bring the interrogation back on course.

"I've always signed my own checks," said Mrs. Cimino stoutly.

"I admire you for it," said Mrs. Wohlsteader firmly. "Money

matters have always been a source of distress to me." She sat back and scowled at the dining room doorway. "But my son insists on telling me about every expense that comes up."

"Is that why you phone him?" said Mrs. Cimino.

"He won't have it any other way," said Mrs. Wohlsteader ruefully. "And it's such a nuisance using the pay phone." She permitted herself a slightly haughty sniff. "We really should have phones in the rooms when they charge us thirty-two dollars a day."

"Thirty-two dollars a day!" Mrs. Cimino's voice was higher pitched than usual.

"It is a scandal, isn't it?" said Miss Schmidt. Involved with unhooking her cane and working her way up from her chair, she took no apparent notice of Mrs. Cimino's surprise.

"It's dreadful," said Mrs. Cimino, regaining control of herself.

"Though the company is generally quite pleasant," said Mrs. Wohlsteader, smiling at Mrs. Cimino as they left the table.

With her usual regal air, Mrs. Wohlsteader led the other ladies past the dangerous center table, nodding affably to Mr. Bjornson and Mr. Ayledotte.

Once outside the dining room, Mrs. Cimino said goodbye to the others and started upstairs, driven by an empty shrinking feeling inside her, very much as though something of great value had been lost or spirited away. The nature walk was coming up soon, but there might still be time to write George a letter: a letter asking for more details about bank accounts, dividend checks, insurance, and other matters. Including the ring, of course: a ring that might well have been stolen rather than mislaid among the various pushings and shovings along the road leading to her little red room.

Wednesday, June 16, 1:15 P.M.

As usual Mrs. Yeager was sitting by the window when Mrs. Cimino came in. Swiveling round, she cocked her small white-thatched head expectantly and held up a longish black strip for inspection.

"Beef jerky?" said Mrs. Yeager. "I'd be happy to break you off

135

a little piece." The brown eyes in her dark face blinked with generous rapidity.

"No, thank you," said Mrs. Cimino. "I have some figuring to do."

Mrs. Yeager shrugged and returned to her inspection of the pine trees on the far hill. Mrs. Cimino sat down on her bed and took out pencil and scratch paper from her night stand. Slowly at first, then with increasing speed, she began to cover the scratch paper with computations.

The central figure in her computations was thirty-two—the basic rate at St. Hild's, according to Mrs. Wohlsteader. She multiplied it by thirty. She multiplied the result by twelve. To that result she added a comprehensive figure covering taxes, utilities, and maintenance for the Elm Street house. She then drew a large circle around what she had done, as though to exile it from her speculations.

Taking up another sheet of paper, she multiplied her Social Security stipend by twelve. To that result she added her yearly dividend income. She underlined the figure several times. But it refused to grow. If anything, the underlining emphasized the frailty of the figure, especially when compared with the contents of her basic-expense circle. Mrs. Cimino put down her pencil, sat there, and grieved for a few minutes.

With a deep sigh she put away her scratch paper. She took out her pen and light blue note paper. She wrote a few words. She stopped and read them through.

Dear George,
I have just been doing some figuring.

She bit her lower lip. She gnawed the end of her pen, almost as though its glossy resistance might offer her the same magical strength that Mrs. Yeager attributed to a hard black piece of beef jerky. With another sigh she put her pen away and crumpled up the piece of light blue note paper.

She picked up her purse, opened it, and took out a white envelope. She emptied out the contents of the envelope on the bed beside her: half dollars, quarters, dimes, nickels, and pennies. She put the pennies back into her purse. The rest she put into another white envelope, labeling it "Change for Phone."

136

She opened the drawer of her night stand. She took out her green address book and looked through it. On her change envelope she wrote a number, labeling it "George's Office." She stood up and smoothed the wrinkles out of her dress. Firmly, purposefully, she took her change envelope and marched out of the room.

The public telephone at St. Hild's lay just beyond Mrs. Nash's office, almost as though Mrs. Nash—Cerberus-like—was charged with guarding the wires leading to the outside world. But it was with confident, cheerful good humor that Mrs. Cimino stopped at Mrs. Nash's doorway.

"Hello there, Mrs. Nash," said Mrs. Cimino. "I thought I'd give this phone of yours a try." She smiled and waved her envelope in front of Mrs. Nash.

"That's what it's there for," said Mrs. Nash. "Do you need any help?"

"I think I can manage," said Mrs. Cimino airily. "I've got my son's number, and I'm sure I have more than enough change."

"Very good," said Mrs. Nash. "Sometimes our best friend is the telephone, particularly when we can't drive."

"Old Mrs. Traynor used to take taxicabs everywhere," said Mrs. Cimino. "But I always felt they were too expensive."

"They certainly are out here," said Mrs. Nash. "You're lucky to have Karen coming in to take you out for shopping and things like that."

"She's been very good," said Mrs. Cimino. "And I hate to bother her father—even on the phone." She looked down at her change envelope thoughtfully. "But there are times when it's wise to talk things over."

"That's true," said Mrs. Nash. She looked at Mrs. Cimino, eyes narrowed behind her dark glasses, as though to read the sequence of thoughts that had led Mrs. Cimino to her doorway. There was a slight touch of invitation in her voice.

"Here I go!" said Mrs. Cimino. She smiled Mrs. Nash's invitation away and hurried on to the phone.

Her preparations were minute and exact: She placed her quarters, dimes, and nickels in neat piles ready for instant access. Then she dialed the Minneapolis number, grimacing a little when the operator came on the line and told her the amount needed.

After putting most of her quarters in the slot, along with two dimes, she stood there listening to the phone ring several times,

137

growing visibly impatient. When a voice finally came on the line, she gave George's extension number. Then she stood there listening to another series of rings. These went unanswered, but she continued to wait, as though her intensity of purpose would somehow force a response.

In time a response came—from the operator, asking for additional quarters, dimes, and nickels. Mrs. Cimino countered with a not unreasonable request: Since her call had not been completed, her money should properly be returned. The operator was not moved by Mrs. Cimino's request, pointing out that the first number had answered and that additional moneys were now justifiably due. Mrs. Cimino permitted herself a few observations on justice, fair play, and the declining quality of service in certain public utilities. Then, still maintaining icy self-control, she hung up and walked back to Mrs. Nash's office.

"Disgraceful!" said Mrs. Cimino. She was breathing heavily.

"Maybe he's still at lunch," said Mrs. Nash.

"I don't see why," said Mrs. Cimino. "It's after one o'clock."

"Maybe you could try after the nature walk," said Mrs. Nash.

"I've used up nearly all my change," said Mrs. Cimino. "And I spent my time waiting and talking to two snippy little girls." Fuming, she turned on her heel and stalked out. There was a soft slap, slap of her rubber-heeled oxfords going back up the corridor.

Mrs. Nash remained pensive for a moment before returning to her paper work.

The rubber-heeled oxfords took Mrs. Cimino back up to her room with more than ordinary directness and speed. There she sat immediately down, took up pen and paper, and began to write.

Dear George,

I have been doing some figuring about what all this is costing. It looks to me as though I will have to start going into the income from the store. I don't want to do this. Simon Montford has always kept that money separate, using any surplus to reduce the mortgage on the building.

Besides, I'm very much in the dark out here. Simon used to send me a detailed monthly set of figures. Have you been getting these?

Mrs. Cimino stopped writing and began to gnaw the end of her pen again. She crumpled up what she had written and began anew.

> Dear George,
> Have you been writing checks on my account for all these expenses?

This effort she broke off right away as too tactless, too accusatory. She took up a third sheet of light blue paper and made another attempt.

> Dear George,
> You and Harold have been very good about taking care of things for me. I am feeling better now, as you know. I'm a little upset over not being told about what's going on at the store and at the house.

Again she stopped, a hard glint coming into her faded blue eyes. The facts were far too uncomfortable to be glossed over with fair language. She decided to try another approach.

> Dear Harold,
> I am *very* upset with your brother.

She paused, charting the sentence to come and the one after that, like a lawyer trying to build a case out of a few small bits of evidence. Ruminatively she put her page on the night stand and sat there a moment on her bed. With a sigh she took off her shoes and stretched out, closing her eyes very tightly. From her chair by the window Mrs. Yeager watched her with interest.

After a while Mrs. Cimino sat up again and put on her shoes. She took out her purse, opened it, and spread out her white envelopes once more. This time she concentrated on her larger denominations: two twenties, a ten, and three fives. These she put into one envelope, putting it back into the purse. She picked up her purse and went out.

Mrs. Cimino's progress down the corridor was slower this time, quieter. If anything, the soft sound of her rubber-heeled oxfords was almost inaudible as she passed by Mrs. Nash's doorway. Had Mrs. Nash been engrossed in her paper work, she would not have noticed Mrs. Cimino. But the paper work had been put aside in favor of a cigarette.

"Going to try again, Mrs. Cimino?"

"Yes, I am," said Mrs. Cimino. "There's no point in letting these little things get me down."

"Very good," said Mrs. Nash, looking at Mrs. Cimino's purse with curiosity. "Do you have enough change?"

"I think so," said Mrs. Cimino.

"To call Minneapolis again?" said Mrs. Nash.

"No," said Mrs. Cimino, smiling as brightly as she could. "This is going to be a local call." She nodded her head as though to indicate a certain amount of intrinsic charm in the notion.

"A local call?"

"For one of your taxicabs, Mrs. Nash." Mrs. Cimino smiled graciously.

"A taxicab?" Mrs. Nash put her cigarette out.

"I think I have enough here," said Mrs. Cimino, gesturing toward her purse.

"Enough for what?" said Mrs. Nash. As though needing a bit of a stretch, she got up from her desk.

"Enough for the taxicab," said Mrs. Cimino. "I've decided to run on home for a little while."

"Do you think that's a good idea, Mrs. Cimino?" By this time Mrs. Nash, moving slowly, had rounded her desk and was standing in the doorway.

"Obviously I think it's a good idea," said Mrs. Cimino, nodding and smiling with even greater good humor than before. "Otherwise I wouldn't be doing it."

"But this is so sudden, Mrs. Cimino." Mrs. Nash smiled down at her with equal good humor. "What about your nature walk?"

"I don't think it will do any harm, Mrs. Nash, if I miss the nature walk today." Mrs. Cimino's smile was beginning to take on a rather fixed, artificial quality.

"But you've always enjoyed our nature walks, haven't you?" There was obvious distress mapped out below Mrs. Nash's dark horn-rimmed glasses.

"I have enjoyed them very much," said Mrs. Cimino. "But I really must hurry along."

"Wouldn't it be a good idea for us to talk about all this?" Mrs. Nash stepped out into the corridor and gestured with manifest invitation toward her office.

"Right now I don't think it's such a good idea," said Mrs. Cimino. "I'm afraid I just don't have time to go into all the whys and wherefores." With some distress Mrs. Cimino noticed that Mrs. Nash was now standing between her and the phone.

"Mrs. Cimino, I really feel you should come in here and sit down for a minute." Again Mrs. Nash gestured invitingly toward her desk.

"I'd like to very much, Mrs. Nash." Mrs. Cimino charged her voice with the utmost sincerity and shook her head with sad regret. "But it's just not convenient right now."

"Mrs. Cimino, I'm afraid I must insist," said Mrs. Nash, her voice quite clear and a little raised in volume.

"Mrs. Nash!" said Mrs. Cimino reprovingly. "You're a lovely person and I'm sure you're quite competent in your work here." She sighed as though reluctant to speak plainly. "But I don't like being spoken to in that tone of voice."

"Mrs. Cimino!" Mrs. Nash's voice was quite loud now. "You must understand that we are responsible for you here."

"Responsible?" Mrs. Cimino looked straight up at Mrs. Nash, a slightly puzzled smile on her face. "I happen to be a homeowner and substantial taxpayer of this state." She gestured back toward the nurses station with an air of authority. "In fact, I was paying taxes and supporting places like this long before you were born." The smile disappeared and the faded blue eyes began to blaze slightly. "Please step aside, Mrs. Nash, and let me by."

"I can't do that, Mrs. Cimino." Mrs. Nash folded her arms as though to indicate that the discussion had been closed.

"I'm sorry to hear you say that," said Mrs. Cimino. She turned as though to go back. "Genuinely sorry."

Her feint accomplished, Mrs. Cimino pivoted quickly and attempted a narrow end run around Mrs. Nash, heading for the main entrance and a road that might take her to Elm Street. Had it not been for Miss Martin and one of the other aides tackling her from the rear, the end run might have been successful, since Mrs. Nash was pretty much off guard. But the two tacklers were strong young women, farm bred, and their teamwork was excellent.

Despite her compact vigor and excellent leverage, Mrs. Cimino was speedily subdued and hauled into Mrs. Nash's office. There, the two young women bracing her against the wall, she was forced to endure a sedating shot from Mrs. Nash. When the orderlies came with a gurney, the shot had already begun to take effect: They had little difficulty carting her back to her room. There she was placed in bed—posies restraining her wrists—and bedrails were installed. By this time Mrs. Cimino was fast asleep.

It was a long time before she woke up.

When she finally opened her eyes the room was dark, timeless, with only Mrs. Yeager's white-thatched head on her left, faintly visible on its pillow. The other shapes in the room were vague, blurred—like the throbbing in Mrs. Cimino's head and the dryness in her throat.

The small tug at her wrists told Mrs. Cimino she had been trussed up, and the bedrails told her she had been returned to some early protective state.

"They got you, didn't they?" Mrs. Yeager's low whisper came threading over toward her.

Mrs. Cimino nodded.

"I told you those vegetarians were clever," said Mrs. Yeager sadly.

There was a long pause. Both elderly ladies lay there in silence, each mulling over the burdens placed upon them.

"It's not a bad place," said Mrs. Yeager finally. "I've been here a long time."

Mrs. Cimino sighed.

"How about a piece of beef jerky?" said Mrs. Yeager. "It helps to chase the blues away sometimes."

"That's very kind of you," said Mrs. Cimino. "But I wouldn't want to put you to any trouble."

"No trouble, dear," said Mrs. Yeager. She got out of bed and went slowly over to the closet.

"Just a wee tiny piece," said Mrs. Cimino. With the yellow light from the hall outside she could barely see Mrs. Yeager's small form rummaging through the closet.

"Here we are," said Mrs. Yeager, whispering her way back to Mrs. Cimino's bedside. She handed Mrs. Cimino a short black stick.

"Thank you," whispered Mrs. Cimino.

"Good beef jerky," said Mrs. Yeager. There was a lilt to her voice. She got back into her bed and stretched out with almost sensuous pleasure in the thought. "Good, good, good beef jerky." Soon she was asleep.

Mrs. Cimino chewed on her gift for a long time, almost as though she were gnawing on the straps that bound her. Turning her head to her right, she looked out the doorway to the corridor, softly lit with a clear yellow light. At the end of the corridor were the stairs, below the stairs were the nurses station and a corridor that led to the main entrance. Outside the main entrance was a road.

Somewhere, leading off from that road, was a dark obscure path that led back to the gray stone house on Elm Street. Mrs. Cimino tried to travel the path back home: It was too winding, too uncertain. She tried to map out a route that might take her from home to St. Hild's, but there were too many blank spots. Even when she closed her eyes and clenched her small hands into fists, the sequence of events refused to take shape.

She gulped down the last of Mrs. Yeager's beef jerky. It was salty, like the taste of tears. She sighed. She let the past drain from her mind: It was of far less concern to her than the future that stretched out in front of her. There it lay: dark, fathomless, like a heavy wool blanket thrust over her face and held there by the hand of some strong, cruel, implacably malevolent child.

Part 3

As soon as they [the Struldbruggs] have completed the Term of Eighty Years, they are looked on as dead in Law; their Heirs immediately succeed to their Estates; only a small Pittance is reserved for their Support; and the poor ones are maintained at the Publicke Charge. After that Period, they are held incapable of any Employment of Trust or Profit; they cannot purchase Lands or take Leases, neither are they allowed to be Witnesses in any Cause, either Civil or Criminal, not even for the decision of Meers and Bounds.

JONATHAN SWIFT
Gulliver's Travels

Saturday, June 26, 10:15 A.M.

From her front porch Mrs. Washburn could see the cars and vans begin to clog the street. Drawn by Mr. Leach's ad, people were arriving early in search of antiques and items suitable for sale at various flea markets.

The large lawn extending down from Mrs. Cimino's house had been converted into a display area: Almost twenty folding tables had been set up. On these were arranged the remains of the Cimino estate, much like an immensely fragmented cadaver laid out for inspection by first-year medical students. The weather was ideal: warm, not too humid, with the clear innocuous blue sky that tents Minnesota for most of the summer.

Mrs. Washburn had no intention of viewing the remains: The notion of strangers picking over clothes and memorabilia had always been distasteful to her. But Joe was late in coming out of the house, and Puddles was restively pulling at the leash. Once down the steps, she found herself edging toward the sale display.

"All set?" said Joe, coming down the steps. For their walk up to the park he had chosen a pleasant costume: light blue slacks, black and white Florsheims, white Palm Beach jacket, and dark blue sports shirt.

"In a minute." Mrs. Washburn, still irritated by the delay, continued to view the comings and goings down at the Cimino house. The prospect of a walk with Joe and Puddles was beginning to lose some of its original attractiveness.

Joe South himself was not an unattractive man. But he was dull. Apart from watching ball games on television, he spent most of his time playing cards and taking care of his wardrobe. Since he changed costumes several times a day, his cleaning bills were high. He had twenty pairs of shoes, each kept in a permanent state of high, glossy polish. Naturally taciturn, he had gradually come to limit himself to monosyllabic judgments regarding hitting, fielding, and duplicate bridge.

"Nice," said Joe, looking up at the clear blue sky.

"They'll have a lot of people there by this afternoon," said Mrs. Washburn.

"Oh?" said Joe.

"Poor Esther's things," said Mrs. Washburn. "Spread out for strangers to pick over."

"Yes," said Joe. He nodded his head in sad assent.

"I've got a good mind to go over there," said Mrs. Washburn.

"Oh?" said Joe, taking the leash from her and trying to restrain Puddles, who by now was in a frenzy.

"Maybe George or Harold will be there," said Mrs. Washburn. "It would be worth it just to hear how Esther is doing."

"Okey-dokey," said Joe. He let Puddles lead them across the street. There he and Puddles explored a neighboring privet hedge while Mrs. Washburn began to wedge her way into the crowd of probing fingers and elbows.

There was a lot to look at: Like many of their era, Frank and Esther had never really thrown anything away, instead allowing the accumulating detritus of forty years to occupy garage, attic, and roomy waterproof cellar. Much of the material was conventional: tools, kitchenware, odd vases and lamps, towels and linens, Mason jars and old cider jugs grown suddenly valuable. Ironing boards, chairs, small tables, cutlery, stuffed animals from distant childhood, electric trains and Tinker Toys—all these could be seen as ordinary sweepings from an old house.

But some of it was unique, stamped more with the features of the original owners. As musicians, Frank and Esther had bought sheet music over the years and kept it—enough to fill up one complete table. Mrs. Washburn found herself staring down at the cover of "The Hukilau Song," with a flattering picture of Jack Owens himself carrying a canoe into the water, assisted by several dark-skinned young men in brightly figured loincloths. Beside him, topping another stack, was "Carry Me Back to Old Virginny," decorated with a sad-faced Freddie Martin holding his golden-voiced tenor saxophone.

"Fabulous, fabulous," squealed a voice attached to an elbow on Mrs. Washburn's right. The hand attached to the elbow reached for the fresh young face of Bing Crosby, staring pensively up at the title "It's Easy to Remember—and So Hard to Forget."

Mrs. Washburn nodded approvingly at these signs of nostalgic respect. But she quailed a bit at the price posted: fifty cents for each piece of sheet music. Apart from Frank's instruction books, there seemed to be over a thousand separate pieces.

"Charming!" The voice was lower, fluted, as though trying to impose a personal mark upon an overworked word. Mrs. Washburn followed the sound over to another table where a willowy young man was going through several stacks of photographs.

Most of the photographs were glossy professional prints: Inscribed with various degrees of affection to Frank Cimino, they bore faintly echoing names like Nick Lucas, Eddie Peabody, Mildred Bailey, Helen Humes, Mike Pingatorre, George van Epps, Spec Red, and Alvino Rey. There were several hundred of these, ranging from national celebrity status to purely local eminence— The Six Fat Dutchmen and Whoopee John Wilfahrt, for example.

Some of the pictures bore no autograph. One of them was of Chief Kona Kai and his Hawaiian Serenaders—all in gleaming white evening dress—with Frank Cimino standing high in the back looking soberly down at his electric steel guitar. Another one, slightly smaller, portrayed three young women with daringly bobbed hair in gold lamé gowns: they were all smiling brightly off to their right at some unseen admirer. A printed legend identified them as the McDonald Sisters—Emily, Esther, Rose—Singers of Songs with Style.

"I love them," said the willowy young man. "I just love them." He picked up a picture of Frank looking thoughtfully at the neck of a four-string plectrum banjo. His companion—an older, chubby man—nodded: The two of them took possession of about fifteen frozen moments and hurried up to the front porch, where one of the bank employees had been stationed with a small adding machine.

Mrs. Washburn scowled: It was as though the sale was somehow rubbing out Esther's past as well as emptying her house. She turned to look back toward the privet hedge. As usual Joe was standing quietly, but Puddles was growing impatient.

"Mrs. Washburn, isn't it?"

She turned back toward the porch again. A spare, white-haired man in his early sixties was coming down the steps.

"Yes, it is." Mrs. Washburn fumbled for the name a moment. "Simon Montford, how are you?"

"Can't complain," said Simon dryly. He stepped aside to let three young matrons crowd through: They were hard-faced, tanned, dressed in incongruously frilly tennis costumes, like large sullen babies grown preternaturally dark and wiry.

"Quite a turnout," said Mrs. Washburn. She gestured round the lawn as though to indicate the knots of people constituted a clear tribute to the quality of life in the big gray stone house.

"I thought some of Frank's guitars might still be here," said Simon. His tone was apologetic, tinged with guilt.

"Is there much inside?" said Mrs. Washburn. She scowled at the open doorway, wondering what quaint curiosities the willowy young man might be gushing over.

"Furniture," said Simon. "The piano's gone."

"Esther always loved that piano," said Mrs. Washburn.

"How is she?" said Simon.

"Not bad," said Mrs. Washburn. "She seems to like it where she is."

"That's good," said Simon. "I think the house was getting to be too much for her." A little awkwardly he began to scrutinize a signed photograph of Lawrence Welk. "And she worried about the store."

"How's the store doing?"

"Can't really say," said Simon. "The bank put in a new manager last month." He laughed a little self-consciously. "One of those young fellows, full of beans. We just couldn't get along."

"That's a shame," said Mrs. Washburn.

"It's not as bad as it sounds," said Simon. "I'm doing instrument repair for Morrisons downtown." He shrugged, not without sadness. "Besides, we're about ready to retire and move to California."

"The winters are hard here," said Mrs. Washburn sympathetically. She gazed down at a photograph of Ray Noble and tried to picture how Joe would look with a mustache.

"That's what we'll do," said Simon. "We'll sell the house and close our little show out." He looked back toward the front porch: The willowy young man and his chubby friend were coming down the steps, arms filled with posters crying the lively attractions of Frank Cimino and his Banjo Buddies. "Better to do it yourself than have someone else do it for you." He gave another self-conscious laugh.

"Much better," said Mrs. Washburn. She found her eyes wandering over toward Joe: Even without a mustache he was a fine-

150

looking man. She waved at him and smiled before going up the steps.

The bottom floor of the Cimino house was crowded with dismantled beds, old night stands, cardboard cartons, and worn pieces of luggage—including two steamer trunks. The rugs had all been taken up. The air was dusty, even though the windows and doors had been opened as though to welcome assault from any quarter. Mrs. Washburn walked upstairs for a moment: The second floor was completely bare.

She walked back down again and went quickly outside, stopping only to look at a table filled with framed photographs. One was of a tall man with long sideburns, stiffly posed in an ill-fitting black suit. She turned it over to see if someone had tagged him with a name: In the lower right-hand corner someone had written "Oscar Johnson, September 4, 1910."

Another framed photograph showed an old-style automobile with a young, thirtyish man at the wheel. Seated directly next to him was a young girl with light brown hair. Calm, self-possessed, she had a faintly superior smile on her lips. In back were two younger girls, both apparently just recovered from a fit of the giggles. Mrs. Washburn turned it over and read: "Papa, Rose, Emily, Esther in Papa's new car. Rose is the one in the front seat."

"The frames alone are worth a couple of dollars apiece," said the young man from the adding machine. "You don't get carving like that these days."

"Very nice," said Mrs. Washburn. "I'm sure you'll get takers for them sooner or later."

"It doesn't matter," said the young man. "After tomorrow we'll turn it all over to one of those West Coast dealers."

"When will the house be ready to be shown?" said Mrs. Washburn, her realtor's eyes beginning to overpower her feelings of distress.

"I think Mr. Leach already has a buyer for it," said the young man.

"I'm not surprised," said Mrs. Washburn. "It's a good piece of property."

She turned away from the young man and hurried on out to the sidewalk. She started toward Joe and Puddles but stopped when she saw a small bent figure approaching from the right.

"Mrs. Simpson!" She waited until the small bent figure got

close enough to peer up at her. "It's good to see you out on a day like this."

"I try my best, dear." Mrs. Simpson cast a rheumy eye toward the table-filled lawn. "But I just wasn't able to get out to poor Esther's funeral." Her wattles quivered disconsolately as she shook her eighty-five–year–old head.

"There hasn't been a funeral," said Mrs. Washburn.

"Not yet?" Mrs. Simpson knit her brows, trying to puzzle the matter out. "I'll have Mary phone the church for me." She sighed and shook her head again. "You just can't trust the newspapers these days."

"Esther's still in the hospital," said Mrs. Washburn, a bit uncertain as to how the situation should be described.

"Still in the hospital?" Mrs. Simpson gave a dry cough, as though to test the efficacy of her own respiratory system. She turned her puzzlement back to the gray stone house. "Why are they selling her lovely things?" Frowning, she squinted up at the front porch. "And where's George? Where's Harold?"

"Harold's still down in Des Moines," said Mrs. Washburn. "George got married again last year."

"Poor dear Esther," said Mrs. Simpson. "Those boys haven't been much help, have they?"

"Not as much as they could be," said Mrs. Washburn.

"I always said she and Frank spoiled them," said Mrs. Simpson, shaking her head regretfully over the irrevocability of poor judgments made in the past. "Bicycles, clothes, games, going away to high-priced schools—that younger one certainly got the cream from the top of the bottle."

"He's done very well," said Mrs. Washburn.

"I know," said Mrs. Simpson. "Esther used to tell me all about it. She was always great for bragging on her kids." Nodding her head with finality, Mrs. Simpson muttered her way on into the display, moving slowly from table to table.

Mrs. Washburn watched her for a minute, marveling at the sharpness of Mrs. Simpson's judgment. Both boys *had* done well, to the degree that Esther was only so much excess baggage.

With old Mrs. Simpson it was different, even though her assets were slim and her house a small frame affair two blocks over on a busy street. Mrs. Simpson's two sons had not blazed forth in great glory: One was a shoe salesman and the other a foreman in a meat-packing plant. Nor had her daughter: Mary had been married once, but that had ended in divorce many years ago. Since that time, bruised by matrimony, Mary had lived submissively with her mother, working as a legal secretary until her retirement two years ago.

To her sons and their families, Mrs. Simpson was still of occasional help, particularly at Christmas and on birthdays. To her daughter, Mrs. Simpson's house and modest income were essential components of a reasonably comfortable existence. Sick or well, rambling or alert, Mrs. Simpson was a valuable item. It was hard to imagine her ever being shunted off to a nursing home, just as it was hard to imagine her children being anything but docile and respectful. And she still had a sharp tongue.

"Here we go," said Mrs. Washburn, hurrying up to Joe and Puddles as though to expiate the sinful amount of time spent.

Tuesday, July 6, 10:30 A.M.

"¿Cómo se dice esta cosa?" Miss Rochester picked up a large yellow pencil and looked queryingly at Mrs. Wohlsteader.

"Un lápiz," said Mrs. Wohlsteader, looking straight at Miss Rochester from behind her gold-rimmed glasses. *"Esta cosa es un lápiz."*

"¿Qué puede usted hacer con un lapiz, Señora Wohlsteader?"

"Con un lápiz, puede escribir," said Mrs. Wohlsteader.

"¿Puede o puedo? Miss Rochester looked sharply down her long Saxon nose at Mrs. Wohlsteader.

"Puedo," said Mrs. Wohlsteader after furrowing her brow a little. *"Con un lápiz, puedo escribir."*

"Muy bien, Señora Wohlsteader."

Mrs. Cimino and Miss Schmidt both hummed soft sounds of approval as Mrs. Wohlsteader sat back, looking very pleased with herself.

Only the three of them were in the room with Miss Rochester. Since they called it an advanced class, Mrs. Cimino had dressed for it with some care: She had forced herself to make the transition back to full-length hose, handling all the snaps and necessary contortions by herself. With her dark blue skirt and ruffled white blouse, she looked very businesslike, very no-nonsense in her approach to the morning's activities.

There was a little more intensity in her manner. The confrontation with Mrs. Nash had steeled her will, even though the smile remained engaging. St. Hild's was a hospital, hospitals were places where you concentrated on getting better; when you improved enough, you went home—it was as simple as one of Miss Schmidt's arithmetic problems. Worries about the house and store were distractions, surfacing only late at night and then not for long.

With George and Harold taking care of things, her job was a simple one: to get well, and to concentrate on this as her first order of business.

The only bad feature of the confrontation had been the required conference with Mrs. Polanski and Mrs. Nash. Hard examiners, working in tandem, they had probed at her. There had been questions, uncomfortable questions, about George, about Lisa, about Harold and Gloria. But she had not broken. She had not given voice to feelings of pain and failure. Bright, cheerful, faded blue eyes full of good humor, she had patiently explained the difficulties under which her two fine sons labored. And she had celebrated their wives, difficult though the task was, as lovely, charming women fit to sparkle at the Governor's Ball.

Her only expressed regret had centered upon the store: She and Frank had expected Harold to come back from college and build it up to giant heights. But he had married a rich man's daughter, choosing to start high up on the beanstalk rather than at the modest altitude of Cimino Music. And yet there were still the grandchildren to think of: By holding on she would be able to pass it along to them. It was a noble dream. The thought of it always made her smile.

When it came her turn, following Miss Schmidt, Mrs. Cimino successfully negotiated the intricate gender distinctions existing between *el lápiz, la mesa,* and *el papel.* Adjusting her hearing aid, she sat back and looked expectantly up at Miss Rochester.

"Our little experiment is off to a good start, isn't it?" said Miss Rochester.

"I for one am quite pleased," said Mrs. Wohlsteader. "Old dogs, new tricks, and that sort of thing." She smiled graciously round at the others.

"That's what they are," said Miss Schmidt. "Tricks." She looked accusingly up at Miss Rochester. "I still don't see the point of it."

"It's not as though we were planning to travel down to Mexico," said Mrs. Wohlsteader. "My last trip was to the Grand Canyon, and that was more than ten years ago." As usual, she was politely determined not to be outdone by Miss Schmidt's capacity for mordant observation.

"But surely you must be proud of yourselves for being able to learn new things," said Miss Rochester, a little pained by the classroom revolt brewing.

"There's not much point in learning new things if they're not going to be useful," said Miss Schmidt. "If I were to give a class in trigonometry, we could make an excellent map of the grounds here."

Even Mrs. Cimino, usually bland and approving, felt impelled to nod her head in grudging endorsement of Miss Schmidt's firm position.

"But why is it so important for things to be useful?" said Miss Rochester.

Now it was Miss Schmidt's turn to look pained.

"I must say, Miss Rochester, that I am shocked to hear you express such a frivolous attitude toward life." Miss Schmidt's voice was unexpectedly deep and resonant, as though she were addressing a joint session of the United States Congress—and scolding them in the special way retired schoolteachers have. "Not that you're a frivolous person yourself," she added kindly.

"You've never been a frivolous person, have you?" said Miss Rochester. She stared thoughtfully at the small, squat, large-faced, white-haired lady in front of her.

"I have certainly indulged myself with a vacation every now and then," said Miss Schmidt. "But I have never been a loafer." She permitted herself a short smile of punctuation before continuing. "Indeed, if I may say so, I have been of substantial service to the community for many years." She sat back, quite secure in her assessment of the matter.

"I'm sure you have," said Miss Rochester.

"If you can't be useful, there's not much point to anything."
Mrs. Wohlsteader looked at Mrs. Cimino for confirmation.

"I really have to agree with Mrs. Wohlsteader," said Mrs.
Cimino. "If it weren't for my health, I'd still be running the music
store."

"But we have to expect health problems as we grow older,
don't we?" said Miss Rochester.

Mrs. Cimino looked over at Mrs. Wohlsteader and Miss
Schmidt, hoping that one of them would comment on the matter.
Mrs. Wohlsteader was staring glumly at the liver spots on the back
of her hand. Miss Schmidt was flashing her a large-toothed professional smile, as though some sort of correct answer was expected.

"Our repair bills are certainly higher," said Mrs. Cimino. She
gave a little laugh.

"Doesn't this mean that we can't be useful in the same ways
that have worked well for us in the past?" said Miss Rochester
softly.

"Exactly," said Mrs. Cimino. "So we have to find new ways
of being useful." She looked over at the others and sat back, feeling
that she had scored an important point.

"And that brings us right back to the Spanish," said Miss
Schmidt. "I still don't see how learning a few strange words is
going to help us be more useful."

Miss Rochester went over to the blackboard and picked up a
piece of chalk. In large bold letters she wrote the word *alert*. She
stepped away from the blackboard and gestured toward it as
though the letters had magical properties.

"That's the first requirement for being useful," said Miss Rochester. "We have to be alert." She looked at them with a close approximation of fierce intensity. "Isn't that right?"

The three elderly ladies nodded, not without distress. Each of
them knew what it was like to be out of touch with what was
going on.

Miss Rochester went back to her blackboard, erased the first
two letters of the word, and wrote two new ones in their place—
the letters *I* and *N*.

"Inert," said Miss Rochester. "That's the danger." She looked
down her long Saxon nose at them, pressing the point. "We need
to remain *alert,* but we run the risk of becoming and staying *inert.*"

Mrs. Cimino shuddered inwardly. She was glad Miss Rochester had not used the term *vegetable*. At St. Hild's there were several rooms with soft white mounds in the beds, turned over from time to time like pancakes on a griddle.

"And what's the difference between these two words?" said Miss Rochester.

"They're spelled differently," said Miss Schmidt, a bit irritated with the laboriousness of Miss Rochester's pedagogy.

"Right!" exclaimed Miss Rochester, as though a momentous discovery had just been made.

"I'm not sure I see just what the point of all this is," said Mrs. Wohlsteader. "It's good to be alert, and it's not good to be inert. Why not leave it at that?"

"Because the spelling gives us a clue," said Miss Rochester proudly. "Something that we can keep in mind, something that we can remember." She went back to the blackboard and circled the letters *I* and *N*. "We'll let these letters stand for the forces that keep us from remaining alert."

"Aha!" said Miss Schmidt. "Like unknown quantities, as in algebra." She nodded at the others to indicate mild approval. "Though I always had much more affection for *X* and *Y*."

"Let's see if we can identify these unknown quantities," said Miss Rochester. "It's certainly not a matter of sluggishness as far as our minds go." She smiled down at the three elderly ladies as though to compliment them on the power of their intellects. "Those minds of yours are busy, busy, busy all the time. Isn't that true?"

Mrs. Cimino nodded without looking at the others. Often at night she had lain awake trying to ease the spinning so that gentle, dreamless sleep could creep in.

"And a lot of it is just plain worrying," said Miss Rochester. "Worry, worry, worry—that's what you do, that's what we all do."

"A person can't help worrying," said Miss Schmidt.

"And it doesn't do any good to tell a person not to worry," said Mrs. Wohlsteader. "Particularly when you really have something to worry about."

"Exactly!" said Miss Rochester. "Intelligent people have a tendency to worry about the future." She went to the board and wrote a large impressive *N*, using it as the first letter of a phrase, "Nagging worries," and going on to write out a complete sentence: "Nagging worries are our first obstacle to being alert."

"That makes sense," said Miss Schmidt. "Thinking about what's going to happen—or what might happen—can be very distracting."

"But that's not all we do," said Miss Rochester. "As we grow older, we often brood over the past." She looked out the window for a moment as though to summon up a vast personal panorama. "We grieve over our mistakes, we fume over the injustices done to us—just as though we were seeing an old movie night after night after night." She went back to the board and wrote a big *I* as the first letter of the phrase "Ineffective anger." She put down the chalk, not with a snap but softly, and her voice was suddenly quite gentle. "But there's nothing we can do to change that movie, is there?"

Mrs. Cimino shook her head sadly. Her own movie had been poorly scripted, poorly staged—particularly at the beginning. Rose had been given the best part, the best clothes. She had always been given the hand-me-downs, which always seemed to be too worn, too out of style, when Emily's turn came along.

And yet she had tried to please, she had tried to be popular with boys. Once she had allowed Eric Augenbraun to walk her home from a high school dance, coming in with pride to announce the existence of her first beau. There had been laughter from Papa, slightly contemptuous laughter, coupled with comments on the social desirability of Krauts and Squareheads. She had not gone to the dances after that, not until her figure had filled out a little more.

They had not been fair. But she had shown them. The store was proof of that. And her sons had been popular, successful, living proof of her value—especially Harold, who had been president of his class. And the grandchildren were beautiful: Ann, Gretchen, Kevin, Patrick—all away at good colleges and certain to move in the best circles. She had been able to revise the script, centering the plot more on herself, supporting her role with attractive characters. By rights, the ending should be a happy one. But it had not worked out that way: Mistakes had been made somewhere, and it was important to ferret them out.

"A person can't stop remembering things that have happened," said Mrs. Wohlsteader, her usually erect frame bowed for a moment.

"Of course not," said Miss Rochester. "But it wastes our energies." She turned back toward them. "Nagging worries and ineffective anger both distract us from what's going on right now." She went up to her desk and pounded on it several times.

"You've admitted yourself that we can't help it," said Miss Schmidt.

"I didn't say that it couldn't be helped," said Miss Rochester. "I said our natural tendency is to let the future and the past distract us."

"Maybe we need something to distract us from our distractions," said Mrs. Cimino, a little nervous over her play on words.

"Why not?" said Miss Rochester. She picked up the yellow pencil once more. "¿Cómo se dice, Señorita Schmidt?"

"El lápiz," said Miss Schmidt, her broad face breaking into a genuine, sustained toothy smile. "And I must admit you have a point." She nodded over at the others. "It was really a most enjoyable half-hour."

"Better than a crossword puzzle," said Mrs. Wohlsteader, not to be outdone.

"But aren't crossword puzzles considered to be a waste of time?" said Mrs. Cimino, trying to put it as tactfully as she could.

"Not by me," said Miss Rochester firmly. She went back to the blackboard, wrote a large A, and used it to initiate the phrase "Active concentration."

"She's right," said Miss Schmidt. "It's very difficult to worry or brood and concentrate on a puzzle at the same time."

"I'd always felt it was better to read good literature," said Mrs. Wohlsteader, allowing her most cultivated tones to wash over them.

"Reading is fine," said Miss Rochester. "But the mind tends to wander off as you turn the pages." Back to the board she went, this time writing a large L as part of the phrase "Limited span."

"Does that include cards?" said Miss Schmidt. "Many older people seem to enjoy playing bridge." She looked over at Mrs. Cimino to underscore the implicit invitation. "And you certainly have to concentrate there."

"Excellent!" said Miss Rochester. "Although it's better to have something you can do by yourself." Hurriedly she erased what she had written and chalked up her design in more symmetrical form. "*Ineffective* anger and *N*agging worries make us *I*nert, but *A*ctive concentration over a *L*imited span of time keeps us *A*lert."

"Very neatly done," said Miss Schmidt. "It's a pity you didn't go into mathematics."

"It sounds to me as though you're talking about exercises," said Mrs. Cimino.

"Of course," said Miss Rochester with great enthusiasm. "Good, wholesome exercises that put the mind to work and distract it from spinning off into confusion." She beamed down at them. "Let's think of some others."

"Solitaire," said Miss Schmidt.

"Not bad," said Miss Rochester. "Not bad at all."

"How about knitting or jigsaw puzzles?" said Mrs. Wohlsteader.

"Fair," said Miss Rochester. "Though there's not much verbal thinking involved in them."

"Here's one for you," said Miss Schmidt. "One of the girls at our school was very strong on memorizing poems."

"Perfect!" crowed Miss Rochester. "Edna St. Vincent Millay used to work at Wordsworth for days at a time."

"Wordsworth!" said Mrs. Wohlsteader, eyes agleam. "I wandered lonely as a cloud . . ."

"But it's not useful," said Miss Schmidt, breaking in with her original irritation unassuaged.

"That's just the point," said Miss Rochester. "Anything that is useful always involves thinking about the future, worrying about whether people will approve of what you're doing. And as we grow older there's less and less of that approval to go round."

"The inward bliss of solitude," murmured Mrs. Wohlsteader, a faraway look in her eyes.

"Solitaire," said Miss Schmidt. Her correction was gentle but firm.

"Solitude," said Mrs. Wohlsteader, still savoring the thought.

"It isn't always inward bliss," said Miss Rochester. "But active concentration over a limited span of time keeps us alert." She went over to the door, opened it, and gestured an indication that the class was over. "As long as we stay alert we can find good ways of remaining useful."

160

"*Hasta mañana, Señorita Rochester,*" said Miss Schmidt, working her way up with the help of her rubber-tipped cane.

"*Muchas gracias,*" said Mrs. Wohlsteader.

"*Hasta luego,*" said Mrs. Cimino, pleased that she could locate an appropriate harmony part.

The three elderly ladies trooped out into the corridor. Mrs. Wohlsteader went upstairs. Miss Schmidt hobbled down to her first-floor room. Mrs. Cimino decided to take a short walk.

Like a general revisiting an old battleground, Mrs. Cimino found herself headed toward the main entrance, walking briskly past the four-bed ward and pausing briefly to look at the public telephone. The door to Mrs. Polanski's office was open. She put on her most engaging smile and peered in.

"Hello there, Mrs. Cimino," said Mrs. Polanski. She was smoking the last cigarette in her morning pack. "How's the new class, how's . . . the . . . new . . . class?

"Very pleasant," said Mrs. Cimino. "Very pleasant indeed."

"Good!" Mrs. Polanski's fair face nodded as though to celebrate a sequence of decisions leading to the small classroom in back of the nurses station.

"I've been noticing that piano over in the corner of the dining room," said Mrs. Cimino. "Is that just for the church services?"

"It's there to be used," said Mrs. Polanski. "Do you play?"

"I used to," said Mrs. Cimino. "But I haven't touched it in years."

"We'd just love to hear you," said Mrs. Polanski.

"I'm afraid I'm dreadfully out of practice." Mrs. Cimino gave a little laugh. "But I might just sneak in sometime and try it out."

"Why not now?" said Mrs. Polanski, rising from her chair with great boisterousness. "If you don't mind a little kitchen noise."

Mrs. Cimino allowed herself to be propelled back down the corridor to the dining room. There Mrs. Polanski ceremoniously opened up a battered Wurlitzer upright, standing expectantly by while Mrs. Cimino sat down at the instrument.

"Go right ahead," said Mrs. Polanski. "See what you can get out of our old cracker box."

Mrs. Cimino remained where she was, flexing her fingers a little.

"Does my being here bother you?" said Mrs. Polanski, her voice softer, less exuberant.

161

"A little," said Mrs. Cimino.

"Then I'll just run along back to my office," said Mrs. Polanski. "I'll leave you here to play for your own amazement." With a great whoop she flew out of the room reiterating the phrase. "For . . . your . . . own . . . amazement."

Mrs. Cimino took a breath and struck a C-major chord. It was a soft sound, barely audible under the clatter of dishes and serving carts. She struck a few more chords. She played a C scale, an F scale, a B-flat scale. By the time she had worked out her F-sharp scale, the girls were beginning to bring out the vases and plastic flowers for the luncheon setting.

Monday, July 12, 3:15 P.M.

Since Karen was working full shifts at Jack In The Box, Alice had volunteered to bring some new hearing aid batteries out to Mrs. Cimino. It was her first visit to St. Hild's.

Her visit to White Towers had been painful: Her words of greeting, her flowers, her attempts at conversation had all gone unrecognized by the small gray bundle sitting in the big chair looking out over the city. She had sighed and left, telling herself that the situation was hopeless.

But Karen's reports had been glowing, enthusiastic. Much of this could be discounted as stemming from the active role that Karen had played in locating the place and in making trips there. And yet Esther's letters had been clear and coherent. So it was beginning to look as though changes were taking place.

Her natural concern had recently been colored by indignation at the estate sale. The silver, the china, the antiques: These should rightly go to Ann, Gretchen, and Karen. And there was the lovely Chickering piano to think of. She boiled at the thought of Lisa's new house filled with stolen family treasures. Karen had shrugged the disgrace away, but the facts were clear: A dear, loving person had been cruelly incarcerated and robbed.

Alice pulled up by the prison and inspected it for a moment. Not even the construction of a new wing could conceal the fact

162

that the building was old, run-down. There were no bars to be seen on the windows, but the isolation of the place might well account for that. At night they probably let the dogs out, great black, snarling beasts that could hold a frail elderly person at bay until white-coated keepers came bustling out with nets and straitjackets.

Taking a deep breath she put her fears aside, got out of her car, and walked up to the main entrance. Down toward the end of the corridor she could see a couple of young women in nurses uniforms: They were much smaller than the beefy Amazons at White Towers. Relieved, Alice went inside and looked for someone to announce her. A door was open on her left. She looked in. A thin-faced woman with dark horn-rimmed glasses was sitting at a desk going over some papers.

"I'm Mrs. Nash," said the thin-faced person. "Can I help you?"

"I've brought some hearing aid batteries for Mrs. Esther Cimino," said Alice, opening up her purse and taking out a small brown package. "Would I be able to visit with her for a while?"

"I think she'd like that very much," said Mrs. Nash. She looked down at her watch and frowned. "Our problem is finding her for you."

Alice smiled as though to indicate that losing a patient here and there was a matter of no great moment. Even when Mrs. Nash picked up a telephone, her spirits remained uneasy.

"Nancy?" said Mrs. Nash. "Could you find Mrs. Cimino and ask her to go up to the new lounge? She has a visitor."

"Mrs. Alice Cimino," said Alice, feeling a little awkward. "My daughter comes out here quite a bit."

Mrs. Nash put down the phone, rose, came out from behind her desk, and extended her hand. "So you're Karen's mother!"

"Yes, I am," said Alice, allowing her hand to be pumped warmly. She seemed to have been identified in terms of an oddly distinguishing mark—like a mole on the left shoulder. Her uneasiness remained with her.

"She's probably out for a walk with Mrs. Yeager," said Mrs. Nash. "But Nancy will find her. I'll show you where the new lounge is."

"Thanks very much," said Alice.

"But first I'd like you to meet Mrs. Polanski, our director."

Mrs. Nash ushered Alice across the corridor to another small office where a middle-sized blonde woman was shouting into the telephone, punctuating her shouts with puffs on a cigarette.

"The specifications clearly call for regular metal pipe, Mr. Sims." The blonde woman took a deep puff and let the smoke out forcefully. "Regular . . . metal . . . pipe."

The blonde woman smiled at them and looked up at the ceiling in dramatic mock dismay while the luckless Mr. Sims attempted to justify himself.

"And that means the sprinkling system too!" said the blonde woman. "The . . . sprinkling . . . system . . . too!"

There was another long pause, during which Alice tried to puzzle out the nature of the strange verbal tic she was listening to.

"You just come over Wednesday and I'll show you," said the blonde woman. "Wednesday . . . Wednesday . . . Wednesday."

After wearing down poor Mr. Sims, the blonde woman hung up the phone, smiled at Alice warmly, and gestured broadly out toward the sparse lawn outside. Alice, following the gesture with puzzlement, took the opportunity to reassure herself that Mrs. Nash was still beside her.

"It's the gophers," said the blonde woman. She snubbed out her cigarette with firm determination.

"They're terrible," said Mrs. Nash. "Just terrible!"

Alice's uneasiness was now replaced by a feeling of near panic: There was a good chance she might have wandered into some bizarre role-playing therapy session.

"They eat plastic pipe just like it was peanut butter candy," said the blonde woman sadly.

"It's common knowledge," said Mrs. Nash, giving Alice an obscure explanatory smile.

"The plumbers know it," said the blonde woman. "And we know it." She lit another cigarette and blew a triumphant ring. "And now they know that we know." She nodded firmly and smiled at Alice.

"Mrs. Polanski," said Mrs. Nash. "I'd like you to meet Mrs. Alice Cimino.

Mrs. Polanski got up from her desk and smiled warmly.

"Karen's mother," added Mrs. Nash.

"Karen's mother!" Mrs. Polanski's bright blue eyes began to sparkle like two little dancing moons. "This is a real pleasure, isn't it, Mrs. Nash?"

"It certainly is," said Mrs. Nash, taking quiet pride in the gift she had just presented.

"We just think the world of Karen," said Mrs. Polanski.

"A fine young woman," said Mrs. Nash, looking at Alice with admiration.

Alice nodded, still trying to get her bearings. Karen a fine young woman? The notion was unsettling, almost as much as the business about the gophers. Not that she was unused to hearing her daughters praised: The accomplishments of Ann and Gretchen had many times been brought to her attention by teachers, relatives, and parents of smitten young men.

But Karen? Her dear little overweight mouse? It was as though an old kitchen chair, long buried in the cellar, had been whimsically appraised by an eccentric collector as a valuable antique. Perhaps the eccentricity of a place like this was infectious, warping the perceptions of those who spent their days working with older inmates. She decided not to debate the matter.

"She's certainly been good about making that long drive out here," said Alice. "I know it's meant a lot to her grandmother."

"A lifeline, that's what she's been," said Mrs. Polanski. "A . . . strong . . . lifeline."

"It's really made a difference," said Mrs. Nash. "And I think you'll be pleased by the progress we've made."

"You haven't seen her yet?" said Mrs. Polanski. She gestured dramatically down the corridor. "Don't let me keep you." She took Alice's hand and pressed it warmly. "Please stop by on your way out. I'd like to talk with you about how things have been going."

"I'd like that very much," said Alice, feeling it was wise to humor the people in this curious place as much as possible.

Mrs. Nash led Alice down the corridor to the new elevator, which was described in glowing terms appropriate for components of an ambitious aerospace program. The elevator took them to the second floor. There Mrs. Nash pointed Alice toward the small lounge at the end of the south corridor.

Alice walked down to the lounge, went in, and sat down in a light green Leatherette chair. The only other person there was a small gray-haired woman absorbed in a copy of *Time,* shaking her head occasionally at the contents. The woman stopped reading for a moment to clean her eyeglasses, wiping them carefully with a pink hankie from her upper left-hand pocket. It was only when she put the glasses back on that Alice recognized her former mother-in-law.

"Why, it's Alice!" said Mrs. Cimino, getting quickly up and coming over. "What a dear you are to stop by!"

"It's good to see you, Esther," said Alice, rising to meet her.

The two women embraced, holding the embrace for a long, wordless time so that the cumulative pain of the past two years could find recognition and then ebb back. When they were able to face each other, Mrs. Cimino led her guest over to a sofa by the window where they could catch what was left of the late afternoon breeze.

"My, my," said Mrs. Cimino. She took out her pink hankie and wiped her eyes. "Dear, dear Alice."

"You're looking well," said Alice. "Very well."

"Do you think so?" Mrs. Cimino looked down at her stocking-clad legs and sighed. "We do a lot of walking but I haven't lost any weight to speak of."

"It's good you can get out," said Alice. She looked out the window at the rolling green country with approval. "I always felt White Towers was a little confining for you."

"White Towers." Mrs. Cimino nodded reflectively. "I had a room to myself there, but it was sort of boring, as I recall."

"This is much nicer," said Alice. "How's the food?"

"Starchy," said Mrs. Cimino. "But the people are friendly."

"I can't get over how well you look," said Alice, still thinking back to the small gray bundle she had visited before. It was as though a compact elderly butterfly had managed to work its way free from its cocoon.

"They say I'm making excellent progress," said Mrs. Cimino. She reached over and patted Alice's hand affectionately. "But tell me about the girls." She smiled in bright anticipation. "What's Ann been up to?"

"She still working on her M.A. in anthropology," said Alice. "This summer she went to Hawaii to do research."

"Research!" Mrs. Cimino clapped her hands in pure delight. "Isn't it wonderful what girls can do now?"

"She's very excited about it," said Alice proudly.

"And what about Gretchen?" said Mrs. Cimino. "Still pretty as ever?"

166

"She's engaged," smiled Alice.

"Engaged!" Mrs. Cimino shook her head in disbelief. "Little Gretchen engaged."

"And a wonderful boy," said Alice, eyes glowing. "He's the captain of the tennis team."

"There's a wedding I'm not going to miss," said Mrs. Cimino, looking out the window as though expecting a pair of handsome, athletic great-grandchildren to come bounding over the fields.

"They haven't set a date yet," said Alice awkwardly.

"Be sure to let me know in plenty of time," said Mrs. Cimino, growing suddenly serious. "I want to help out as much as I can."

"That's very kind of you," said Alice.

"Kind?" Mrs. Cimino looked puzzled. "With my own grand-daughter? I'd be hurt if you didn't let me."

Overcome, Alice reached into her purse for a Kleenex. It was as though Esther had judged the divorce and found her as blameless as she knew herself to be.

"It's so much nicer when you can use family things at the reception," said Mrs. Cimino. "And between the two of us we should have more than enough silver and china."

Alice nodded, still overcome, as much by shock now as by sentiment. It was clear Esther had not been told about the estate sale. To her original maternal indignation was now joined a just rage both fierce and capacious. Her ex-husband, his postadolescent wife, and the ice-cold Mr. Leach from the bank: They had conspired and continued to conspire in keeping the truth from a dear, saintly person.

But she was loath to be the bearer of evil tidings. Perhaps Esther had been told but had chosen to cloak the bitter news with reassuring fantasy. Perhaps the staff at St. Hild's had judged it wise to keep the truth from her until she improved more. It was certainly something to take up with Mrs. Polanski.

"They're lovely things, Esther," said Alice, deciding to temporize.

"I've spelled it all out in my will," said Mrs. Cimino happily. "Ann and Gretchen are to get most of the silver, while Karen gets the Haviland china. Does that sound fair to you?"

"Very fair," said Alice. "You certainly wouldn't want to break up a set like that."

It was monstrous! A will with nothing left to distribute, heirs with nothing left to inherit, a homeowner with no home to go back to! And here was Esther prattling away, looking fit and well, more so than at any time in the last three years. Alice looked down at her watch. She would have to cut her visit short before Mrs. Polanski left the office.

"Your Mrs. Polanski asked me to stop by on my way out," said Alice. "I really should go if I want to catch her."

"She's our big boss," said Mrs. Cimino archly.

"She seems very nice," said Alice, getting up for one last embrace.

"She is." Mrs. Cimino's tone was flat, judicial. "But she smokes."

The two women said goodbye with deep affection. Mrs. Cimino returned to her *Time*. Alice walked out of the room and then accelerated her pace, trying to recapture as much of her customary classroom authority as possible. By the time she reached Mrs. Polanski's office, her sharp nose and chilly blue eyes signaled a steel intensity of purpose.

"Mrs. Polanski!" Alice tried very hard to smile and remain tactful. "May I come in?"

"Please do." Mrs. Polanski gestured to a chair beside her small, distressingly untidy desk. "How does she seem to you?"

"She seems fine," said Alice. She sat down and caught her breath for a moment. "Much better than before the eye operation."

"We don't win them all," said Mrs. Polanski. "But she's got plenty of spirit, and she's very much in touch with things, very . . . much . . . in . . . touch."

"In touch with *everything*?" said Alice.

"I would say so," said Mrs. Polanski, not without pride. "She's one of our most alert residents now."

"If you think she's so alert, why have you chosen to keep things from her?"

"What things?" Mrs. Polanski's fair face grew solemn. She stared thoughtfully at the chilly blue eyes boring in at her.

"*Her* things!" Alice bit out the words like pieces of raw carrot from an underdone classroom stew. "Her house, her silver, her china, her family pictures!"

"Has something happened? Has there been a fire?" Mrs. Polanski pushed back her chair, ready to go into action and man the pumps.

168

"There's been a sale," said Alice, speaking coldly and distinctly. "There's been an estate sale." She looked suspiciously at Mrs. Polanski. "Don't tell me you didn't know about it."

Mrs. Polanski shook her head. She got up and went over to a filing cabinet. She came back with a folder. She sat down again. She lit a cigarette.

"Everything she owns," said Alice, still biting the words out to force the enormity of the offense into the consciousness of this fuzzy-minded person.

"When?" said Mrs. Polanski.

"Just a couple of weeks ago."

"Karen's been coming out in the evenings and on weekends," said Mrs. Polanski. "I haven't seen her in almost a month." She opened up the folder and looked through it. "There's a letter here from Mr. Leach, the trustee, dated June thirtieth, questioning the hair-styling charges we put on." She closed the folder. "That's all we have."

"So you had no way of knowing?"

"That part of it is up to Mr. Leach," said Mrs. Polanski. "It would have been better if he had talked it over with us." She shrugged, not without a touch of helplessness. "But he's the one running the show as far as her assets are concerned."

"That's criminal!" said Alice, still unreconciled.

"It may be immoral," said Mrs. Polanski. "But it's not criminal." She smiled at Alice as though to gentle the harshness of the matter. "We're lucky he doesn't decide to take her out of here and put her someplace else."

"Can he do that?" said Alice, aghast at the stout cords woven around her mother-in-law.

"Under the court order, Minneapolis Southern Bank has the power to act in her best interests," said Mrs. Polanski.

"Best interests!" Alice was incredulous. "She could be living in her own home right now."

"She could," said Mrs. Polanski. "Particularly if she had a companion there with her."

"So how is selling her home in her best interests?"

"That's not for us to decide," said Mrs. Polanski. "Mr. Leach makes those decisions now, subject to the approval of the court later on. And the court generally approves everything the trustee does."

"This is dreadful," said Alice. Her voice was small, bewildered, almost fearful.

"It's going to make it harder for us," said Mrs. Polanski thoughtfully. "I don't know how she'll take it when we tell her."

"So you *are* going to tell her."

"We have to," said Mrs. Polanski. "If she found out by chance, it might set her back a great deal."

"But what is she going to do?" Alice was almost in tears. "Will she have to stay here the rest of her life?"

"Sometimes that's the way it works out," said Mrs. Polanski. She got up from her desk and put Mrs. Cimino's folder back in the filing cabinet, softly sliding the drawer shut. "And sometimes they slip back into confusion again."

"As bad as when they came here?"

Mrs. Polanski nodded. Still standing by the file cabinet, she lit another cigarette.

"That must be pretty discouraging for you," said Alice, finally breaking into the silence that had crept upon them.

"It is," said Mrs. Polanski. She took a deep puff and watched the smoke drift aimlessly up toward the top of the window. "But I get to go home at night."

Tuesday, July 13, 4:00 P.M.

It was not a scorcher. But the air was muggy, almost saturated with moisture aching for the ground yet unable to get there. There were small beads of perspiration on Mrs. Cimino's upper lip: They clung to its soft white down until brushed away, and then crept back like truant children. So she came down to her appointment with a fresh, clean blue hankie.

That morning she had pulled out a few whiskers: long, gray bothersome shapes that seemed to slink out of her chin every now and then. And she had meticulously shaved under her arms the day before. But she still felt sweaty, gross, uneasy.

As she walked down the corridor to Mrs. Polanski's office, her uneasiness mounted. It was like being summoned to the principal's office, there to be questioned and scolded. Perhaps it had been a mistake in judgment to collaborate with Mrs. Yeager in caching the beef jerky outside. But Mrs. Yeager was a dear, kind soul: Her vegetarian views were harmless enough, and a daily walk out to the far grove of sycamore trees seemed to do her good.

Mrs. Cimino stopped just before the four-bed ward. She took out her blue hankie and chased a few more beads of sweat away. She polished her eyeglasses. She adjusted her hearing aid. She smoothed a couple of wrinkles out of her pink-striped cotton dress. She put on her most engaging smile and strolled pleasantly into Mrs. Polanski's office, much as though she were stopping by the store to pass the time of day with Simon Montford.

"Here I am," smiled Mrs. Cimino, taking a friendly yet forceful initiative.

"You're looking very well," said Mrs. Polanski. She got up from her desk and motioned Mrs. Cimino to a chair. "Do you mind if I close the door?"

"It's hot," said Mrs. Cimino. She smiled at the doorway as though it represented the one avenue along which a cool, drying breeze might proceed toward the two of them.

"Dreadful!" said Mrs. Polanski. "Just dreadful!" She closed the door and turned on a small electric fan. "Is that better?"

"Much better," said Mrs. Cimino. She turned her face toward the fan's domain and let the rush of air scratch at her for a while.

"We could do with some air conditioning," said Mrs. Polanski. She frowned at the fan.

"We have it at the store," said Mrs. Cimino. "But I always felt it was too expensive for a big house."

Mrs. Polanski transferred her frown from the fan to a folder in front of her. She was obviously in no mood to discuss the air-conditioning matter further. Mrs. Cimino took out her blue hankie and polished her eyeglasses again.

"I wanted to talk about your progress here," said Mrs. Polanski.

Mrs. Cimino felt immediate relief: Mrs. Yeager's small deception was apparently still safe. Perhaps, principal-like, Mrs. Polanski was concerned about the Spanish. With Mrs. Wohlsteader's background in French and Miss Schmidt's forceful intellect, she knew herself to be at the bottom of the class.

"I'm enjoying those classes very much," said Mrs. Cimino. "Your Miss Rochester is a lovely young girl."

"She says you're doing very well," said Mrs. Polanski. For the first time a broad smile lit up her fair face. "We all feel you're doing well."

"My daughter-in-law seemed to think so," said Mrs. Cimino. She paused to chart the relationship more precisely. "Perhaps I should call her my ex-daughter-in-law." She smiled a polite confusion. "But she's a dear person."

"I met her yesterday," smiled Mrs. Polanski.

"Very dear, very sweet," said Mrs. Cimino, resolved to give the room a genial ambiance.

"We had a nice talk," said Mrs. Polanski. "And it reminded me that your position here is a little difficult."

Mrs. Cimino's smile disappeared. She had tried to put the money worries out of her mind and take each day as it came. With George and Harold to handle things for her, she had concentrated on getting better. But bills had a way of mounting up, and finances had a way of going wrong. She tightened her small hands and waited for the bad news.

"So I gave Mr. Leach a call this morning," continued Mrs. Polanski. "I wanted to make sure I had everything straight."

"Is he one of your people at the downtown hospital?" said Mrs. Cimino. "Someone in the accounting office?" She smiled pleasantly, resolved to make Mrs. Polanski's task as easy as possible.

"Not exactly," said Mrs. Polanski. She sighed and looked down at the folder again. She picked up a pencil. She drummed on the desk with the pencil.

"If there's a problem about the money, I'm sure it's just a temporary mix-up," said Mrs. Cimino gently. "Why don't you give George a call? Or Harold?" She gave a little laugh. "He's the businessman of the family."

"Let's take stock a minute," said Mrs. Polanski. Her tone was suddenly brisk. "How much do you remember about the hospitals you've been in over the last six months?"

"Let me see," said Mrs. Cimino. She gave another little laugh, more embarrassed than the first. "First there was the cataract operation in Minneapolis Presbyterian. Dr. Sandoval did that. Then I went home."

"Where'd you go next?"

"I stayed home for a while." Mrs. Cimino's nose wrinkled

with distaste. "There were bandages, and I had trouble walking."
Her lips pursed thoughtfully. "I had a fall—not too bad, but Dr.
Peterson put me back in Presbyterian again."

"And then?"

"I went home again," said Mrs. Cimino, a distant look in her
eyes. "And George got some girls to come in and help." She shook
her head firmly. "That didn't work out." She gave another embarrassed little laugh. "I guess I was pretty hard to get along with."
She looked appealingly at Mrs. Polanski for reassurance.

"You'd had some bad blows," said Mrs. Polanski. "When
you're up in years, they're not easy to take."

"Anyhow," said Mrs. Cimino. "They put me in Minneapolis
Central and then in White Towers and then in here at St. Hild's."
She shook her head in mournful contemplation of the expense.
"I've sure been in a lot of hospitals."

"Do you remember the hearing at Minneapolis Central," said
Mrs. Polanski. "With Judge Schultz?"

"A judge?" Mrs. Cimino smiled good-humoredly, eyes sparkling a little. "Down at the county courthouse?" She giggled in
delighted memory. "The last time I was there was four years ago
when Michael Ryan and I took one of the tenants to court."

"Sometimes the judge comes right to the hospital," said Mrs.
Polanski. "Particularly for a competence hearing."

"Competence hearing!" Mrs. Cimino was suddenly less genial,
less sparkling. "That's for crazy people, isn't it?"

"Crazy, incompetent, not responsible—those are just words,"
said Mrs. Polanski. "All they mean is that someone needs help in
handling business matters."

"That's what bankruptcy proceedings are for," said Mrs. Cimino. "For people who can't handle their business properly."

"That's a cop-out, Mrs. Cimino." Mrs. Polanski's fair face
neared her, eyes boring right into her own. "You can't tell me you
don't remember anything about the hearing they held for you."

Mrs. Cimino sighed. Try as she might, she could not summon
up anything more than a vague picture of going down in an elevator to a room with a flag. It was like fumbling through a dark
closet for a loose shoe that had drifted out of place. She began to
feel a little panicky.

"Don't you remember anything?" said Mrs. Polanski, pressing
her.

"There was a man who asked me a lot of foolish questions,"

said Mrs. Cimino. "I thought he was a psychologist or something like that."

"He was a judge," said Mrs. Polanski. "Judge Schultz. And he appointed Minneapolis Southern Bank as your trustee, or conservator, as some states call it." She gestured toward the folder. "Mr. Edward Leach is the trust officer in charge of handling things for you."

"But I thought George was handling everything for me," said Mrs. Cimino. "And I'd made up my mind not to bother him until I got out of here."

"He couldn't do it, not without a court order," said Mrs. Polanski. "And the court decided you needed a trustee."

"Well, I don't need one now," said Mrs. Cimino. "And I don't want one." Her mouth was firmly set, ready to scold someone.

"The decision has already been made," said Mrs. Polanski. She shook her head and sighed. "It's something you're going to have to live with." She paused, healingly, stretching it out.

"I suppose it could be worse," said Mrs. Cimino bravely, finally breaking the silence. "Those banks are good about handling investments, and I've always tended to worry about money." She began to glow in anticipation. "With the house paid for, I really don't need much to live on, once I get out of here and go home."

Mrs. Polanski sighed and began to drum with her pencil again.

"It's not that I haven't liked it here at St. Hild's," continued Mrs. Cimino. "You've all been very sweet, but I still sort of like to come and go as I please." She looked anxiously at Mrs. Polanski, fearing she had transgressed the bounds of tactfulness. "You understand how it is, don't you?"

"I understand," said Mrs. Polanski. "But I'm not sure Mr. Leach understands. And he's the one who makes the decisions now."

"What decisions?" said Mrs. Cimino. There was something in Mrs. Polanski's voice that made her uneasy, fearful.

"The decision to sell your house." Mrs. Polanski said it flatly, then hurried on to safer, more neutral language. "Mr. Leach feels your property should be converted into income-producing assets."

"Sell my house!" Mrs. Cimino rubbed the back of her neck, acutely conscious of the summer heat weighing heavily upon her. "Don't I have something to say about that?"

174

Mrs. Polanski shook her head. It was an awkward, wordless moment.

"House." Mrs. Cimino closed her eyes tightly, trying to force its features to stay in her mind. "What about the furniture?" Opening her eyes, she stared accusingly at the fan. "The china, the silver, the jewelry—did they just cart it off to some kind of storage place?"

"Not exactly," said Mrs. Polanski slowly, choosing her phrasing with care. "Mr. Leach consulted with your family about what should be sold and what should be kept."

"But they didn't consult with me." Trying to control herself, Mrs. Cimino bit her lower lip to keep it from quivering. "It's almost as though they were settling my estate." Struck by the logic of the matter, she raised her voice. "What about my will? That china and silver was supposed to go to the girls."

"Your will doesn't apply in a situation like this."

"Then it's worse than being dead," wailed Mrs. Cimino, letting the tears well up. "I never expected anything like this to happen. . . . never!" She shook her small head rapidly and made fierce gurgling cries, like an old gray dog's resurgent frenzy at a strange intruder.

Mrs. Polanski bowed her head and remained quite still.

"It just doesn't make sense." Mrs. Cimino's voice was oddly high: a half-throttled yelp that barely took the imprint of consonantal mouthings in its rush toward speech. Following it, she got up from her chair and began to pace the floor.

"Things like this happen," said Mrs. Polanski. She watched Mrs. Cimino pace off the room like a sentry intent upon a ritualized preciseness.

"Terrible things," cried Mrs. Cimino in a loud voice. She came to a halt and challenged Mrs. Polanski with her faded blue eyes. "What they've done is almost as bad as what that young man did. . . ." She looked out the window in horror as a vaguely careening picture took clearer shape in her mind: much as though she were staring—voyeurlike—at a strange, crazed, toothless creature, strapped down and helpless under the hovering white assault of the ambulance attendant.

As though to escape from the sight, Mrs. Cimino sat down and buried her face in her hands: Great, slow, rasping sobs convulsed her small body like the ponderous tolling of a big church bell that shakes both loft and tower.

Quietly, almost shyly, Mrs. Polanski came over and took Mrs. Cimino in her sturdy arms, trying to cushion the impact of each sob.

"Those boys, those boys," gasped Mrs. Cimino. She shook her head slowly, pityingly. "My poor, dear, foolish boys." Taking a hankie from Mrs. Polanski, she dabbed at her eyes and sniffled. "They should have talked it over with me first."

"Maybe they didn't want to upset you," said Mrs. Polanski. She returned to her desk, fair face a bit drawn, and picked up her pencil.

Mrs. Cimino got up and began to pace the floor again, trying to put her spinning mind into some sort of consistent orbit. She felt as though the past and future were beginning to take on sharp, distracting colors: reds, greens, dark purples that made her dizzy with fear and anger. She came back to her chair. She tried to smile. And she searched for pacific words. After a long time, they came: slow, low-pitched, oddly distant from the tear-streaked face.

"I'm sure George and Harold did what they thought was right," she said sadly. "But it seems to me that everyone made up their minds about me in an awful hurry."

"It looks that way," said Mrs. Polanski. "But you've improved a great deal since the hearing."

"Are you saying that the judge would make a different decision if he talked to me now?" said Mrs. Cimino.

"He might," said Mrs. Polanski. "But that still wouldn't solve the problem of how and where you're going to live when you leave St. Hild's." She sat back: thoughtful, speculative.

"I think I'd better talk this over with George and Harold," said Mrs. Cimino. "Harold's always full of good ideas." She got up and looked thoughtfully at the fan, allowing it to ruffle her dress a little. "He was after me to move south a few years ago." She gave a little laugh and smiled at Mrs. Polanski. "Too bad you had to be the one to give me the bad news."

"I was a little worried as to how you'd take it," said Mrs. Polanski. A smile had come back to her fair face, and she had put her pencil down.

"I think I must have sensed something," said Mrs. Cimino. "Karen seemed a little upset the last time she was out." She shrugged, took out her blue hankie, and dabbed at her eyes for a moment. "Who knows?" Fearful of breaking into a flood of tears, she began to edge toward the door.

"Is there anything we can do?" said Mrs. Polanski, concern beginning to replace her relieved smile.

"No," said Mrs. Cimino. "This is something I'll have to work out with the boys. I'm sure that Mr. Leach will listen to what they have to say."

She said goodbye and walked out, turning toward the main entrance. She went outside to the sparse lawn and sat down on one of the old wicker chairs there. A slight breeze had come up to blunt the edge of the heavy, moist, suffocating warmth. She unbuttoned the top two buttons of her dress and let the moving air lave her neck. She could hear footsteps, light footsteps, coming up behind her.

"Has Mr. Anderson come yet?" It was Mrs. Anderson. Drawn by the breeze, she had wandered around from the back.

"I don't know," said Mrs. Cimino. "Is this his day to come?"

"He's supposed to come on Sundays and Thursdays now," said Mrs. Anderson.

"Then he won't be coming today," said Mrs. Cimino. "Today is Tuesday."

"Are you sure?" said Mrs. Anderson. She shaded her eyes and looked expectantly up the road.

"I'm sure," said Mrs. Cimino. "It's Tuesday, and it's almost dinnertime." She got up, stretched, and smiled at Mrs. Anderson. "Why don't we walk back together?"

"Tuesday," said Mrs. Anderson.

The two elderly ladies walked around the west side of the building to the new wing's rear entrance. The ground for their journey was uneven, and some of the big roots lay exposed above it. They progressed slowly—but surely, taking each step with thoughtful, deliberate care.

Part 4

An unpracticed observer expects the love of parents and children to be constant and equal; but this kindness seldom continues beyond the years of infancy: in a short time the children become rivals to their parents. Benefits are allayed by reproaches and gratitude debased by envy.

SAMUEL JOHNSON
The History of Rasselas, Prince of Abyssinia

Friday, July 23, 9:30 P.M.

"In the long run we'll all be dead," said Professor Palmer cheerfully. "And that's the first postulate of Keynesian economics." He looked agreeably around the Radisson Grill as though expecting the occupants of each table to rise and genuflect in his direction.

"I know," said the visiting agronomist. "But what else can you expect from an old queen who spent most of her time running after Lytton Strachey's young men at Cambridge?" He smiled at Mrs. Palmer.

Mrs. Palmer smiled back. Good arguments were her husband's stock in trade, fattened like bullocks in graduate seminars and then let loose in professional journals to stampede decorously through both conservative and liberal china shops. She sipped her Tia Maria and watched the two men beam at each other: her husband sleek, rubicund, just a shade on the heavy side; the visiting agronomist older, slightly desiccated from laying miles of irrigation pipe in alien cornfields.

They had brought the visiting agronomist to the Radisson at departmental expense: In university folklore good food and drink had long been celebrated as the soil from which Nobel Prizes grew, such as the one stemming from a social encounter between a physicist and an Egyptologist. Well-schooled, Mrs. Palmer had learned to let a smile of reverential attention participate in the discussion for her.

Behind the smile her mind was far away: Mark, their eldest son, had just dropped out of his pre-law program to take a job as a telephone company lineman. Stubborn, irresponsible —Mark was beginning to grieve her greatly.

"I always knew economics was a dismal science," said Professor Palmer. "But a moral science?" He chuckled roguishly.

"Adam Smith was a professor of moral philosphy, wasn't he?" said the visiting agronomist.

"Beautiful!" said Professor Palmer. He took out his leather cigar case and offered one in homage to the visiting agronomist.

181

Mrs. Palmer smiled approvingly as the visiting agronomist accepted the gift with a chaste reluctance quite fitting for a high-ranking consultant to the Department of Agriculture. There were lots of good cigars in the Radisson Grill that evening, vapors of success rising up from tables where well-dressed men and women deftly fenced with one another—a far cry from Mark's pitifully modest goals of fresh-air work and tackle football under the lights at night in a neighboring park. Even Dr. Brinning, an adjunct professor of psychiatry, had shaken his head sadly over Mark's failure to respond to treatment.

Mrs. Palmer continued to smile and nod appreciatively as the two men droned away at each other. Mark's defection retreated from her consciousness as her ears began to pick up a conversation from the table in back of them. There were two men at that table: She had seen them come in. A tall man with long sideburns and a shorter, stocky man—expensively dressed—with heavy eyebrows. But she was not sure which of the two belonged to the slow, deep voice.

"According to Dr. Gonzalez, she's in good physical shape," said the slow, deep voice. "All she takes is a little mild medication to control her blood pressure."

"For his zero-sum game to work," said Professor Palmer. "Von Neumann introduced one player who was supposed to do all the losing."

"The taxpayer?" said the visiting agronomist.

"Nature!" crowed Professor Palmer. "The invisible losing player is called Nature."

"Lovely!" said the visiting agronomist. He winked at Mrs. Palmer: Dutifully, she smiled back at him.

"I don't know," said a higher, crisper voice from the table in back of Mrs. Palmer. "Maybe we should run her down to the Mayo Clinic for a complete work-up."

"Leach wouldn't go for that," said the slow, deep voice.

Mrs. Palmer smiled at her husband with affectionate pleasure: She was now convinced that the slow, deep voice belonged to the tall man with sideburns. It was tentative, worried; while the higher crisp voice went well with the expensive clothes and air of authority worn by the shorter, stocky man with heavy eyebrows. She eased herself back in her seat so as to pick up the conversation more effectively.

"We shouldn't allow ourselves to be hurried into anything," said the crisp heavy eyebrows. "You said yourself she's doing well where she is."

"But she doesn't want to stay there," said the deep long sideburns.

"I know that," said the crisp heavy eyebrows. There was a touch of irritation in his voice. "But we have to consider what our options are."

"Do we have any choice?" said the deep long sideburns. Mrs. Palmer sketched herself a clear picture of the puzzlement on his face.

"Of course we have a choice," said the crisp heavy eyebrows. "It's a simple matter of looking at the situation logically and coming to a decision." There was forceful assurance in the voice now. "She wants to leave, and she can't go back to Elm Street, so she's asked us to work something out for her—that's the situation.

"Did she ask if she could come down there with you and Gloria?" said the deep long sideburns.

"She knows it's out of the question," said the crisp heavy eyebrows. "Her friends are up here, her trustee is here, she has good medical care here, the girls are here, you're here. Coming down to Des Moines just doesn't make good sense."

"She and Gloria have always gotten along," said the deep long sideburns. "And you've certainly got plenty of room."

"I don't think it would work out," said the crisp heavy eyebrows. "I sincerely feel she'd be happier with you and Lisa."

"But she hardly knows Lisa," said the deep long sideburns, still puzzled by the direction the conversation was taking. "I don't think they would get along."

"That's not my fault," said the crisp heavy eyebrows.

Mrs. Palmer nodded sympathetically to herself. There was obviously an aged relative involved here—an aunt, probably. And the two men were trying to decide where she should go. Decisions like that had serious consequences, sometimes quite unexpected. Her own grandmother had moved in with her aunt and uncle at the age of eighty-five: Lively, alert, matriarchal—she had stayed on for thirteen years.

"It's a question of social perceptions," said the visiting agronomist. "Most of them can't handle a unit larger than the family or tribe."

183

"Lerner ties all that in with women's emancipation," said Professor Palmer.

"Who's talking about fault?" said the deep long sideburns.

"I suppose it correlates," said the visiting agronomist. "But I don't see a causal link."

"We're talking about logical alternatives," said the crisp heavy eyebrows smoothly. "And Des Moines is not a logical alternative."

Mrs. Palmer nodded emphatically at the visiting agronomist, trying to shake his words out of her ears. She was much more interested in how the two men were going to dispose of their aunt.

"What if she visited back and forth?" said the deep long sideburns. "Maybe six months with you and six months with me?" His voice seemed to brighten a little at the notion.

"It wouldn't work," said the crisp heavy eyebrows. "Believe me, I've thought about it. And I've talked it over with the psychiatrist. It just wouldn't work out."

"What psychiatrist?" said the deep long sideburns. "Did they have a psychiatrist come in and look at her?"

"Gloria's psychiatrist," said the crisp heavy eyebrows patiently. "All that responsibility might be too much for her."

"But what about *your* responsibility?" said the deep long sideburns. "Mother and Dad worked hard at that store." The voice grew suddenly strong and righteous. "And so did I. They put you through school, and Mother was always running down there when Kevin and Patrick were little."

"I don't think you're being fair," said the crisp heavy eyebrows in an injured tone. "That was a long time ago, and we have to deal with the situation at this point in time."

"What's so fair about insisting that she move in with Lisa and me?"

"I'm not insisting," said the crisp heavy eyebrows. "I merely stated it as a logical alternative." His voice resumed its customary smoothness. "If we work together, I think we can come up with other alternatives."

"But what about inflation?" said Professor Palmer. He nodded to the red-coated waiter for another pair of brandies. "You can't increase production without greater capital investment."

"What alternatives?" said the deep long sideburns.

"Very simple," said the visiting agronomist. "You bring the labor force to where the capital investment already is—the way they've been bringing Spanish and Arab workers into France."

184

"So the third world all moves to Minneapolis?" said Professor Palmer, as always kittenishly combative.

"To Los Angeles, I would think," said the visiting agronomist.

"Brilliant!" said Professor Palmer.

"I would think a church-related retirement home would be our best bet," said the crisp heavy eyebrows. "Meanwhile she can stay on where she is."

"But she wants to get out," said the deep long sideburns. "Mother wants out now. That's what she told me the last time I was out there, and that's what she told you."

"She wants to have something to look forward to," said the crisp heavy eyebrows. "As long as she feels we're working on something, she'll be just fine."

"Do you think so?" said the deep long sideburns.

Mrs. Palmer found herself growing uneasy: Cast as sons rather than nephews, the two men seemed almost clinical in their detachment from the central agony of the matter—like accountants disputing the proper allocation of costs in a corporate statement. Not that such disputes ever grew heated: The skill lay in handling problems with a minimum of guilt and recrimination. The alternatives were always there, and the well-dressed people in the Radisson Grill searched until a mutually acceptable solution was reached. The emotions stayed under the table: If they surfaced it was only for rhetorical effect, like docile porpoises bounding up from the water at the signal of their mentor.

"I'll have my secretary write for brochures," said the crisp heavy eyebrows. "By next spring she may be ready to be put on a waiting list somewhere."

"She might slip back again," said the deep long sideburns. "Lisa says these psychological things are tricky."

"Very tricky," said the crisp heavy eyebrows. "That's why Gloria's psychiatrist feels she's better off where she is."

"What's he know about it?" said the deep long sideburns.

"He took his work at Harvard," said the crisp heavy eyebrows. "So he's much more into the basic research than that crazy Polish woman."

"She is pretty strange," said the deep long sideburns. "She . . . is . . . pretty . . . strange."

It was apparently a joke of some kind. The two men laughed, obviously in good humor with each other and with the temporizing solution they had located. They were both good-looking men:

185

Their voices were cool, intelligent. The elderly lady—whoever and wherever she was—had raised sons to be proud of: clever sons, successful sons, sons who met for dinner at the expensive Radisson Grill. In the best sense of the word, the two men had been educated—nourished in the clear light of reason. But in that light the frail bonds of affection had seemed to wither all too quickly, much like a small white thread wisping into smoke under the steady unwinking gaze of a magnifying glass on a brilliant July afternoon.

"We'd have plenty of computer time available," said Professor Palmer, casually broaching the subject he proposed to take up in detail next day.

"Lovely!" said the visiting agronomist. Now on his third brandy, he was beginning to smile slyly at Mrs. Palmer.

Mrs. Palmer smiled back. But she pulled her legs over, a little farther away from the visiting agronomist: As the wife of a full professor she was no longer required to endure such small social indignities. But she had endured them, and she knew that endurance—masked with good humor—was the common denominator linking computers, law degrees, and the Radisson Grill.

One endured. But one resented. And sometimes the resentment might fly off toward an innocent target of opportunity. She turned her thoughts back to Mark: He was manly, he was self-supporting, he was doing what he wanted to do—not what she and her husband wanted Dr. Brinning to get him to want to do. Why not let him go? Let him go. And love him for it—not in spite of it. Years later—in spirit, at least—those strong wings might beat their way back with good cheer.

Friday, August 27, 3:00 P.M.

"I think we might as well get started with our little program," said Miss Rochester. As she rang her small hand bell, the hum of conversation gradually stilled. Mrs. Cimino and Miss Schmidt walked slowly over to a table on the right side of the room and sat down.

The left side of the room had been cleared: On the far end was a cut-glass punch bowl set out on a white-covered table, flanked by trays of cookies and finger sandwiches. Mrs. Wohlsteader and her family were standing at the near corner: From this informal reception area Mrs. Wohlsteader had been flitting around the dining room, returning from time to time with various residents and staff members in tow.

It was not the first graduation party for Mrs. Wohlsteader: Every April her son would bring her in for what Mrs. Polanski called her refresher course, and every August he would reappear, taking her back with him to Eau Claire, Wisconsin. But it was a good excuse for everyone to dress up. Mrs. Cimino was glad she had worn white gloves along with her sky-blue suit.

"Is there anyone who doesn't have a song sheet?" said Miss Rochester. She had decked out her blue uniform with a small orchid in honor of Mrs. Wohlsteader's achievement.

The achievement, as always, was substantial: Mrs. Wohlsteader's arrival in late April was invariably accompanied by jars of tranquilizers and symptoms of disorientation. After a month, when both the pills and the dependency patterns of the past year had been put away, she became reasonably alert. After three months, she was again her usual vigorous, opinionated self, writing letters of cultural comment and protest to newspapers as far removed as Dubuque.

"We need a couple of those song sheets down here," said Mr. Bjornson, carefully raising his hand so as not to split the seams of his black jacket. He was sitting at a table midway back, together with Mr. Patterson and Mr. Ayledotte, a seventy-eight-year-old wheelie possessed of impressive poker-playing skills acquired in construction camps over numerous decades. Miss Martin hurried over with more song sheets, prudently making sure her back was not turned to Mr. Patterson.

"Any more needed?" said Miss Rochester, raising her voice to meet the competition offered by Mr. Stewart's table. Even though Mr. Stewart had done honor to the occasion by wearing a plaid tie, he still tended to whoop when excited. Mr. Monsour had supplemented his soft "baby, baby, baby" with a louder "yeah, yeah," much to the dismay of old Mrs. Kenniston and Mrs. Yeager nearby.

All the ladies were nicely turned out: Mrs. Kenniston's black dress was handsomely set off with a fine string of pearls, and Mrs. Yeager had dug into her part of the closet for a plum-colored dress.

Mrs. Anderson, at the same table, was proudly wearing a chrysanthemum corsage her son had brought over. At the other tables small pieces of jewelry, full-length hose, and newly done hair testified to hours of preparation and planning.

Mrs. Cimino looked down at her song sheet: The material printed there had been composed by some of the residents. In the great American tradition of the Kiwanis, the Lions, and Job's Daughters, inspirational lyrics had been fitted to well-known melodies. It was the first time she had seen these secular hymns, and she was greatly relieved that Mrs. Polanski had not asked her to play the piano.

"Ladies, ladies and gentlemen," said Miss Rochester, ringing her bell again to quiet a newly risen hum. "I think 'Keep in Touch' would be a good one to start out with."

Mrs. Cimino reached over and patted Miss Schmidt's hand: Miss Schmidt had written the words herself, using the tune "As the Caissons Go Rolling Along." With Miss Rochester to lead them, they all sang with gusto.

> Keep in touch, keep in touch—mental effort means so much,
> As the years keep a-rolling along.
> Work or play, in our way, we stay with it every day,
> As the years keep a-rolling along.
> So we say each one, that the best is yet to come.
> Count off our numbers loud and strong—
> > eighty-one, eighty-two,
> > eighty-three, eighty-four
> > There's lots do do—brother, sister this means you,
> As the years keep a-rolling along.

As usual there was great applause, beamingly acknowledged by Miss Schmidt: A shrill grandstand whistle came spiraling out of Mr. Kappelhoff's table, smilingly endorsed by Mr. Salves. Old Mr. Higgins, not yet finished with his newspaper, had gone so far as to roll it up into a small truncheon with which he belabored the table vigorously.

"Very good," said Miss Rochester. Mrs. Nash, brightening her white uniform with a red scarf, nodded approvingly. She was standing in the near corner with Mrs. Wohlsteader and her family.

It was a good-looking family. Mrs. Wohlsteader's son, a man in his middle years, had a large, pleasant face, his wife was dressed very smartly in pink and white. Beside them, standing awkwardly to the rear, was a well-scrubbed young man in a Coast Guard officer's uniform. Like Mrs. Wohlsteader, they were all on the tall side—taller even than George.

Mrs. Cimino thought with pleasure of her own family and of how their long-range plans had been set in motion. Sooner or later there would be a graduation party for her, and the boys would whisk her off to some sort of delightful surprise. Right now, as Harold had put it, they were exploring various options, bringing her elaborate brochures from the Methodists in California, the Presbyterians in Ohio, and the Episcopalians in Arizona. But she was sure that they would soon drop these in favor of a small apartment in either Minneapolis, or Des Moines. It was a shame Harold always insisted on making things complicated.

"Any requests?" said Miss Rochester.

"How about that one about the doctors?" boomed Mr. Bjornson, giving Mr. Ayledotte a friendly pat that would have propelled Mr. Ayledotte across the room had not his brakes been on. It was Mr. Ayledotte who had written the special lyrics to "When Irish Eyes Are Smiling." Nodding agreeably, Miss Rochester got them all together on pitch and started them off.

> *When doctors smile and tell you*
> *There is nothing to be done,*
> *And attempt to tranquilize you*
> *With a dose of Librium.*
>
> *Don't let them patronize you,*
> *Or pretend you're getting well.*
> *Tell your doctor when he's smiling,*
> *That he just can go straight to Hell!*

The last strain was sung with magnificent spirit, even by the most decorous ladies—old Mrs. Kenniston and Mrs. Wohlsteader included. And it was with pleasure that Mrs. Cimino noted Mr. Ayledotte's barbershop tenor high F at the end, nobly buttressed by Mr. Bjornson's deep, rich B-flat.

"Better than Lawrence Welk!" said Miss Rochester.

"How about Fred Waring?" said Mr. Patterson, who had taken his M.A. at the University of Pennsylvania.

"How about Frankie Yankovic?" shouted Mr. Stewart. Despite his dour Scotch background, he had immense enthusiasm for polkas, largely because he had seen wheelchair people executing square dances and polkas on the *Today* show.

Mr. Stewart was something of a problem: In his more lucid moments he was noisy, forward, and disagreeable. On various occasions he gave way to spells in which he fancied himself a major general in the FBI. As a major general he had worn a plumed hat to his large insurance office, insisting that his employees—as well as his nieces and nephews—snap to attention and salute him.

In spite of his bizarre behavior, Mr. Stewart was at St. Hild's for purely medical reasons: He continued to phone his lawyer once a week to make sure all was progressing satisfactorily with his business affairs. He had been—and continued to be—an excellent judge of the stock market. And he had prudently inserted a very sensible clause in his will: It called for the immediate disinheritance of his nieces and nephews in the event that any court found him mentally incompetent. The alternative heirs, a local clutch of hard-shell Baptists, had once attempted to hail Mr. Stewart into court, but the nieces and nephews had loyally rallied round to his vociferous defense, pointing out that the plumed hat seemed to have a magic effect in increasing the net worth of the defendant each year. Swayed by this incontrovertible evidence of sanity and good sense, the judge had rejected the petition.

Mrs. Cimino was a little nervous in the presence of Mr. Stewart. But he was a very knowledgeable conversationalist about legal matters, and he seemed to have a high regard for Michael Ryan, urging her to correspond with him regarding her legal situation. She had laughed the suggestion aside, as well as the notion that placement in a nursing home could be warded off through the same sort of testamentary coercion he had used.

"How about Mrs. Polanski?" said Miss Rochester, gesturing dramatically to the other side of the room. There Mrs. Polanski stood, dressed quite formally in a long skirt and flowered blouse. To great applause she strode forward, took a commanding position in front of the punch bowl, and addressed the group.

"Residents, staff, honored guests." Mrs. Polanski bowed

slightly in the general direction of the Wohlsteaders. "We are called a convalescent hospital, a . . . convalescent . . . hospital. And that is what people do here. They convalesce, get better, move upward as far as they can go."

Mrs. Cimino looked over at Mr. Salves: He was getting around in a walker now. Mr. Bjornson would be going back to New Oaks soon.

"Sometimes our residents can only travel a short way," continued Mrs. Polanski. "As we grow older, physical limitations close in on us and sometimes bring us down." She smiled around the room, touching lightly on Mr. Stewart, Mr. Ayledotte, and the other wheelies. "But we rarely allow negative attitudes to bring us down."

There was mild applause at this, to which Miss Schmidt contributed by banging the tip of her cane on the hard wood floor.

"What are these negative attitudes?" Mrs. Polanski glared rhetorically around the room, as though to smell the creatures out and call them to account. "Where do they come from?" She paused and lowered her voice conspiratorially. "What can we do about them?"

Mrs. Cimino smiled brightly at Miss Schmidt. There were certainly no negative attitudes at their table. If there were, Miss Schmidt could scold them away herself.

"Age-ism!" Mrs. Polanski struck a bold monitory pose like that of the Statue of Liberty. "There's too much age-ism in society, in the medical profession, and in ourselves."

"Is that like communism?" whispered Mrs. Cimino to Miss Schmidt.

"It's a branch of capitalism," said Miss Schmidt, who had always admired Emma Goldman.

"Our age-ist society says that older Americans are by definition frail and feeble-minded," said Mrs. Polanski. She looked challengingly around the room. "Is that true?"

"No!" came back a chorus of reaction, under which Mr. Bjornson's low-voiced growl could clearly be heard.

"Our age-ist doctors say that older Americans should be treated with tranquilizers but not with respect." Mrs. Polanski paused for a deep breath. "Is that true?"

"No! No!" came back another chorus.

"Sue them for malpractice!" shouted Mr. Stewart.

"Tranquilize *them*!" shrilled Mrs. Yeager, her white-thatched dark face suddenly contorted with rage. "Tranquilize those poisoners!"

"Quite so," said Mrs. Polanski quietly. She waited for the room to cool down. "But what about age-ist attitudes in ourselves?"

This time there was no general reaction. Most of the residents looked glumly down at the floor, as though they had been caught with the evidence of petty theft on their person.

"What about it?" continued Mrs. Polanski. "What about our desire to be taken care of? What about our desire to play games with our families? What about our desire to give up and crawl back into a safe little nest where nobody will ever ask us to do anything?" Again she paused, took a breath, and let her eyes make contact with everybody in the room. "Give up? Is that what you want to do?"

"No! No! No!" The chorus rang out as Mrs. Polanski led them with the broad gestures of a conductor directing the finale of Beethoven's *Ninth Symphony*. Caught up, Mrs. Cimino pounded on the table along with all the others.

"Good!" said Mrs. Polanski firmly. She turned her blue eyes over to the Wohlsteader family, where the young Coast Guard Wohlsteader was cowering somewhat. "And good for you, Marie Foster Wohlsteader!" She picked up a small scroll from beside the punch bowl. "Come on up here and receive your St. Hild's graduation certificate!"

All aflutter, Mrs. Wohlsteader walked slowly up, almost as though the strains of "Pomp and Circumstance" were pacing her steps. She did not exactly glitter as she walked, but she had several additional diamonds and a beautiful gold bracelet to harmonize with her basically regal bearing. Her hair, with a slight blue tint, had been done up early that morning, and her daughter-in-law had brought over a very elegant black dress. To sustained applause, she took her certificate from Mrs. Polanski's hand and walked back to her family.

"How about a closing song, Miss Rochester?" said Mrs. Polanski, stepping back for Miss Rochester to dominate the room.

"Do you all have your song sheets handy?" said Miss Rochester, waiting a minute for the group to get them out. "Let's finish up with 'From the Shores of California.' "

Mrs. Cimino looked down at her sheet. Their closing song had been written to the tune of "The Marines' Hymn," with lyrics by Mr. Stewart. Well loosened up by Mrs. Polanski's near incitement to riot, she joined in the singing with great force, almost as though she were voicing her rage at the forcible theft of her diamond ring.

From the shores of California
To the Massachusetts Bay,
We have paid our country's taxes
And worked hard in ev'ry way.

Though the politicians fool around
And the young folks scream and kick,
We are proud to say that it's not us
But the country that is sick.

"Very, very good!" said Miss Rochester. "And congratulations again, Mrs. Wohlsteader!"

After another round of applause, Mrs. Wohlsteader made her exit, marching out the front entrance to her son's car. There she waited for her daughter-in-law and grandson to get in the back seat. She waved goodbye, gave Mrs. Cimino, Mrs. Anderson, and Miss Schmidt affectionate hugs, and got into the front seat beside her son. The others went back inside, but Miss Schmidt and Mrs. Cimino stood there, under the roof of the old carriageway, waving goodbye until the Wohlsteader car disappeared down the road.

"It's certainly a blessing when your family looks after you," said Miss Schmidt, not without a touch of wistfulness.

"Yes, it is," said Mrs. Cimino.

"There she goes," said Miss Schmidt. She turned to go in. "I suppose you'll be driving away like that one of these days."

"Yes, I will," said Mrs. Cimino firmly. She had suddenly decided to explore a few options on her own. "I'll be leaving soon."

The two ladies started down the corridor to the elevator, Miss Schmidt taking her usual solid, cane-supported steps. Short, squat, she looked brightly up at Mrs. Cimino.

"I have only a couple of nieces now," said Miss Schmidt. "And they're very far away."

"I have two sons," said Mrs. Cimino. "And they're very, very busy." Her faded blue eyes were thoughtful.

Monday, August 30, 3:45 P.M.

As usual Mrs. Yeager and Mrs. Cimino took a circuitous route to reach the sycamore grove. After coming out of the rear entrance, they made their way up to the sparse front lawn. There they arranged themselves on an old white wicker settee as though to carry on a quiet afternoon chat. From this vantage point Mrs. Yeager was able to scrutinize the red brick building and ferret out an empty space among the comings and goings that centered on the main entrance.

At an appropriate time Mrs. Yeager nodded: The two elderly ladies rose and walked over by the new wing, pausing to admire it for a moment. Then they struck out on the nature-walk path, winding up a slight incline until they came to a break in the split-rail fence on the left. Here Mrs. Yeager stopped and looked back, making sure they were unobserved.

Her security precautions satisfied, Mrs. Yeager led the way through tall grasses that almost masked them completely until they reached the small group of trees. There Mrs. Cimino waited while Mrs. Yeager walked on alone: Safely packed into a small tobacco can, the beef jerky had been cached in a private hiding place. Mrs. Yeager was accustomed to break off a piece, return the can to its nest, and rejoin Mrs. Cimino. But today she came quickly back, the can in her hand.

"They found it!" Mrs. Yeager's dark face was lit up with excitement.

"Squirrels?" said Mrs. Cimino. From what she could see of the can, it looked as though the top had been pried off and the contents nibbled at.

"Hardly," said Mrs. Yeager. There was just a touch of suspicion in the dark eyes blinking rapidly at her companion.

"That's dreadful," said Mrs. Cimino.

"I think they must have known all along," said Mrs. Yeager thoughtfully. "But they waited until I made a slip."

"What kind of slip?" said Mrs. Cimino.

"I shouldn't have spoken up like that at the party," said Mrs. Yeager. "It was my fault for bringing it out into the open." She shook her white-thatched head. "Even a poisoner doesn't like to be called one."

194

"Are you sure?" said Mrs. Cimino. She peered at the can a little more closely. "Those claw marks look like a raccoon's to me."

"Of course they look like a raccoon's!" said Mrs. Yeager. Her grim crack of a smile appeared. "I never said they weren't clever."

"I guess a person has to be careful," said Mrs. Cimino. Though unconvinced regarding the pervasiveness of the vegetarian conspiracy, she was resolved not to debate the matter. "And yet our walks out here have been pleasant."

"We'll keep up the walks," said Mrs. Yeager. Her dark eyes blinked with rapid thoughtfulness, like little dots of fast-moving circuitry. "But I'll hide all of it in the closet now." She gave a short, harsh laugh. "It'll drive them crazy."

"Shall we go back?" said Mrs. Cimino. "I have a letter to read through before I mail it."

"Why not?" Mrs. Yeager hurled the can into a nearby bush and started over toward the access road. Only thirty yards away, it would bring them back to the main entrance again. "But watch out for that poison oak."

Mrs. Cimino carefully followed Mrs. Yeager, skirting the dangerous oily green leaves that threatened her ankles. An experienced campaigner, Mrs. Yeager knew her foe well: wild carrot, nightshade, Dutchman's-breeches, mugwort—she could name them all and itemize their maleficent properties.

She set a brisk pace, small though she was, but Mrs. Cimino followed along without difficulty. Even though there was still a touch of plumpness to her, her wind was better and her legs were firm. The two elderly ladies came up to the building, marching Indian file along the side of the road, and went in the main entrance. As they passed by Mrs. Polanski's office, Mrs. Yeager waved cheerily as a deceptive indication that nothing of moment had occurred.

When they reached their room, Mrs. Yeager went directly to her chair by the window, pulling it around so that she could get a reasonably good view of the pine trees. Mrs. Cimino picked up her letter, already folded, and placed it in a stamped, addressed envelope. Still not satisfied with it, she wanted to read it through once more before sealing it up and sending it off.

It was her third attempt at stating her position: The first two had been long, wordy, and the margins had wavered a bit. This one, though concise and friendly, still seemed a little incomplete, a little tentative. After carefully polishing her glasses, she read it through with a slow, critical eye.

Michael Ryan, Esquire
Attorney at Law
The Broadloom Building
759 State Street
Minneapolis, Minnesota

There seemed nothing wrong with the salutation: She had gotten the address out of the Yellow Pages from the phone book in Mrs. Nash's office. Even though it took up space on her large white sheet of paper, it signaled a firm, businesslike purpose. And the omission of the zip code ought not to cause a problem.

Dear Michael:
I hope this letter finds you and Martha in good health. As you can see from my address, I am writing you from St. Hild's Convalescent Hospital. I have had good care here and Mrs. Polanski, the director, tells me I am in excellent shape.

Not bad, she concluded. A personal touch, implicitly presenting a due bill for thirty years of friendly commerce. And a clear opportunity to check any statements made with a responsible, professional person. This part could certainly stand as written.

In March my health was not good. At that time Judge Schultz appointed Minneapolis Southern Bank as a "trustee" to manage my assets. A Mr. Edward Leach is the trust officer directly responsible for running the store and paying my bills.

Mrs. Cimino paused and bit her lower lip. There might be a little too much private anger in those quote marks around *trustee*. And the indignation of the expression "a Mr. Edward Leach" was surely obvious. On the other hand, Michael was a feisty sort: Like any veteran of the Great Depression he had a wholesome distrust of

196

banks and bankers—interest-gouging rascals battening like maggots on their helpless victims. She decided to take her chances with what she felt were the basic urges of her reader.

My understanding is that Judge Schultz's decision can be reversed. In view of my complete recovery, I feel it should be reversed. I would like you to represent me in this matter, so I will phone your office next week and arrange for an appointment at a mutually convenient time.

Please remember me to Martha and to Philip—if he is still in the office with you.

Sincerely,
Esther
(Mrs. Esther M. Cimino)

Mrs. Cimino sighed. She took off her glasses and rubbed her faded blue eyes for a moment. She looked over at Mrs. Yeager, as though seeking wise counsel: Mrs. Yeager was still peering intently at the pine trees. There was so much to say, and yet she had filled up two pages. The reference to Philip was far too vague: She should have kept better track of that boy, but it seemed logical for him to remain in practice with his father. The mechanics of the appointment were murky: Somehow she would have to find a time intersecting with both Michael's schedule and Karen's availability.

Could she do better? Should she call first, perhaps, and run the risk of an impertinent secretary's voice? Mrs. Cimino sighed again, put her glasses back on, and sealed up her small subversion of the order imposed on her from outside. As though in fear that her resolve might again weaken, she got up quickly and went downstairs with the letter.

She placed the letter in the mail basket, address side down so as not to excite comment. She stood there at the nurses station, almost ready to unveil her project to the admiring eyes of young Miss Martin. Miss Martin was absorbed in checking temperature charts. Anxious, fluttery, Mrs. Cimino decided to soothe her spirits with a little Active concentration over a Limited span of time. She walked over to the dining room entrance, peeked in, and wandered idly over to the battered Wurlitzer upright in the near right-hand corner.

She had never been a bravura parlor pianist, with a repertoire of Chopin and Liszt—Emily had always been the family *Wunderkind*. But she knew chords and how they moved, and she was able to pick out melodies and accompany them with a modest swing bass in the left hand. Softly, unobtrusively, she began to play.

"Isn't that 'Poor Butterfly'?" It was Mr. Ayledotte. In his usual gentlemanly way, he had waited until the closing chord before speaking.

Mrs. Cimino, never able to handle music and speech together, rounded things off with a final A-flat arpeggio. With pleasure she noted that Mr. Ayledotte was smiling happily in his wheelchair.

"I guess the tune is buried somewhere in there," said Mrs. Cimino. She gave one of her embarrassed little laughs.

"With those good old songs," said Mr. Ayledotte, "the tune just floats out at you."

"They don't write melodies like that anymore," said Mrs. Cimino.

"They sure don't," said Mr. Ayledotte. He looked at her expectantly. It was clear he wanted her to play another song.

There was the sound of wheels, followed by a slight skid. Mr. Stewart had just come up on her right.

"Music, music, music!" said Mr. Stewart, rocking excitedly back and forth in his wheelchair. "How about a polka?" He looked around the dining room, quietly serene and set for dinner. "Let's liven the place up."

"I'm not much good at polkas," said Mrs. Cimino shyly.

"You can do it," said Mr. Stewart. He began to clap his hands in tempo. "Polka, polka, polka!"

"Polkas are better with an accordion," said Mrs. Cimino, "It's hard to keep the rhythm going on the piano." She tried to smile engagingly at Mr. Stewart's sandy eyebrows.

"Come on!" said Mr. Stewart. "Give us something like 'Liechtensteiner Polka' or 'Helena Polka.'" Growing even more frenetic, he began to clap and sing. "Helen, Helen, Helen, you're the only girl for me, only girl for me, only girl for me."

"We don't need a polka," said Mr. Ayledotte. "Let her play what she wants."

There was silence for a moment as the lyrics of "Helena Polka" faded away. From Mrs. Cimino's right, Mr. Stewart looked over to her left as though noticing Mr. Ayledotte for the first time.

198

"Who asked you?" said Mr. Stewart, sandy eyebrows knit truculently over his watery gray-green eyes.

"Nobody asked me," said Mr. Ayledotte, his face reddening a little under his sparse white hair. "I just made a general comment."

Mrs. Cimino had never liked arguments. But she was clearly trapped there on the bench with Mr. Stewart on her right and Mr. Ayledotte on her left.

"Polkas are lots of fun," she said weakly. Her throat was suddenly quite dry.

"As far as I'm concerned," said Mr. Stewart, scowling over at Mr. Ayledotte, "you can keep your general comments to yourself."

"You don't have to listen if you don't like it," said Mr. Ayledotte, smiling fixedly.

"Is that so?" said Mr. Stewart.

"That's right." Mr. Ayledotte nodded as though to enforce the sweet reasonableness of the matter. "You can wheel yourself over to the other side of the room." He gestured expansively toward the array of tables that stretched out toward his left.

"I'll wheel myself wherever I damn well want," said Mr. Stewart. Suiting action to the word, he backed up and wheeled over to Mr. Ayledotte's side of the piano.

"And that includes where you're not wanted, I suppose," Mr. Ayledotte wheeled quickly round so that he was facing Mr. Stewart.

"That's for me to decide, buddy." Five years younger, Mr. Stewart glared at Mr. Ayledotte, who appeared to be effectively backed up against the piano.

"What's the matter, Stewart?" said Mr. Ayledotte softly. "Having trouble with names again?"

It was a low blow. Mrs. Cimino tried to shut her ears against the torrent of profanity she knew Mr. Stewart was capable of unloosing.

But there was no profanity, no countering insult. Mr. Stewart merely nodded and looked over toward the kitchen in a manner that invited Mr. Ayledotte to follow his gaze. It was almost as an independent entity that Mr. Stewart's right fist lashed out and caught Mr. Ayledotte on the cheekbone.

"Bastard!" Mr. Ayledotte cried out. "Dirty bastard!" He began to sob, more out of surprised humiliation than pain.

"Poor dumb gimpy slob," exulted Mr. Stewart. Unclenched,

his freckled right hand protruded a long, bony finger which he shook under Mr. Ayledotte's nose. "I could buy and sell you."

With the right side of her bench now cleared, Mrs. Cimino got up, wondering if she could get round in back of Mr. Stewart and wheel him away before further violence took place. But before she could take action, Mr. Ayledotte—still sobbing—pushed blindly out with both hands toward Mr. Stewart. Since Mr. Ayledotte was well braced against the piano, his push sent Mr. Stewart, chair and all, careening across the room about ten feet, bumping with a loud crash into the daisy table and sending the small vase shattering to the floor.

"My back!" cried Mr. Stewart. "You've damaged my back!"

"Tough beans!" said Mr. Ayledotte. He appeared to be suddenly in much better humor.

"I'll have my lawyer sue you for everything you've got!" screamed Mr. Stewart, careful not to reapproach the piano. "And I'll have the FBI on your tail from here to doomsday."

"Tough, tough beans with sugar on them," said Mr. Ayledotte, smiling cockily at Mrs. Cimino. A gentlemanly fellow, he had never developed an extensive vocabulary of insult.

By this time the kitchen staff had hurried out and Mrs. Polanski had been sent for. But Mr. Stewart was still yowling threats like an old calico cat on a high, safe picket fence.

"We'll come after you with tanks and airplanes, buddy!" Mr. Stewart shook his freckled fist in emphatic threat. "And I'll get a lien against your house!"

Mrs. Cimino's small body was shaking all over, but she managed to escape from the piano and work her way down the wall to the entrance, shrinking back as Mrs. Polanski came running in.

"Mr. Stewart, Mr. Stewart, Mr. Stewart!" said Mrs. Polanski, overpowering his willful promises with her loud voice. "Mr. Stewart, Mr. Stewart, Mr. Stewart!"

"Ask him to say it back," shouted Mr. Ayledotte, "Five to one it comes out sounding like Napoleon."

"You!" Mrs. Polanski turned on Mr. Ayledotte like a spotlight from a prowling police car. "Timothy Ayledotte!" There was cold contempt in her voice for the apprehended culprit. "Acting like an overgrown schoolboy!"

Mrs. Cimino slunk out, not without a measure of guilt, since she knew herself to be the prime mover behind the disturbance. Even though she closed the door behind her, she could still hear Mrs. Polanski's voice rising, falling, pausing dramatically here and there, shaping longer and longer stretches of silence in which the docile, shamefaced responses might be inserted. And it had all started with a simple song.

Mrs. Cimino, eyes clouded, face flushed, walked over to the nurses station.

"Fireworks," smiled Miss Martin, looking up from her charts.

Mrs. Cimino shrugged and tried to smile, much as though she had merely happened to wander by that afternoon. She remained standing at the counter.

"Is there something I can help you with?" said Miss Martin.

"The mail's gone out, hasn't it?" said Mrs. Cimino.

"Yes, it has," said Miss Martin. She smiled down at the empty mail basket as though to indicate its contents were already winging their way to far-off realms.

"Oh, dear," sighed Mrs. Cimino. "I put a letter in there I wanted to look at again." She smiled up at Miss Martin appealingly. "I'm not sure I remembered to put the stamp on."

"No problem," said Miss Martin. "They'll send it back to you."

"Or maybe I had the address wrong," said Mrs. Cimino reflectively.

"It'll take longer," said Miss Martin. "But it'll still come back." She paused, trying to read the worried eyes looking up at her. "But we could phone the post office if it's really important."

"No," said Mrs. Cimino. "It might just as well go the way it is." She smiled at Miss Martin and nodded firmly. "Thanks anyway."

Mrs. Cimino walked over to the stairs, feeling a little foolish over her impulsive urge to retreat. What was wrong with seeking legal counsel from a knowledgeable, experienced family friend? Upon what reasonable basis could reprisals come her way? The courts of this country were there to hear the plea of the widow, of the orphan, of the cruelly mistreated. A day in court was something to look forward to, not shrink from.

As she went up the stairs, she scolded herself roundly for allowing chance timing to confirm her decision. She knew fear would come upon her again. But when next it came, welling up from the dark reaches of childhood, she resolved to face the creature down.

By the time she reached her room with the red door, she was in high spirits, ready to do battle with the aid of a good lawyer. Very softly under her breath she murmured Miss Rochester's talismanic phrase: Ineffective anger and Nagging worries make us Inert, while Active concentration over a Limited span of time keeps us Alert.

To that soothing litany she added one mild qualification: Righteously effective anger is a proper duty, wholesome in its origins and thoroughly respectable in its consequences.

Tuesday, September 14, 2:00 P.M.

Mrs. Cimino was more than a little disappointed in the offices of Ryan and Ryan, Attorneys at Law. They were in the Broadloom building, just as they had always been; but they were now on a different floor, lower down, as though the occupants had been demoted from the respectable seventh grade to the irresponsible fifth.

And the decor was different: Michael had always favored solid woods, but the young, blonded secretary had seated Karen and her on a red-cushioned couch precariously supported by slender metal pipestems. There was no give to it, no air of discreet wisdom. It was like a dentist's waiting room. A nervous, skinny young thing in Capri pants sat across from them weeping softly into a thick mat of Kleenex; beside her was a middle-aged woman with a hard, craggy face that looked as though it had worn out three bodies.

"Mr. Bronkowski will see you now," said the blonded secretary to the skinny young thing and the hard, craggy face. She motioned them into the offices of Bronkowski, Chalmers, and Johns—a team of matrimonial surgeons who apparently specialized in property settlement extractions. Mrs. Cimino frowned at her granddaughter, as though to warn her against the griefs attendant upon lapses of judgment and good sense.

She replaced her frown with a slightly uncomfortable smile: Her own good sense seemed vulnerable to question. After writing to Michael and waiting a decent interval, she had phoned his office, expecting a cheery greeting and a firm promise that all would be speedily set right. But Michael had left town, running off to Boca Raton, Florida, with Martha: It was young Philip who spoke to her on the phone, and young Philip had always been shy, even for a trumpet player. It was hard to imagine him standing up in a courtroom and snapping back at the judge with his father's bright legal wit.

She gave Karen's hand a pat: It was an awkward situation for the girl, almost conspiratorial—like Mrs. Yeager's excursions out to the sycamore grove. She had not actually pledged Karen to silence, but she had gone ahead without talking it over with George and Harold. If there were anger, some of it might come Karen's way. Mrs. Cimino sighed: Despite the expense, it might have been better to have taken a taxicab in from St. Hild's, or a bus.

"Mrs. Cimino?" It was the blonded secretary, trilling professionally. "Mr. Ryan will see you now." She motioned toward a small door on the left.

"Thank you," said Mrs. Cimino. She gave Karen's hand a final pat and got up.

"Are you sure you don't want me to come in with you?" said Karen. Her eyebrows, always puzzled, had more of a tilt to them than usual, and there was clear concern in her light brown eyes.

"Later on, perhaps," said Mrs. Cimino, trying her best to smile reassurance. "But I think this should be my own little show."

"Good luck," said Karen. She smiled brightly and reached for a copy of the *New Yorker*. Two years old, it was an obvious legacy from the Michael Ryan domain.

Mrs. Cimino smiled once more at her granddaughter before going in the door. Karen was really a lovely girl: fifteen pounds lighter now, chestnut hair a bit longer with more of a wave to it; a quicker smile, a bolder walk, and a figure rich with promise. Nicely turned out, too, in a light green skirt, a high-necked dark green sweater, and a gold chain. Still working at Jack In The Box mornings, now that the semester was about to start, she seemed to have thrived on the responsibility. Frank would have been pleased: He had always distrusted skinny women, and it was clear that

Karen would never be a screamer. With a sudden feeling of contentment, Mrs. Cimino walked into young Philip's office.

"It's good to see you, Mrs. Cimino." Philip Ryan came out from behind his desk and shook hands warmly.

"I suppose it's not very tactful to say that you've grown," said Mrs. Cimino, putting on her most engaging smile. "But you have."

"It's been a long time," said Philip. He motioned her to a sturdy leather chair: another bequest, she surmised, from Michael's office.

"Do you still play the trumpet, Philip?" Despite her fears, Mrs. Cimino felt it would be wise to establish a degree of friendly authority.

"I still *have* the trumpet," said Philip. He smiled ruefully. "But I haven't practiced in a long time."

"A Conn, wasn't it?" said Mrs. Cimino.

"That's right," said Philip, pleased and obviously impressed. "It's a Conn—just like Harry James used to play."

Mrs. Cimino sat back in her chair with a small sigh of relief. Rapport had been established. She took a closer look at Philip: He had grown, but not much. Slender, slightly taller than Michael, he was a bit more slanted toward the Black Irish side of the family. His hair was dark and so were his eyebrows; they topped a slightly ruddy face whose basic bent was serious. Dark blue suit, white shirt, striped tie: nothing at all like the tweeds his father used to favor. It was as though Michael's poteen flamboyance had been diluted in a half-gallon of weak tea brewed at Yale or some other effete eastern place.

"Well, here I am," said Mrs. Cimino. She clapped her hands in a clear signal that it was time to get down to business.

"It's good to see you," said Philip. He went back to his desk as though it was a safe haven for him. "You're looking very well."

"Everyone says I *am* well," said Mrs. Cimino, looking steadily at him.

"Then we might as well get started," said Philip with sudden resolution. "First of all, I want you to tell me again exactly what you want from the court." He looked at a sheet of yellow legal paper as though to refresh his memory. "Then we'll put our heads together and work out some sort of strategy."

"I spelled it all out in the letter," said Mrs. Cimino, a little irritated at being asked to retrace her steps.

"I know," said Philip. "But I want to hear it again." He sat back in his chair; smiling, receptive, as though the story were something that merited pleasurable retelling.

"I want that Judge Schultz to reverse his decision," said Mrs. Cimino, pointing her finger directly at Philip in stern admonishment. "I'm perfectly competent to manage my own affairs, and that's what I want to do."

"Fine," said Philip. "You want the judge to declare you mentally competent, and you want the judge to dissolve the trust he established for you." He sighed and looked down at his sheet of paper. "This is not going to be easy."

"What's so difficult?" said Mrs. Cimino. "It's a matter of simple justice." Her irritation was beginning to grow. "Aren't you experienced in handling cases like this?"

"Cases like this are very rare," said Philip, refusing to bristle at the implicit questioning of his legal capacities. "And I'll tell you exactly why, Mrs. Cimino." He tried to take the sting out of his words with a warm smile. "It's a matter of fees."

"Fees!" said Mrs. Cimino. "I'm no pauper. And that father of yours has certainly gotten enough out of my late husband and me." She looked around the room as though to call the absent Michael Ryan in for a scolding.

"That's very true," said Philip quietly. "And that's the reason I'm going to take on your case."

"Good," said Mrs. Cimino, suddenly relieved and sorry for her little explosion. "I didn't mean to imply any dissatisfaction."

"You've been a good client, and a good friend," said Philip. "When I talked to Dad on the phone, he was delighted that you were better." Philip bent forward to emphasize his position a bit more. "But an ordinary attorney would never touch a petition like yours."

"I don't understand," said Mrs. Cimino. "There can't be that much involved, can there?"

"It's generally just a petition and a hearing," said Philip. "But the judge is the one who determines what the fees will be, and he rarely awards the petitioner's attorney more than a couple of hundred dollars."

"I'd be glad to pay much more than that," said Mrs. Cimino. "Within reason, of course," she added with thrifty haste.

"But you can't pay any more," said Philip patiently. "At this point anything you have is under the control of Minneapolis Southern Bank."

"Who pays for *their* lawyer?" asked Mrs. Cimino suspiciously.

"You do," said Philip. "Or rather your estate does." He sighed. "And the court generally awards them a fee ranging from eight to twelve hundred dollars."

"For the same hearing, for the same court appearance, for the same amount of work?" Mrs. Cimino was incredulous. "It doesn't make sense."

"It's a way the court has of discouraging actions like this," said Philip. "Once a trust or conservatorship is established, they don't like to break it up and then maybe have to establish it again."

"But why would the bank want to oppose my petition?" said Mrs. Cimino. "It's my money, not theirs."

"But they have control of it now," said Philip. "It's not just the fees they charge as much as it is the discretionary power they have in handling your assets."

"Like selling the house," said Mrs. Cimino, glowering at the thought. "And Karen tells me they've put a new manager in charge of the music store."

"It all adds up," said Philip, smilingly evoking a picture of his client's assets churning away in a basement cauldron stirred by black-suited wizards and goblins. "So that I'm sure they'll oppose any petition involving dissolution of your trust."

"What if they do?" said Mrs. Cimino, thoroughly prepared to cudgel Mr. Leach and his fellow rascals.

"It would mean delaying tactics," said Philip. "They could drag things out for a couple of years."

"A couple of years!" Mrs. Cimino was aghast. "I'd be almost eighty by the time I got my checkbook back!" She sighed, she shook her head, she took out a pink hankie and wiped her eyes for a moment. "What am I going to do?"

"My advice is to concentrate on one objective at a time," said Philip. "I think we should go after the mental competence thing and leave the trust as it is for a while."

"But what's the point?" said Mrs. Cimino, at the brink of tears. "The bank would still have my money, wouldn't they?"

"They'd have to give you an adequate stipend out of your income," said Philip. "And you'd be able to spend it the way you saw fit." He smiled at the notion for a moment. "You'd certainly be able to write your own checks again."

"It's not much," said Mrs. Cimino. "It's like getting an allowance from someone."

"You'd be able to transact business," said Philip. "Change your will, if you wanted to."

"Oh," said Mrs. Cimino. She gave her eyes a final dab and put her pink hankie away. "I suppose it's better than nothing." She stared back at him, not without implicit accusation.

"And remember," said Philip, pressing the point. "Later we can always go in and ask to have the trust dissolved."

"All right," said Mrs. Cimino. "We'll do it your way." She sighed deeply over the canker of corruption eating into the American polity. "But it's still a scandal!"

"Let's get started, then," said Philip. His manner was brisker, more authoritative, a little more like his father, as he reached into a drawer and took out a sheaf of legal forms. "I want you to sign these now, before you leave, and I'll have the secretary type in the necessary information."

"Now?" said Mrs. Cimino. She drew back. "Maybe I should think it over for a while."

"I'd advise you to sign them now," said Philip. His voice was serious, firm. "This way you're certain to be protected."

"Protected?" Mrs. Cimino's hands began to moisten a little under her white gloves. "Protected against what?"

"It's hard to say," said Philip. "But I'd certainly feel better if we got all your forms signed today." He gestured toward the documents. "Power of attorney so that I can act for you, your petition to Judge Schultz, and a restraining order just to be on the safe side."

"Safe side?" Mrs. Cimino moistened her lips. "You make it sound sort of risky."

"It won't be," said Philip. "But estate matters can be just as emotional as divorce actions." He began to check the appropriate lines for his client's signature. "There was a case here in Hennepin County a few years ago where an elderly lady told her trustee she was going back into court."

"How could he stop her?" said Mrs. Cimino. "It's a free country."

"He stopped her," said Philip. He looked straight at Mrs. Cimino as though to underscore the parallel. "He took her out of a local nursing home and moved her by plane to a nursing home in California."

"But they can't do that, can they?"

"They certainly can," said Philip. "Unless you have an attorney empowered to act in your behalf." He pushed the first document over toward her. "Right after each X, please."

Mrs. Cimino busied herself with signing the documents, trying to make her signature as bold and as commanding as possible. The whole business was as bad as poor dear Mrs. Yeager's vegetarians, except that the rascals were somehow able to wrap themselves in the American flag, coming out into the open and flaunting their villainy.

"Why didn't I have an attorney at the original hearing in March?" said Mrs. Cimino, pushing the documents back for Philip to check. "I think I could have used one."

"You were in no condition to hire one," said Philip. "And this state makes no provision for any sort of representation." He finished checking the signatures and put the documents in a neat pile. "In Pennsylvania the court often appoints attorneys to represent elderly people, but it's an exception."

"Are you saying that in most states they can wheel you in and lock you up for good—just like that?" Mrs. Cimino was growing indignant. "That's incredible."

"Happens all the time," said Philip. "It happened to you, didn't it?"

"Yes," said Mrs. Cimino. Her voice was low, discouraged. "It happened to me." Her eyes wandered off behind Philip, coming to rest on an autographed picture of Harry S Truman. "I don't see why George and Harold were in such a hurry about all this."

"I wouldn't be too hard on them," said Philip. "They acted upon what the hospital people told them."

"Do you think so?" Mrs. Cimino found comfort in the thought. "They're really very fine men." She sighed. "But they

208

seem to be busy, busy, busy. I don't know how I would have managed if it hadn't been for Karen."

"Did she drive you out here from St. Hild's?" said Philip.

Mrs. Cimino nodded.

"Did you tell her what you had in mind?"

"I told her it was legal business," said Mrs. Cimino. "But I didn't want to say anything more than that."

"I think you should tell her right away." Philip gestured toward the documents as though the legal wheels were already beginning to turn. "And I think you should be prepared to tell Judge Schultz exactly where and how you're going to live when you leave St. Hild's."

"What kind of allowance am I going to get?" said Mrs. Cimino. "Am I going to have to ask that Mr. Leach for spending money?"

"I'm sure I can get him to accept a basic stipend in the neighborhood of eleven hundred a month," said Philip. "That's probably under what your total expenses are now." He rose and started to walk Mrs. Cimino out to the door.

"That sounds fine," said Mrs. Cimino. "For a start." She opened the door and smiled cheerily at Karen. "Karen, I want you to meet my lawyer, young Philip Ryan."

Still a little mystified, Karen got up and shook hands. Philip saw them out the waiting-room door and directed them to the elevator. They walked down toward it in silence. The skinny girl in Capris and the craggy-faced woman were there, waiting for the elevator to come. When the elevator finally arrived, the four women got in, ranging themselves on either side like small opposing armies, the skinny girl sobbing quietly in a far corner.

"How did it go?" said Karen, trying to make the ride a little more palatable.

"Fine," said Mrs. Cimino. She lowered her voice a little. "We're going to court." There was an air of firm decision to her voice.

"Good!" said the craggy-faced woman. She scowled approvingly at Mrs. Cimino and Karen. "Good for you!" The craggy-faced woman turned upon the skinny girl and exhibited Mrs. Cimino to her like a curiosity from the university primate laboratory. "If she can do it at her age, you can do it at your age."

Mrs. Cimino shrank as far into her corner as she could.

"It's never too late to get what's coming to you," said the craggy-faced lady. As the elevator doors opened, she pushed the still-sniffling skinny girl on ahead of her.

Mrs. Cimino and Karen followed them, hanging back a little.

"But Momma, the banks are closed," said the skinny girl.

"No problem," said the craggy-faced lady. "I'll come round first thing tomorrow morning after he's gone to work and we'll have those accounts transferred to your name by eleven o'clock."

"But what about tonight?" said the skinny girl. "What will I say to him?"

"Be nice, sugarplum," rasped the craggy-faced woman. "It never does any harm to be nice."

The craggy-faced woman pushed her daughter on out of the building into the sidewalk traffic. A bit reluctant to venture forth, Mrs. Cimino and Karen stood there a moment.

"She's right," said Mrs. Cimino, nodding at the vanished harpy and siren combination.

"About being nice?" Karen looked over at her grandmother, shocked at the apparent approval of a conspiracy starting up.

"No," said Mrs. Cimino. "It's never too late—she's dead right on that." She took Karen's arm with an affectionate pat. "What do you say we get a little snack and I'll tell you all about these strange goings-on?"

They walked out of the building, standing back a minute to stay clear of the stream of pedestrian traffic that poured past them. Busy, needled slightly by the small chills of early autumn, the people jostled and shoved their way along. Like Alaskan sourdoughs, they all seemed imbued with the notion that to stop moving was to terminate existence itself; so that motion became a proper goal, almost as important as the end to which it was directed. Moving, moving, moving, keep moving: This was what they scowled at slower folk who dared impede them, for this had been established as their cardinal rule of social intercourse. And it was still fairly warm.

But Mrs. Cimino could smell winter in the air: shoveled drifts along the sidewalks and ashes strewn down at the intersections. With the house gone, it might make good sense to search out something warmer, a place where one could walk all year round with quiet certainty.

Chief Kona Kai had once played a split week in St. Petersburg,

Florida, before moving on to Miami Beach. And Miss Schmidt had spoken highly of it. As Mrs. Cimino and Karen braved the traffic on their way to the parking lot, a sudden gust of wind whistled down upon them. Pulling her light brown camel's-hair coat more snugly around her, Mrs. Cimino found the notion of warmer climates unusually attractive and reassuring.

Wednesday, October 13, 10:50 A.M.

Mrs. Cimino's second competence hearing was staged with much more flair than the first: The American flag was larger, the bailiff was neatly uniformed, and the lighting was excellent. There was even an audience of sorts seated in the rear—elderly gentlemen, for the most part, who habitually wandered from courtroom to courtroom in search of entertainment.

Judge Schultz tended to frown at these elderly gentlemen. Even though they were neatly dressed and clean, some of them coughed inopportunely and all of them whispered back and forth, not unlike a Greek chorus chanting lugubriously while the action took place on the apron in front of his high perch.

By the time the Cimino action was called, he had reached an unusually high pitch of irritation: The previous matter had taken up almost fifty minutes of genteel wrangling, so he was already far behind schedule. And he was in pain: Just above the area where his body made contact with his padded chair was a large boil, vulnerably sensitive to the small movements made by his left buttock as it shifted from one position to another.

He had examined Mrs. Cimino's petition with distaste: It represented the intrusion of ambiguity into a domain already mapped out, much like the elderly gaffers hawking and grunting on the back benches. Not that he blamed Mrs. Cimino personally. It was the law itself which thrust the ambiguity in front of him, since the notion of competence was fundamentally a creature left over from early common-law pastoral gardens: gardens in which free men and women roamed, unfettered, unrestricted, gathering their fruits and storing them in stout bins built with the materials of responsible social contract.

That garden was now a jungle. Only trained professionals could cut their way through the vines and thickets of the tax structure. And there were predators to consider: artful and designing persons, as the decorous language of the law termed them. In that jungle, early pastoral notions of competence offered little help in determining whether or not an elderly petitioner should be allowed to venture forth alone and unprotected.

Judge Schultz looked down at the petitioner and her attorney. They had stepped out from the seating area and were now standing behind a large table directly below his bench. A respectable, grandmotherly sort, wearing a navy blue polka-dot dress with matching navy blue jacket, she seemed a far cry from those wild-eyed, smock-clad furies of the Monday sessions at Central Hospital.

The attorney was unfamiliar to him: Philip Ryan of Ryan and Ryan. This would be the younger one, taking over a greatly reduced practice now that Michael had decided to take it easy. About thirty, conservatively dressed in brown, probably not as lively as the father. That was good: Michael had always favored bringing evidence in from left field at the last moment. But he had been good company.

"You would be Michael Ryan's son, wouldn't you?" Judge Schultz frowned speculatively down at the younger man. A couple of older attorneys down in the seating area looked up with interest.

"Yes, Your Honor, I am," said Philip.

"It's a pleasure to see you here," said Judge Schultz. "Please remember me to your father and mother."

"I shall, Your Honor," said Philip. "And I'm sure they'll be very pleased."

"I've read the petition, Mr. Ryan," said Judge Schultz. "Is there anything you want to say before I talk with the petitioner?"

"If it please Your Honor," said Philip. "I should like to point out that the petition is unopposed by the petitioner's family."

"Are any of them here?" said Judge Schultz. Very gingerly he shifted position so as to peer round the room.

"The petitioner's granddaughter, Miss Karen Cimino, is here," said Philip. He turned toward his right and gestured in the direction of a young woman sitting on the aisle halfway back. "And I should also like to point out that our petition is unopposed by her trustee, Minneapolis Southern Bank."

"I take it you've been in contact with them," said Judge

Schultz. Again he shifted position, grunting inaudibly, and squinted down at the document.

"Yes, Your Honor," said Philip. "I've talked this over with Mr. Edward Leach, one of their trust officers." Philip gestured toward the papers on the table in front of him. "We've come to a mutually satisfactory agreement regarding the petitioner's monthly living stipend."

"Good," said Judge Schultz. "Then you make no allegations as to mismanagement or malfeasance on the part of the trustee?" Although his words were directed to Philip, he looked straight at the petitioner, as though expecting her to burst forth in a rage of paranoia. Apart from a slight tightening of the jaw, she appeared to be in reasonable control of herself.

"The trust which you established, Your Honor, seems to be working quite well," said Philip. "But the stigma of incompetence is a source of humiliation to both the petitioner and her family, particularly in view of the fact that they have been residents of this city for many years."

"The point is well taken," said Judge Schultz. "And this court has no desire to stigmatize unnecessarily any citizen of this county." He continued to stare directly at the elderly woman in front of him, but his voice was raised enough to be clearly audible to the venerable Greek chorus clustered in back. "I must remind the petitioner, however, that this court did not seek to assume responsibility for her welfare."

"We are aware of that, Your Honor," said Philip.

"The original petition was made by a member of the present petitioner's family," continued Judge Schultz, looking straight into the faded blue eyes down below him. "As a result of that action, this court is now responsible for seeing that the best interests of the petitioner are protected." He looked over at Philip for a moment. "Is the petitioner aware of this?"

"I have been careful to point this out to her, Your Honor." Philip nodded reassuringly to the elderly lady beside him.

"Very well," said Judge Schultz, subsiding somewhat. "But I must remind the petitioner that this court does not take that responsibility lightly."

"I am sure she understands that the court's primary concern is for her protection and welfare, Your Honor." Again Philip nodded reassuringly.

"And I hope she understands that any questions put to her in this court are put to her solely with the purpose of determining where her best interests lie." It was a preamble that Judge Schultz had given many times before, so it rolled trippingly from his tongue, despite his present condition of acute distress. "Does she understand this?"

"I have explained the procedures to her, Your Honor," said Philip.

"Very well," said Judge Schultz. He nodded to the bailiff, a husky young man in a brown uniform, and the bailiff escorted the elderly lady up to a high-backed black leather chair on his left. Judge Schultz leaned toward her and smiled as warmly as his boil would permit.

"Would you state your name for us, please?" said Judge Schultz."

"My name is Esther McDonald Cimino," said the elderly lady.

"Would you state your present address, Mrs. Cimino?"

"Right now I'm living at St. Hild's Convalescent Hospital," said Mrs. Cimino. "But I have owned a home in this city for many years."

"Do you understand the purpose of this hearing?"

"As I understand it, Your Honor, it's supposed to decide whether I'm mentally competent or not," said Mrs. Cimino.

"That is correct," said Judge Schultz. "And that is why I must ask you a few routine questions."

"I'll answer them the best I can, Your Honor."

"Very well," said Judge Schultz, moving once more into drearily familiar territory. "Can you tell us when you were born?"

"February tenth, nineteen hundred, Your Honor," said Mrs. Cimino, just a touch of snappishness in her voice.

"Can you give us today's date?"

"Today is Wednesday, October thirteenth, nineteen hundred and seventy-six," said Mrs. Cimino. She was careful to invest each syllable with appropriate weight and significance.

"I must apologize for this next question, Mrs. Cimino." Judge Schultz tried to smile in a twinkling way at the tastefully dressed elderly lady. "But would you tell us how old you are?"

"I've already given you my birthdate," said Mrs. Cimino. She looked round the room as though to seek supportive comment on the idiocy of the proceedings. "And nineteen hundred from nine-

214

teen hundred and seventy-six leaves seventy-six." She looked back at Judge Schultz in a scolding manner. "Simple arithmetic ought to tell you that I'm seventy-six years old."

There were a few coughs and clearings of the throat from the backbenchers at this. Judge Schultz chose to ignore them.

"Can you tell us the name of the President?"

"Do you mean the President of the United States or the president of General Motors?" said Mrs. Cimino, disregarding Philip's frown in favor of playing to a larger audience.

"I mean the President of the United States of America," said Judge Schultz. He was careful to enunciate the question slowly, as though putting it to a small child.

"At the present time, the President's name is Gerald Ford," said Mrs. Cimino. She nodded knowingly at the coughers and throat-clearers. "But that state of affairs is certainly subject to change."

A cluster of coughs this time, a couple of wheezes, and one softly voiced cackle. Judge Schultz looked sharply up and stared his Greek chorus into immediate silence. Then he mumbled something into his desk.

"What's that, Your Honor?" Mrs. Cimino turned more directly toward Judge Schultz and fingered her hearing aid. "My hearing isn't quite what it used to be."

"I'm sorry." Judge Schultz raised his voice and looked directly at her. "What I said was 'two heads are better than one.' "

"What about it?" Mrs. Cimino was clearly mystified. There was a low sigh from one of the seats in the back.

"What does it mean to you?" Shifting uncomfortably, Judge Schultz smiled thinly down at her.

"It's a proverb, an old saying," said Mrs. Cimino. She looked desperately at Philip and Karen.

"I know it's a proverb," said Judge Schultz impatiently. "But I want to know what it means."

"Couldn't you look it up somewhere?" said Mrs. Cimino. She tried to smile engagingly. The back benches were quiet. Even the attorneys in the nearer seating area had begun to look up.

"Mrs. Cimino!" said Judge Schultz. His voice was thick with irritation now. "My impression was that you understood the purpose of this hearing."

"I understand the purpose, Your Honor," said Mrs. Cimino. "But I don't understand this question."

"Let me put it to you again," said Judge Schultz. "Please tell us how you interpret the expression 'Two heads are better than one.' " He sat back, wincing a little, and scowled at his uninvited, uncooperative Greek chorus, much as though the riddle had come from the Sphinx on down to the present.

It was a hard proverb: much harder than "too many cooks spoil the broth" or "a stitch in time saves nine." And even these posed a substantial challenge to literal-minded elderly people—which was why the county psychologists had begun to use them, like new mazes designed to tax the capacities of irritatingly quick-witted, beady-eyed gray creatures.

He could see that Mrs. Cimino was taken aback and that her attorney was visibly shaken. And he began to regret the low blow: If his boil had not been bothering him, he would never have asked it.

"Take as much time as you want," he added, a touch of regretful kindness in his voice.

"An interpretation?" Mrs. Cimino sighed and paused, trying to collect her thoughts. "Two heads are better than one." She nodded as though trying to gnaw the wisdom out of it. "I'd say it means the judgment of many people together is better than the judgment of one person alone." She looked around the quiet courtroom for a moment. "And that's why we have elections and juries in this country."

There was no applause, no dramatic response, except the continuation of the silence. But there was a broad smile on Philip's usually serious face, and an emphatic nod from the black robe high above her.

"And laws, too, Mrs. Cimino," said Judge Schultz. He looked around the room and smiled approvingly. "Wouldn't you include the law as well?"

"Yes, Your Honor," said Mrs. Cimino. Her voice was low, deferential. "I would certainly include the law."

"Very well," said Judge Schultz, almost forgetting his boil for a moment. "As far as this court is concerned, you are obviously in full command of your faculties and as mentally competent as any citizen of this county needs to be." He raised his hand as though to stay Mrs. Cimino from leaving the high black leather chair pre-

216

maturely. "Yet we are still responsible for looking after your welfare."

"But I'm not on welfare, Your Honor," said Mrs. Cimino. "I'm a taxpayer, a property owner, and I'm able to look after myself."

"Those are brave words, Mrs. Cimino, and I respect you for them," said Judge Schultz. "Have you made any plans?"

"I can't go back home," said Mrs. Cimino. She looked up at the judge accusingly. "That trustee of yours sold my house."

Judge Schultz looked uncomfortable.

"And my furniture," continued Mrs. Cimino inexorably, before allowing her expression to soften. "But I don't think I could have endured another Minnesota winter."

Judge Schultz sighed and smiled with manifest relief.

"So I've been in correspondence with the President Jefferson Hotel of St. Petersburg, Florida," said Mrs. Cimino. "It's been highly recommended to me."

"I'm glad to hear it," said Judge Schultz. "And I'm sure that your trustee will give you every bit of help possible in living a comfortable life down there." He looked out toward the elderly backbenchers and paused dramatically before going on. "Petition granted!"

"Thank you, Your Honor," said Philip, as the rap of Judge Schultz's gavel set off a small flurry of comings and goings by other attorneys and their clients. Stepping forward, he guided Mrs. Cimino down from the high black leather chair and down the aisle to Karen's congratulatory hug. He motioned them to go on ahead and wait in the corridor outside. With his papers gathered up into his briefcase, he followed them quickly and elatedly.

Judge Schultz was not elated, but he was reasonably content: Most matters ended up with one of the adversaries dissatisfied, while the Cimino matter had managed to avoid active opposition from either the bank or from members of the family. And there had been a nice touch of drama, too.

He smiled for a moment—almost cheerfully—before turning once again to the subject uppermost in his mind: that large, painful, slyly positioned, unwholesomely pink excrescence which a bleak, merciless providence had seen fit to inflict upon him. Frowning, he considered the matter. By lunchtime, he decided, he would be able to do execution upon the culprit.

Tuesday, November 16, 10:30 A.M.

Mrs. Cimino watched her two large suitcases disappear from sight as the conveyor belt carried them off. They were new suitcases, unfrayed, ungouged, and she feared for their safety on whatever jostlings and jumblings lay before them. The whole business was like a roller-coaster ride: smiling attention from the ticket taker, a placid approach, and a final imprisoned series of dips and swirls from which there was no escape.

"You're sure this is better than taking the train?" she said to Karen as they walked over to a red Leatherette couch and sat down.

"Much better," said Karen. "The trains are slow and they're uncomfortable."

"I guess they are if you say they are," said Mrs. Cimino, looking around to take stock of where she was.

The waiting room was pleasant enough: couches, low tables, and a ramp that led up to the boarding passage. But it fell far short of the massive stone cathedrals she remembered from her days on the road with Frank. There, under one large vault lined with shops and services, travelers had communed together before hurrying variously off into the darkness where the trains waited, mist-shrouded and steaming impatiently.

The dining cars had used solid silver, gleaming white napery. And there had been flowers—sometimes long-stemmed roses—set neatly at the window edge of each table as an implicit admonition not to push and shove, not to bolt one's food, not to take the journey as anything other than a civilized progress through the fields and towns of a many-kingdomed realm. Davenport, Peoria, Texarkana, Memphis, Chattanooga, Altoona: just to hear the names intoned with high conductor's pomp memorialized the land in all its rich vulgarity.

But the conductors, red-faced and gruff, were all gone now: their places taken by young, smilingly antiseptic attendants in pastel uniforms. The smiles were attractive; but each was clearly a surface gesture, very much like the professional grimace of a nurse coming in to inflict a prescribed humiliation. And the humiliation was complete, not only for the traveler, strapped in and powerless, but also for the land itself: a land whose towns and villages were now reduced to a gray, nameless blur that devoured the traveler, ground him up, and then spit him out in crowded gobbets onto a carpeted surface indistinguishable from the one he had just left.

Mrs. Cimino was not by nature a conservative person; but she had flown before, and she knew the airplane for what it was: a mean-spirited, worrisome way of getting from one place to another.

It was quite apparent that her fellow travelers were nervous: Across from them was a middle-aged man alternately looking at his watch and at the waiting-room clock in an attempt to reconcile some minute disparity. To his right was a young woman in skintight yellow pants with a face stretched thinly over her high cheekbones and fragile chin, so that the bones themselves appeared on the verge of bursting through. She was smoking cigarettes, long brown ones.

"Mrs. Polanski seemed to think it was a good idea," said Mrs. Cimino reflectively. "And so did Mrs. Nash." She looked up at the entrance ramp, still suspicious, as though she were being pushed there by consensual committee action.

"Are you getting cold feet?" said Karen. She reached over and patted her grandmother's small hand.

"Strangers," said Mrs. Cimino. She watched the skintight young woman walk slowly over to check her departure time again. "I've always been shy in getting acquainted." She gave one of her embarrassed little laughs.

"You never had any trouble at the store," said Karen.

"That was different," said Mrs. Cimino. "I'd be on one side of the counter and the customer would be on the other." She looked at Karen appraisingly. "You should know how that is from working at Jack In The Box."

Karen nodded.

"How do you like it?" continued Mrs. Cimino. It seemed appropriate to fill the time with something other than the rehearsal of small fears.

"It's not bad," said Karen. "I'd be an assistant manager if it weren't for my schedule at school."

"Assistant manager!" Mrs. Cimino nodded with approval, as though to fix the magnitude of the feat in her mind. "They must think very highly of you."

"I get there on time," said Karen.

"That's half the battle," said Mrs. Cimino. "And how's the college going this semester?"

"It's all right," said Karen. "But it seems sort of pointless."

"Why's that?" said Mrs. Cimino. "Don't you like the idea of becoming a teacher someday?"

"That was mostly Mother's idea," said Karen. "And it looks to me as though the schools won't be hiring teachers by the time I get my credentials."

Mrs. Cimino was silent. She searched for comfortable words but found none. Ann and Gretchen had been able to move quickly and gracefully through college, while Karen plodded along. And part of the plodding had involved trips out to St. Hild's with stamps, stationery, and even beef jerky for dear Mrs. Yeager. It was as though Karen had been sucked into a vacuum of her grandmother's making, there to struggle faintly, like a moth in a jar.

"I should have helped out with your education," said Mrs. Cimino in a low voice. "I should have done that instead of worrying about the store so much."

"That's all right." Karen gave a little laugh. "I was never much of a student anyway." She gave her grandmother's hand another pat. "I like what I'm doing."

"I bet you would be good at the store," said Mrs. Cimino. She shook her head at the way matters had been knotted up. "It's too bad Simon Montford isn't there anymore."

"I'm sure the bank has everything under control," said Karen.

"I hope so," said Mrs. Cimino. She looked up the ramp again, darkly, as though her departure would be the signal for immediate disorder, like a teacher's closing of the classroom door. "I'd feel a lot better if you were looking after things."

"But I don't know anything about running a music store," said Karen. She shook her head and smiled at the fancifulness of the notion.

"You could get there on time," said Mrs. Cimino, smiling archly at her granddaughter as though the feat were rare and beautiful.

Karen laughed, pleased at her grandmother's return to good humor.

"And you could learn the rest of it," continued Mrs. Cimino. "It's not that different from Jack In The Box." She nodded forcefully, underscoring the parallel. "All you have to do is use good sense and keep good people with you."

"Like Simon?" said Karen.

"Simon was with us for years," said Mrs. Cimino. He's one of the best repairmen in town. And we always had good teachers, too." She shook her head again in mournful contemplation. "It was a good little business."

"It still is," said Karen. "Believe me, everything's going to be all right."

"People keep saying that to me," said Mrs. Cimino, looking bleakly around her. She tried to brighten a little. "That's what they all said at the party."

"It was a wonderful party," said Karen with conviction. "We were all very proud of you."

Mrs. Cimino smiled, partly to keep herself in good humor and partly out of pleased recollection. Her graduation party had been held the previous afternoon. George and Lisa had been there, Lisa in black skirt and high boots like a dark-haired fugitive gypsy. Restless, a bit irritated over not being the center of attention, she had insisted on serving punch and cookies to Mr. Stewart and Mr. Ayledotte. But she had made the mistake of turning her back, skirts swirling, on Mr. Patterson: His affable, exploratory pinch had evoked a shocked shriek, not at all assuaged by Mr. Monsour's comment regarding meat and potatoes. Eyes snapping, face thunderously dark, she had flounced immediately out to the Porsche, there to make detailed plans for George's subsequent chastisement.

George had stood there, dressed in leather, smiling fixedly, but still a fine figure of an older son. If anything, he had seemed to respond favorably to Mrs. Polanski's speech: It had celebrated one of her favorite themes, "it's never too late." Karen had been quiet, as usual, but her smile had been warm, genuine; and Miss Schmidt—never one for idle praise—had pronounced her to be attractive, poised, and personable. While the exit had been lacking in the drama of Mrs. Wohlsteader's departure, the party as a whole had been appropriately noisy and cheerful.

"I'll miss that place," said Mrs. Cimino, trying to imagine what it would be like not to come back to a room with a red door. "Mrs. Yeager and I used to take such good walks together."

"You wouldn't be able to do much walking in the snow," said Karen.

"I'd forgotten about that." Mrs. Cimino smiled ruefully. "Florida it is, then," She opened up her purse and took another look at her little white envelopes. "I hope I don't run out of money."

"You'll be fine," said Karen. "You've got a hundred dollars in cash and a thousand dollars in travelers checks." She pointed to the two largest envelopes. "And Mr. Leach will send you a check for a thousand dollars on the first of every month."

"I hope so," said Mrs. Cimino. Again she was dispirited. "There's nothing worse than being stranded in a strange town without any money." For a moment she scowled at the memory of the evaporative Chief Kona Kai and her first lean winter in Minneapolis.

"Mr. and Mrs. Bales sound like lovely people," said Karen. She took out one of the envelopes, extracted a sheet of paper, and began to read it aloud.

Dear Mrs. Cimino:

We acknowledge receipt of your deposit for Room 105. It will be a pleasure to have you with us for the season and for longer, should you wish to stay on.

Please let us know your arrival time. Mrs. Bales and I will feel better if we meet you at the airport, since this is your first visit with us.

Our guests are a congenial group. Many of them have been coming down to the President Jefferson for years, and some of them are now staying here permanently, since the installation of our air-conditioning system. We look forward to having you among them.

Cordially,
Richard N. Bales
Manager

"Air conditioning," said Mrs. Cimino. "That's a good thing to have in the summer, especially in a store."

"And here's your ticket and baggage claim," said Karen. She put them firmly in her grandmother's purse and closed it up. "Remember, there's an hour's layover in Kansas City, but you don't have to get off the plane."

"Kansas City," said Mrs. Cimino. Her voice was soft, thoughtful. "We played the Muehlbach Hotel there."

"And remember, too," said Karen, raising her voice a little. "I'm going to phone the President Jefferson Hotel when I get home, so they'll be sure to meet you. And I'll call tonight to make sure you're there and settled."

"Don't worry about me," said Mrs. Cimino. Sensing the departure time was upon them, she smiled encouragingly at her granddaughter. "Everything's going to be just fine."

"Do you have something to read on the plane?" said Karen, still nervous, still a bit reluctant to have her guardian role curtained off.

"Miss Rochester gave me a crossword puzzle book," said Mrs. Cimino. "And I'm sure they'll have magazines."

"Then we're all set." Karen patted her grandmother's hand.

"I know it's silly of me," said Mrs. Cimino. "But I wish Harold and Gloria could have been at that party."

"Maybe they'll stop and see you on their way back from the Bahamas," said Karen.

"That would be nice," said Mrs. Cimino. In her mind's eye she saw herself parading Harold and Gloria around the President Jefferson Hotel—both of them tanned, both of them dressed with the expensive casualness of those accustomed to command tip-seeking deference. She had always enjoyed basking in the glow of their success, even at a distance, feeling it was as much her fire as theirs.

Even before the plane was called, the middle-aged man across from them was up by the ramp, boarding pass in hand as though to whip the airline into more rapid flight. And the skintight young woman was not far behind: Hastily discarded, her long brown cigarette had been speared into the small sandy desert of an ashtray beside her seat.

Mrs. Cimino and Karen were slower, waiting until the anxious ones were well aboard. After talking with the stewardess Karen boarded the plane with her grandmother, located the seat, strapped her in, and sat there beside her for a moment.

"Here we go," said Mrs. Cimino. She patted her purse, finding reassurance in its bulk.

Karen, wordless, kissed her grandmother goodbye. She squeezed her way up and out against the flow of late arrivals, turning to wave a final farewell before she stepped out the door. Out in the waiting room she went directly to the window, standing there with her nose almost pressed against the cold glass. Face intent, she quietly willed the long argosy safely aloft and on its journey south.

Vigil finished, she started back to the main concourse. It was a long, well-lit tunnel flanked with level, moving walkways. The walkways were filled with people going and coming, most of them carrying hand luggage, and all of them strongly adjured by voices above to eschew erratic movement.

Karen walked down the middle of the tunnel, setting a good pace, arms swinging, feet pointed directly ahead. There was a young man hurrying toward her, business-suited, attaché case in hand. Despite his haste, he took time out to smile. And so did a young marine, ambling more slowly, fresh-faced and crew cut. It was not until she had passed them both by that Karen realized the smiles had been meant for her. And by then it was too late for even a distant acknowledgment.

Wednesday, November 17, 9:15 A.M.

Mrs. Cimino had breakfasted late. Lacking the cheery goading of Miss Martin and the other aides at St. Hild's, she had lain abed, lazily inferring the height of the sun as the light from outside gradually crept across the bed. It was not a large bed. And it was not a large room. Nor was the bathroom anything more than a small closet decked out with the necessary plumbing fixtures. But the room was adequate, private, a cellular retreat from the communal movements below.

By the time she finished her poached eggs and coffee, the dining room was almost empty: Most of the breakfasters had sauntered out in twos and threes, leaving only a portly red-faced man still glowering at the financial pages, and a pair of seventyish ladies, hennaed and rouged in a mildly flirtatious manner.

Not sure of whether to leave a tip or not, Mrs. Cimino stole a glance at the uncleared table on her left. She could see nothing. She waited for one of the girls to come over and scoop up whatever silver might be there. No one came. She gave the matter thought. Finally she opened her purse and extracted a quarter from the appropriate envelope: overly generous, probably, but a bold gesture seemed called for.

She got up from her table in a direct, purposeful manner. She walked out to the lobby, standing in the doorway for a moment to inspect the temperature of the water before diving in. It seemed safe, quiet. Nearly all the overstuffed chairs and sofas were empty, with the exception of the far corner. There two elderly ladies were looking at the newspaper. One of them had a pencil in her hand.

Directly across from her and slightly to the left was the reception desk. A stack of newspapers was on the counter. And Mr. Bales, a welcome point of reference, was standing behind the counter sorting mail into a wall of boxes on his right. He did so with what seemed to be a professional flourish: reading the address ruminatively, tapping the letter several times against the stack, and then flipping it into a relatively small target. Not wishing to disturb his accuracy, Mrs. Cimino waited until he finished.

"Good morning, Mr. Bales," said Mrs. Cimino. Resolute, she smiled engagingly.

"Feeling rested, Mrs. Cimino?" said Mr. Bales.

"Just fine," said Mrs. Cimino. "And I want to thank you again for picking me up at the airport."

"We like to do it," said Mr. Bales. "Sometimes the taxicabs take our guests the long way round." He smiled down at the small person in front of him. "And it's a good way of getting acquainted."

Mrs. Cimino smiled back. Her host was a slight, trim man in his early sixties. Short gray hair, small mustache, surprisingly unjowled, with brown eyes and a ruddy complexion. In his white shirt and dark tie, Mr. Bales still carried the flavor of a retired commander, even though he had been dry-docked out of the Navy in 1961. At that time he had shrewdly sought a berth in the Tampa Post Office, staying there until 1975. With his two pensions—Navy and federal—he had then moved into the private sector in order to qualify for social security. Politically, he was a strong Republican. But Mrs. Cimino had forgiven him this after the first five minutes of their ride together.

"I think I'll take a look at one of your papers," said Mrs. Cimino. She opened her purse and tried to fumble unobtrusively through her change envelope. It was only after sustained tactile exploration that she emerged with the requisite fifteen cents. Pondering the matter, she resolved to revise her accounting system.

"There's a good activity page in the back," said Mr. Bales.

"That sounds interesting," said Mrs. Cimino. She picked up her paper and started away.

"What about your mail?" said Mr. Bales.

"Too early for that, isn't it?" Mrs. Cimino gave one of her embarrassed little laughs.

"We had one come a couple of days ago," said Mr. Bales. He reached up into one of the boxes and brought down a large white envelope.

"Isn't that something!" said Mrs. Cimino, taking it from him with puzzled delight.

"You must be a popular lady," said Mr. Bales, drawing upon his substantial store of post office charm, faintly approximating the intimate style of a small-town butcher handing over a pound of ground chuck.

"I wouldn't say that," said Mrs. Cimino, warming to the exchange. "But it's always nice to get a letter."

She put off looking at the letter, fearing that it might be from Mr. Leach, until she picked out a good reading spot. It was not an easy choice: Too close to the other ladies might be taken as intrusive; too far away might define her as unduly distant. She finally decided it would be appropriate to share the window with them, so she walked directly over and sat down.

It was with pleasure that she recognized the letter as coming from St. Hild's.

Dear Mrs. Cimino:

I'm writing this to you a couple of days before your graduation party. I want it to be waiting for you in St. Petersburg when you get there, so I'm marking it "Hold until 11/17."

It should go without saying that you are one of our *favorite* people. And your progress has been *wonderful*. I'm sure you remember how discouraged and *confused* you were when you came to us in April.

You should also remember that the confusion can always come back. For older people it's always waiting, like a *tiger* ready to jump out at you. If you don't want that tiger to get you, here are some things to keep in mind.

1) Watch your medication. Older people often react to harmless drugs in unusual ways.

2) Stay physically active. Walking—plenty of it—is your best medicine. *And don't shuffle!*

3) Forget about the past. The retirement homes of this country are filled with people telling the same stories again and again. *Who cares!!*

4) *Stay in touch with what's going on!!!* Read the newspaper every day! Even the bad news!! And force yourself to concentrate on small mental tasks. (It's better to *write* letters than read them.)

5) Stay lucky! There's not much we can do to control this part of it.

That's about all I have to say, except that you have to depend on yourself more and more as your horizons shrink. Most people plain don't care, and that goes for our families, too. So you can't expect to keep going on the basis of letters and visits. Being old is like being locked up in prison. The only company you have is your mind and your body, so you'd better be careful who you take in there with you. It's a grim thought, but there's no point in *copping out* about it!!

We're proud of you. We've got your picture hanging up there with all the others who've managed to get out of here. And all of us—Mrs. Nash, Miss Rochester, Miss Martin, and the others—wish you the best. *You certainly deserve it!!!!!*

Affectionately,
Irene Polanski

It was time for a hankie. Mrs. Cimino reached in her purse and fished out a white one. It was a dear letter, filled with love and concern, but a frightening one. It was the kind of letter they might hand an astronaut before they locked him into his capsule: a final checklist to take with him into the limitless unknown. It made her yearn for the sight of Miss Schmidt bravely hobbling around. And for dear Mrs. Yeager, quietly enduring her fancied persecution.

She picked up her newspaper and held it up in front of her so that she could weep unobtrusively into the second and third pages. She stole a glance at her neighbors: They were still absorbed in working the daily crossword puzzle together. She leafed through the paper until she found the crossword puzzle. It was a blur to her.

Not that her eyesight was poor: The new glasses were working quite well. And the hearing aid was in good order. But her will power was wanting: While the flesh was strong enough, the spirit was weak this morning. A little more in control of herself, she put the paper down and took stock of her new home.

Like most of the people in it, the President Jefferson Hotel had seen better days. The furnishings of the lobby, as well as those of the TV lounge just beyond it, were dark. And so was the woodwork, handsomely carved and shaped as would have been deemed proper for a middle-sized Georgian building put up a few years before the First World War.

At that time rail connections to St. Petersburg were far superior to those extending south to Ft. Lauderdale and Miami. And the President Jefferson had been considered an elegant refuge for propertied gentry coming down from Boston and New York. Even after Henry Flagler transformed his sand and mosquitos into an oceanside Shangri-La, St. Petersburg continued to attract its fair share of snowbirds. So the President Jefferson continued to employ a uniformed doorman and a salon orchestra in the evenings.

But the Second World War came. The city grew, and nearby Clearwater Beach became the prime winter haven in the area. Like other modest luxury hotels, the President Jefferson drifted downward to become a rooming house—or residence hotel, as the Tolliver family preferred to call it. As such, it opened its doors from November to April, offering modest accommodation to thrifty elderly folk wishing to escape the bitter Illinois and Ohio winters.

Only recently had the President Jefferson begun to offer year-round sanctuary to these grizzled robins. For the city now offered a rich variety of programs for its guests, and old Mr. Tolliver, the present owner, had wisely chosen to put in air conditioning and to provide informal supervision for a growing permanent clientele. The supervision was little more than a kindly checking of medications and movements. But it defined the place as an effective halfway house lying somewhere between the coercive attentions of a hospital and the mindless anonymity of an apartment building.

It had been a good choice for Mrs. Cimino. She was grateful to Miss Schmidt for recommending it to her. But the lack of structure—regimentation, Mrs. Polanski would have called it—was still upsetting. With breakfast behind her, the day was a large canvas waiting for an inventive mixture of umbers and ochres. And it was far too early to think about lunch. She looked out the window: The street was bathed in sunlight, but she could not bring herself to take a walk. She stole another glance at the two crossword puzzle ladies.

"An instrument for Andres," said the elderly lady with the pencil. "Now what could that be?"

"Who could it be?" said the second lady. "André Baruch, maybe, along with André Kostelanetz."

"André Baruch?" The lady with the pencil stared solemnly at her companion.

"The radio announcer," bubbled the second lady happily. "And so good-looking!"

"But it asks for an instrument," said the lady with the pencil.

"The microphone?" The second lady was tentative. "That's kind of an instrument."

"It's only six letters," said the lady with the pencil. Obviously wearied by her companion's flights of fancy, she looked over at Mrs. Cimino and smiled. It was a clear plea for assistance.

"How about *guitar?*" said Mrs. Cimino, a bit overcome by her own quickness and daring. "That would go with Andres Segovia."

"It would indeed," said the lady with the pencil. She gestured to a neighboring chair. "Would you like to come over and help us?"

"I'd enjoy it very much," said Mrs. Cimino. She smiled shyly, picked up her purse, and walked over to participate in their collaborative Active concentration over a Limited span of time.

"We never work them all the way through," said the lady with the pencil. "But we do our best." She rose and gave a slight, formal bow.

"I'm Mrs. Gatlin," said the second lady. Her manner was brightly effusive. "And this is Mrs. Hinckle."

"My name is Mrs. Esther Cimino, and I've just come down from Minneapolis." Like a new girl in school, Mrs. Cimino felt obliged to identify herself in more detail.

"We're both from Evansville, Indiana," said Mrs. Hinckle. She put her pencil down, signaling that the puzzle could wait until social commerce was more firmly established.

Mrs. Hinckle was on the tall side, five foot five shrunk down from an original five foot seven, probably. Her hair was quite white, simply done. It topped a long, narrow face heavily crisscrossed with lines but with a translucent parchment glow to it, not unlike a firmly done hard-boiled egg. Though close to eighty, she stood quite erect. Despite her slender, almost emaciated form, she reminded Mrs. Cimino very much of her dear friend Mrs. Wohlsteader.

Her companion, Mrs. Gatlin, was younger, shorter, plumper, more coquettish, with big blue eyes that still managed to sparkle continuously behind her rimless eyeglasses. Her hair was slightly tinted and extravagantly curled, though tastefully so. And she was a far cry from the two bizarre ladies of the dining room. She was wearing a bright yellow frock, trimmed with white and flounced at the bottom. Mrs. Cimino searched through her store of acquaintances for an analogue and found one. Mrs. Gatlin reminded her a little of Myra Flint back in Jamestown: a bit on the boy-crazy side, Myra had been, with a smile that always seemed on the verge of bursting into a giggle.

"My late husband's younger brother lives in Minneapolis," said Mrs. Gatlin, working herself up to a high pitch of enthusiasm. "Herb Gatlin?" She sat back, eyes fluttering expectantly.

Mrs. Cimino had to shake her head and confess ignorance.

"He's in insurance," added Mrs. Gatlin. "And he's also one of the Tailtwisters in the Lions Club."

"My husband was in Kiwanis," said Mrs. Cimino apologetically.

"Minneapolis is a big city," said Mrs. Hinckle.

"I have a cousin in Terre Haute," said Mrs. Cimino, trying a long shot. "Ira Johnson," she added.

"Terre Haute's pretty far from us," tinkled Mrs. Gatlin. "We're practically in Kentucky." She giggled a little in the magnolia-ridden manner of an elderly southern belle.

"I grew up in Jamestown, New York," said Mrs. Cimino, electing to lead from a geographically closer suit. "And that's practically in Pennsylvania."

The three elderly ladies shared a merry laugh over the minute shadings of geography that served to blur the categories of mapmakers.

"Pennsylvania," said Mrs. Hinckle. "There's a lovely state for you."

"My father came from Uniontown," said Mrs. Cimino. "But it's quite small."

"So is Kittanning," said Mrs. Hinckle, watching her closely for some sort of response. "My niece lived there for many years before she moved to Glendale."

"Not Glendale, California!" said Mrs. Gatlin, quite overcome and almost refusing to accept so farfetched a possibility.

"Glendale, California," said Mrs. Hinckle with deep satisfaction.

"But that's near Santa Monica," said Mrs. Gatlin. She fairly quivered with excitement. "And Santa Monica is where my brother's wife grew up.

"And isn't Santa Monica right up the coast from Long Beach?" said Mrs. Cimino, wanting to get her facts straight before moving delightedly on.

"It certainly is," laughed Mrs. Gatlin.

"Long Beach is where my late husband's brother moved to!" Secure, Mrs. Cimino sat back in her chair. "They used to send us oranges at Christmas."

"Isn't that something?" said Mrs. Hinckle, serene joy in her gray eyes. Struck by a sudden thought, she turned to Mrs. Gatlin. "You never told me you had relatives in Santa Monica."

"Didn't I?" Mrs. Gatlin's small giggle crested into a high surfer's wave. Only when it subsided was she able to continue. "But you never told me you had relatives in Glendale."

Suddenly secure in the discovery of safe common ground, the three ladies discussed the attractions of California for a while, centering largely upon the weather and upon tales of film stars seen among the lettuce and radishes of the markets there. In firm agreement they concluded that Florida weather was superior and that the smog of California—already in Arizona—was threatening to reach the Mississippi. Shaking their heads over the prospect, they went back to their puzzle.

It had not been a trivial exchange. At the President Jefferson it was important to establish who you were in terms of valid reference points, like a house taking on its character from well-known nearby landmarks. Friends, family, hairdo, clothes: These were the quarterings of respectability, the gules and hatchings of bourgeois heraldry.

They had not been needed at St. Hild's, but they were essential here. It was obvious to Mrs. Cimino that the purchase of new clothes must take place without delay.

"Not bad," said Mrs. Hinckle. She put her pencil down and sat back. "Only fifteen unfilled squares this time."

"Better than yesterday," said Mrs. Gatlin.

"We had help," said Mrs. Hinckle. Graciously she inclined her head and smiled at Mrs. Cimino.

"It certainly makes the morning fly by," said Mrs. Cimino.

"They used to have a big jigsaw puzzle," said Mrs. Gatlin. "Spread out on a table over there." She directed Mrs. Cimino's gaze down toward the TV lounge. "Nearly everyone would stop and work a little on it."

"And in three or four days it would be done," said Mrs. Hinckle.

"Except for that modern art one," giggled Mrs. Gatlin. "We never did finish that one."

"People got discouraged," said Mrs. Hinckle. "With horses or boats you have something familiar to work with."

"This is quite a town for boats, according to Mr. Bales," said Mrs. Cimino. Secure in her role as new arrival, she smiled warmly.

"Mr. Bales ought to know," said Mrs. Gatlin. "He's a Navy man." Her big blue eyes fluttered at the thought of Navy men in white parading through the streets.

"They're really a sight to see," said Mrs. Hinckle. "Especially out on the bay."

"Are we far from the water?" said Mrs. Cimino.

"Goodness, no!" exclaimed Mrs. Gatlin. "We're only six blocks from the big waterfront park."

"Small blocks," added Mrs. Hinckle.

"I think I might just walk down there this evening and take a look," said Mrs. Cimino. "Before it gets dark," she added, her voice accented with tones of good sense.

Despite the qualification, Mrs. Hinckle looked at Mrs. Gatlin, who giggled back at Mrs. Hinckle. The two of them looked at Mrs. Cimino, then back at one another. Mrs. Cimino blushed.

"Not in the evening," said Mrs. Hinckle finally. "Not unless you have someone with you."

"You mean a person has to be . . . careful?" said Mrs. Cimino.

"Very careful, my dear," said Mrs. Hinckle firmly.

"And that includes sitting on the park benches," giggled Mrs. Gatlin. "Even in the daytime." Her giggle modulated into a titter.

"But what about all these programs down at the center?" said Mrs. Cimino. "Aren't most of them held at night?"

"They are," said Mrs. Hinckle. "And that's why we generally walk down in small groups."

"And even then we walk down the middle of the street," added Mrs. Gatlin merrily. "That's so no one can jump out at you from one of those dark doorways."

"Good heavens!" said Mrs. Cimino.

"It's a jungle," said Mrs. Hinckle. Her gray eyes clouded at the thought.

"And we just can't run as fast as we used to," said Mrs. Gatlin, who was now quite beside herself over the humor of the situation.

Mrs. Hinckle permitted herself a dry laugh at Mrs. Gatlin's high spirits. She looked over at Mrs. Cimino's purse. Her face was somber.

"That's a nice-looking purse you have there," said Mrs. Hinckle finally.

"I'm glad you like it," said Mrs. Cimino. "My granddaughter helped me pick it out."

"Would you mind showing me how you propose to carry it?" said Mrs. Hinckle.

Puzzled, Mrs. Cimino picked up her purse, rose, and slung it casually over her shoulder. She took a few steps over toward the door, wheeled smartly around, and returned to where the other ladies were sitting.

Mrs. Hinckle shook her head. "That won't do." She got to her feet and beckoned for Mrs. Cimino to give her the purse. "You must turn the flap side *in,* my dear, and make sure your arm is on the *outside* so that it prevents any swinging back and forth." In demonstration, she took the same journey, walking very erect with her gray eyes flashing opposition to any invisible assailant.

"That makes good sense," said Mrs. Cimino. Retrieving her purse, she attempted to duplicate Mrs. Hinckle's protective measures.

"Much better," said Mrs. Hinckle. An approving smile brightened her wrinkled face. "Don't you feel more secure that way?"

"I certainly do," said Mrs. Cimino. She smiled warmly up at the taller Mrs. Hinckle.

"Not too secure, I hope," said Mrs. Gatlin archly. She began to giggle again. "Someone could come along and take the purse . . ." Her giggle threatened to overwhelm her words. ". . . and its owner at the same time." Still on the couch, she collapsed into complete hysteria at the bold notion. Only after reaching into her own purse for a lace-trimmed hankie was she able to recover her rational powers.

"You've both been very kind," said Mrs. Cimino. "I'm beginning to feel very much at home." She smiled at the two of them. "Except that there it's the cold weather that keeps us cooped up."

"That's very good," said Mrs. Gatlin, commencing still another round of giggles.

"Perhaps they should call us the snow chickens instead of the snowbirds," said Mrs. Hinckle, permitting herself a sustained bit of genteel laughter.

"Snow chickens!" squealed Mrs. Gatlin. "Snow hens and snow roosters—that's what we are!" Almost prostrate with amusement, she shook her head helplessly. It was only the sight of Mr. Bales peering round from the desk that brought composure to her.

In great good humor, Mrs. Hinckle and Mrs. Gatlin said goodbye to Mrs. Cimino. With the crossword puzzle behind them, they purposed a short walk within the safe environs of the hotel. Mrs. Cimino declined their invitation in favor of her newspaper.

She had enjoyed getting acquainted. But she felt it unwise to intrude further into the company of the Evansville ladies. Mrs. Polanski's prison reference was still on her mind, and she resolved to work her way through the newspaper's first section.

She managed to get through the third page before her attention wandered again, this time back to St. Hild's and the green rolling country which ringed it round. In that happy rural seat there were no purse snatchers. Nor were there dark doorways grayly shadowing evil men. All was safe there. All was secure. And the day was neatly sectioned off into calm recurring patterns.

Now on the couch, she noticed that her purse was way over at the other end. She reached out and pulled it closer to her. Reassured, if only slightly, she resumed her reading.

Monday, November 22, 10:00 A.M.

Another lovely day! Another bucket of sunshine splashed down over the sidewalks, there to puddle brightly among small islands of shade. And to think the same sky was scowling down snow on Mrs. Washburn back there in Minneapolis! Mrs. Cimino stopped to look at a pair of open-toed blue shoes pointed toward her in one of the store windows. Feet planted firmly, she stretched up on her own toes for a minute, feeling the muscles in her calves tighten. On these level sidewalks a slightly higher heel might well be called for.

The urge to shop was on her: the urge to confer with clerks in carpeted rooms, gravely weighing alternatives until the right choice emerged, almost like a command that would not brook denial. But her cash was almost gone, though not frivolously: After Mrs. Gatlin's dinner treat, it had seemed more than proper to stand for the Ferrante and Teicher concert on Sunday. With only fifty dollars left out of her original hundred, Mrs. Cimino had decided to translate her travelers checks into the more convenient idiom of a local bank account.

The local branch of Florida Security Bank was close: only a few blocks away at the corner of Third Street and Eighth Avenue. Unimaginative though the street names of St. Petersburg were, they provided her with a running check as to where she was. Starting out from the hotel's position at the corner of Fifth Street and Sixth Avenue, she had worked her way down to Eighth Avenue already and was now turning right for the second leg of her trip.

Eighth Avenue, more than the others, was lined with shops: Small ventures, they formed a modest commercial estuary in the forest of apartments and residence hotels that populated this section of the city. But it was still a leisurely street, not nearly as busy as downtown Minneapolis. There were benches here, not just at the bus stops but all along the way. And these were filled with folk, old and young, passing the time of morning in casual talk, just as though it were Sunday rather than a working day.

But the cars were still a hazard. And the street crossings, with their uneven curbs, demanded wariness and strategy. At the first two she had slyly waited until others came along to ford the stream with her, since it was well known that automobiles rarely attacked people in groups. Emboldened, she decided to attack the Fourth Street stoplight by herself, looking cautiously to her left to make sure nothing would take her by surprise.

As she reached the middle of the street, a young man coming up behind her slowed his pace and accompanied her the rest of the way. Southern gallantry, she smiled to herself, a little like Mr. Bales: never in too much of a hurry to stop for a small kindness.

There was something to be said for the South, for the sunshine, for the placid unconcern with scheduled gettings and spendings. Once across, she slowed her own pace to more of a saunter, taking time out to smile at the people coming toward her.

Just as Mr. Bales had described it, the bank was a small light brown stucco building. She stood still for a moment, assessing the three wide steps that led up to the entrance. Feeling quite brave, she declined the support of the balustrade and went directly in. The business area was conventional enough: a counter at the right for the tellers and a carpeted section at the left with desks for the officers and special services. At her near left was a young woman seated behind a desk labeled "New Accounts."

"Good morning," said Mrs. Cimino, flavoring her businesslike manner with her best smile. "I think I might like to open an account with you.

"I think we'd like that very much," smiled the young woman.

She rose—a promising sign—and motioned Mrs. Cimino to a chair. With her brown hair, fairly short, she faintly echoed Karen: just a girl, really, but well started in the world.

"Here's my situation," said Mrs. Cimino, immediately investing the matter with high seriousness. "I've always lived in Minneapolis and done business there."

The young woman nodded with appropriate solemnity.

"But now I'm living here." added Mrs. Cimino. "At your President Jefferson Hotel." She gestured toward the door as though to bring the place in to confer with them. "Do you know it?"

"It's a lovely place to stay for the winter," said the young woman. "And we're very happy to have you with us."

"I came down here with travelers checks," said Mrs. Cimino. She leaned forward in a confidential manner. "But I think they're going to be a dreadful nuisance."

"They're fine for a short stay," said the young woman. Her sympathy was manifest. "But it certainly makes sense to open a checking account if you're going to be here any length of time." She picked up a small green brochure and handed it over to Mrs. Cimino. On the cover was a sketch of an ecstatic elderly couple beaming up at a large balloon labeled "Senior Citizen Sunshine Accounts." Beside the balloon was a swordfish whose cheerful smile promised that the balloon would not be punctured, even in jest.

236

"Isn't that something!" said Mrs. Cimino, noting with a practiced eye that the first twenty checks were not charged for. "You seem to have it all worked out." Her disappointment at not being able to discuss the problem at length was more than balanced by her delight at the apparent thrift of the arrangement.

"It's a very practical account plan," said the young woman. "Unless you're going to be writing a lot of checks every month."

"Not me," said Mrs. Cimino. "Without a house, you don't have all those bills to look at. I just want to do a little shopping every now and then."

"Fine." The young woman smiled and took out the appropriate cards for Mrs. Cimino to sign.

Mrs. Cimino straightened her glasses and went to work, reaching down into her purse for the envelope in which she had her addresses written down. After filling out the cards, she took out her envelope of travelers checks: She had decided to use eight hundred dollars in opening the account, keeping the rest in reserve.

"Is the President Jefferson going to be your permanent address?" said the young woman.

"I think so," said Mrs. Cimino, still busy endorsing her travelers checks. "They have air conditioning now, and they seem like very pleasant people."

"I'm sure you'll enjoy it a great deal," said the young woman.

"I'll certainly enjoy the winters," said Mrs. Cimino. "I still can't believe I'm out in the middle of November without a coat."

The last check endorsed, she looked brightly up at the young woman. "Here they are," she said.

"Fine!" The young woman checked the signatures and made out a deposit slip. Then she got up. "I'll be right back with your temporary checks," she said.

Mrs. Cimino, smiling, watched her walk over to one of the tellers on the other side of the room. The bank was not busy as yet: It looked to be girding itself for a denser flow of traffic later on. Many of the customers seemed to be elderly people like herself. She felt very much in place.

When the young woman came back, there was a young black man with her. Mrs. Cimino's natural suspicions were somewhat allayed by the fact he was neatly dressed in what appeared to be a Dacron suit. He was slender, slightly taut, with heavy eyebrows bristling out over a solemn face. Like Philip Ryan, he appeared to be habitually serious, awkwardly so, unskilled as yet in the traditional banterings that lubricate American commerce. The locker-room style, Harold had called it: a style of controlled aggressiveness under a perpetual veneer of joviality.

"This is Mr. Harris, our assistant manager," said the young woman.

"Welcome to Florida, Mrs. Cimino." Mr. Harris tried very hard to smile warmly.

"It's a pleasure to be here, Mr. Harris." Relaxed, perfectly in control, Mrs. Cimino smiled her most engaging smile. "I think I'm going to like this bank of yours very much." She looked over toward the tellers and writing tables with a cheerful proprietary air.

"We'll do our best," said Mr. Harris. The smile in his solemn brown face came more naturally, more easily, this time. "I just wanted to get acquainted."

"That's very kind of you," said Mrs. Cimino. "But I'm afraid I'm not going to be one of your big spenders here." Her faded blue eyes twinkled merrily.

"I'm sure you'll be one of our favorite customers just the same," said Mr. Harris. He smiled even more as he found himself drawn into the small orbit of polite badinage.

"Isn't that something!" Mrs. Cimino smiled at the young woman this time, as though sharing a private delight. She picked up her packet of temporary checks, a sceptre with which to take leave of her court. "These southern gentlemen are all so charming and nice." She looked back at Mr. Harris, determined to broaden his smile even more. "It must be the water."

Her chorus of appreciative laughter well shaped, Mrs. Cimino started for the door. Mr. Harris, his day brightened beyond measure, escorted her. Before going down the steps, she beamed upon him again.

"And I just love this sunshine of yours," said Mrs. Cimino. She walked briskly down, sure of his admiring, respectful gaze.

Quite at ease, she walked back to the Fourth Street stoplight: she felt recognized, defined as something more than a transient. It would be good to go through the rituals of banking once more: the deposits, the withdrawals, the balancing of statements. And it was good to be called by name, to be treasured as a customer. As she

238

waited for the light to change, she began weighing the advantages of opening a small savings account in this warm, hospitable climate.

It was just as the light flashed green that she felt a wiry hand on her wrist, pulling it back with a sharp, jolting snap.

Her purse had been well positioned in the manner prescribed by Mrs. Hinckle. But she had not been prepared for the force with which her left arm would be wrenched from its socket. She turned her small body around, following the pull. It was a young man: dark-faced, expressionless, impassive, except for teeth bared by the effort involved in the assault.

She had always thought that criminals never got up before noon: The attack came as a profound surprise.

"Ah, ah," came Mrs. Cimino's high-pitched resistant whimper.

"*Sssssss,*" came the attacker's biting intake of breath. In a half-second he had worked the strap almost off her small arm.

"Hey!" came a loud voice from over her right shoulder, as though a truck wheeling left were warning her back.

There was a sudden release of pressure. The dark face—hard-eyed, straight-haired—disappeared off to her left. She staggered backwards, knowing that the curb was behind her. Braced to lose her footing and fall, she feared for the press of traffic grinding upon her even more than the fall itself. Bad luck, long deferred, had come upon her once more.

But there was no fall, no jolt of the head against solid pavement. There was a grunt and a heavy pressure against her back and a hand cupping her right elbow in support. Almost cradled against the solid flesh in back of her, she found herself still erect, still on her feet. It had been wise to wear the oxfords: High heels would surely have given way and brought her down.

"It's all right," said a deep, mellow voice. "It's going to be all right."

The pressure against her back disappeared. But she remained erect, grateful for the support still there under her elbow.

"Are you feeling all right?" said the voice. It was softer, more concerned, now that the immediate crisis had been faced.

Speechless, still gasping for breath, Mrs. Cimino nodded. Turning slightly to her right, she could see that the deep, mellow voice belonged to a tall, well-built sixtyish gentleman in a neat seersucker suit. Under his broad-brimmed planters hat she could see a strong face, still flushed from its effort. The face was well cared for: light hazel eyes and a trim, pencil-thin white mustache.

"You need a chance to catch your breath," said the gallant gentleman. He helped her over to a nearby bench and sat down beside her.

"Dear me, dear me," said Mrs. Cimino. Her pulse was racing.

"And so do I," said the gentleman. He took off his planters hat and mopped his brow. "I'm not as young as I used to be." He was breathing heavily.

"Dear me." Mrs. Cimino took a few more composing breaths. "What kind of place is this?"

"A dangerous place," said the gentleman. Still puffing, he looked up Eighth Avenue in the general direction of the assailant's flight. "Don't try to talk until you get your strength back."

Mrs. Cimino nodded assent. She managed a weak smile for her rescuer before returning to her task: taking deep breaths and trying to relax the tense, visceral mobilization of her small body. She rubbed her left wrist. She rubbed her left shoulder and worked it a little: The ache, dully arthritic, would stay with her for weeks. But she was alive.

It was a hazardous place, Florida: an alien land, far from the constraints of Saxon law and commerce. Unseasonably warm, studded with odd names like Tallahassee, Boca Raton, and Pompano. A tropic land, filled with strange birds, coral snakes, alligators: a land where seasons, wet and dry, replaced the natural shadings of spring, summer, autumn, and winter. And in such a place, cleared though it might be, the jungle was always near, ready to creep back. And along with the jungle came the jungle people: unfriendly folk with savage ways and savage lusts.

Lustful men, sly men: They had even found their way up to the big northern cities, working under cover of darkness. And there, through force and guile, they had often seized young girls, carrying them off—bound and drugged—to lives of shameful degradation. Warned against these men, she had always been wary, fearful of abduction whisking her off to Brazil or Argentina. But she had never imagined making the journey by choice. And here she was, well on the road to permanent residency!

Bones intact, purse safe, breath almost regained: Mrs. Cimino sat quietly on the bench. She did not look over at the man in the seersucker suit. She looked down at her oxfords. She shook her head as though to drive both the incident and the humiliation out of her steaming hot, fiercely spinning mind.

Monday, November 22, 10:45 A.M.

Mrs. Cimino moved tentatively on the bench: Apart from her shoulder there were no major twinges. And her purse was safe. She began to relax a little more and take stock of her rescuer in the seersucker suit.

"It's awfully good of you to sit here with me," she said to him. "But I don't want to keep you from your business."

"Young hoodlums like that are everybody's business," said the man in the seersucker suit. His hazel eyes were still intent on the assailant's escape route. "You should really report this to the police."

"Police!" Mrs. Cimino's returning strength drained quickly from her.

"They'll want my name, too," said the man. He pulled out a handsome leather billfold and took out a business card. He handed it to Mrs. Cimino and sat back, his face softening with concern. "Are you sure you feel all right?"

"I'm all right," said Mrs. Cimino, absorbed in the card for a moment. In neat, slightly Spencerian script it announced the bearer to be Roger J. Desmond, Judah Benjamin Building, Atlanta, Georgia. It was a thoroughly respectable business card.

And so was the owner. Mr. Desmond had the look of someone substantial: His hair was well-trimmed, his white shirt was of good broadcloth, and his carriage was erect and forceful. Obviously a business executive of some sort. Or a retired admiral, maybe.

"Atlanta," she said, smiling at the notion of a fellow stranger. "I'm from Minneapolis."

"Minneapolis!" said Mr. Desmond, showing his clear white teeth in a brilliant smile. "My business has taken me there many times."

"I'm Mrs. Esther Cimino," she said, smiling at his courtly bow of acknowledgment. "And I'm very, very grateful to you for stepping in the way you did."

"Glad to do it," beamed Mr. Desmond. "It's all part of being a good citizen."

"A good citizen," nodded Mrs. Cimino, still feeling uncomfortable over the police report idea. She looked up Eighth Avenue, very much clogged with traffic now. "And you feel I should report this to the police?"

"It could help them," said Mr. Desmond. "Each report gives them a better picture of what's going on. And then sooner or later . . . pow!" He clapped his hands forcefully together as though trapping an elusive mosquito. Pleased with his bit of drama, he smiled down at Mrs. Cimino.

"I guess I'm up to doing that," said Mrs. Cimino. She tried to invest her small, weak voice with brave authority.

"If I had the time I'd go down to the police station with you," said Mr. Desmond. He looked regretfully down at his handsome gold watch and paused. Struck with a happy thought, he looked back up and smiled. "I've got it!"

Mrs. Cimino smiled back, mystified but taking pleasure in the boyishly exultant snap of his fingers.

"We'll make your report over the phone," continued Mr. Desmond, gesturing to a coffee shop across the street.

"But I wouldn't want to take any more of your time," said Mrs. Cimino, inwardly much relieved.

"No problem there," beamed Mr. Desmond. "The gentleman I was supposed to meet here is over an half an hour late already." He looked at his watch and nodded, as though confirming an opinion previously reached. "I had a feeling he wouldn't show up."

"That's very kind of you," said Mrs. Cimino, allowing herself to be helped up.

"It's a pleasure," said Mr. Desmond. "And it's part of being a good citizen." He looked darkly back at the spot they were leaving.

They made it across Eighth Avenue and into the coffee shop. There Mr. Desmond commandingly took a booth and insisted she sit down. When the waitress came he ordered a cup of hot tea for Mrs. Cimino and a large glass of iced tea for himself. Preliminaries over, he took out a small note pad and very meticulously set down the circumstances of the crime: location, time, and description of the assailant.

"You certainly have a good eye for detail," said Mrs. Cimino admiringly.

242

"It's part of my business," said Mr. Desmond. Seriously intent upon his duty, he did not amplify the matter. He got up, note pad in hand, and went over to the public telephone: Mrs. Cimino could see him talking there, tapping on his note pad for emphasis. After a few minutes he came back, obviously very pleased with himself.

"Just as I thought," he said. "Our description is going to be very helpful to them." He raised his glass of iced tea as though to toast their success. "Here's to law enforcement!"

"There's a lot of crime these days." Mrs. Cimino sipped her hot tea and looked around the coffee shop suspiciously: Over at the counter were two young men, bare-armed and with long hair. The waitress, a stocky young woman, was joking with them. It was a comfort to have Mr. Desmond smiling at her from across the table.

"And more and more people who just don't want to be bothered," said Mr. Desmond, his voice tinged with bitterness. "Especially when it comes to cooperating with the authorities."

"That's not good," said Mrs. Cimino. Despite her original impulse to let the matter go, she was beginning to feel like a thoroughly responsible citizen.

"It's our biggest problem," said Mr. Desmond. He leaned toward her, lowering his voice. "I'm in that field myself."

"A policeman?" Mrs. Cimino's eyes widened.

"Heavens, no," laughed Mr. Desmond. "I'm far too slow to catch purse snatchers." He took another sip of iced tea, hazel eyes sparkling. "I'm with the Federal Reserve System, traveling out of Atlanta."

"How interesting!"

"We go after the big fish," said Mr. Desmond. "The embezzlers."

"I suppose that's quite a problem now," said Mrs. Cimino, thinking of what a grand story she would have to unfold to Mrs. Hinckle, Mrs. Gatlin, and Mr. Bales.

"It's getting worse and worse," said Mr. Desmond, reaching tactfully for the check. "That's why we offer rewards to the good citizens who help us in catching and convicting the rascals."

"Really!"

"And even that doesn't always do the trick," said Mr. Desmond. "In my day a fifty-dollar reward was a lot of money."

"It's still a lot of money," said Mrs. Cimino stoutly.

"Not to my volunteer, apparently, or he would have shown up on time." Mr. Desmond pushed his glass over to the side and put his note pad back into his pocket. It was clear he was getting ready to leave.

"That's a shame," said Mrs. Cimino. "And here you've wasted even more time helping me out."

"That's the way it goes," said Mr. Desmond. He looked down at his watch. "Are you sure you're feeling all right now?"

"I'm fine," said Mrs. Cimino. "But I wish there was something I could do about all this."

"You really mean that, don't you?" Mr. Desmond's deep mellow voice was soft with wonderment.

Mrs. Cimino nodded.

"It just might work," said Mr. Desmond, a faraway look in his eye. "In fact, it might work very, very well." He stopped suddenly and looked closely at her. "Are you sure you feel all right?"

"I feel fine," said Mrs. Cimino. "Perfect, and I really want to make all this up to you." She looked around the coffee shop again, taking in the stocky waitress, the young men, and the telephone up front.

"No," said Mr. Desmond suddenly. "You've been through enough today." He gestured courteously toward her. "Let me get you started home first. Then I'll move on."

"But what would I have to *do?*" said Mrs. Cimino, aquiver with excitement and determined not to see the matter closed off in uncertainty.

"Very little," smiled Mr. Desmond, relaxing and sitting back for a moment. "All we ask our volunteer to do is to deposit some marked currency with the teller we suspect of doing the embezzling."

"Up here at Florida Security?"

"Your own friendly neighborhood bank," said Mr. Desmond, not without a cynical smile. "But once the embezzler spends some of those marked bills . . . pow!" Again he clapped his hands together, trapping another elusive mosquito.

"Is that all there is to it?" Mrs. Cimino was incredulous. "Anyone could do that." She was stunned by the elegant simplicity of the plan.

"Anyone who would not arouse the rascal's suspicions," said Mr. Desmond, correcting her kindly.

"I see what you mean," said Mrs. Cimino, a shrewd conspiratorial glint in her eyes. She smiled brightly and clapped her hands, catching her own criminal mosquito. "I'll do it!" She laughed at her boldness. "You just give me that marked currency and I'll go right over and make that deposit for you."

"Wait a minute," smiled Mr. Desmond. "We have to make sure our suspect's on duty." He looked down at his gold watch before reaching for his broad-brimmed planters hat. "The rascal might be out to lunch."

"I hope not," said Mrs. Cimino. She got up and accompanied Mr. Desmond to the door. There she waited while he paid the check and went back to their booth, apparently for the purpose of leaving a generous tip.

The two of them left the coffee shop and went back across Eighth Avenue. They walked up to the bank building: Mr. Desmond slowly, Mrs. Cimino straining at the leash. At the foot of the stairs, just by the balustrade, Mr. Desmond stopped and held up a warning hand.

"That's far enough," he said. "You wait here and I'll go in to check things out." He patted her hand reassuringly. "We don't want to arouse suspicion," he added.

"I understand," said Mrs. Cimino in a low voice. She watched him stride purposefully up the steps and into the building.

What a story this would make! She could see herself in the lobby of the President Jefferson dramatizing it from beginning to end: the purse snatcher, the near fall, the rescue, the coffee shop. This alone would make for a fascinating narrative. And the addition of the embezzlement plot would carry it to even greater heights, capped only by the final revelation that civic virtue in this case even carried with it a handsome monetary reward. It was beautiful!

Almost immediately, it seemed, Mr. Desmond was back, face set and hazel eyes serious.

"We're in luck," he said. "He's still on duty." He gestured in toward the entrance. "The young fellow down at the end. He's wearing a light blue shirt and a striped tie."

"Light blue shirt, striped tie," said Mrs. Cimino, just as though she were reciting items from one of Miss Rochester's menus.

"Are you sure you feel all right?"

"I feel fine," said Mrs. Cimino. She started to go up the stairs but stopped, puzzled. "Where's the marked currency?"

"That's our first step," said Mr. Desmond. He nodded encouragingly at her.

"I don't understand," said Mrs. Cimino. "I thought you were going to give me the marked currency to deposit."

"I am," said Mr. Desmond. He paused and looked at her searchingly. "Didn't I explain that to you in the coffee shop?"

"I don't think so," said Mrs. Cimino, trying to bring the conversation back in full detail.

"About the government regulations?"

"No," said Mrs. Cimino, feeling on firmer ground. "We didn't go into that."

"It must have been the timing element that distracted me," said Mr. Desmond, snapping his fingers in self-irritation. "But we're forbidden to use government money for the purpose of entrapment."

Mrs. Cimino nodded, still quite confused.

"And there's always a chance that one of our volunteers might decide to skip out the back door with that government money."

"I never thought of that," said Mrs. Cimino.

"Probably because you have a trusting nature," said Mr. Desmond. "But the government has to think of everything." He reached into his coat and pulled out an oversize brown envelope. "That's why we have to follow our standard procedure."

"What's that?" said Mrs. Cimino. She looked up toward the bank entrance, fearful that the suspect might come out the door on his way to lunch.

"First the volunteer withdraws a sum of money." He tapped the envelope as though the money was safely sealed up in it.

"How much?"

"It doesn't matter," said Mr. Desmond negligently. "The important thing is to make the withdrawal from one of the near windows."

"One of the near windows," said Mrs. Cimino. "So the embezzler won't become suspicious."

"Right!" said Mr. Desmond, obviously pleased with her quickness. "Then the bills are brought out to me." He took out a large pen. "And I make each one with our special ultraviolet code number." Hurriedly he returned both enevelope and pen to his inside pocket. "Then the volunteer goes back and redeposits the money with the suspected teller." He stopped suddenly and looked down at her again. "Are you sure you feel up to all this?"

"I feel wonderful," said Mrs. Cimino, underscoring her words with great emphasis. "But how much should I withdraw?"

"It doesn't matter," said Mr. Desmond. "Except for calculating the reward."

"Of course," said Mrs. Cimino, trying to look immensely altruistic. "I'd almost forgotten about the reward."

"Ten percent now," said Mr. Desmond, "And ten percent on conviction."

"That sounds fair." Mrs. Cimino did a quick sum. "How does four hundred dollars strike you?"

"Pretty high," said Mr. Desmond. "It would give you forty dollars right now and forty dollars later on." He sighed and shrugged. "But it's government money, not mine."

"How about seven hundred dollars?" said Mrs. Cimino, eyes glistening with excitement.

"Whatever you're comfortable with," said Mr. Desmond. As always, his manner was easygoing and gracious. "But get it in twenties." He took out a cigar and lit it. "They're a nuisance to mark, but they give us a better chance at apprehension and conviction."

"I think I have it straight," said Mrs. Cimino. Her voice crackled with sudden authority. "I make the withdrawal from a teller near us, I bring the bills out here, you mark them with your special pen, and I take them back for deposit at the window where the teller is wearing a blue shirt and striped tie."

"Perfect!" said Mr. Desmond. There was clear respect in his deep, mellow voice. "But are you sure you feel all right?" He raised his hat to a pair of elderly ladies coming down the steps toward them.

"I feel splendid," said Mrs. Cimino, not without impatience at his cloying concern.

"I think I'd better walk up the steps with you," said Mr. Desmond, taking a leisurely puff on his cigar. "I'd feel better if you could see me while you're in there."

He gave Mrs. Cimino his arm and escorted her up the steps. She went to one of the desks in the middle. There she opened up her purse, took out her check packet, and made out a check to cash for seven hundred dollars. She looked back outside. Her Mr. Desmond was clearly there: broad back, seersucker suit, planters hat, and even a visible ring of cigar smoke.

Reassured, she took her check to one of the near windows,

handing it to a young woman in a pink ruffled blouse.

"This must be a new account," said the pink ruffled blouse.

"Yes, it is," said Mrs. Cimino. Looking outside again, she could see Mr. Desmond—poised, unconcerned—tipping his planters hat to someone.

"I'll have to check this," said the pink ruffled blouse. She closed her cash drawer and walked over to where the files were.

Certain of Mr. Desmond's sentinel position, Mrs. Cimino stole a glance down toward the end of the counter. Sure enough, there were the blue shirt and striped tie, damning signs of overly expensive taste in a bank employee. She looked back at Mr. Desmond. He was now facing her, smiling slightly. She gave a faint, barely perceptible nod of recognition.

"Mrs. Cimino!" The voice came from in back of her.

She turned quickly round and found herself staring up into the solemn face of young Mr. Harris. The pink ruffled blouse was beside him, her check in hand.

"Is there anything wrong, Mr. Harris?" Mrs. Cimino resolved to put up a bold front.

"This is a very large check," said Mr. Harris, taking it from the pink blouse. The pink blouse left them and returned to her window.

"It's good, isn't it?" said Mrs. Cimino.

"Certainly it's good," said Mr. Harris. "But do you mind my asking you the purpose of such a large withdrawal—and so soon?"

"I don't see that it's any of your business, young man." Mrs. Cimino's eyes blazed with righteous anger.

"The safety of our customers is always a matter of concern," said Mr. Harris firmly. He gestured over toward his desk.

"Then you should do something about the purse snatchers in this city," snapped Mrs. Cimino.

"There are other kinds of criminals in St. Petersburg," said Mr. Harris. "And some of them are very smooth talkers who specialize in tricking elderly citizens out of their hard-earned money."

"What kind of tricks?" said Mrs. Cimino. She turned back toward the entrance: There was no trace of Mr. Desmond, not even a faint remnant of cigar smoke.

"All kinds," said Mr. Harris. "If you'll sit down for a moment, I'll tell you about some of them."

"Maybe I'd better," said Mrs. Cimino. Weakly, slowly, she allowed herself to be led over to Mr. Harris's desk. There she learned that Mr. Desmond would have substituted an envelope filled with paper for the envelope filled with twenty-dollar bills. It was this second envelope that she would have taken back in for redeposit. In the meantime Mr. Desmond would have vanished—along with her seven hundred dollars.

"But he's a fine gentleman," said Mrs. Cimino, not quite convinced. "Look at how he stepped in and rescued me from that purse-snatching hoodlum."

"An accomplice," said Mr. Harris. "His rescue was a necessary step in winning your confidence."

"And I thought it was just a chance encounter," said Mrs. Cimino, shaking her head at her own stupidity.

"It was certainly just chance that the attempt was made on the same day you opened your account," said Mr. Harris. "That's the only reason the teller brought it to my attention."

"I'm terribly grateful to you," said Mrs. Cimino. She rose and tried to smile engagingly. "This is my second rescue today, and I'm sure it's not going to get me into trouble like the first did."

"It won't," said Mr. Harris. His solemn young face lit up with a smile. "But I want you to promise me to be careful about making any substantial cash withdrawals." He got up and escorted her to the door.

"You've been very kind, and I promise to be more sensible," said Mrs. Cimino. She waved goodbye and started down the steps, indulging herself in the welcome support of the balustrade this time.

On her way back to the hotel, purse tightly clutched, she debated whether or not to tell Mrs. Hinckle and the others about her narrow escape. It was far from being a flattering story, or even an amusing one—despite any little joke she might make about there being foxes in among all the snow chickens. And yet it might be a good cautionary tale: helpful in warning her friends of new dangers outside the safe confines of the President Jefferson.

It was not until she reached the hotel door that a decision came finally, irrevocably, upon her: She would keep silent, keep the shame to herself. Even when all helpful allowances had been made, it was clear the incident depended upon its central character: a foolish, gullible, greedy old woman. To see that old woman in the harsh light of a morning mirror was bad enough; to put her on public display was unthinkable.

Quickening her step, she walked in and smiled brightly at Mr. Bales.

"Out on the town this morning?" Mr. Bales was quizzical, not without irony.

"Out in the big city, Mr. Bales."

"And how did you like it?"

"Fine," said Mrs. Cimino. "Everything went very well." She paused and looked back out the window, nodding her head as though to approve of the entire arrangement. "And I just love your sunshine."

"That's what keeps us going," laughed Mr. Bales.

"We can't ask for much more than that, can we?" smiled Mrs. Cimino. With her last ounce of pep she forced herself to walk briskly on to her small room.

Friday, December 3, 8:00 P.M.

Mrs. Cimino was more nervous than she appeared: It was her first important social engagement, and the terrain was unfamiliar. And it was very dark, too. Like most expensive watering places, the dining room of the Clearwater Beach Hotel favored subdued lighting and large vases dangerously positioned. It was good to have the white jacket of the maître d' up ahead, gleaming like a trainman's lantern as it guided them to an appropriate siding.

And it was certainly good to have Michael and Martha Ryan at her side. From Boca Raton, Michael had phoned her a few days before, explaining they would be passing through St. Petersburg and asking her to join them for dinner. Happily, she had splurged on a modish powder blue suit the week before, along with a pair of stylishly daring new shoes. Dear Mrs. Hinckle had helped her get dressed, insisting upon loaning her a necklace and brooch for the occasion. With a more flattering bra than the functional devices she had always favored, Mrs. Cimino felt reasonably elegant.

Once seated at a table with cushioned chairs, her confidence began to wane somewhat. As her eyes became accustomed to their new setting, she could see that most of the elderly women there were wearing long gowns. And there were jewels, lots of them, catching the light and bending it back like tropical fish drifting slowly in the warm currents of a safe aquarium. These were snow-birds of brilliant plumage: peacocks, certainly, and she but a spar-row in their midst. She tried to make her left hand as inconspi-cuous as possible, hoping that Martha would not notice the absence of her diamond.

Martha herself had worn a short dress, mildly brocaded, to-gether with a tactful string of pearls. A former librarian, she had never been much for dressing up, preferring instead to keep a well-ironed wintry look all the year round. Like Michael, she was in her early sixties, middle sized, with small features and clear gray eyes. Her gray hair was pulled straight back into a bun, almost defiantly, as though to assert her independence of the conventions of charm.

Michael was wearing a quiet, dark blue suit. He was a short man, bantamlike, not much taller than Martha, with a way of looking around appraisingly at his surroundings like a wary inves-tor on the verge of making a substantial commitment.

"An orchestra!" said Michael. He nodded down toward the end of the room. A small stage was there, dark for the moment. But the instruments on it were clearly in readiness.

"Not too loud, I hope," said Martha. She looked forbiddingly round the room as though to quell whisperers in her library stacks. "We're here to visit with Esther."

Mrs. Cimino straightened her glasses and examined her menu. It was a big one, bound up with gold lettering and printed on rich-textured paper. It reminded her of the grand hotels she and Frank had stayed at long ago, except that the waiters here were all on the young side: slim, tight-trousered, and with elaborately styled hair.

And the clientele was different: The couples were older, less flushed with immediate prosperity, more like apples left out on the windowsill a little too long. Their postures were less graceful: A fine-looking gentleman over toward her right had his chin tilted consciously up, stretching the wattles out so that the neck appeared smooth, unlined, but giving his eyes an unnecessarily haughty downward cast. The woman with him, slightly younger, seemed pleasant enough, but her smile was small, careful, so that the upper lip and cheeks would not run risks of premature wrinkledom.

Wrinkles! An enemy to be kept at bay, even at the cost of surgical pain. The creams, the exercises, the hair pulled back and back to stretch the loosening skin tight over the bones beneath. And as a last resort the actual sewing and stitching, brilliant in its execution, with only a faint tilt to the eyes left behind as evidence. It gave the eyes an Oriental look, filling the dining room with candidates for the leading role in the life story of Anna May Wong or Madame Chiang Kai-shek.

Not all the dragon ladies were there with escorts of the same age. Up by the dance floor Mrs. Cimino could see a richly bejeweled woman in a long white gown. Beside her were two young men in their early thirties: One was slender, blond, very handsome in a perfectly fitting Harris tweed; the other was dark, a little on the chubby side, but very personable and animated in his conversation. All three of them were clearly having a splendid time.

"Quite a place," said Michael, who had also taken time out to look around after giving their order to a slim, slightly pouting young man in a form-fitting costume.

"Do these people come down here for the whole season?" Mrs. Cimino's thrifty spirit found such sustained expense hard to comprehend.

"Most of them do," said Michael. "The weather's lovely, and the boating is a major attraction, along with fishing and golf."

"It must be very pleasant for them," said Mrs. Cimino. Over in a far corner she had caught sight of another elderly lady—wearing a tiara—courted by a younger male entourage. "Especially when the children and grandchildren come down to visit."

"It's pleasant for some," said Michael, following her gaze with a faint smile. "But most of them hate it."

"Michael has a lot of sympathy for retired well-to-do people," said Martha, not without a touch of irony.

"I can't see why," said Mrs. Cimino. "They all seem healthy enough, and they certainly don't have any money worries."

She smiled approvingly at the table next to them, offering it as persuasive evidence. It was occupied by two elderly couples. One of the women was wearing a dark blue gown with short matching jacket. The other—also in her early seventies—was tastefully impressive in a dark wine-colored evening dress set off by an expensive string of pearls. And the men were striking, too. Well-barbered, well-mannered, tuxedoed: They had the look of prosperous

252

retired executives enjoying a well-deserved reward for hard work and shrewd management. As a group, the four of them could have been painted by Holbein in the rich, full textures reserved for clients of obvious social consequence.

"Exactly," said Michael, again following her gaze. "No worries, and no action." He nodded to her as though his point were self-evident. "It drives them crazy."

"Do you mean they're so used to working that they can't sit back and take it easy?" There was sympathy in Mrs. Cimino's voice, together with an affectionate remembrance of Miss Schmidt.

"It's not the lack of work," said Michael. "You can get that out of a garden."

"And a few callouses wouldn't do him any harm," interjected Martha. She nodded firmly at Mrs. Cimino, as though to enlist her support of the Minnesota ethic.

"It's power," said Michael. He smiled sympathetically at their neighbors, who had just ordered a second round of drinks. "When you're used to cracking the whip, it's no fun to get out of the driver's seat and turn the reins over to someone else." He nodded at the tuxedoed gentleman nearest them. "There's a man who probably floated on a sea of flattery for twenty years. And now he can't even fire anybody—heartbreaking!"

"Is he serious?" said Mrs. Cimino, looking over at Martha.

"I'm always serious," said Michael, pleased with his flight of fancy. He beckoned them toward him as though about to reveal a bit of scandal. "Last year I sent a Christmas card to a former client who had just retired as vice-president in charge of purchasing for a large department store chain. And I added a brief note, wishing him well."

"That was very kind of you," said Mrs. Cimino, her thoughts skidding over to a consideration of how to manage Christmas and Christmas presents on her modest budget.

"It was apparently an act of total benevolence," said Michael, sitting back expansively. "Do you know that I got back a two-page letter thanking me?"

"It was certainly nice of him to be so appreciative," said Mrs. Cimino. "But I don't see where the benevolence comes in." Again she looked over at Martha. Martha shrugged and looked skyward. It was clear she had endured the story many times.

"But Esther," said Michael, "here was a man who probably

got over five hundred Christmas cards as long as he had the power to make purchasing decisions. And expensive gifts, too!" He smiled like a magician on the verge of completing his trick. "The moment he retires, steps down, all those cards disappear."

"Except from a clever Irish attorney who wants to handle his probate work," added Martha, nodding at Mrs. Cimino to signal her deeper understanding of the matter.

"My impulse was genuine," said Michael blandly. "If I profit from it, so much the better."

As their food arrived, served poutingly but gracefully by the slim young man, Mrs. Cimino pondered the matter. She took another look at the lady in the dark blue gown and at the lady in the wine-colored evening dress. Two drinks behind them, they were sipping wine and poking quietly at their food. There was an air of restraint, of refinement, to the group: a marked contrast to some of the tables with young men at them, where the talk was beginning to grow vivaciously audible. And the orchestra was beginning to set up their gear. She let the noise wash the topic away for a while.

Midway through dessert there was a loud squeal from the blond young man over at the elderly bejeweled woman's table. His chubby, dark fellow courtier had taken up one of the bejeweled woman's bracelets. Using it as a monocle, he was peering aristocratically around the room.

"Dreadful!" said Mrs. Cimino. "I certainly wouldn't want my grandchildren carrying on like that."

"If I know this place," said Michael. "Those are no grandchildren."

"We had no business coming here," sniffed Martha.

Mrs. Cimino examined the courtiers around the room more closely. It was clear that her original impression needed rethinking: The young men, on second thought, did not really qualify as dutiful relatives taking an aged grandmother or aunt out to dinner. She nodded toward the bejeweled woman.

"Would you say those young men over there are . . . peculiar?" Is was the best euphemism she could think of.

"Peculiar!" Michael's blue eyes sparkled. "What's so peculiar about a simple matter of statistics?"

"Statistics?" Mrs. Cimino looked helplessly over at Martha

again. All she got was another shrug and another patient look skyward.

"It's very simple," said Michael. "Hubby leaves wifey well-fixed, so wifey can afford to treat her young friends to expensive dinners and nice presents." He smiled around the room expansively. "Multiply this by five million and you have the whole economy."

"Well, you don't have me," said Mrs. Cimino. Her tone was stoutly dissenting.

"Maybe not—or maybe not yet," smiled Michael. "It all depends upon whether you get your money back or not."

Mrs. Cimino gasped at the suggestion that she might find herself queening it over a group of lavender young men.

"It's true, Esther," he grinned. "Most of the country is owned by well-to-do elderly ladies, each with a retinue of interior decorators, hair stylists, business advisors, and smooth-talking company."

"And the lawyers," interjected Martha. "You mustn't forget the lawyers." She smiled at him in affectionate challenge.

"The lawyers don't count," said Michael. "They're too argumentative."

"He has a point," said Martha. She looked over at Mrs. Cimino as though to enlist her sympathy.

Mrs. Cimino nodded, not so much out of sympathy as out of embarrassed recollection: Mr. Desmond had been a smooth talker, and she had lapped it up like an old tabby going after thick cream. There had been flattery, attention—much more than she had ever had at Elm Street or at St. Hild's. At a lower price, it would have been attractive.

The orchestra began to play. There were five of them: all slim, graceful young men dressed in tight-fitting black trousers and white mess jackets. They were not very good: The pianist was too flowery and the drummer too unsteady. But they all smiled refulgently, and they kept their tempos up high enough to infuse energy into the gathering. Society tempos, Frank had called them: businessman's bounce, a sort of two-beat perpetual motion that reduced all melodies to one monotonous common denominator.

The bejeweled lady was one of the first to take the floor, gliding sedately in her long white gown while her dark, chubby escort executed quivering feats of footwork around her like an ecstatic moth flitting round a proud stately flame. When his blond fellow courtier relieved him, the chubby young man made his way up to the bandstand. There he remained, watching the dancers and shouting melodious treble cries of encouragement. Savoring the music even more, he began to sway in rhythm, extending his arms and moving his head like a huge misshapen flamingo about to take flight.

"It's worse than Boca Raton," said Martha.

"I'm surprised the management doesn't stop it," said Mrs. Cimino. She looked toward the maître d's station, half expecting to see him hurry up, flanked by burly white-coated folk from the kitchen.

"Not with a steady customer like that," said Michael. "I bet she's in here two or three times a week."

"It's dreadful for a woman her age to carry on like that," said Mrs. Cimino. Disbelieving, she had watched the bejeweled woman take up the maracas and shake them delightedly while her two courtiers wiggled sensuously to "Begin the Beguine."

"Not envious, are you?" Michael's blue eyes were dancing with pleasure, fueled slightly by Martha's clear disapproval.

"I should say not," said Mrs. Cimino, still watching the display, to which was added the spectacle of the elderly lady with the tiara, slightly askew now. Despite the Latin rhythm, she had made up her mind to do the Charleston, which she performed to the enthusiastic applause of her own retinue. Not to be outdone, the bejeweled woman began to shake her flabby flesh, uncorseted, along with the maracas.

"Good!" said Michael. His tone was avuncular, mockingly approving. "Then the bank doesn't have anything to worry about."

"What's the bank have to do with all this?" Mrs. Cimino looked around the room, her gaze resting affectionately on their four neighbors. Dinner over, they were quietly drinking brandies.

"As long as you're happy, there's no reason for you to go into court and cause trouble." Michael smiled at her, as though to goad her into becoming another litigious Mr. Stewart.

"But what's so bad about having a trustee?" said Martha. "You've set up plenty of them in your day."

"There's nothing bad about it," said Michael. "From the family's point of view, it makes sense, good sense." He smiled over at

256

Mrs. Cimino, eyes intent upon her. "But from Esther's point of view, it's not good at all."

"You're a troublemaker," said Martha, turning away in mock disgust.

"Just a minute," said Mrs. Cimino. "What's not good about it?"

"It's your money," said Michael. "Why shouldn't you do what you want with it?" He gestured round the room as though to indicate that any excess was permissible.

"I'm not so sure I trust my own judgment anymore," said Mrs. Cimino. Her manner was diffident, as though Judge Schultz's lecture was still in her ears.

"Nonsense!" said Michael firmly. "You don't really believe that, and neither do most of my clients—after they've thought about it for a while."

"That's when you stop talking long enough to let them think," chimed in Martha. She patted his hand to take the sting out of her words.

Intent upon his point, Michael waved her aside and leaned forward. He smiled knowingly at Mrs. Cimino.

"Every now and then," he said, "an elderly widow comes into the office with a jim-dandy idea her children have thought up. And that is to start signing assets over to these dear children."

"Why shouldn't she do that?" said Mrs. Cimino. "It's a good way of avoiding taxes."

"It's also a good way of losing control, of losing power," said Michael. "Do you know how long it takes me to talk a client out of an idea like that?"

Mrs. Cimino shook her head. It was an idea, eloquently supported, that Harold had often put forth. She had always felt guilty in turning it aside.

"Fifteen minutes," said Michael, sitting back magicianlike again. "All it takes is fifteen minutes." He gestured expansively. "Then they walk out of there, head held high, determined to hold on to what they have as long as they can."

"According to Philip, I'm stuck with the trustee business," said Mrs. Cimino. "I don't think that can be changed."

"You never know," said Michael. "But I'd start pushing them a little."

"How?" said Mrs. Cimino. "I can't go back to court again."

"You don't have to," said Michael. "Start by asking for more money." He chuckled at the thought. "That always makes them nervous."

"That's an idea," said Mrs. Cimino, looking over at Martha for support. "I could do with a little more."

"And I'd also get Karen or someone to keep an eye on what's happening at your music store," said Michael. "You and Frank put a lot of work into that business, and there's no reason for them to play games with it."

"What kind of games?" said Mrs. Cimino suspiciously.

"Don't ask me," said Michael, suddenly pious. "Bankers make up their own games." He looked over at Martha and smiled wickedly. "Look at what they've done to the interest rate."

"Madness!" said Martha, starting to get ready for departure. "This man has been reading too many detective stories."

"It's been lovely, as far as the evening goes," said Mrs. Cimino, beaming at the two of them taking Martha's hand. "You're such good company."

"You're a good audience," said Michael.

"And he needs that," said Martha, smiling with patient understanding.

"That's why I'm going to practice law a little more," said Michael thoughtfully. "Philip will still handle nearly all of the Minneapolis work, but I want to do some of the estate planning and try a case here and there."

"You were always good at it," said Mrs. Cimino.

"I got by," said Michael, grinning mischievously. "And it's a good chance to bore people and make them pay you at the same time." He rose, coming round to pull her chair out for her.

They headed for the door. Martha and Mrs. Cimino stood there while Michael got their wraps. While they were waiting Mrs. Cimino looked back for a moment at their somnolent, brandy-drinking neighbors. With distress she noted that the lady in the wine-colored evening dress had now passed out completely: Both of the tuxedoed gentlemen were slowly coming over to her aid. Quietly, almost as a matter of course, they dragged their limp object of concern out a side door, her wine-colored evening dress trailing them like a magnificent coronation train.

Under the circumstances it was really a very dignified exit, much more graceful than an ambulance.

Her own exit from the Ryans' Cadillac was reasonably graceful: She said goodbye quickly, without lamentation, and went directly into the hotel. Miss Featherstone, the night supervisor, was on duty at the desk. There Mrs. Cimino signed in her arrival time, as was the custom for guests at the President Jefferson.

Wednesday, December 8, 10:45 A.M.

"We need the space," said Brian. He smiled over at his father-in-law as though the proposition were self-evident.

Mr. Leach looked at the toy store with distress. It was a nice little store, run by the wives of two local pediatricians as a self-supporting hobby. Bolstered by its indirect professional authority, he had bought his new grandson, now two months old, a clinically endorsed busy board there. To invade it seemed a cruel assault upon a generation of physicists and astronauts presently cooing happily in their cribs.

One of the frau-doctors opened the door and came out for a moment. Seeing Brian, she went immediately back in, slamming the door with modest force. Brian shrugged, implicitly advancing another self-evident proposition regarding the curious habits of toy-store proprietors.

"Cold!" said Mr. Leach. He blew on his hands and put them back in the pockets of his black coat. He looked over at the beauty salon on the far end of the building. He looked at the toy store again. He looked at Cimino Music, solidly occupying the end nearest him.

It was not a small store: almost fifty feet of frontage and plenty of window space. The window space was filled with amplifiers now—giant ones—flanked by smaller gadgetry. Moog, Farfisa, Fender-Rhodes, Altec-Lansing, Ampeg: The names were oddly built, almost otherworldly, far removed from the productions of Mr. Conn, Mr. Selmer, and Mr. Gibson. And the objects themselves were big black things, ominous. It was hard to imagine them singing out songs about sunshine and the need for kindness to whales.

They went inside. The floor space was also filled: with amplifiers, keyboards, and rows of guitars hanging from the ceiling like gourds left out to dry. And so was the back of the store, where once Simon Montford had done his repair work and where the teachers had forced young hands into the shaping of bar chords and paradiddles. Here the amplifiers were smaller, some of them scratched and frayed: These had been taken as trade-ins or on consignment, mutely waiting until a likely prospect should wander by.

"You can see we've really built up the stock," said Brian proudly. From the back he gestured up toward his invasion force. "We must have almost a hundred and fifty thousand dollars worth of name equipment here." He sighed happily. "I'm figuring that on the basis of list price."

Mr. Leach nodded. A figure like that would add materially to the impressiveness of his report to Judge Schultz.

"It's a simple thing to knock out the partition," said Brian. He rapped three times on the toy store side to underscore his point. "And then we'd be able to go after the rest of the major franchises."

"They have a lease," said Mr. Leach. "You wouldn't be able to do anything until summer."

"No problem," grinned Brian, looking for all the world like a friendly pirate in his long mustache. "They've been bugging us about the sound for the last three months." He looked at the wall as though it were nothing more than a curtain to be lifted. "If we goose it up a little more, they'll be glad to split."

"To vacate," said Mr. Leach, correcting his son-in-law automatically. He had tried to introduce sound business terminology into Brian's diction, replacing terms like "up front" and "bottom line" with more chaste accounting-based neutralisms.

"How about it?" said Brian as they walked back to the front of the store.

"I don't know," said Mr. Leach. He looked at his watch. He looked at his Oldsmobile parked out in front. "I'm going to have to think it over." He looked at Brian, trying to smile encouragingly. "It's not that I don't believe in you, but I have to make sure our cash-flow position is protected."

"Cash flow." Brian mouthed the phrase as though it were an old friend. "Cash flow is the name of the game, isn't it . . . Grandpa?" He smiled brightly, blue eyes atwinkle, and walked his father-in-law out to the Oldsmobile.

Mr. Leach drove off, still thinking about cash flow, about the various tributaries that found their way down into the net-income figure for Mrs. Cimino's estate. The stocks were doing well enough, and the proceeds from the house showed a respectable yield, even though they had been placed on demand deposit with Minneapolis Southern. And there was the Social Security, together with the rental income from the other occupants of the building. Just as he had projected, there was more than enough to carry Brian and the store.

But the rents were in danger of drying up: The chiropractor upstairs had moved out in September, replaced by a coin dealer in November at a slightly smaller figure. The loss of the frau-doctors would be serious, even if set off with a short-term loan. Judge Schultz might shake his head at that: not violently, but enough to indicate his displeasure with an irregularity introduced into an otherwise smoothly running arrangement.

Mr. Leach's steep, retreating hillside of a forehead was furrowed as he carefully pulled into the parking lot of Minneapolis Southern Bank. But his spirits revived at the sight of familiar surroundings: the marble floors, the discreetly clothed officers, the ebb and flow of humble traffic. With an approving nod he walked over to his small office in the trust department. The morning's mail was laid out neatly on his desk.

The third letter brought the furrows back.

St. Petersburg, Florida
December 6, 1976

Dear Mr. Leach:

I am glad to see that both Sun Oil and ITT have increased their quarterly dividend. With this additional income, I am sure you will have no difficulty in *increasing* my monthly allowance.

I have had to buy new clothes down here—almost a complete wardrobe, since nearly all my things were sold this summer, *through no fault of my own.* (I don't blame you for this, but it *has* created a problem.)

Also, with Christmas coming up, I want to send each of the grandchildren a proper gift.

261

Finally, I want to help my granddaughter, Karen, with her education. She has been very good to me, and I think some help would give her a better start in life.

The stipend increase can wait until January. But I would like an extra *thousand dollars now* (two hundred dollars apiece for the five grandchildren—Kevin, Patrick, Ann, Gretchen, and Karen). For Karen, I would like *two thousand dollars,* but there's no rush about that. (You can go into the rental income for it.)

Please give this matter your prompt attention.

Yours truly,
Esther Cimino

Mr. Leach tried to rub the furrows away with his pudgy left hand. His small eyes grew even smaller as he squinted at the sudden harassment thrust upon him. If the legal department had listened to him, there would have been no harassment: The old woman would have been safely immured at St. Hild's. But Mr. Emory—lawyer-like—had recommended letting the hearing go through without opposition, fearing total loss of the trust in the event of a full-scale battle.

He picked up the phone, called the legal department, and asked the secretary to have Mr. Emory stop by his office sometime before lunch.

He read the letter through again: To his feelings of harassment were now joined feelings of strong moral disapproval. The old woman's desire to deck herself out with silks and satins was simply disgraceful. And the need to purchase affection through extravagant gifts was downright pitiful! But most upsetting was the blatant tone of ingratitude: Rather than appreciating his role in freeing her from responsibility and worry, she clearly resented everything that had been done with her immediate and long-term welfare in mind.

It was not the first time that his selfless efforts had been whined at. Nor was this the only area in which old people posed a problem. Year after year they insisted on hanging on. Reluctant to let go, they clogged the waterways of progress like huge gray, unsightly weeds, slowing the movement of able younger folk. Even in the bank there were senior officers still ensconced in positions of power and authority. Far better to have an oubliette built in below those large mahogany desks, opening up at the proper time and letting the occupant slide down a greased runway to far-distant sunny exile in Arizona.

And they could be difficult. Aged airline pilots, supported by hungry legal talent, fought to keep their quavering hands on the controls. Cranky, irascible academic people, secure in their burrows of tenure, snarled viciously at reasonable suggestions that they turn over their seminars to able young scholars. In that climate of resistance it was best to proceed carefully, supported by good advice wherever possible.

When Mr. Emory came in, Mr. Leach grimaced and pushed Mrs. Cimino's letter across the desk toward him.

"Do we have a legal problem here?" he said. He sat back and waited for Mr. Emory to render judgment.

Mr. Emory read the letter slowly, impassively, in the special way lawyers have of searching out tricky subordinate clauses and pronouns of uncertain reference. He was a fortyish man, tall, frecklefaced, with a rawboned farmer look to him that was still the despair of his wife, who had taken great care to clothe him in Brooks Brothers suits. But he was a first-rate attorney. And he loved legal conflict: It was the only time his right heel ceased tapping.

"She's mad about something," said Mr. Emory. He put the letter down and smiled at Mr. Leach.

"Mad?" said Mr. Leach. "I'd say she was greedy."

"No," said Mr. Emory. "I'd say she was mad."

"About what?" said Mr. Leach.

Mr. Emory shrugged, as though a cow had gotten lost when someone else was supposed to be looking after the pasture. He picked up the letter again.

"Who knows," he said finally. "Maybe some of her new friends have more to play with than she does."

"That's not our fault," said Mr. Leach.

"But she's still mad," said Mr. Emory. His tone was gentle.

"What do you advise?" said Mr. Leach. His manner was dignified, as though to return the conference to a more proper fiduciary plane.

"Be nice," said Mr. Emory. "Send her some money."

"But Ryan agreed to the present arrangement," said Mr. Leach. He took off his glasses and looked at Mr. Emory with a long-suffering, injured countenance.

"I know that," said Mr. Emory. "But she'll feel better if you send her some money." He nodded philosophically, and his heel tapping slowed for a moment. "People always like to get money."

"We don't have to if we don't want to," said Mr. Leach, his feeling of unjust injury overpowering his dignified diction temporarily.

"Send her a fourth of what she's asking for," said Mr. Emory, scrutinizing the letter again. "That ought to cool her down for a while." He put the letter down and looked at Mr. Leach. "And I'll tell you why."

Mr. Leach sat back, relieved that a more coherent legal opinion was about to sail across the desk toward him.

"These things are never final," said Mr. Emory, his heel slowing to a mild pavane. "She could petition the court for an increase, she could write the judge a letter, her family might get into it." His gray-green eyes looked off toward the window as though to summon up a swarm of minor irritations.

"But Judge Schultz would never dissolve a trust like this," said Mr. Leach. "It's all set up, running beautifully."

"I didn't say he would dissolve the trust," said Mr. Emory. "But he doesn't like trouble, and he doesn't like to appoint trustees who get into trouble." His freckles bunched up to let a smile appear. "How many of these things do we get from him a year?"

"From Judge Schultz?" Mr. Leach's furrows came back for a moment. "Between thirty and forty."

"That's more than our share," said Mr. Emory. "Why not try to keep it that way?"

"I'll do it," sighed Mr. Leach. He looked at Mr. Emory and tried to smile, like a small boy looking at a dentist who has just discovered an obscure cavity.

"Good," said Mr. Emory. His heel began to race as a signal for departure. "Send her some money." He got up, straightening his newly wrinkled Brooks Brothers suit. "Write her a nice letter."

Mr. Leach watched Mr. Emory's tall, rawboned frame go out the door. He scowled. He scowled down at Mrs. Cimino's letter. He tried to smile, to summon up thoughts of niceness, of kindly import. They did not come, not until he pictured his grandson, Edward. Smiling at that dear chubby face, he tried to hold the feeling with him as he drafted a nice letter to the source of his distress.

Dear Mrs. Cimino:

In response to your letter of December 6, I am very happy indeed to report that your principal shows strong growth and promises an adequate yield in the future. In terms of our responsibility to the court, your affairs are on a sound basis. I am sure this knowledge will be of great comfort to you down in the Sunshine State of Florida.

I am sending you a check for two hundred and fifty dollars to use for Christmas presents. I wish it could be more, but we've had a number of high costs in getting the trust set up. I seriously question the wisdom of singling Karen out for special help in her education. My own feeling is that Karen should be encouraged to work her way through school, since I have always believed that young people do better when forced to rely on their own resources. In Karen's case, I am sure that her character will be greatly strengthened by the experience.

It makes me very, very happy to tell you that I feel justified in raising your stipend to twelve hundred dollars a month. I am sure you will want to save some of this.

Let me close by wishing you the best of luck down there in St. Petersburg. Our own winter is quite bad this year, and there have been many accidents. I myself dented a front fender as the result of a skid last week.

Sincerely,
Edward Leach
Assistant Trust Officer
Minneapolis Southern Bank

It was a nice letter. Unusually nice, particularly the closing personal touch. Even though grandson Edward's face had disappeared midway through, the feeling had sustained him, giving the whole thing a warm, positive tone.

He gave the draft to his secretary and started to go through the rest of his correspondence. Most of it was routine, with the exception of a letter from Aetna Insurance announcing an increase in the rate for Cimino Music. The increase had been called for because of the recent theft of ten large amplifiers.

The furrows came back to Mr. Leach's forehead.

He rubbed them quickly away. But he made up his mind to tell Brian—tactfully—that the locks on the doors should be changed.

Friday, December 24, 8:00 P.M.

"Very nice," said Mrs. Hinckle, examining Mrs. Cimino's Christmas party attire. "For something like this, a little color never hurts."

"Not too flashy, is it?" Mrs. Cimino took a few steps in her new yellow dress. She had bought it, along with shoes and earrings, on the basis of her small bonanza from Mr. Leach.

"Not for a party," said Mrs. Hinckle. Although still committed to dark blue silk, she had chosen to lighten it with a handsomely beaded gray sweater.

From the dining room they could hear the hum of voices and the exploratory sounds of a saxophone tuning up. An annual Christmas party was a tradition at the President Jefferson, begun under the Tollivers and now sustained by the expert attentions of Mr. and Mrs. Bales. Mrs. Bales, originally from South Carolina, still retained the ability to invest modest circumstances with charm.

"Here I am!" said Mrs. Gatlin, coming breathlessly up.

The other two elderly ladies courteously cooed with high admiration: Mrs. Gatlin, small and plump, was wearing a pleated white skirt and navy blue jacket. Her hair, more deeply tinted than usual, was swept back daringly to reveal a pair of little ears from which sparkling diamonds dangled. Giggling, she spun around before them, so that the skirt swirled out like a partially opened parasol.

"Adorable!" exclaimed Mrs. Cimino.

"Very nice!" said Mrs. Hinckle, always more restrained in her enthusiasms.

Supporting one another with mutual praise, the three ladies walked into the dining room. At the doorway they paused, taking in the spectacle for a moment.

Most of the rugs had been taken up, so that the old oak parquet floor gleamed out with much of its original elegance. Around the dancing space thus cleared were positioned tables for the celebrants, and these were set with good white linen. Directly across from them was a long buffet, with crystal punch bowls at either end. In the middle, behind the buffet, was Mrs. Bales: Wearing a long black skirt and white blouse, she beamed invitation to partake of small refreshments preliminary to those scheduled for later on.

266

Over in the corner to their right was the orchestra: piano, drums, and saxophone. They were playing a lively fox trot, "Hello, Dolly," and had already seduced a number of guests into circling the floor. Since the balance between ladies and gentlemen was uneven, a few ladies had already coupled themselves together, much on the order of freshman high school girls. And the two henna-haired ladies, even more dauntless, were dancing alone: one in an exotic turban, beneath which her red ringlets peeped out like small flames about to ignite a larger conflagration. Her friend, heavily rouged, affected a long boa, executing bizarre movements therewith on the order of Isadora Duncan and Martha Graham. From time to time their paths would cross, generally right in front of the orchestra, and they would bow together toward the source of their pleasure.

"Lovely!" said Mrs. Gatlin. She executed a solo spin of her own and smiled archly at her companions.

"I think we should find a table," said Mrs. Hinckle, taking immediate charge and leading Mrs. Gatlin and Mrs. Cimino over to a table in the far left corner. "This way we'll have a good view of the Christmas tree when they call out the gifts."

Mrs. Cimino, her gaze drawn toward the dancers, had not paid much attention to the Christmas tree. Once seated, she inspected it with approval: It was large, whitely flocked, and decorated with red and green lights that artfully echoed the streamers crisscrossing the room up above them. Beneath the tree were packages, gaily wrapped, one for each guest.

She had drawn Mr. Sanderson, a retired stockbroker from Milwaukee. Seated over by the orchestra with Mrs. Sanderson, resplendent in Spanish lace shawl and comb, he had decked out his portly frame in red trousers and plaid jacket, much like British regimentals donned to bedazzle the colonials. Not sure of what to buy him, she had finally settled on a small pocket calculator: It seemed an appropriate item for a gentleman who found pleasure in watching televised market transactions.

But Mr. Sanderson's conversation was interesting: he shook his head over the misfortunes of ITT and sagely commented on the soundness of Dow Chemical. She had enjoyed discussing her own modest holdings with him, though the enjoyment had been tainted by the knowledge that those holdings were now firmly under the control of the stingy Mr. Leach. Following Michael's prodding, she had written to Karen, asking her to keep an eye on how the music store was doing. And she had written to Philip: a careful letter, in which she expressed a desire to see her legal Bastille stormed and leveled whenever sufficient strength could be assembled.

"That band is yummy!" said Mrs. Gatlin, bouncing her plumpness up and down in her chair. "I hope they play a Paul Jones."

"They have good rhythm," said Mrs. Hinckle. "And they're not too loud."

"For three pieces, they do very well," said Mrs. Cimino, looking down at the three musicians at the other end of the room. "It always helps to have a tenor saxophone."

"Is that what that is?" said Mrs. Gatlin, smiling over at Mr. Bales, whose white Navy commander's uniform gave him the look of a dignified refugee from a musical comedy.

"It's certainly better than a trumpet," said Mrs. Hinckle approvingly. "Those things have a terrible screech to them sometimes."

"It's a tenor saxophone," said Mrs. Cimino. "And he's very good." She nodded pleasurably as the instrument cajoled its way through "Stairway to the Stars."

Though loyal to her husband's guitar, she had always liked the sound of a tenor saxophone. It was a strong, full, manly voice: Its basic range was that of the singing baritone, melodic in its movement yet capable of rapid soarings and witty effects. Sometimes sentimental, with vibrato widened, it generally seemed to smile at its own music, as though the popular idiom were there as an old friend—to be treated with affection, yet never too seriously. By itself it could fill a room. With two supporting musicians, it could fill an evening with rich variety. Mrs. Cimino began to tap her foot and hum quietly.

"The fleet's in!" giggled Mrs. Gatlin as Mr. Bales came up, ramrod-straight and splendidly ribboned.

"Which will it be, ladies?" Mr. Bales gestured over toward the buffet. "The near one or the far one?"

"Is there any difference?" said Mrs. Gatlin. She fluttered her big blue eyes in an attempt to make the question as personal as possible.

"There's a difference," said Mr. Bales. He bent over and whispered softly. "The punch on the far end has something in it."

268

"Do you mean it's . . . strong?" giggled Mrs. Gatlin.

"I mean it's . . . popular," smiled Mr. Bales, ruddy face a little more aglow than usual.

"And so are you," said Mrs. Gatlin, her giggles controlled enough to allow another fluttering of her big blue eyes. "There's something about a uniform, you know."

"It fits you very well," said Mrs. Hinckle. "Do you get much chance to wear it?"

"I belong to one of the Coast Guard auxiliary squadrons," said Mr. Bales. "And we have formal meetings several times a year." He smiled down at Mrs. Gatlin. "Just enough to keep me out of mischief."

"Isn't he terrible!" squealed Mrs. Gatlin, looking at her companions for immediate confirmation.

"He's very much in demand, I'm sure." Mrs. Hinckle smiled reprovingly at Mrs. Gatlin, reminding her that Mr. Bales would have to be shared by all the unattached guests.

"I'm very much in charge of seeing that everyone gets started," said Mr. Bales, gesturing up toward the buffet.

In great good humor, he led the three ladies up to the buffet, urging the alcoholic punch on them with tactful restraint. It was Mrs. Gatlin who made the decision for them, twinkling up ahead and pronouncing the contents innocuous. After making sure that they were safely back at their table, he strode off masterfully, intent on directing his flotilla of elderly craft into a wholesome social maneuver.

"All set, everyone?" Mr. Bales shouted from the bandstand down at them in his best hailing voice. "Mrs. Bales and I are going to start off our first mixer." He paused dramatically. "A snowball dance!"

The tenor saxophone took the pick-up notes into "A Pretty Girl is Like a Melody," and Mr. Bales led Mrs. Bales gracefully around the floor for a half chorus. Then the music stopped. They separated, each choosing a partner from the group. The music began again, and then stopped again, so that the four dancers could each select new partners from those seated. In a short while the floor was filled with people, some bobbing up and down, some taking long swooping steps in classic ballroom style.

Mrs. Cimino had ended up with Mr. Sanderson, a conservative

bobber-up-and-downer. Very much out of practice, she was pleased to see that her basic box step still did the job. When the snowball finally melted away into silence, she sat down, flushed and lively. It was with little difficulty that Mrs. Gatlin persuaded her to take a second cup of punch from the far end of the buffet, risking whatever strange effects might lie in its mysterious mixture of grenadines and rums.

Back at the table, she felt quietly animated, tapping her feet and feeling half-forgotten dance steps march themselves into her awareness. And she began to listen more closely to the music, almost as though it were a friendly voice at her table, chiming in along with Mrs. Gatlin's giggles and Mrs. Hinckle's decorous comments. The melodies were familiar, most of them, and they urged their lyrics into her mind together with the recollection of Tiffany-lit ballrooms and larger orchestras.

"What's that song they're playing now?" said Mrs. Hinckle, never one to allow unnecessary uncertainty to prevail.

"It's 'Poor Butterfly,' " said Mrs. Cimino with pleasure. "I'm surprised they know it."

"If it's an old one, they should know it," said Mrs. Hinckle. She nodded toward the bandstand. "There's no generation gap down there."

Mrs. Cimino stopped her internal wanderings long enough to adjust her glasses and take a good look at their three-piece orchestra. Despite the energy and endurance of their playing, they were all reasonably elderly gentlemen.

The drummer was the youngest, in his early sixties, but with a full head of wavy gray hair. Like many drummers, he affected an absent smile and elaborate twirlings of his sticks and brushes. But he was competent: He stopped at the same time his companions did—always a sign of consummate musicality in a drummer, according to Frank.

The piano player was the leader: heavy, about sixty-five, he was quite bald and jowled. He smiled incessantly, punctuating his more ambitious moments with skyward glances of adoring gratitude to a private muse overhead. A big, flashy ring on his right hand bore witness to his years of homage to Eddy Duchin, Carmen Cavallero, and other busy-fingered masters. But his playing this evening was tasteful, rhythmic, offering an effective background for the melody instrument of their trio.

270

The tenor saxophonist was the oldest: late sixties or early seventies. A short man with thinning gray hair and slightly protruding ears, he had made a necessary concession to his age by propping himself up on a high drummers stool, thus avoiding the lusterless effect of sitting down to play, while at the same time avoiding the exhausting consequences of standing straight up for three hours.

"I suppose there's a tune there somewhere," said Mrs. Gatlin, giggling away. "But I can't tell where it is."

"He's improvising," said Mrs. Cimino, still watching the instrument, held out with the bell slightly tilted, as a flood of runs and arpeggios poured out.

"Improvising!" said Mrs. Hinckle. "Doesn't the man know what he's doing?"

"He's just trying to make it more interesting," smiled Mrs. Cimino.

"He's cute," announced Mrs. Gatlin. "But I wish I knew what he was playing."

"I think it's 'Body and Soul,' " said Mrs. Cimino. She gave one of her embarrassed little laughs. "But I'm really not sure."

"I suppose you can't expect too much from local fellows," said Mrs. Hinckle, not without a touch of patronage. She had always been a loyal supporter of Hal Kemp and Guy Lombardo, and had once been heard characterizing the great Lawrence Welk as a cheaply derivative newcomer.

"I wouldn't be surprised if they turned out to be professional," said Mrs. Cimino. "That saxophone player might have played with some big bands in his day."

There was a familiar look to the saxophone player, though it was hard to imagine his appearance with a full head of dark, curly hair masking those protruding ears. In her days on the road with Frank, there had been many musicians casually met.

Many musicians, many orchestras, many ballrooms, hotels, and theaters: back when the great names of Paul Whiteman, Isham Jones, Coon-Saunders, and Orville Knapp had glittered and beckoned. By train at first, later by chartered bus, these and others had traversed the land, pulling into town like small circuses, each equipped with advance men, wardrobe attendants, band boys, and even rehearsal pianists.

And as with circuses, the spectacle was central, almost as important as the music itself. Elaborate lighting, ornately scrolled music stands, bold uniforms glistening with gold braid and sequins: Like a massed bank of flowers, these formed a setting in which a central jewel—the orchestra leader himself—commanded awestruck reverence and admiration. There he would be: sometimes athletically waving his magic baton, sometimes quietly still, overwhelmed with feeling at a tender moment.

The music was trivial: thin, popular stuff for the most part. But the execution was superb, like the choreography of a well-staged professional football game. Clean, powerful brass work, rhythm that always stayed on the cutting edge of the beat. And above all the saxophone sections: four or five instruments phrasing as one, like a supple-voiced choir of traveling angels. In one of those sections, given the camaraderie of musicians, she might well have met a lively young man whom the years had seen fit to transform into an elderly gentleman with a bad back.

"I think it's your turn," said Mrs. Gatlin archly as Mr. Bales sailed up to their table and winked at Mrs. Cimino.

"How about it?" said Mr. Bales. He gestured invitingly toward the dance floor. "This is the last dance before intermission." He smiled down at Mrs. Gatlin. "And who knows what's going to happen after that?"

"You're a rascal!" giggled Mrs. Gatlin.

"Surprises?" said Mrs. Hinckle. After her third cup of punch from the far end, her tall, slender frame was beginning to unbend and sway to the music. "I bet this man is good at surprises."

Mr. Bales, his arm around Mrs. Cimino's small form, disengaged himself for a moment. Looking first to one side, then to the other, he bent over and whispered softly to his admirers.

"The hokey pokey," he said. "We're going to have a hokey pokey, and I'm going to make sure that both of you get out there and do some hokey pokeying!"

"He's terrible," trilled Mrs. Gatlin. "Simply terrible!" She collapsed immediately into a strong fit of the giggles.

"At least . . ." Mrs. Hinckle began to giggle herself. "At least that's better than the hanky-panky."

Temporarily overcome, Mrs. Hinckle giggled her tall frame over to the left, almost losing her balance. But she recovered herself, looked quickly around, and resumed her usual dignified bearing. Smiling and nodding encouragement, the two of them waved Mr. Bales and Mrs. Cimino off to the dance floor.

Mr. Bales was a good social dancer: At times he would whirl, at times he would glide, at times he would stop and sway, passing polite remarks to other couples, much like an automobile pausing at a red light to exchange pleasantries with a fellow traveler. And Mrs. Cimino was able to follow him effectively: When the tune ended with both of them positioned down by the bandstand, she applauded warmly and smiled up at the tenor saxophone player.

With professional courtesy he smiled back. Quickly he bent over and whispered something in the piano player's ear. The piano player nodded. They waited for the dancers to leave the floor.

Mr. Bales escorted Mrs. Cimino back to her table. He looked down toward the bandstand, as though expecting the musicians to take their intermission. But the musicians went into another song.

"Another dance!" squealed Mrs. Gatlin. "And here you are, Mr. Bales." She shook her finger roguishly at him.

"Why not?" said Mr. Bales. "As long as you promise to be one of the first out on the floor for our hokey pokey."

"I promise," giggled Mrs. Gatlin, bouncing up with great good will. "Even though I'm really very, very shy."

Even Mrs. Cimino found herself giggling along with Mrs. Hinckle as she sat down. So intent was she upon watching Mrs. Gatlin dance and flutter her big blue eyes simultaneously that several bars of music went by before she recognized the tune as "Lovely Hula Hands." And it was almost a full chorus before it dawned on her that the tenor saxophone player was Barney Feldman.

It had to be Barney. The height was right, and the movements were right. And with a full head of hair the face would be right. Barney had played lead alto on the Kona Kai band and had been one of Frank's closest friends. Many times, even during the last lean year, they had gone off to ball games together during the day, coming back for improvised dinners over a hotel room gas jet. And he had held George spellbound with tales of Polish wizards and warlocks. A lean year it had been, but the company had been first-rate.

A fourth cup of punch? Mrs. Cimino decided to get one: partly as an excuse to take her up by the bandstand, partly to give her Dutch courage to introduce herself. But Barney was apparently preempting her move: horn placed on its stand, he was sauntering across the dance floor toward her table. To encourage him she rose and smiled, faintly embarrassed, as though she and her girl friends had come to the dance with the hope of being picked up by one of the musicians.

"Esther?" Barney's tone was querying, uncertain.

"It certainly is, Barney." Mrs. Cimino smiled warmly and took him by the hand. "Esther Cimino, same as always."

"I thought so," said Barney. "But I didn't think you'd recognize me." Ruefully he smoothed back his thin strands of gray hair.

"I did," said Mrs. Cimino. "But the 'Hula Hands' tune made me sure of it." She turned to Mrs. Hinckle and Mrs. Gatlin. "This is Mr. Feldman, a very dear friend of my late husband's."

Her two companions smiled and moved over in clear invitation for Barney to join them.

"How exciting!" bubbled Mrs. Gatlin.

"And touching," added Mrs. Hinckle, nodding philosophically. "I bet it's been a long time."

"Ages!" said Mrs. Cimino. A bit overcome, she reached into her small beaded purse for a hankie. She shook her head. She sighed. "I don't know what to say."

"Florida!" said Barney, gazing around the room. "Everyone comes here sooner or later." He looked back at Mrs. Cimino. Slowly, a little stiffly, he sat down next to her.

"It's very nice," said Mrs. Cimino, a bit more in control of herself.

"Is this where you're staying?" said Barney. "We play here every Christmas."

"I just came down from Minneapolis last month," said Mrs. Cimino, happy to be on safe, detailed ground.

"It's a good room," he said. "Good acoustics, and Myron says the piano's not bad."

"I haven't even tried it out," said Mrs. Cimino.

"Do you play?" squealed Mrs. Gatlin. "The only thing I ever learned to play was the phonograph!" She giggled happily and the climate lightened even more.

"We've really enjoyed your music," said Mrs. Hinckle. "And the rest of the people certainly seem to like it."

"We try to keep them dancing," said Barney, still looking at Mrs. Cimino. "And throw in a little jazz every now and then."

"Red hot!" giggled Mrs. Gatlin, shaking her head and fluttering her hands, flapperlike. "And are you really going to play a hokey pokey?"

"First thing," said Barney urbanely. "First thing as soon as we go back."

"Wonderful!" said Mrs. Hinckle. "It's always good to get everybody out on the floor."

"That's what we're here for," said Barney. He smiled over at Mrs. Cimino as though to indicate his words had been spoken many times, in many different ballrooms. "We want to see everybody have a good time."

He looked back up at the bandstand. The piano player was sitting down on his bench, carefully adjusting the bright red cushion he habitually carried with him. He struck a few chords, bell-like, following them with a very short one-finger phrase.

"Recognize that?" smiled Barney, looking at Mrs. Cimino.

Mrs. Cimino nodded.

"It's a little tune musicians use," he explained to the others. "A way of saying that it's time to get back to work."

With that, he was up and on his way to the bandstand. Mrs. Cimino watched him as he sauntered back—still lively, but bent, his dark blue suit a little frayed around the cuffs. There was no air of prosperity to him, no feeling of investments safely squirreled away to take him through the winter. But he still played well.

There was a crisp press roll from the gray-haired drummer. A cymbal crash. Mr. Bales hopped up to the bandstand and faced his crew with forceful enthusiasm, gleaming forth in his Navy whites like an end man from a minstrel show.

"President Jeffersonians!" he said, smilingly acknowledging the round of applause coming at him from all quarters of the room. "President Jeffersonians, are you having a good time?" Still greater applause now, punctuated by whistles and glass thumping.

"Then you're ready for a special treat." More applause at this.

"Are you finally going to put something in that punch?" came a voice from the side. It sounded suspiciously like Mr. Sanderson's.

"We're going to do better than that," said Mr. Bales, not at all taken aback. "We're going to put some punch in this party, my friend!" He waited until the applause thinned out completely before holding up his hands for silence. In a low voice he continued. "But I want to warn you that this next dance has been thoroughly tested by the Mayfair Clinic of this great city." He paused again before going on in a rapid shout. "And the management of the President Jefferson will not take responsibility for any case of lumbago or cardiac arrest resulting from overindulgence in this activity!"

More whistles, glass thumping, and applause at this.

"How about a case of Bourbon?" cried another voice from the side.

"I'll drink to that!" came the Mr. Sanderson voice, quickly silenced by an irate wifely hiss.

Mr. Bales held up his hands again, shaping a calm before his next verbal storm.

"So we want you all out here," he said. "All of you, out here in a big circle." He looked imperiously down at Mrs. Cimino's table. "Come on, Mrs. Gatlin. How about that promise of yours?"

Giggling and bubbling, Mrs. Gatlin bounced her way out to the floor.

"Come on up, Mrs. Hinckle," insisted Mr. Bales. "No one gets to sit this out. And that means Mrs. Cimino also."

Blushing, but good-humoredly, Mrs. Hinckle and Mrs. Cimino came out, and so did the rest of the guests, milling around until they had formed two circles: a large one facing in, and a smaller one facing out.

"Wonderful!" said Mr. Bales. "All you have to do is follow the words of the song. And if you can't make out the words, just watch Mrs. Bales over here." Mrs. Bales came up just below the bandstand, looking very much like a magician's assistant prepared to smile her way through a Chinese torture chamber trick.

The music started up, and Mr. Bales, voice booming, began to sing out the hokey pokey words as a recipe for the assembled dancers.

It was a simple dance, more of an awkward eurhythmic exercise than anything else. The words called for movement of the right foot first, followed by a hand-fluttering turning around of the body. This turning-around movement, or hokey pokey, served to punctuate other actions: movement of the left foot, of the right knee, left knee, right hip, left hip, and on up the body, waxing gross and elemental.

Simple, but marvelously effective in loosening the inhibitions. Mrs. Cimino found herself hokey pokeying each time with greater and greater abandon, throwing her small body around and contorting it far beyond its normal capabilities. Even when the tempo speeded up at the end, she stayed with the movements, tongue protruding a bit in rapt concentration. And so did Mrs. Gatlin, Mrs. Hinckle, and Mr. Sanderson, to say nothing of the two henna-haired ladies, each of whom affected great rollings of the eyes and other facial gestures.

A simple dance, but an eloquent dance. A basic dance. A dance weathered down from far-off times: from the kermess, from the mad folk of Lübeck, garbling the liturgy from *hoc est corpus* to *hokus pokus* and other strange cries. And before that, from even earlier circlings on the moors and in flame-flickered caves, ending as always with a mixture of delight and exhausted reverence.

"Wasn't that something!" said Mrs. Hinckle, her clear-toned, pale face flushed with joy. "I haven't jumped around like that in years."

Mrs. Cimino, breathless, merely nodded as she helped Mrs. Hinckle weave her way to the security of their table.

"That Mr. Bales, that Mr. Bales," giggled Mrs. Gatlin delightedly. "He's so bad!"

But there was worse to come as the orchestra grew violent. Polkas! A monstrous legacy from eastern Europe. And the tarantella from Italy. From Mexico, *La Raspa*—more familiarly called the Mexican shuffle. A few hardy souls even attempted the hora, circling and weaving with what little energy they had left. And all the way through there was Barney's tenor saxophone urging them on: big-voiced, biting, always just a little ahead of the beat and daring them to catch up.

To Mrs. Cimino it was a blur, even the exchange of gifts—a welcome respite graciously supervised by Mrs. Bales. But she survived: She danced and clapped, clapped and danced, sipped her punch, waved to Barney every now and then as she circled by. And the time flew: Before she knew it the saxophone went deeply into the melody of "Good Night, Sweetheart" as a signal that the evening was officially over.

Limp, the three ladies sat at their table, trying to assemble sufficient force to take them to their rooms. They watched the musicians closing up shop: the drummer fitting his gear into two cases, the piano player restoring the top and bottom which he had removed from the piano. And there was Barney, swabbing his instrument out, his back to them.

"He's not much of a talker," said Mrs. Gatlin. "But he sure is cute when he plays that sousaphone."

"Saxophone," said Mrs. Cimino. "It's a tenor saxophone."

"Think of Rudy Vallee," said Mrs. Hinckle, trying to be helpful.

"It was a megaphone he played," said Mrs. Gatlin thoughtfully. "Or something like that."

Mrs. Cimino left her friends to recover their clarity of mind and walked up to the bandstand. His instrument put away, Barney had loaded up case, drummers stool, and music stand onto a small luggage frame with wheels.

"What do you think?" he said to Mrs. Cimino, directing her attention to his package.

"Very nice," said Mrs. Cimino. "Very practical."

"It's really not the weight," said Barney, looking at his saxophone case. "It's the way it tilts you over to one side."

"It was wonderful to see you," said Mrs. Cimino. "After all these years," she added lamely.

"Jerry Teitleman carries an amplifier, too," said Barney, still looking at his saxophone case. "I don't see how he does it."

There was a pause. Ready to go, Barney eased his little cart down off the bandstand and smiled at Mrs. Cimino.

"It's been a long time," he said.

"Yes, it has," said Mrs. Cimino.

"And you live here?" He looked around the room and down toward the doorway leading into the lobby.

Mrs. Cimino nodded. There was another pause.

"I'll give you a call," said Barney finally. "Maybe we can have a cup of coffee together."

Wednesday, December 29, 11:15 A.M.

"I know it's a drag standing in line," said Barney. "But we won't have a waitress bugging us once we sit down."

"I don't mind," said Mrs. Cimino. She smiled, partly at the sound of musician slang coming incongruously forth from an elderly stooped gentleman. Yet it had always been Barney's way of talking. Frank's too, until the business proprietor had buried the itinerant sideman.

"And the Muzak here is the best in town," said Barney, looking approvingly around Clifford's Cafeteria. "None of that Longines or Melachrino Strings stuff."

"It's very nice," smiled Mrs. Cimino.

They were positioned along the right-hand.wall of the cafeteria. Even though the cafeteria had opened its doors at eleven o'clock, there were four or five people ahead of them waiting to pick up their trays, still slightly hot and moist from the dishwasher. And there were between twenty and thirty people spread out over the large eating area, much as though they had each staked a claim on a private space insulated from the others by surrounding empty tables.

The tables were bare: no flowers, not even plastic ones, as at St. Hild's. Only a functional centerpiece composed of salt and pepper. But there were centrally spaced storage shelves on which could be found the other condiments: the mustards, the ketchups, the sauces—all gleaming brightly and ready for crafty use. From these shelves the proper combination of tools could be assembled: tools with which to jerry-build high-spiced idiosyncratic housings for blandly chosen properties. And ketchup itself was practically a vegetable, some said, giving substance to the thinnest soup.

The people were thin, taken as a group. And they were old, most of them over seventy, coming early to avoid the rush of noontime traffic. Some ate somberly, faces bowed over their food, muttering to themselves. Others ate sporadically, peering around from time to time like bright-eyed toads at morsels flitting by them. There were groupings, fluid ones, joined by late arrivals in high spirits at seeing a salon already established. At Clifford's the lonely, the crazed, the gregarious could all find their way to a table, each cautiously carrying a tray filled with a shrewd-budgeted selection from the morning's offerings.

The budgets were thin, too. Macaronis and stews were great favorites, sometimes supplemented at home with gleanings from the trash bins of local markets. There bruised cabbages could be found, and carrots: good stuff for hearty soups and artfully contrived ragouts. But cooking was hard in a third-floor flat. The ventilation was poor; and greases baked themselves, year after year, into the woodwork. Once there, like a deep dye, they stayed on and on with a faintly acrid smell that not even scraping and repainting could remove. It was much better to eat out.

And the serving line at Clifford's was a joy; cheerful, gleaming with metal and glass, it offered rich variety. Squash, eggplant, zucchini, muffins, rolls, breads and cheeses, salads small and large, fruited mixtures, hams and ribs of beef, spaghetti, macaroni, cannelloni, pork pie, beef pie, lamb pie. As Barney ushered her along, Mrs. Cimino calculated prices and options, noting that the portions were all small enough to fit the elderly taste. It was with a signal feeling of accomplishment that she ended up with stuffed bell pepper, clam chowder, peas, tea, and crackers—all for well under a dollar and a half.

"Great!" said Barney, pleased that everything could fit onto one tray. He picked up a toothpick and led the way over to a table by the far wall.

Mrs. Cimino followed, trying to strike the right balance between distance and friendliness as she threaded her way through a bunched group of elderly gentlemen in suit coats with ill-matching trousers.

They sat down. Barney dealt out the provender, laying each plate down like a card from a triumphant gin rummy hand. He took the tray over to a waiting stack and returned, nodding his head in time to the music.

"Eighty beats a minute," he said. "That's a good basic pulse for you."

"It's very pleasant," said Mrs. Cimino. She brushed a wisp of hair back with her left hand, furtively making sure that her hearing aid was turned up as high as it could go without squealing.

"Florida!" said Barney. He dug into his chicken fricassee with energy. "They're freezing in Chicago."

"And in Minneapolis, too," smiled Mrs. Cimino.

"Minneapolis!" Barney stopped eating and smiled at her for a moment. "That was some cold town."

"It's nice in the summer," said Mrs. Cimino loyally.

"It gets hot here," said Barney, stirring a little sugar into his iced tea. "But I don't mind." He nodded as though to convince himself that the humidity could gracefully be endured. "It's good for the oranges."

"And you have orange trees?" said Mrs. Cimino, hoping to hear more about Barney's little house.

"Two of them," said Barney, "with a lemon branch grafted onto one." He smiled proudly. "I can pick my own oranges for my own breakfast."

"Isn't that something!" said Mrs. Cimino.

"Sure beats Chicago," said Barney.

Barney was not a native of Chicago. But he had ended up there. And the settled-down coherent portion of his life had been spent there: on the South Side, about a mile from the University of Chicago, where wild-eyed émigrés had been building bombs at the same time he was playing first tenor on Don McNeil's Breakfast Club radio show.

When the Kona Kai band folded, Barney had hopped a freight back to New York. There he had descended upon his father's Brownsville flat, seeking succor and a stake. Neither had been forthcoming, only imprecations and reproaches. But a friend's room had opened up, a fellow alumnus of Pat Foster's Harmoni-Kiddies, where Barney had started out in the music business at the age of fourteen. There had been casuals to play, enough to get by on. And finally there had been a steady job playing in the pit for a long run of *Girl Crazy.*

There had been a wife in New York: a tap dancer, good-looking but heavy-legged, with a brain jolted loose from all that jumping up and down on hard wood surfaces. It had seemed wise to try Chicago.

Chicago had been great: It had been the hub from which all the big shows radiated, showering the Midwest and points beyond with a constant deluge of *Guiding Light, Myrt and Marge, Hoosier Hot Shots* and countless other blendings of music and drama. And there were road companies, too, settling in for long runs. Plenty of work for a good reed man, and lots of club dates to fill in the empty spaces.

There had been another wife: a vibraphone player, really good, too. Tay Voy had praised her highly, and Red Norvo had stopped in to hear her one evening. She had even been listed two years running in the *Down Beat* polls. But she had been a drinker—the Irish in her, possibly. She had finally run off with a short-order cook to Yakima, Washington. So he had stayed in Chicago.

But after the war the shows had all moved to the West Coast: A gradual process, it ultimately left the local musicians stranded as irrevocably as Chief Kona Kai's sudden departure from Minneapolis. Not wanting to go on the road again, Barney had concentrated on casual work and small clubs, playing as much jazz as possible. During the days he had gone into a friend's real estate office and kept busy. It was a good field for someone who didn't like to get up too early in the morning.

The third wife had also been a nighttime person: She'd been Hungarian, a waitress at the College Inn. But she had been a good woman, thrifty and sensible. With her there had been twenty-one years of comfort and happiness, ending when she died of cancer in 1965.

Children? There were four. A son from the dancer, raised by a grandmother in Newark, New Jersey. He owned a bar, but they had lost touch over the years. From the vibraphone player there had been a daughter, living in Riverside, California, the last time he had heard—two Christmases ago. And from the Hungarian two more daughters, both in their thirties now and both good Catholics. Of these, one was still single and the other lived with her husband and two children just across the bay in Tampa.

Money? Not bad, though it had come and gone, what with support payments and high living in the pre-Hungarian years. But he had prospered a little, ending up with a couple of rentals and some mutual funds. With Social Security, there had been more than enough to justify moving down to the sunshine seven years ago. He'd bought three bungalows, all fairly close together. In the smallest of these he lived and practiced, looking after his garden and his pets: two Siamese cats—Fazola and Chumish—along with a nondescript spanielish dog named B-Flat.

"And you still play!" Mrs. Cimino looked at him admiringly. "Isn't that something!"

"I get a few calls," said Barney. "But the driving at night is a problem." He took out a pair of metal-rimmed glasses and fitted them over his protruding ears. "That's why I like to work with Myron—he has a good commercial style and he lives close."

"Doesn't it get tiring for you?" Mrs. Cimino's eyes were filled with concern.

"The tenor is a killer," said Barney, shaking his head. "That's why I carry the stool."

Mrs. Cimino nodded.

"But I don't do much more than a wedding here and there or a Bar Mitzvah—four nights a month, maybe five." He pushed his chicken fricassee, cleanly picked, to one side. "The rest of the time I spend practicing the clarinet." He smiled happily at the notion. "There's an old man's horn for you. It's light, portable, doesn't take too much wind, and you can always lay out a good story on it, as long as you woodshed a little each day."

Mrs. Cimino smiled. It was an expression Frank had always used: woodshedding, hours spent alone practicing, active concentration over a demandingly extended period of time. As the business had grown, the time available for woodshedding had diminished. But he had still managed to carve out space for himself: space in which to voyage off away from her in search of a better tone, a neater fingering, a more inventive harmonic movement. Away from the instrument, he had been able to make the journey: At night she had sometimes seen his hand tapping softly on the blanket, weaving a backdrop for the parade of notes that were silently marching through his head.

Musicians! They were kindly men, nearly all of them, even when they drank. But they never really made their home with a woman. Underneath all the kindness, all the gentle concern, it was always the instrument that came first, even when it stayed locked up in its case, like a beautiful mistress in a distant castle securely invulnerable to attack.

Other men could be cranky, indolent. But they needed their home as a refuge from the winds that blew outside. For them it was a place where the armor, rusty or not, could be taken off and the true face shown. Musicians were different, and she was sure that Barney also had kept a private world somewhere in his mind, unknown, unknowable, unshared with the woman who lay beside him at night. She wondered how many times the Hungarian had screamed out her jealousy and anger at Barney's hurt, uncomprehending face. Or sat across from him at table, grimly silent.

"Very good," said Mrs. Cimino, finishing up the last of her bell pepper. "Do you eat out much?"

"Not as much as I used to," said Barney. "What with taxes up on the property, I have to watch it. Not that I don't have it coming in," he added hastily. "But I like to have something laid back for an emergency." He smiled and traced a small design on the table with his toothpick. "You know how it is."

"Yes," said Mrs. Cimino. "I know how it is." She thought of

how clever they all were in labeling unpleasant certainties with placid-sounding names: *Emergency* always meant nursing home, just as *see-ay* meant cancer, and *needs help* meant incontinent.

"Breakfast and lunch are fine," said Barney cheerfully, his dark brown eyes lighting up a little. "And I generally go over to my daughter's on Sundays."

"How about dinners?"

"Frozen-food city most of the time," said Barney, shaking his head at the spectacle of endless refugees from Mexico and China coming out of his oven. "And that instant spaghetti is a heartbreaker."

"Remember how I used to fix it in the hotel room for you and Frank?" said Mrs. Cimino. She smiled for a moment at the memory of covered pans stacked severally above one gas jet.

"Sure do," said Barney quickly. "And what a panic, with little Georgie crawling around!" He laughed at the picture summoned up. "But it was always tremendous!"

"I don't get to do any cooking at the hotel," said Mrs. Cimino. Even though the invitation was clearly implicit, it was important to choose her words carefully. "So I'd really like to come over and fix you a good meal sometime."

"Out of sight!" Barney beamed happily, then paused. "But it wouldn't be too much trouble for you, would it?"

"No trouble at all," said Mrs. Cimino. "As long as you help me a little with the shopping."

"Great!" said Barney. "That's what the car's for—fetching and carrying." He paused, snapped his fingers, and smiled broadly. "How's next Monday hit you?"

"Just fine," smiled Mrs. Cimino. "I can't wait to see those oranges of yours."

Part 5

There are only two basic needs for regularity of
sexual expression in the 70- to 80-year-old woman.
These necessities are a reasonably good state of
health and an interested and interesting partner.

WILLIAM H. MASTERS AND VIRGINIA E. JOHNSON
Human Sexual Inadequacy

Thursday, January 6, 1977, 11:00 A.M.

Karen was a cold-weather girl. She liked the feeling of wool: sweaters, skirts, slacks, mufflers, earmuffs, and heavy caps. Like bold harbingers of spring's return, the colors brightly spoke to her of a people resolute in reds, greens, and yellows despite the land twisting and turning beneath them, as stormwhite needles sewed capes and shrouds with which to mask the homely landmarks of their commerce with each other.

She pulled the storm door of Philip's office building open. She went inside and stood there a moment, breath steaming. She shook the snow, feeble and slushy now, from her parka and boots. She waited for her face to come alive with color, like a fresh morning glory opening up after hooding itself against the night's cold scrapings.

The elevator was there, but she chose the stairwell, prancing up the four flights like a mettlesome pony. She stopped to catch her breath just outside the office door before she opened it and went in. Philip was in the waiting room talking to the coolly professional secretary he shared with Bronkowski, Chalmers, and Johns. He smiled and ushered her into his office.

"That's a big package," said Philip, looking at the large manila envelope Karen had in her hand.

"I'm not sure there's much in it," said Karen. She opened it and took out three white folders, each filled with papers. "But it might be useful."

Philip made no move to examine the folders. He looked over at the autographed picture of Harry S Truman as though seeking inspiration. He looked back at Karen appraisingly.

"I'm not an accountant," he said.

Karen's face fell. It was as though her laboriously handcrafted gift had been quickly scanned and found wanting.

"But neither is Judge Schultz," Philip continued. He smiled again. "He likes things simple—simple questions, simple answers." He took the folders from her and moved them over to the side of his desk. "We'll go through these—and carefully—later on, but for now I'd like to get a picture of what all this means to you."

Karen nodded, still disappointed. She had expected her material would go immediately into a brilliant legal hopper, there to be sifted down into malleable impressive form.

"Let's start with how the store was running before the bank assumed control," said Philip. "Would you say it was running well?"

"Very well," said Karen, feeling a little more confident.

"Why?" said Philip.

"It was making money," Karen gestured at one of the folders. "The accountant let me Xerox some of the tax returns."

"But why was it making money?" said Philip.

"I see," said Karen. "You're trying to get at the basic approach that Grandmother and Simon were using."

"Exactly," said Philip. "That's the reason it was a good idea to talk it over with Simon."

"He likes to talk," smiled Karen. "And I took down pages and pages of notes." She gestured toward the biggest folder, not without dismay.

"But what did *you* get out of it," said Philip, pressing his point.

Karen paused. Simon Montford had given her almost a complete history of Cimino Music. Fires, thefts from petty cash, troubles with wholesalers, shoplifters, teachers who showed up drunk and breathed heavily upon twelve-year-olds earnestly working their way through Mel Bay's *Fun with the Guitar:* In a couple of evenings he had given her a panorama of what it was like to run a small music store in a provincial city. But it had not been a simple picture.

"I'd say it made money because it did more than just sell musical instruments," said Karen slowly.

"What did it do?" said Philip. "And how did it tie in with the moneymaking part?"

"The teaching part of it was good," said Karen. "They had the four studios in the back, and between five and seven teachers working there, depending on who was available."

"How did that help?" said Philip. "They never charged much for those trumpet lessons, as I remember."

"You bought your trumpet there, didn't you?" said Karen.

Philip nodded.

"And guitar players are always moving up from one instrument to another," continued Karen. "Folk guitars, classic guitars, twelve-string guitars, four-string banjos, five-string banjos, to say nothing of all the electric stuff."

"That makes sense," said Philip. "They made a little money off the teaching program and a lot of money over the long haul from the customers it brought in." He nodded, trying to distill a basic principle from the evidence. "Like a Ford agency running a driving school on the side."

Karen laughed, not without admiration. She could see how it was trickling down: from Simon to her, from her to Philip, and from Philip to Judge Schultz, ending up with a few drops of high-proof brandy pressed out from the many grapes gathered.

"What else?" said Philip. "And how did that help?"

"The repair shop," said Karen firmly. "After a sale, they would be right there to make any minor adjustments necessary, and later on they would be able to handle any major work."

"There's our Ford agency again," smiled Philip, growing more and more pleased with himself. "A service department to keep the customer happy."

"A lot of times people would come in and order right out of the catalog," said Karen. "So they didn't really have to stock very much."

"Small inventory, good service, good customer base," said Philip. "There's nothing wrong with that."

"Will Judge Schultz be able to understand it?"

"*I* understand it," smiled Philip, "and more important, *you* understand it." He nodded and took out a sheet of legal note paper. "Your familiarity with the business could be a very persuasive element of any case we might present."

"Do we have a case?" said Karen breathlessly.

"It depends on how the bank is doing with it," said Philip. He looked over at Harry S Truman again. "Are they doing all right?"

"I don't know," said Karen. "But I can't see much sense to what they're doing."

"Why?" said Philip.

"They've loaded up with a lot of big items," said Karen. "All the new speakers and keyboard things."

"Maybe those are more popular now," said Philip.

"They are," said Karen. "Just as brass instruments were more popular when you took lessons there—along with accordions." She paused to evoke a picture of hundreds of miniature Lawrence Welks parading in and out, all playing "The Sharpshooter's March" and "Tico Tico." Encouraged by Philip's smile, she continued.

"But they've closed down the teaching and the service department, and they've started to take a lot of trade-ins."

"Is that bad?" said Philip.

"It's risky, according to Simon," said Karen. "A lot of those things can sit there for months waiting for someone to come along. Meanwhile you have the space tied up, along with a higher insurance risk."

"Would you say they have a high inventory and high turnover?"

"I don't know," said Karen. "What's high?"

"I don't know either," said Philip. "And I'm sure Leach has the records set up so they wouldn't make any sense even if we could get at them."

Karen looked crestfallen.

"How about employees?" he continued. "Who do they have working there?"

"There's the manager, Brian Markle," said Karen. "And two other salesmen." She scowled at the notion. "Plus a lot of people who wander in and out."

"Customers?" said Philip.

"Friends," said Karen. "Sometimes they have rock bands rehearsing there at night."

"How do the other tenants like that?"

"They don't," said Karen flatly. "Especially the toy store next door. They've called the police several times."

"You've done a good job," said Philip. He sat back, still serious in his sober brown suit.

"Do we have a case?" said Karen again.

"Not yet," said Philip. "But we're close."

"It's a clear case of mismanagement, isn't it?" said Karen. "They've turned a good little business into a playground for unemployed musicians." Suddenly righteous, she fumed at the spectacle of vacant-eyed young men assaulting the neighborhood with harsh, tuneless sounds.

"No," said Philip, shaking his head.

"I'm sure they're not doing nearly as well," said Karen.

290

"They don't have to," said Philip. "The only thing required of a trustee is that he be a prudent man." His serious, slightly ruddy face smiled at the decorous legal phrase.

"I don't see anything prudent about wrecking a business," sniffed Karen. She looked over at her folders, ready to stuff them back into the manila envelope and retreat home.

"A prudent man is permitted to take reasonable risks in the exercise of his fiduciary role," said Philip, savoring the phrase somewhat. "That's the way the law looks at it."

"You're the lawyer," said Karen. "But I still don't think it's right."

"It's not just a matter of the law," said Philip. "We're dealing with a judge, a particular judge."

"Judge Schultz," said Karen, shoulders drooping. "And he likes things simple."

"He also likes to keep things going," said Philip thoughtfully. "He doesn't like to see businesses liquidated, people put out of work—at least that's the picture I get from studying his decisions."

"That's a point," said Karen. "With the teachers there, the store had nine employees."

"I think it's a key point," said Philip. "If it were just a matter of the building and the stock portfolio, I don't think your grandmother would have much of a case."

"Banks are used to handling those, aren't they?"

"They are," said Philip. "But they're not used to managing music stores." He smiled cheerfully. "So you really can't blame them if things go wrong here and there."

"Why don't they sell it?"

"Judge Schultz wouldn't like that," said Philip, becoming more animated. "Even though he might go along with it in the absence of any other alternative."

"But there *is* an alternative," said Karen. Her light brown eyes were aglow with excitement now.

"Exactly," said Philip. "Dissolve the trust, return control of the store to the Ciminos, and put all those nice people back to work."

"But what about Grandmother?" said Karen. "Would she have to come back to Minneapolis?"

"Many owners of family businesses spend most of their time

away," said Philip. "As long as they have someone else in the family to look after things for them." He leaned forward and looked directly at Karen.

"I hadn't thought about that."

"Start thinking about it," said Philip. He pulled the folders over and bunched them neatly together. "You certainly know how it works now. And I'm sure you could get a clear picture of present trends if you nosed around in the library and talked to some of the other store owners."

"I could do that," said Karen.

"At the same time I'll do some checking on what's been going on," said Philip. "You'd be surprised what turns up on a simple credit report."

"But I hadn't thought much about going into the store," said Karen. "I'm not sure I could handle it."

"You'd be able to hire Simon back, wouldn't you?"

"Simon!" Karen brightened. "Why can't he come back as manager again?"

"This has to be a long-range plan," said Philip. "Besides, Simon's not one of the family."

"I don't know," said Karen. She looked around the room, fixing for a moment on a shelf of books. "I was thinking of becoming a teacher."

"Do you want to do it?"

"I think so." Karen laughed, an embarrassed laugh, not unlike her grandmother's. "But it's hard to see myself selling a fifteen-year-old boy one of those complicated electric guitars."

"How about a thirty-year-old man?" smiled Philip.

"I thought you played the trumpet."

"I could be convinced to change." Philip stood up and started to put the folders back into the manila envelope. "Why don't we give it a try over lunch?"

"I'd like that," said Karen. Forcefully, directly, she got up and took the envelope from him. "I'd like that very much."

As they bundled up and walked out together, she took a closer look at him. Out from behind his imposing desk, he seemed smaller, less formidable. Old enough to be married, or to have been married. Overly serious. Perhaps this was out of deference to his father: It had been Michael who was the star, and it had been Michael who wrote the script, for Philip as well as himself. But

292

now with Michael away, Philip was beginning to come into his own.

They were a pair, a pair of contrasts. Philips' life had been planned, guided, from college on through law school to a secure position in his father's firm. Rudderless, she had been set adrift early with no one at the helm but herself. Helping hands could be overpowering, but they might be better to have aboard than emptiness.

As they got into Philip's MG, Karen restrained her urge to scoot over closer to the lean, furred body at the wheel. She felt herself sinking back, no longer driven to impose her will upon the snow and wind outside. She watched the window frost up with the vapor of their two breaths: a sign of palpable warmth between them, welling up from young lungs and sustained by strong young blood coursing beneath fair, unblemished northern skin. To Karen, not yet twenty, winter was a joy.

Monday, January 17, 10:00 P.M.

Mrs. Cimino had not realized how much her lower back ached. The pain must have lain dormant for a long time, like a tulip bulb staying low until spring reached down and touched it into life. But there was no denying it, once Barney's strong fingers began to work their way into a small soft part about two inches to the left of the base of her spine.

She permitted herself a few sighs and monosyllabic directions.

"There," she said. "That's it. Right there."

"There?" The voice came from high up on the bed, right behind her. It seemed oddly far away, almost detached from the service it directed.

"There," she said. She sighed again, with great finality this time.

Bodies were strange. The back was certainly a curious place. She had always thought of it as a specific territory mapped out into high, middle, low, right, and left subdivisions. But those were only general sections: Within them she now became aware of countless separate addresses, defined as such by myriad individual bones, nerves, and muscles. And Barney's fingers, searching through them, were like a caller in an unmarked, unlit neighborhood, knocking at many different doors before finding grateful welcome.

"How's this?" said the faraway voice.

"Oh!" Her own voice, suddenly loud, seemed like an intruder. "I can feel that all the way down to my toes."

But there was really not that much separateness. The whole arrangement was more of a network of interconnected passages: A bell might be rung in one location, but the window would light up somewhere else, sometimes surprisingly distant.

The pressure stopped. The fingers withdrew. A slight resentment came upon her. But a broad, suave visitor took their place: It was Barney's palm. Gently, it traversed the long road down from her back to just above her left knee. It was a pleasant journey, slow, replete with pauses and side trips. And she was happy to see its progress repeated again and again, and then again.

Quiet, somnolent, she felt no urge to speak.

Kindness roused her: the desire to be generously active. She turned, freely, so that she was now on her right side. From there she burrowed down until her hands could reach Barney's feet. She took the right foot first, cradling it. Her fingers worked upon it, squeezing the big toe first and then moving on to the others. If the back could speak to the feet, she reasoned, the reverse might hold true.

"Oh!" The sigh came from very far above her, just as she reached the middle toe. "That's the one, that's the one!"

"There?"

"There." The voice was soft now. There was relief in it.

Obedient, serviceable, her fingers stayed with the middle toe, a dearly found new friend. But there were other tasks: The fingers moved on farther to press deeply into a point midway down the arch. There they lingered without response. But a fraction over to the left brought forth a quick cry—half groan, half whimper.

"That's it!" said the distant voice. "That's it!" Up above her she could feel arms thrashing.

"Does it hurt?" Within, she nursed a secret delight in her new-found power.

294

"Oh, yes, yes," said the voice. "But I didn't know it until now." There was a laugh. "Don't stop, don't stop!"

Her fingers stayed there, sometimes pressing long and deep, sometimes pressing even deeper before courteously withdrawing to a point of neutral presence. Only temporarily did they leave to stroke the heel and ankle, even going as far as the calf at times. Always they came back to the tirelessly greedy point of original discovery.

And the silence grew.

So it was time to move on to the other foot, staying there a decent space. Then upward in stages: hand leading the body, body beckoning the hand, until her head regained its rightful place on the pillow beside his. The breathing was soft, a sure sign he was sinking deeper and deeper into a quiet twilight of mind and limb. Wishing to join him there, she leaned over, kissed his forehead. She gave a sigh and lay back, comfortably supine, waiting.

As she lay there, she found herself thinking of Frank and of what their nights had been like through the years. Young, supple, he with spear, she with snare, they had hunted each other in the darkness. Eyes closed for the most part, though sometimes winking open to stare glazedly toward a strange nearby creature of intimacy. Kindly yet distant, Frank had played her, pleasured her, almost as though she were an instrument from which he sought to draw forth the music slipping from his own life. Unable to enter or possess that odd private ground of his, she in fair defense had always held a part of herself back.

And so their moments together had never been true meeting places: Stopovers they were, on the way from past to future, encumbered with the baggage of unvoiced regret. As the years pulled them along, the world outside came more and more into their chamber, leaving incrustations of habit strong upon them. They had been friends, never abrasive, never untrue, never wandering off to pick the flowers.

Lying there, drowsily listening to Barney's breathing, she felt slightly disloyal to Frank, to their life together. The thought was painful. And yet she felt free, unconstrained, unreluctant to share her body's warmth with this new dear, good, needful friend. She turned toward him, letting him sleepily snuggle up, right arm encircling her, head buried between her breasts.

For a long time they lay there, quiet, unmoving, with only an occasional pressure from Barney's hand to indicate that conscious awareness still linked them together. In time his hand began to busy itself again: slow strokings for the most part, but every now and then taking time out to press and probe, bringing once again those dear strong fingers into play. Gracious, tactful, they worked their way down to her lower back. And even further: to the sheathed tip of the tail bone itself.

"Ah!" Her voice was soft, drawn out, a shading of whimper to it. It was a most exquisite intrusion. The muscles of her legs tensed in homage and her back arched a little.

The intruding finger stopped, withdrew. There was a long pause before it resumed its commerce, lighter than before, almost diffident. There was need for welcome: With a slight rippling movement of the hips, she found herself urging—even demand-ing—a return to the original intensity. It came, gladly, and sent its taut message quivering through her body, rousing her to more di-rect response.

It was then, heeding the call, that her own hands began to stroke Barney's head, to search each hair from root to tip, moving on to explore the ears and venture even farther on down to the chest. There her left hand stayed, gentling that good gray plain like the summer wind kissing waves of wheat, descending only rarely for a strong rub, a sly pinch. And these intended merely to throw into sharper contrast the softness of their congress.

With delicate good sense her hand moved down, far down, hoping to find growth in their small garden. Sometimes the plant remained quiescent, merely nodding at their ramblings. And at other times it grew in playful wise before subsiding quickly into soft retreat. But tonight the stem stood hardy, firm, proud, taking her fingers as much as they took it.

With joy, she knew herself to be both garden and gardener here: the earth in which to bed that strong life and the hands with which to raise it up. Constant care was needed: the closeness, the comfort, the serviceable exchange of touch. And in time they yielded harvest.

But by now Barney's fingers were beginning to work their own way downward, raising only the slightest hint of private entry as she tightened the muscles of her stomach and pressed up toward them. Like rich loam newly turned, there was moistness waiting, hinting of an earlier welcome had the journey not been pleasantly deferred.

Seriously intent, no longer playful, their caressing hands came back to guide their heads and lips together: These were gentle nuzzlings, mouthings here and there at first. But they culminated in one strong sustained embrace, leaving thighs and legs to grope blindly for each other. The key reaching for the lock, as the lock the key.

Finally there was contact: there on the doorway like a shy guest waiting to be invited in, yet nourishing a keen desire to force entry even at the expense of friendship. Proud, secure, she thrust herself forward and took him into her, pillowed to assist his searching out her farthest corner, deepest wall.

Staying there, albeit cherished, until pushed out, that dear presence returned again and stayed, leaving quickly to come back once more. And yet again, again: With hastening importunity their journey moved, taking her with high gasps up and up toward one sharp final moan that seemed wrenched from far away in the darkness above her. Then his brief fury, long deferred, followed by stillness, throbbing, slightly tense: a stillness that spoke of good fruit and warm reward. Smiling, triumphant at their precious harvest, she held the limpness there for a while before letting it depart, like a child sent back to play, secure in the drowsy knowledge that with proper nurture it would again grow to fierce man's estate.

Barney's farewell caresses still remained: long strokings, small pats, fainter and fainter as he drifted off into peaceful, sighing sleep. Almost there herself, Mrs. Cimino looked down through the darkness at what she could make out of her body. The contours, the valleys, were less firm than long ago, but there was smoothness yet, warmth, softness that could speak to the touch and bring a glass of comfort to the spirit behind that touch. And yet that warmth had lain unused, dissipated in lonely beds and rooms, like a light left burning in a solitary mountain cabin.

It was good to have someone in that cabin again: someone strong and yet not overwhelming, someone who needed to be warmed and could still couple something of his own to it. Before falling finally asleep, she raised up: She looked around the room, taking in the soft outlines of the dresser, of the doorway just beyond it. These were not her things, this was not her room: It was not her home, it was not her land. Yet it was good to be here. And it was good to be alive, to lie back and dream fresh new dreams, almost young, resting up against that dear good kind sweet flesh.

Friday, February 4, 11:00 A.M.

"Bingo," said Mr. Bales. "We missed you at bingo last night." From behind the reception desk he smiled down at Mrs. Cimino.

"I bet that was fun," she smiled back, determined to keep the exchange on a surface level. "Did you have a good crowd?"

"A dandy crowd," said Mr. Bales. He pushed the sign-in sheet over toward her. "Mrs. Gatlin won two tickets to the Ice Capades show next week."

"Isn't that something!" said Mrs. Cimino, as she put down her time of arrival and initialed it. "And isn't she the lucky one!" She beamed engagingly at Mr. Bales as an indication that her enthusiasm for the President Jefferson's social program continued strong and unabated.

"It's good to be lucky," said Mr. Bales. He reached over to the mailboxes. "And that's what you are today." He handed her the letter with the air of someone delivering a personal gift.

"This will be my good news, then," smiled Mrs. Cimino. "So I'll just take one of your newspapers to balance things out." She took out her change purse and deftly extracted a dime and a nickel.

"The market's up," grinned Mr. Bales.

"We can certainly use that," said Mrs. Cimino, paying implicit homage to the stock market as a topic of concern among her fellow guests. She picked up her letter and her newspaper. The sofa by the window was free, so she went directly over and sat down.

The letter was from Karen. Nicely typed and spaced, too.

February 1, 1977

Dear Grandmother,

Just a note to tell you how everything's going. But first give yourself a hug and a Happy Birthday in case this doesn't get there in time!

Mom and Dad are fine. Dad just finished building a shed in back of the place that he and Lisa bought. They had me over for a cast party a couple of weeks ago. It was for one of the Chekhov Club shows—a rock-and-roll version of *Little Women,* I think. Anyhow, Lisa had a good part in it. Everybody was happy and enjoying themselves.

Mom is still busy at school, but she likes it. And she's on the curriculum committee developing new courses in consumer education for the system. Gretchen's wedding is scheduled for June, but it's still not decided whether it will be here or in Eureka, California. Ann is still working on her anthropology M.A.

I haven't seen Uncle Harold, but Dad told me he bought a warehouse business a month or so ago. Kevin is taking what they call a sabbatical from Williams College to work there for a year and write a paper about it. Aunt Gloria won a golf trophy. I don't know what Patrick's doing. Still away at school, I guess.

I'm still working at Jack In The Box and going to school. I'm taking business courses now. The accounting courses are the hardest ones, but I'm starting to get the hang of it.

As for the store, there's not much that I can tell you, except that they've loaded up with a lot of expensive items. From what I can find out, a lot of the musicians here in town are beginning to order their equipment direct from the big East Coast wholesalers. It's very hard for local stores to compete with this, so I think the store is in for trouble.

Philip Ryan tells me he wrote you a few weeks ago about your wishes regarding going back to court. Have you changed your mind? We both feel you have a pretty good case, but it might make sense to let things go for a while, particularly if you like it down where you are.

Well, take care of yourself and watch out for the park bench Romeos in the sunshine. It's still cold here.

Your loving granddaughter,
Karen

Mrs. Cimino sighed. It was good to get the news from home, but there was a feeling of tugging to the letter, as though small hands were pulling at her to come back to Minneapolis. Philip's letter had arrived two weeks ago: She had read it, thought about it, and then put it away for further study later on.

She had certainly intended to make up her mind about the court business. It was clearly the thing to do, and apparently it could be done, according to Philip. But the days had drifted by, like white-winged sailboats out on the bay, leaving her decision docked in a small unattractive narrow. It might be a good idea to talk it over with Barney.

"And what do you think of our market now?" said Mr. Sanderson, coming up and pointing to the paper beside her. His portly frame was decked out in canary yellow slacks and blue cashmere golfing sweater.

"Better," smiled Mrs. Cimino. It was as though they were discussing the fortunes of a mutual friend: a friend hospitalized and going through one crisis after another, feebly rallying only to sink back again.

"It's a start," said Mr. Sanderson. He sat down heavily across from her. "But I think it'll be a long time before you see the small investor return."

"That's what I am," said Mrs. Cimino. She gave one of her embarrassed little laughs. "One of your small investors."

"Backbone of the country," said Mr. Sanderson piously. "Fighting against inflation, fighting to keep the tax-paying businesses of the economy going." His incipient lecture on the matter was interrupted by the sound of an auto horn outside: Apparently a signal, it pulled him up to his feet and cheerily out the door.

Mrs. Cimino picked up her paper. She did not look at the financial pages. The small-investor role was one she had chanced into, and she was a little irritated with herself for allowing the charade to continue. There were other charades she began to think about: the slightly awkward signing in each time she came back from Barney's, along with Barney's dropping her off a block away so as to avoid undue notice. Though only a short time in Florida, her life had become webbed with petty deceit.

Suddenly resolute, she put down the paper, rose from the sofa, and marched up to her room: There she took out Philip's letter and read it through again, chewing on each paragraph as though it were a tough, resistant piece of dear Mrs. Yeager's beef jerky.

January 15, 1977

Dear Mrs. Cimino:

As you may recall, I wrote you in response to your letter of December 15. In my letter I stated that I would give serious thought to your wishes regarding court action addressed to the dissolution of the trust established for you by Judge Schultz. Since then I have investigated the matter and discussed it with your granddaughter Karen.

An action of this sort is generally quite difficult to bring off, so I don't want to get your hopes up prematurely. Nevertheless, I believe we can work out an effective strategy. I suggest that you begin thinking about coming back to Minneapolis in the spring for a visit and for a conference, since a persuasive component of our case would be your demonstrable capacity to make such trips.

My father and mother tell me that their dinner with you was quite pleasant. They also say that your health and spirits seem to have prospered in St. Petersburg.

With the weather what it is, I should emphasize that there is no haste in this matter. I would, however, like to hear from you soon, so that we can begin to assemble our case—if that is still your desire.

Sincerely,
Philip Ryan
Attorney at Law

Lawyers! How they reduced everything to one gray soup of legal sentences with a few ambiguities floating on top! She had told the boy what she wanted, and here he was writing back to ask her if that was really what she wanted. And the worst part of it was that she wasn't sure now.

Procrastination! That's what she had indulged herself in, taking the pleasures of the moment as they came in hopes that the future would somehow work itself out for her. She looked out of her window and scowled at the sunshine: Perhaps the Florida climate was beginning to bake the gumption out of her! Certainly the choleric Mr. Stewart back at St. Hild's would never have wheeled aside from the prospect of litigious combat.

And power! Here was a chance to get it back. A chance to become something more than Poor Esther barely getting by on her allowance from Mr. Leach. With power, with the ability to give or withhold, Poor Esther would find a ready welcome at weddings and parties as Dear Esther. And if she wanted to buy gold or travel madly, she would do so.

Firm of purpose, she reached into her night stand for pen and paper.

Friday, March 11, 3:00 P.M.

Mrs. Cimino shifted her chair a little over to the right. The sun had been in her eyes: a clear Minnesota sun that angled in from Philip's window more intent on nuisancing honest folk than forcing the ground's hardness to retreat. It came in patches, small swaths, leaving large blocks of coldness still in the room. Too warm for a coat, too cool for a sweater, the day had irritated her with its lack of definition.

She looked over at Karen beside her: The girl had good color to her, a vividness in the face that sang out over the brown skirt, light green sweater, and suede jacket.

She looked at the folder Karen had brought along with her. It was a thick folder. She looked at Philip, sitting solemnly behind his desk like a quiet fisherman waiting for her to bite. She looked back at the folder again. She shook her head.

"Seems awfully complicated to me," she said. "Why can't you call it mismanagement and leave it at that?"

"We don't really have enough evidence," said Philip. His manner was patient. "And we can't subpoena the records until after we bring action."

"But then it would all be down in black and white," said Mrs. Cimino, still feeling it was her duty to bring banks and bankers to the bar of justice.

"The case wouldn't be crystal clear," said Philip. "If we object to the present management, the bank can immediately change the manager before we appear."

"And if we object to Mr. Leach," said Karen, "the bank can simply assign another trust officer to run things for you."

Mrs. Cimino paused, sulking a little. The trip had been discouraging right from the start. Barney's station wagon had overheated on the way to the airport, so she had almost missed the plane. And Mr. Bales had expressed collective disappointment that she would be missing the Spring Gala with which the President Jefferson said farewell to all the April-departing snowbirds. So she had left St. Petersburg feeling low.

The arrival in Minneapolis had not raised her spirits: Only Karen had turned out to greet her, taking her directly to a hotel like an anonymous thief come in to do secret mischief. Philip had counseled her not to see George and Lisa or even dear Alice on the grounds that the decision should be made and the papers filed without a family discussion. Only in the case of St. Hild's had he relented, allowing Karen to drive her out for a visit on Thursday afternoon and dinner that evening. And the hotel room had been cold, noisy, with street sounds right outside her window.

She looked over at Karen's folder again. In a way it was like trading one trustee for another. She tried to smile.

"You two seemed to have it all worked out," she said.

"We've had to," said Philip. "Someone like Judge Schultz isn't going to reverse a decision he's already made unless we give him reasons he'll feel comfortable with."

"A grown man ought to be able to admit it when he's made a mistake," said Mrs. Cimino stoutly.

"Judges don't make mistakes," smiled Philip. "The only thing they're willing to admit is that circumstances may have changed."

"It's my store and my money," said Mrs. Cimino. "That hasn't changed."

"But you've changed," said Karen. "That's something Judge Schultz will have to recognize."

"Do you think so?" said Mrs. Cimino. She brightened, inwardly thanking Mrs. Hinckle and Mrs. Gatlin for helping her to pick out her colorful plaid blouse and gray tweed skirt.

"You're looking quite fit," smiled Philip. "And you've certainly handled things very well down in Florida."

"I haven't had much to work with," said Mrs. Cimino. "There've been times when I've barely made it through the month."

"That's another change in circumstances," said Philip. "Inflation, along with the difficulties in communicating with your trustee."

"And there's the change in music retailing," added Karen, determined to bring her folder into play. "The young musicians are spending more of their own money today—not their parents—so they're more interested in buying at a heavy discount, even if it means calling a toll-free number in Philadelphia."

"Doesn't that prove the bank is wrong?" said Mrs. Cimino. "If they're trying to sell all those expensive things here in Minneapolis, they obviously don't know what they're doing." She sat back, satisfied that she had scored an important point.

303

"But it also proves that you and Karen are fully aware that your approach is practical and up-to-date," said Philip.

"Karen seems to be more aware than I am," said Mrs. Cimino, not without sadness.

"That's the most important change," said Philip, waxing enthusiastic for the first time. "Now you have someone in the family able and willing to assist you in keeping the business going."

"And this is what you want?" said Mrs. Cimino, looking closely at Karen. "I know you can handle it." She nodded approvingly over at the big folder. "But will you want to be bothered with it in a few years?"

"It's a wonderful opportunity," said Karen.

"Do you really think so?" said Mrs. Cimino, finding great comfort in the implication that her store was of equal prestige with advanced degrees, teaching credentials, and warehouse firms.

"With Simon to help me, and with you to advise me, I'm sure I can make it go," said Karen.

"Quite a change from last year, don't you think?" said Philip, addressing his remarks to Mrs. Cimino but smiling at Karen. "One of the reasons Judge Schultz established your trust was that no one in the family was able to take care of the store for you."

Mrs. Cimino nodded. She reached for the folder and started to page through it. Karen had done a good job organizing the material: She had surveyed other stores, large and small, and had made a good case for the balance between music instruction, instrument repair, and instrument sales. As well, there was a strong case made in favor of continuing her own involvement—even from a distance. Karen had certainly changed during the last year: from a sullen, neglected girl to a responsible, attractive young woman.

Even Mrs. Nash had noticed the change in Karen: She had commented on the pounds lost, on the more direct manner of expression. So there had been a little triumph in the return to St. Hild's, taking Karen around and seeing old friends once more.

Some of them had left: Mr. Bjornson, Mr. Salves, and Mr. Monsour among others. But Mr. Ayledotte was still there, along with Mr. Stewart. And so was old Mrs. Kenniston, though it seemed doubtful that she would make it through another winter. It had been good to see Mrs. Yeager and Mrs. Anderson, both about the same as far as their private little worlds went. Miss

Schmidt had left the month before, going to her long-awaited apartment in an Ojai, California, community for retired teachers.

There had been some deaths: Mr. Higgins and Mr. Kappelhoff, along with a number of the white mounds whom she had never known by name. And there had been other changes: Mrs. Polanski had taken a position with the government in Washington, and had been replaced by Dr. Ralston, a young gerontologist from Alabama. He seemed pleasant enough. But he had increased the size of the director's office and staff. Everyone wore white uniforms now, even Miss Rochester.

That part of it had been distressing: In her mind St. Hild's had always stood as a final safe retreat, a place where someone would tell you not to shuffle and yet take your hand until you got your balance back. But without Mrs. Polanski, fair-faced and bold, the place seemed dull, uninspired, fighting a rear-guard action at best against confusion and weakness. In spite of the new construction, the changes there gave her an empty feeling, much as though a dear friend had suddenly moved away.

Everyone moves away. The boys, wet and glistening in their baths, each a small joying piece of herself: They had wandered off, their places taken by deep-voiced young men coming in late at night from unknown, unknowable secret places. And these had left, giving way to older men: balding, graying, familied, coldly distant from her home.

And she from them.

Mrs. Cimino put the folder back. She smiled at Karen. She clapped her hands once with an air of businesslike finality.

"It makes sense," she said. "Rather than say what they've done wrong, we'll tell them what we're going to do right." She sat back, relaxed, pleased with herself for summing up matters so neatly.

"Exactly!" Philip nodded and sat back, sighing with obvious relief.

"Do you think the judge will have confidence in me?" said Karen, still a bit shaken by her grandmother's original lack of enthusiasm.

"I don't see why not!" snapped Mrs. Cimino. "*I* have confidence in you, and my judgment ought to count for something."

"It certainly should," said Philip. "And that's why the court is going to be concerned about your competence to make important decisions."

"My competence!" said Mrs. Cimino. "I thought that was all settled." She sat straight up and scowled at Philip. "Is that Judge Schultz going to sit up there and ask me questions about the President again?"

"Certainly not," laughed Philip. "But my bet is that the bank's attorney will make his case along those lines."

"That I'm incompetent?" Mrs. Cimino was still fuming at the notion.

"Not in so many words," said Philip. "But they're going to argue that the trust is really there for your own good."

"I don't see how," said Mrs. Cimino stoutly. "They're wrecking my business, bleeding me with charges for this and that, and they won't give me anything to live on."

"But you're still protected," said Philip. "And so is your estate."

"Against what?" said Mrs. Cimino incredulously.

"Against the influence of artful and designing persons," said Philip. "People who might take advantage of you."

"Are there many artful and designing persons down there in St. Petersburg?" said Karen, smiling at the quaintness of the notion as much as at the language.

"We've had a couple of mutual fund salesmen come by," said Mrs. Cimino. "But Mr. Bales always sends them packing." She joined Karen in mild laughter.

"It's not a trivial point," said Philip. His eyes were serious. "I know that Judge Schultz has strong views about the need for protecting elderly people from costly mistakes in judgment."

"Well, he's wasting his time as far as I'm concerned," said Mrs. Cimino. She snapped out the words in a valiant attempt to suppress her memory of the suave Mr. Desmond.

"Then we're all set," said Philip. He sat back and smiled confidently at the two of them. "As it stands, I think we have a good case for returning your assets to your direct control." He reached for a stack of legal forms and began to check the places for Mrs. Cimino to sign.

Mrs. Cimino, suddenly tired, sat back in her chair and closed her eyes for a moment, listening to the two young people chatter

306

on about the need for a little more investigation of the store and its personnel. Once made, her decision had defined her as a quiescent, passive member of the partnership, buoyed along by the optimism of the others. Like a remorseful purchaser, she began to worry about the move, much as though a line were being let down into deep water, there to snag on some dim piece of wreckage far below.

She felt chilly. So she moved her chair back over to the left again, letting the sunshine wash over her lower face and neck. It felt good. It reminded her of Barney's orange trees and what a pleasant curiosity it was to get up, walk out back, and return with two oranges freshly picked for breakfast.

Papers ready, she carefully signed her name at the appropriate places, thinking of how Mrs. Polanski would have applauded her resolution. A good afternoon's work behind them, she and Karen said goodbye to Philip. Karen driving, Mrs. Cimino dozed slightly on her way back to the hotel, thinking of a good meal, a warm bath, a good night's sleep, and a quick journey back the next morning to her Florida oranges.

She had meant to tell them about Barney. But there had been many other matters to discuss. And the subject itself had never come up.

Friday, March 18, 8:30 P.M.

The workout at Golden Wing Spa had gone well. With sweating intensity, George Cimino had pushed his lean, still-muscular body through a highly ritualized sequence of bench presses, back lifts, and sit-ups. And the sit-ups—thirty of them—had been done on a tilted board, so that gravity slanted in upon him as a fell antagonist. Between each straining effort, as custom and good sense demanded, he had gulped huge, healing drafts of air. And he had held them long, sucking each one deep into his lungs and treasuring it before snorting it out, not unlike a weight lifter driving himself to command one final massy challenge.

There were mirrors all around the place.

He had not avoided them. Nor had he postured before them, as some of the younger men did, striking graceful poses and eyeing their reflections with covert pleasure. He had merely fought a skirmish, nothing more, but enough to repel for a while the softly decaying self that bided its time within.

He showered, singing to himself, and put on his clothes. Lisa had picked them out: a gray turtleneck sweater and light blue slacks. And she had picked out the gold chain to wear with them, a solid badge of office fit for the Lord Mayor himself. Or for a trusted general, standing solemnly in the wings, there as backing for the bright sparklings of his lovely queen. It was in keeping with this collective image that Lisa had urged the briar pipe upon him: so that he would have something to do with his hands at parties.

He got in the Buick and drove home. Lisa's Porsche 912E was in the driveway. He got out and looked at the Porsche. Even with the faint light from the house, he could make out what appeared to be a new scratch on the right fender. He walked into the house, determined to maintain the cheerful momentum set in motion by his workout.

"How was the spa?" said Lisa. Still intent on the latest issue of *Better Homes and Gardens,* she did not look up as he came into the living room.

"Pretty good," said George. He heaved a leftover deep breath. "The old machine is still working for me."

"It ought to," said Lisa. She put down her magazine, stretched back on the couch, and looked coolly up at him. "You spend enough on maintenance."

"Well worth it," said George. "Do you realize I haven't had a cold this year?"

"That's all psychological," said Lisa. "If you wanted to have a cold, you'd have a cold."

"Some people who have colds aren't very happy with them," said George, wondering what kind of spiral Lisa was initiating. Quick, wordwise, she had ways of taking him into awkward corners and leaving him there to work his way out.

"That's what they tell you," said Lisa. "But they don't always mean what they're saying."

"They're lying?" said George, thinking of how Alice had complainingly snuffled her way through many a winter.

"To themselves," said Lisa. Her slim body stretched gracefully out on the couch, and her long dark hair was brushed back to frame her new position. "Most people lie to themselves all the time."

"Gosh!" said George, wondering whether or not his own response was tainted with insincerity. "I'll have to think about that."

Shaking his head, he walked on past her and out to the kitchen. It was not that his workout had made him hungry. Nor did he yearn for a conventional snack: cookies, crackers, pie with cheese. But some sort of oral satisfaction was certainly in order: a methylcellulose wafer, perhaps, or a couple of chocolate diet candies.

He opened the cupboard door and examined their health section. The contents were impressive. There was vitamin C with and without rose hips, brewer's yeast, various other forms of protein, kelp pills, iron pills, vitamins E and B-10, along with the conventional aspirins, laxatives, and bulk supplements. Not all these were in use. But their magical properties required them to be held and never thrown away, lest their mana fall by chance into heathen hostile hands.

"Are you fixing yourself a drink?" Lisa's voice was tinged with suspicion, as was often the case when her snapping brown eyes could not train directly on George.

"Just a little apple vinegar and water," said George, still resolutely cheerful. "Can I get you something?"

"No," said Lisa.

"Some wine, maybe," said George. "A beer, a glass of water."

"We're not communicating," said Lisa. "Didn't you hear me say I didn't want anything?"

Vinegar-water and coaster in hand, George came back into the living room and sat down across from her.

"I heard you," he said. "But I didn't know whether you meant it or not."

"I meant it," said Lisa. She sat up in one fluid motion and stared intently at him, a half smile on her face.

George sipped on his vinegar-water and smiled back at her.

"Mr. Leach called again," said Lisa finally. "And before that a Mr. Emory."

"He's a lawyer," said George. "I talked to him in Leach's office a couple of days ago."

"Aren't you going to phone him?" said Lisa.

"I'll phone him," said George. "But I need time to think all this over."

"That hearing is scheduled for the seventh of April," said Lisa. "It's less than three weeks away." There was a slight edge to her voice.

George sipped his vinegar-water some more. He stared at the floor, avoiding Lisa's direct gaze. He looked around the living room, handsomely furnished with things from the Elm Street house. Over to his left, leading off from the hallway, was their dining room: solid oak table, cane-bottomed chairs, buffet, and a special display cabinet for the rare pieces of china. It was a lovely place. And Lisa was lovely in it, entertaining graciously and slowly working her way up to the top of the Chekhov Club social hierarchy.

Both Mr. Leach and Mr. Emory had spoken darkly of his mother's petition. They had urged him to join with them—partnerlike—in opposing the action: an action that threatened to erode the established order like a spring flood washing down from a high hill and gnawing at the subsoil beneath foundations previously deemed secure. They had given him reasons, good reasons, logical and compelling reasons.

But he had not yet given them an answer.

"I don't know," he mused. "I just don't know." He sighed and shook his head.

"I can't do it for you," said Lisa. "She's your mother, not mine."

"She's your mother-in-law," said George. "That ought to count for something." In making the decision, he wanted very much to have someone out on the branch with him, there to sit securely or to tumble down if misfortune bit it off.

"Esther means a great deal to me," said Lisa. "And her welfare means a great deal to me." She picked up her magazine again and began thoughtfully looking for her place. "But she is not really my mother-in-law."

"She's not?" George looked over at the magazine, trying to bounce his gaze up from the pages into Lisa's downcast eyes.

"She's Alice's mother-in-law," said Lisa. Her place located, she nodded with firm approval, still looking down.

"But I'm not married to Alice anymore!" said George. He was

beginning to feel shaky, as though his personal history had suddenly been rewritten by a whimsical team of directors and novelists. "I'm married to you."

"What about Karen, Ann, and Gretchen?" said Lisa. She looked up, straight at him, face set.

"What about them?" said George, quite confused by now.

"They're Esther's grandchildren," said Lisa. "Isn't that right?"
George nodded.

"And Alice is still their mother. Right?"
George nodded again.

"If Alice is still their mother," said Lisa, "Esther is still Alice's mother-in-law."

"I'll have to think about that," said George. "But it doesn't sound quite right to me."

"I'll rephrase it," said Lisa. Obviously intent on clearing up the matter, she put her magazine aside. "Alice is still Esther's daughter-in-law."

"Alice, Alice!" said George with irritation. "Why are you so worked up over Alice?"

"Because it's not going to be easy for me to sit back and watch you knuckle under to her," said Lisa sadly. "Not after all those things she did to you."

"Alice?" George put his vinegar-water down on the coaster with a firm click. "Alice has nothing to do with Mother's petition."

"And Karen?"

"Karen will be helping," said George. "I don't see anything wrong with that."

"Helping herself," said Lisa airily. "And handing it right over to Alice, Alice, Alice." She intoned the name with mock reverence, as though it still exerted talismanic charm over her husband.

"You think so?" George looked at her, trying to puzzle things out.

"I think your Mr. Leach is right when he says we're going to end up on the short end if that trust is dissolved," said Lisa.

"But it's her money," said George defensively. "Why shouldn't she do what she wants with it?"

"*Her* money!" Lisa laughed and shook her head, eyes sparkling, her long dark hair swirling over her shoulders. "It is *not* her money and you know it."

George stared at her blankly. This new puzzle was worse than the business about Alice.

"Your father built up that business," continued Lisa. "And you helped him do it."

"I didn't help that much," said George.

"Did Harold help in the store?"

"No," said George, scowling a little. "But things were better then."

"Better for Harold," said Lisa. "Harold, Harold, Harold."

"What's he have to do with it?"

"He'll be right there with another master investment plan," said Lisa, smiling cheerfully. "Otherwise he'd be opposing this with you."

"Mother wouldn't go for his schemes before," said George loyally. "Why should she now?"

"She's different now," said Lisa, growing thoughtful. "She's down in Florida." The slim young body sprang up and darted over to the side of the room, framed in the archway like Joan of Arc in the midst of her troops. "And that's why it's not her money now."

George continued to stare at her, still unable to comprehend the annunciation being thrust upon him by this strangely posturing creature.

"That's it!" said Lisa, almost to herself, as the scene began to take shape. "A dear woman, your father's wife, worked for that money." Sure of itself, the voice began to acquire vibrant force. "She worked hard, she saved, she took what your father left and made it grow into a fine estate." The brown eyes looked off toward the side, as though Mrs. Cimino were about to step out and acknowledge praise justly due her.

"I respect that woman," continued Lisa. "The woman who raised you, the woman who worked at the store, the woman who did without so that her sons could prosper." She paused and looked directly down at George. "And I just don't want to see a strange old lady down in Florida make a mockery out of all that woman did."

"Gosh!" said George. There was awe in his voice.

Lisa smiled. She came over to him. She bent down so that her long dark hair washed over his face. With her hair still between them, veil-like, she kissed him, softly but letting her small red tongue part the strands like a sly elf stealing through the summer grasses to explore what lay beyond. She let him pull her down to his lap, lifting her slightly so that her long legs swung round and flowed over the side of the chair like the tail of some dark mermaid come over to find solace in a landsman's strong arms. There was silence, draining some of the harshness away.

George sighed, gently stroking her back. Leach had been tactful, but he had alluded unequivocally to evidence linking his mother with a St. Petersburg gentleman, Barney Feldman by name. And now Lisa had conjured up dismal possibilities within the family itself.

"I don't know," he finally said. "It still doesn't seem right."

"What doesn't seem right?" Lisa's voice was drowsy, far away.

"Going into court and telling the judge your own mother can't be trusted," said George.

"Isn't that what you had to do last year," said Lisa. The voice was soft, sympathetic. "And all alone you were, too."

"I had you," said George, still stroking her back. "But it was different."

Under his hand, he could feel the back muscles tighten as a signal that she was going to pull away. She did not pull away quickly, but she straightened up and faced him with eyes grown cold again.

"It was the same kind of hearing," she said. "The same judge."

"But it was in the hospital," said George lamely. "It was more . . . informal."

"No lawyers," said Lisa. "Is that what you mean?"

"That's part of it," said George.

With one movement she swiveled round and took the floor, going directly back to the couch. There she sat down, crossing her legs in a posture of complete relaxation, as though St. Joan had suddenly been followed by Noel Coward in a Chekhov Club potpourri. Long fingers smoothing back her dark hair, she smiled at him, unoffended, eyes glowing with amused recognition.

"It's the biggest part," she said. "That's what you're afraid of."

"You don't understand," said George. "You don't have to walk in there and face your own mother and your own daughter."

"Are you afraid she'll spank you?" giggled Lisa.

"I'm only trying to do what's right," said George, reddening a little.

"Right for whom?" said Lisa, still mocking him.

"Right," said George helplessly. "You know what I mean."

"Right for Alice? said Lisa. "Right for Harold? Right for that seventy-two-year-old Feldman beatnik cozying up to her in the Florida sunshine?" With a quick leap she was on her feet again and glaring at him. "And when are you going to start thinking of what's right for *us*?"

"There's nothing wrong with our life just the way it is," said George in a suddenly injured tone.

"There's a lot wrong," said Lisa. "When are you going to stop lying to yourself?"

"I'm not lying to myself," said George. "I'm very happy."

"*I, I, I*," said Lisa. "But we were talking about *us, us, us*."

"I thought *we* were very happy, then."

"What about our goals?" said Lisa fiercely. "What do we have to look forward to?"

"There's my retirement," said George. It was clear he found comfort in the notion.

Lisa shrugged, let her arms fall to her side in complete despair. After looking heavenward with an expression of martyrdom, she stared at him and shook her head pityingly.

"It's not far off," he continued. "We could sell this place at a good profit, move into the cabin, and travel four or five months out of the year."

"That's not a goal," said Lisa, her voice filled with wonderment. "That's a surrender."

"Surrender!" said George, deeply wounded now. "I've earned it, and I don't see why I shouldn't enjoy it."

"What about me?"

"You would enjoy it, too."

"Enjoy it!" Lisa stepped back, appropriately aghast. "Up at the lake! That desert! With a bunch of middle-aged drunks who come up from the city on the weekends to put on cowboy hats!"

"Then we'll stay here in the city," said George, growing desperate.

"Why this city?" said Lisa. She looked out through the window with undisguised contempt. "This overgrown railroad town."

"This is where we live," said George.

Lisa was quiet for a moment. She took a breath. She went back to her couch and resumed her Noel Coward manner.

"We could move to New York," she said airily.

"New York!" said George. "I don't know anybody in New York."

"That's what I mean," said Lisa. "You're afraid." She stood up quickly, young breasts taut, tempting. "You're afraid of life, afraid to take what's there to be taken."

"I don't have to take *this*," said George, getting up himself and wondering if his blood pressure was being affected.

"But you *are* taking it," glared Lisa. "That's one of the things you've done all your life."

George glared back. He took a deep breath and tried to unclench his left hand. It was time to rechannel the discussion.

"There's another scratch on the Porsche," he said.

"I put it there," said Lisa. "And I was wondering how long it would take you to get up the courage to ask me about it."

"That's not a theater prop!" roared George, finding his voice at last. "That's a new car, and a damned expensive one!"

"What are you going to do?" said Lisa. "Hit me?" Lips slightly parted, she stepped even closer to him, breathing with anticipation.

Like a shy, gangly boy ringed with bystanders and forced to confront his principal tormentor, George stood up to her, almost touching her, moved mightily to do her bidding: to slap, to pinion, to carry her struggling out of the room to whatever farce she had designed for them. But he remained still, quiet, taking deep Golden Wing Spa breaths that made his chest heave toward her. When it came, his explosion was coordinated, magnificent: In one smooth motion of his own, he turned round and picked up the armchair he had been sitting in. Holding it high up, he gave it a medicine-ball throw that took it across the room, where it brought down a floor lamp with the crash of a felled Douglas fir.

Without a word he rushed outside and started up the Buick, sitting there while the motor warmed up. The lake was less than an hour and a half away, and it beckoned him. Once there, he would sort matters out. And he would fish.

Inside, Lisa went back to her *Better Homes and Gardens*. It had been a good scene, almost as good as Edward Albee. And a much better range than the ingenue roles they had been giving her at the Chekhov Club.

With pleasure, she heard the sound of the Buick's motor being turned off. She concentrated on her magazine as her husband came

315

in, walked by her into the kitchen, and returned to darken the space in front of her. After a while she looked up at him, quizzically, as though nothing of moment had happened.

"I forgot my kelp pills," said George. He held up the small jar as a palpable symbol of strong domestic ties pulling him back.

Lisa put her magazine down. There was deep concern in the brown eyes and a slightly furrowed brow under the dark hair.

"Forgetfulness is a bad sign, dear," she said. "Maybe they're having the hearing for the wrong person." It was with great tenderness that she smiled up at him.

There was nothing more for George to throw. His only recourse lay in slamming the door as he went out. It was a good slam: loud, authoritative. And it rattled most dangerously the valuable pieces of china in the dining room display cabinet.

Thursday, April 7, 10:30 A.M.

Judge Schultz sat in his chambers waiting for the two attorneys to come in. From the window behind him—mid-morning light streamed in to illuminate his bald head with a slightly askew, saintlike aureole. The Cimino file was on his desk, open, with Minneapolis Southern Bank's response on top.

It was not a large file. But it promised growth: Matters like these could wax multifoliate with charges and countercharges. Judge Schultz did not like files thrusting upward like huge unsightly weeds. So he tended them carefully, circumscribing and defining the areas of contention as much as he could. In this wholesome task, a pretrial conference had always worked well for him.

The attorneys came in together: Philip Ryan for the petitioner, followed by Mr. Emory for the bank, stepping courteously back to allow his junior to precede him. Briefcases in hand, they came up to his desk and sat down. Emory eased his rawboned frame into a chair on the shadowy side of the room, sitting there like a familiar, comfortable part of the furniture. Young Philip Ryan sat closer: solemn, stiff. a little nervous.

"I don't want this to take all day," said Judge Schultz. He looked grimly at the documents in front of him. "And I don't see why it can't be resolved here and now."

"We're prepared to be reasonable," said Mr. Emory, his freckled face a smiling study in cheerful accommodation. "How does a generous increase in her living stipend strike you?" His right heel began to tap softly on the carpet, inaudible but setting a tempo for Philip's reply to follow.

"Who decides what's generous?" said Philip. He smiled at Judge Schultz. "I'm sure Your Honor doesn't want to waste the court's time haggling every year over the size of a monthly allowance."

"Are you saying she'd be back again next year even if we worked something out now?" said Judge Schultz. His gaze at Philip was intent, tinged with suspicion.

"I'm saying that the present arrangement is humiliating to her," said Philip. "And besides . . . "

"Just a minute!" broke in Mr. Emory. "This doesn't make any sense." He looked at Judge Schultz with clear distress at the foggy quality of younger legal minds. "No one denies the trust is a basically humiliating arrangement." His gray-green eyes were bland, sympathetic. "Our concern here is with Mrs. Cimino's best interests."

Judge Schultz did not respond. He had found it was best to let the attorneys wrangle, wallow in argument for awhile, Fretful, tired from their exertions, they would be more receptive when he stepped in to guide the case back to solid ground. He nodded at Philip and sat back in his chair.

"She's already been found competent by Your Honor," said Philip. "And she's now ready to look after her own best interests."

"This is a complicated estate," said Mr. Emory. "The trust was established to protect it and her."

"I agree it's complicated," said Philip. "And the major complication is the music store." He looked pleasantly at Mr. Emory. "If it weren't for the music store, I don't think we'd be here."

"An elderly lady of questionable judgment has no business running a Minneapolis store from a hotel down in Florida," said Mr. Emory.

"There's nothing wrong with my client's judgment," said

Philip, growing heated. "And the store was doing very well up to the time she was hospitalized last year—hospitalized, I might add, as a direct result of serious errors in medical judgment."

"But Your Honor," said Mr. Emory, smiling again, "the medical profession is not on trial here."

"That's right," said Judge Schultz. "Let's stick to the issues." He looked over at Mr. Emory. "What about this store?"

"We'll be reasonable there as well," said Mr. Emory. "If Mrs. Cimino has some views on how it should be run, we'd welcome her help."

"Maybe we could work something out here," said Judge Schultz. He looked at Philip hopefully.

"With all respect, Your Honor, the bank cannot work both sides of the street at the same time," said Philip. "If Mrs. Cimino's judgment equips her to assist them, it certainly qualifies her to cash her own dividend checks."

Judge Schultz nodded. It was clear the store was a central issue. He pursed his lips and took another look at Mrs. Cimino's petition. It was a straightforward document seeking to have the conservatorship set aside and the assets therein returned to the petitioner's direct control. In support of this request, the petitioner pointed to the fact that she had been found mentally competent in a previous hearing and to the fact that she was presently living on a completely independent and functioning basis.

As for the store, the petitioner pointed out that it was a family business—Cimino Music—and that said business had been in operation for almost fifty years. At the present time, the petitioner proposed to manage this business with the help of her granddaughter, Karen Cimino. In support of this proposal, the petitioner attached a detailed plan for the operation of the business under Miss Karen Cimino's direct supervision. The plan itself was asserted to meet the needs of both the community and the employees, in addition to demonstrating the present capabilities of the petitioner.

Judge Schultz put the petition aside and rubbed his eyes. He looked over at Mr. Emory, not without irritation.

"Are you having trouble with this store?" he said.

"None at all," said Mr. Emory. "It's doing very well."

"I've tried to subpoena Mr. Leach, the trust officer in charge," said Philip. "But he's been unavailable." He looked over at Mr.

Emory as though the fact indicated a clear weakness in the older man's case.

"The man's on vacation," said Mr. Emory. "Perhaps we should have a continuance." He smiled soothingly back at Philip.

"I think we can get by," said Philip cheerfully. "I've subpoenaed the present store records along with the manager, Mr. Brian Markle."

"But you're not alleging mismanagement, are you?" said Judge Schultz a little nervously. Sometimes the newspapers took up allegations like these and magnified them, making everybody—court included—look disreputable.

"Not in the least," said Philip. "I merely want to demonstrate that the petitioner's proposal is clearly based upon a recognition of what present conditions are."

"Your Honor, this could take all week!" said Mr. Emory. "The real issue here is Mrs. Cimino's present capacity, not a plan she's drawn up."

"In the interest of saving time," said Philip, "I'd certainly be willing to let Mr. Emory question my client on how she proposes to run things."

"How about that?" said Judge Schultz to Mr. Emory.

He watched the attorney for the bank with interest, wondering if the bait would be taken. In his experience, the elderly often proved to be embarrassingly detailed in their command of facts regarding stores and other businesses. The questions might be few, but the answers could be voluble, lecturelike, glossing the present in terms of the past again and again.

"I'm prepared to concede Mrs. Cimino's general knowledge of the business," said Mr. Emory. "I'd rather question her on how things have been going for her in Florida."

"What's Florida have to do with it?" said Philip, not without suspicion.

"The central issue here is her basic capacity," said Mr. Emory. "I don't think the court is going to be comfortable unless it's sure that she's able to take care of herself today, tomorrow, and the day after that." His smile, directed primarily toward Judge Schultz, was one of the affectionate concern.

"Then you're prepared to concede the efficacy of her plan?" said Philip.

"I didn't say that," said Mr. Emory, tapping his heel on the carpet a little faster. "I merely said I was willing to concede her general knowledge of the business."

"Then you'll have no objection if I question Mr. Markle regarding specific conditions," said Philip, pressing the point.

"I don't see any point to it," said Mr. Emory. He looked appealingly at Judge Schultz. "He just told us that there was no mismanagement involved."

"I'm not suggesting that there is," said Philip quickly. "But I think the court needs this information in order to evaluate the plan."

Judge Schultz looked at his watch. He took another look at the bank's response. The response was a little vague about the present operation of the store, preferring instead to focus upon the petitioner's present age (seventy-seven) and to raise the dark prospect of custodial care sometime in the future. In terms of the future, the response pointed to the court's wise continuation of the trust at the hearing which found the petitioner technically competent within the letter of the law.

As far as the spirit of the law went, the bank's response reminded the court that elderly people such as the petitioner were in general deemed unusually vulnerable to the influence of artful and designing persons. In view of this vulnerability, the response submitted it would be most improper to remove the petitioner from the protection of the court and from the trust set up on her behalf.

Judge Schultz looked at Mr. Emory, freckled face intent, heel tapping gently on the carpet. He looked at young Philip Ryan, less nervous now that things were out on the table. The two men had been fencing. It was time to step in and move matters along.

"I've heard enough," he sighed. "I think I'll let Mrs. Cimino be questioned first, and then we'll hear from Mr. Markle."

He looked at Philip and then over at Mr. Emory. Both attorneys seemed satisfied with the sequence.

"After that I'll hear closing arguments for the petition and against," he continued. "Then I'll either make a decision or postpone matters pending a more detailed study of these records."

"Thank you, Your Honor," said Mr. Emory, first on his feet and already started toward the door.

"Thank you, Your Honor," said Philip. A little more slowly, he checked his briefcase to make sure everything was there before walking briskly out, almost a half a minute behind Mr. Emory's tall, rawboned frame.

Judge Schultz did not hurry. After the attorneys left he continued to sit at his desk, stretching a little here and there, almost as though the bar association had designed special isometric exercises for use in judicial chambers. Relaxed, he rose and went over to the full-length mirror that graced the left wall of the room. There he put on his black robe, making sure that its generous drape hung freely.

He was not a dramatic man. But he was conscious of the dignity of his office. And he knew a proper entrance was always necessary. After checking his watch again to make sure that everyone would be expectantly in place, he gathered up his papers. Papers firmly in hand, he swept quickly out of his chambers, setting a well-paced tempo right from the start.

Thursday, April 7, 11:00 A.M.

Mrs. Cimino had chosen her costume with care. Her dress was a soft wool, mauve-colored, with pleats along the sides that gave her short, sturdy frame the effect of modest height. With her black purse and shoes, she stepped up to the witness stand and took her seat with an air of springlike dignity, lying somewhere between the austere restraint of Mrs. Hinckle and the bright feathers of Mrs. Gatlin.

Even though her feet were barely able to touch the floor, she was comfortable. Philip's preparation of the case had been thorough, and the dark possibility of George or Harold's opposing her had not materialized. It would have been good to have them with her, smiling up from the seats below, but Karen was enough. Prepared to endure her small ordeal with understanding and good humor, she nodded pleasantly to Mr. Emory as he approached her.

"Florida seems to agree with you, Mrs. Cimino," said Mr. Emory. "You're looking quite fit."

Mrs. Cimino blushed a little under her tan. She had expected someone more hostile, chilly in the way that bankers were. But this gentleman was wholesome: He had something of the Johnson look to him, a tall, rawboned, freckle-faced flavor of honest work that argued well for their exchange.

"We walk a lot down there," she said, smiling pleasantly at both Mr. Emory and the people seated in the back, much as though a primary reason for her visit was to celebrate the virtues of sun-drenched leisure.

"Good!" said Mr. Emory approvingly. "I'm really sorry you've been put to the inconvenience of coming up here before our spring has settled in."

Mrs. Cimino, not sure of what to say, bent her small head, softly coiffed. She looked over at Karen: Karen was smiling. She looked down at Philip: He was solemn.

"And I also regret having to ask you a few questions," Mr. Emory continued. "After all, it's your money." He laughed in a shy, apologetic way, like a big farm boy asked to come up before the class and recite. "But we want to be sure we're doing the right thing."

Mrs. Cimino nodded. Relaxed, she sat back and folded her hands.

"We know you're not happy with the trust arrangement," said Mr. Emory. "Would you mind telling us why?"

"Gladly," said Mrs. Cimino, smiling at him to take the sting out of her words. "I just don't like the idea of someone else making decisions for me."

"Can't blame you for that," laughed Mr. Emory. "I feel the same way myself." He chuckled a little more before moving on to his unpleasant duty. "But apart from the principle of the thing, can you give us a specific example of where your trustee has acted contrary to your wishes?"

"Christmas," said Mrs. Cimino firmly. "That Mr. Leach of yours refused to let me give my grandchildren the gifts I had planned for them."

"Did he?" Mr. Emory appeared to be quite shocked. He paused and went back to a number of papers scattered carelessly on the table. "And you asked him this in a letter?"

"I certainly did," said Mrs. Cimino.

"But he answered your letter, didn't he?" said Mr. Emory, fishing out a document and holding it up. "And he also enclosed a handsome check for you to spend on your grandchildren."

322

"It was less than I had in mind," said Mrs. Cimino. "Less than I asked him for."

"But he did not actually refuse you, did he?"

"No, not if you want to be technical about it." Mrs. Cimino pondered the matter, then brightened. "But he completely refused to allow a gift to Karen for her education."

"Didn't he give you a good reason for that?" smiled Mr. Emory. He paused and stepped back for a moment. "Or don't you remember what he wrote you?"

"Of course I remember," snapped Mrs. Cimino. "He said that her character would be strengthened if she relied on her own resources."

"Your memory's very good," said Mr. Emory. He nodded around the courtroom as though to call attention to his elderly prodigy. "But are you telling us that you feel Mr. Leach was wrong?"

"I think he was wrong to do what *he* wanted to do rather than what *I* wanted him to do," said Mrs. Cimino. She smiled gently at him, feeling that she had escaped from a small trap of some sort.

"Don't you trust Mr. Leach's judgment?" said Mr. Emory. There was a look of pain on his freckled face.

"I'd rather trust my own judgment," said Mrs. Cimino.

"And how would you describe your judgment last spring?"

"Last spring?" Mrs. Cimino, suddenly ill at ease, looked down at Philip in a clear appeal for help.

Philip was on his feet at once, not irate but firm in his objection.

"Your Honor!" he said. "The petitioner's condition last spring is a matter of record." He looked witheringly at Mr. Emory, who had retreated in pained dismay to just in front of his place at the counsel's table. "My understanding was that Mr. Emory's questions were going to deal with the present."

"I'll put it another way," said Mr. Emory, smiling over at Philip. He came quietly up to Mrs. Cimino and smiled again at her. "Would you say that Mr. Leach's judgment last spring was trustworthy?"

"No," said Mrs. Cimino flatly.

"Why?"

"He sold my house without even asking me," said Mrs. Cimino, newly seething under the recollection of the action.

"Where were you at the time of this sale?"

"In the hospital," said Mrs. Cimino. "St. Hild's Hospital, about forty miles north of here."

"Did you like it there?" said Mr. Emory.

"Very much," said Mrs. Cimino. "They have a wonderful program."

"Yes, they do," said Mr. Emory quickly. "And your present state of improved health and vigor is directly due to that program, isn't that right?"

"It certainly is," said Mrs. Cimino, glad to be once again in positive territory.

"And it was Mr. Leach who urged your transfer from White Towers to St. Hild's," said Mr. Emory. "Isn't that true?"

"I guess so," said Mrs. Cimino slowly. "But it was Karen who visited St. Hild's and recommended it."

"Of course," said Mr. Emory. He turned and smiled at Karen. "But it was still your trustee who urged and approved the move." He smiled as though to recapture and cherish the action. "I'd say that was darn good judgment on Mr. Leach's part, wouldn't you?"

"Yes," said Mrs. Cimino in a low voice.

"We don't expect a medal," said Mr. Emory. "That's what a trustee is supposed to do." He looked around to embrace the room with his remarks. "A trustee is there to protect you and to look out for your best interests." He turned back to Mrs. Cimino and moved closer to her. "Don't you want that protection any more?"

"I can look out for myself," said Mrs. Cimino stoutly.

"How have you been handling your money?" said Mr. Emory.

"I pay my bills," said Mrs. Cimino. "And I keep my checkbook balanced."

"That's more than a lot of us do," said Mr. Emory laughingly. "And where's your checking account?"

"Florida Security Bank."

Mr. Emory put his tall, rawboned frame in motion and went back to his papers on the table. He picked up one and returned with it.

"That's right!" he said, almost with pleased surprise. "And you opened it on November twenty-second. Isn't that right?"

"I think so," said Mrs. Cimino, growing a bit nervous.

"Do you remember how much your original deposit was for?"

"Eight hundred dollars," said Mrs. Cimino, feeling more at ease as she demonstrated her command of matters.

"Right again!" said Mr. Emory, as though she had just shown great classroom brilliance. "And did you make any withdrawals that day?"

"No," said Mrs. Cimino. She looked over at Philip appealingly. But Philip merely looked back at her: smiling, slightly puzzled.

"Did you *attempt* to make any withdrawals?"

"I might have," said Mrs. Cimino, faded blue eyes misting a little.

"According to Mr. Harris, the assistant manager of your local branch of Florida Security, you attempted to withdraw seven hundred dollars less than an hour after you opened the account." Mr. Emory's voice was low, almost confidential, as though reluctant to trumpet the facts forth.

The court stenographer paused and looked up at Judge Schultz. Judge Schultz looked down at her. He scowled and looked over at Mr. Emory.

"How much?" said Judge Schultz.

"Seven hundred dollars," said Mr. Emory. "That's what you tried to withdraw, isn't it?"

"I guess it is if you say it is," said Mrs. Cimino. She gave one of her embarrassed little laughs. She did not look at Philip. She did not look at Karen. She did not look at the friendly elderly gentlemen in the back of the room. She looked down, examining the tips of her black shoes with sudden interest.

"But Mr. Harris persuaded you not to make this withdrawal, didn't he?"

Mrs. Cimino nodded.

"He acted in what he thought were your best interests," said Mr. Emory. "And that's what we're trying to do here." He moved very close to her, almost protectively so. "Some of this may be embarrassing, even painful, but it's necessary in helping the court reach a wise decision."

Mr. Emory paused and looked round the room. It was quiet. He looked at Philip Ryan: Philip was somber, thoughtful. He turned back to Mrs. Cimino.

"I want you to take your time here, Mrs. Cimino," he said.

"But I'd really like you to tell us the circumstances leading up to your attempted withdrawal of these moneys."

Philip sprang up, face aglow. He rounded his side of the table and stood there looking up at Judge Schultz.

"I don't see the point of this, Your Honor," he said. "No money was lost, no error in judgment was involved." He stopped for breath and looked angrily at Mr. Emory. "And you certainly can't expect the petitioner to have complete recall of an incident that took place almost five months ago." He remained standing, forcing the point.

"I'd say it's Mr. Ryan who's trying to work both sides of the street here," said Mr. Emory softly. "First he objects when I ask the petitioner about her circumstances in Minneapolis last spring, and now he objects to my asking her about her circumstances in Florida."

"It's an eight-hundred-dollar deposit and a seven-hundred-dollar withdrawal an hour later?" said Judge Schultz, looking bemusedly at Mrs. Cimino.

"An *attempted* withdrawal," said Philip firmly. He sat down.

"I'd like to hear about it," said Judge Schultz. "but I think, Mr. Emory, that you could be more direct in developing this information."

"Thank you, Your Honor," said Mr. Emory. He turned to Mrs. Cimino, still gentle in his manner. "Didn't you tell Mr. Harris you had been assaulted by a purse snatcher after making your deposit?"

"Yes," said Mrs. Cimino in a low voice.

"And didn't you also tell him that a gentleman stepped in to rescue you?"

"Yes."

"And didn't you tell Mr. Harris that this gentleman solicited your participation in a scheme to entrap an embezzler at Florida Security?"

Mrs. Cimino nodded.

"What credentials did this gentleman offer you?" said Mr. Emory, his freckled face creased with puzzlement. "Who did he say he worked for?"

"He said he worked for the Federal Reserve," said Mrs.

Cimino. Recovering her equilibrium somewhat, she faced Mr. Emory more directly. "I was so upset from the purse snatching that I believed him."

"But he was really an unscrupulous confidence man," said Mr. Emory. "And he enticed you into withdrawing seven hundred dollars for use in his scheme. Isn't that correct?"

"Just a minute," said Philip. "No withdrawal was actually made."

"I'll grant that," said Mr. Emory smoothly. "But he did entice you into filling out and presenting a withdrawal slip. Isn't that the way it worked out?"

"Yes, sir," said Mrs. Cimino. "That's what happened."

"Fortunately, no harm was done," said Mr. Emory. "beyond a little embarrassment then and now. I sincerely regret having to bring all this out." He smiled around the room, taking in the backbenchers, all grown quite silent. "So let's drop it and get a picture of how things are going for you right now down in St. Petersburg." He went back to his table and picked up another sheet of paper. "You're staying at the President Jefferson Hotel?"

"Yes, I am," said Mrs. Cimino, breathing more easily now that the Mr. Desmond ordeal was over.

"Would you say they take good care of their guests?"

"Yes," said Mrs. Cimino. "They're lovely people."

"Mr. Bales is the manager, isn't he?"

"Yes, he is," said Mrs. Cimino, growing uncomfortable again. For a Minneapolis banker, Mr. Emory seemed to have learned a great deal about St. Petersburg recently.

"They're good about reminding their guests to take their medication, aren't they?" said Mr. Emory, looking at his paper as though it were a descriptive brochure.

"Yes, they are."

"And I believe they have an arrangement for signing out and signing in when guests are gone for any length of time. Isn't that true?" Mr. Emory continued to look at his brochure, nodding approval at the wholesome concern it displayed.

"Yes, they do," Mrs. Cimino's voice moved into its low register again.

"Have you yourself done any signing out and signing in?"

"Yes, I have," said Mrs. Cimino wearily. Not wanting to look at either Philip or Karen, she fixed her gaze on a point halfway up the back wall.

"And these records show that your visits during the last three months have nearly all involved overnight stays at the home of a friend." Mr. Emory smiled, put down his papers, and came up to her again. "Is this friend a lady friend or a gentleman friend?" There was a light archness to his tone.

"A gentleman friend," said Mrs. Cimino stoutly, "and a very old friend."

"Old?" said Mr. Emory. "He's younger than you are, isn't he?"

"I'm not sure how old he is," said Mrs. Cimino, growing flustered. "What I meant was that Mr. Barney Feldman is a gentleman whom I first met many, many years ago."

"Have you discussed marriage with this younger man?" said Mr. Emory pleasantly. "Or other sorts of financial arrangements?"

"We've discussed many things," said Mrs. Cimino, bristling in spite of herself. "And I can't see that it's any of your business."

She looked over at Philip: Philip was looking down at his notes. She looked over at Karen: Karen was looking up at her with pained bewilderment, brow furrowed and small, sensitive mouth slightly aquiver. She looked over at Judge Schultz: He was quiet, pensive, handpropping his chin.

"Your welfare and best interests are certainly our business," said Mr. Emory, unoffended. "With all respect to your proper desire for privacy, I must remind you that you are presently under the protection of this court." He smiled up at Judge Schultz and moved slightly away from her. "And it is this court which has appointed a trustee to protect you from artful and designing persons."

At the phrase, remembering Philip's use of it, Mrs. Cimino felt her cheeks grow hot.

"There are lots of these rascals around," continued Mr. Emory, widening his range of concern to include the whole room. "Sly men, younger men, younger men with clever ways of victimizing older women." He shook his head sadly and returned his gaze to Mrs. Cimino. "Speaking for myself, I can only say that I truly regret the fact that you have seen fit to involve yourself in this sort of relationship." He paused, frowning at the spectacle evoked.

328

With manifest effort he brightened, smiled at her, and gestured once more, this time as though to present her in full dignity to the assembly. "But I want to thank you, Mrs. Cimino, for the courtesy with which you have answered these questions. You're a charming lady, and I'm sure you recognize our intentions are respectful and concerned."

With that, Mr. Emory wheeled round and walked directly to take his seat behind the counselors' table. Mrs. Cimino started to get up, but Judge Schultz stayed her with a gesture and a shaking of the head, as he looked expectantly down at Philip. Philip got immediately up and came over, trying to look very confident and reassuring.

"Exactly how long have you known Mr. Feldman?" said Philip. "When did you first meet him?"

"Fifty years ago," said Mrs. Cimino. "He was one of my late husband's closest friends."

"Fifty years ago!" said Philip, looking down at Mr. Emory. "And he was over twenty then?"

"Yes, he was."

"And so our younger man turns out to be well over seventy," said Philip to Judge Schultz. He turned again to Mrs. Cimino. "Does he own property? Is his income sufficient for his needs?"

"He owns his own home," said Mrs. Cimino. "And he also owns some other pieces of real estate in St. Petersburg. I would say he lives quite comfortably."

"Did he encourage you in any way to initiate this petition?"

"He did not," said Mrs. Cimino firmly. "I first met him down there at our Christmas party, and I had written you well before that time."

"Quite right!" said Philip, emphatically and with obvious relief. "Your recollection is quite correct—as my office records will show." He turned once more to Judge Schultz. "And so is this relationship, which Mr. Emory seeks to taint with scandal. Two old friends meet, they break bread together, they share one another's company." He raised his voice and looked round the room. "It should be clear to any reasonable person that what we've heard here reflects great credit upon the petitioner's state of mind and health."

Mrs. Cimino sighed gratefully and looked at him as he held out his arm to assist her down. Still beet red with shame and humiliation, she felt unsteady on her feet, and the distance to her seat seemed uncommonly long and fraught with danger. But she dropped his arm and stood there, making sure her balance was steady before setting out.

Her progress back was slow, her steps small, in marked contrast to the way she had bustled up, fashionably frocked, filled with confidence. And she was slightly sweaty after her public display of foolishness, past and present. But she made it: without stumbling, without faltering, and with even a chilly smile for the freckle-faced gentleman in the Brooks Brothers suit.

Thursday, April 7, 11:30 A.M.

Philip Ryan tried to mask his irritation as he looked through his notes prior to beginning his examination of Brian Markle. The exchange between Mr. Emory and Mrs. Cimino had been damaging. And it had made his own lack of preparation embarrassingly obvious to everyone there: including Karen, before whom he had posed in a slightly knowing, overbearing way. He tried to shake off the thought of how his father would chide him for failing to probe beneath the surface of his client's words in stating the circumstances.

As quickly as he could, under the pressure of time, he tried to reshape his approach. It would not be easy to neutralize the picture Mr. Emory had painted, squeezing each pigment out from Mrs. Cimino's Florida stay and packing it heavily upon the canvas with bold, lurid strokes. But he was hopeful, and he gave Mrs. Cimino's small hand a reassuring squeeze before focusing his attention upon Brian.

Despite his newly won executive post, Brian still wore his dark hair quite long. And his drooping mustache still had a fearless piratical flavor. His clothes, carefully chosen for the occasion, were those of a New Mexico sheepherder, except that they were made of brushed denim and had cost over three hundred dollars. Not even the small gold earring in his left ear could detract from the air of prosperous confidence that accompanied him to the witness stand.

"I want to thank you, Mr. Markle, for taking time out from your busy schedule to appear here," said Philip. "The store is still keeping you busy, isn't it?"

"Sure is," said Brian, looking around the courtroom as though to invite the spectators down to try out assorted guitars and amplifiers. "We really have it swinging now."

"I'm sure you have every reason to be proud of yourself," said Philip. "And I'm sure the bank is equally proud of you," He took a minute to look over at Mr. Emory, as though seeking enthusiastic support. Mr. Emory's freckled face was impassive.

"When did you assume the managership of Cimino Music?" continued Philip.

"The first of May," said Brian.

"Was Simon Montford connected with the store then?"

"Yeah," said Brian. "He was there,"

"Did you consider him competent in his work?"

"He was a pretty cool dude about fixing things," said Brian, "But he kept hassling me about the new image."

"Did you fire him?"

"No," said Brian. "I just told him to come in and leave through the back door so he wouldn't make the place look tacky." There were a couple of appreciative snorts from the far side of the courtroom, where two young women and a young man were sitting. The bailiff, a large muscular man, stared them into immediate silence.

"In other words, you had a conflict in professional judgment. Isn't that right?"

"That's right," said Brian. "We just couldn't make it together."

"And you felt your professional judgment was superior to his. Isn't that right?"

"Right again," said Brian, blue eyes sparkling proudly. "After all, I'm the manager."

"What's the name of the music store you manage?"

"Cimino Music," said Brian.

"And why is it called Cimino Music?" said Philip, looking down toward his small client.

"Because Mrs. Cimino owns it," said Brian. He nodded chummily at Mrs. Cimino. Mrs. Cimino did not nod back.

"If Mrs. Cimino owns it, don't you think her judgment should prevail over yours?"

"Your Honor!" said Mr. Emory, unwinding his tall, rawboned frame and putting it combatively on the floor. "Mr. Ryan is asking for a general opinion here."

"On the contrary," said Philip. "I'm asking for a *professional* opinion regarding the management of a music store." He looked at Mr. Emory and then up at Judge Schultz, looming above him. "It seems to me my question is just as valid as Mr. Emory's question of Mrs. Cimino regarding Mr. Leach's judgment."

"I'm sorry," said Judge Schultz, looking at Brian speculatively, "but I have to agree with Mr. Emory. Try to focus on the present condition of the store."

"Very well, Your Honor," said Philip. He turned back to Brian. "Under your managership, Mr. Markle, the store has begun to deal in a number of new merchandise items. Isn't that true?"

"That's right," said Brian. "We're very much into heavy amplifiers and keyboards now." He beamed complacently round the room.

"Doesn't that take up a lot of space?"

"That's our main problem," said Brian.

"And you've tried to solve that problem by using space formerly devoted to instrument repair and music instruction. Isn't that correct?"

"It's helped," said Brian. "But we could still use more."

"Hasn't your solution meant some loss in income?"

"Not in terms of the bottom line," said Brian. "We've also cut out a lot of salary expense."

"By salary expense, you mean the jobs of two repair people and five teachers, don't you?"

"A lean operation is a clean operation," smiled Brian. "And we're pushing for more of a contemporary feeling."

"Can you give us an example of what you mean?"

"T-shirts!" said Brian, brightening enthusiastically. "Up-to-date body language!" He threw open his jacket and pointed to a yellow undergarment with compelling purple lettering across the front.

" 'See Cimino for what's Cool and Keen-oh,' " read Philip aloud in a slow monotone. "That's very catchy." He looked around the room as though about to take a vote on the slogan's effectiveness. "Is this part of your customer relations program?"

"The kids love 'em," said Brian.

"And how about your relations with other tenants in the building?" said Philip.

"We've had a few bad vibes here and there," said Brian, shrugging.

"Weren't there complaints about the noise?"

"Not noise!" said Brian. There was pain in his blue eyes. "We're talking about music."

"According to police records, the complaints have been using the words *excessive noise*."

"Your Honor!" said Mr. Emory, on his feet again. "Mr. Ryan is wandering off again. Please instruct him to focus on the present condition of the store."

"But Your Honor," said Philip. "There's been more turnover in the tenancy of the building this year than in the previous five years combined. And we must remember that the assets in question include both the store and the building that houses it."

"It's a proper area for questioning," said Judge Schultz.

"Thank you, Your Honor," said Philip. He went back to his table and picked up a piece of paper. "I see you've had a couple of insurance claims filed."

"We've had some bad luck," said Brian, shrugging again.

"Your last claim was for a theft of thirty thousand dollars' worth of equipment, wasn't it?"

"A real downer," said Brian, shaking his head sadly.

"But the police report shows no signs of breaking and entering," said Philip. "How do you explain that?"

"I've already explained it," said Brian in an injured tone. "To the police, to the insurance people, and to the insurance people again." He squirmed a little in his seat and then sat up very straight. "Someone must have forgotten to lock up that night."

"That's an expensive oversight, isn't it?"

"Your Honor!" Mr. Emory rose. "Mishaps like these constitute normal hazards of doing business. I suggest that Mr. Ryan is unfairly attempting to belittle this fine young man."

"But Your Honor," said Philip quickly. "Mr. Emory implied a serious lack of judgment on the petitioner's part when she had a close escape from a comparatively small loss, seven hundred dollars. Here we have a thirty-thousand-dollar loss, clearly due to poor judgment, and Mr. Emory asks us to be understanding."

Philip paused, looked at Mr. Emory a moment, and then raised his voice a little.

"And I agree with Mr. Emory," he continued. "I think we should be understanding, particularly since natural errors in judgment are bound to occur in unfamiliar surroundings."

"You're losing me," said Judge Schultz, leaning forward a little and peering down at him. "What do you mean by your reference to unfamiliar surroundings?"

"I mean, Your Honor, that the music store itself is as much an unfamiliar setting for Mr. Markle as a crowded, hostile street corner is for Mrs. Cimino."

"You haven't established that for us," said Judge Schultz, sitting back and looking at his watch.

"I think it should be clear from what we've heard that Mr. Markle took over a business with which he was unfamiliar," said Philip. "A business with nine employees; a business with an ideal balance between sales, service, and instruction. Not knowing how to run it, he converted it into a stable of expensive electronic white elephants with only three keepers to watch them!"

"Irrelevant, irrelevant!" said Mr. Emory, shaking his head. "We're dealing with the trust, not with the qualifications of a manager who can easily be replaced." He sat down, gray-green eyes coldly fixed on Brian.

"I suggest it's highly relevant to point out the contrast between Mrs. Cimino's approach and Mr. Markle's approach," said Philip. "After all, it is Mrs. Cimino's judgment that has been of such concern to Mr. Emory."

"It's a matter of concern to us all," said Judge Schultz, looking reflectively down at Mrs. Cimino. "Are there questions you can put to the witness that deal with his qualifications?"

"Yes, Your Honor," said Philip, quickly turning toward Brian again. "Mr. Markle, have you ever managed a music store before this?"

"Not exactly," said Brian.

"What do you mean by that?"

"I mean I managed a music group," said Brian. "And that's

sort of like a music store," he added cheerfully, "as far as the equipment part of it goes."

"Very interesting," said Philip. "But who hired you for the managership of Cimino Music?"

"The bank did," said Brian, nodding down toward Mr. Emory.

"Who at the bank?" said Philip.

"Mr. Leach," said Brian.

"That's Mr. Edward Leach, isn't it?" said Philip. "And his home address is 4456 Crescent Drive, isn't it?"

"I guess so," said Brian. He slouched down in his chair a little.

"I would think your recollection ought to be quite clear," said Philip. He raised his voice a bit. "Didn't you list that address as your own home address on a credit application last January?"

"I suppose I did," said Brian ruefully.

"So you and your wife were living at the home of Mr. Leach." Philip smiled over at Mr. Emory for a moment. "Mr. Leach is your father-in-law, isn't he?"

"Yes," said Brian. He looked appealingly down at Mr. Emory. Mr. Emory's freckled face was set, and his heel was tapping to a lively tempo.

"Don't you think it was very generous of your father-in-law to give you a well-paying managerial position in a field where you had no previous work?"

"I guess so," sighed Brian.

"I quite agree," said Philip firmly. He turned back to the courtroom at large. "But some people might say, as Mr. Leach himself said to my client, that your character would be more strengthened if you relied on your own resources."

From the back of the room, chokings and wheezings could be heard as the chorus of elders commented. But they were soon frowned into silence, after which Philip walked over to where Mrs. Cimino was sitting.

"It should be clear, Your Honor, that Mr. Emory is attempting to judge the petitioner by artificially high standards," said Philip. "In terms of those standards, she is expected to avoid natural hazards such as purse snatchers. And she is expected to avoid natural slips in judgment. And she is certainly expected to avoid natural relationships based on affection and friendship." He paused and gestured up toward Brian. "But thanks to the testimony of this fine young man we can see that these artifically high standards do not really apply to the bank itself."

He paused, looking around the courtroom for a moment to let the import of his words sink in. And it was with reasonable confidence that he smiled up at Judge Schultz, who was still scowling over at Brian.

"I have no more questions, Your Honor," said Philip. He sat down and gave Mrs. Cimino's hand another reassuring squeeze.

"Mr. Markle!" said Mr. Emory, on his feet almost immediately and determined to salvage matters. "You were a professional musician for many years, were you not?"

"That's right," said Brian, brightening a little.

"And what was your instrument?"

"I played the guitar," said Brian, suddenly putting his hands in position to sound an opening chord on an invisible assembly of wood and wire.

"Splendid!" said Mr. Emory, beaming round at everybody. "Are you aware that the late Mr. Cimino was also a professional guitarist for many years?"

"That's what they say," said Brian, obviously relieved to be in laudatory, friendly hands.

"So it would have been reasonable for Mr. Leach to conclude that your professional background equipped you for this position, wouldn't it?"

"I think so," said Brian, nodding his head ruminatively.

"And isn't it also true that Mr. Leach was assigned to this trust around the first of April?" said Mr. Emory, looking up at Judge Schultz.

"That's right," said Brian.

"Acting under the pressure of time, it would certainly have been reasonable for Mr. Leach to take advantage of his relationship with you, rather than engaging an unqualified stranger at such short notice. Don't you agree?"

"I think so," said Brian, confidence almost completely recovered by now.

"I think so, too," said Mr. Emory firmly. "And I think the bank was unusually fortunate in securing the services of someone with the same background as the late Mr. Cimino, particularly on such short notice. And I also think our Mr. Leach was fortunate in

336

finding someone whose relationship with him insured the kind of trustworthy performance necessary in our fiduciary responsibility."

Tall, impressive in his Brooks Brothers suit, Mr. Emory looked around the room, almost as though he were about to evoke a round of applause for his witness. Smiling easily at Judge Schultz, he stepped back to his place at the table.

"I have no more questions, Your Honor," he said.

"Very well," said Judge Schultz. "You may step down, Mr. Markle."

With a bland, neutral gaze, Judge Schultz watched Brian uncoil himself and saunter over to his small claque. Even after Brian had squeezed into his seat, Judge Schultz continued to gaze around the room, almost as a conductor shapes his silence before attacking a busily frenetic overture.

"We'll resume after lunch," he said. "at which time I'll hear your closing arguments for and against the petition."

He paused again, nodding round the room, as though to fix the faces of everyone there in his memory.

"This court stands adjourned until two o'clock!" he said finally, punctuating the matter with an authoritative rap of his gavel and a quick movement up from his chair.

Not surprisingly, he reached the parking lot well before any of the others got as far as the elevator door.

Thursday, April 7, 2:00 P.M.

The courtroom had begun to fill up. Over to the right, behind Karen, the chorus of elderly backbenchers had swollen to over half a dozen. And on the far left several middle-aged ladies had variously come in, not unlike solitary visitants to a large cathedral in the afternoon. In between were four or five attorneys, briefcased and well barbered, checking their materials and coming up from time to time to confer with the court clerk regarding the status of the docket.

Karen had expected her grandmother would be sitting back with her: comfortable, farther removed from the arena. But Philip had insisted she resume her place beside him at the counselor's table. He had not lunched with them, preferring to spend the time in revising the draft of his argument. He had stopped by only to share a quick cup of coffee and voice reasonable optimism regarding their prospects.

She looked over at him, trying to read their fortunes in his bearing.

He seemed relaxed, more so than Mr. Emory, whose right heel was tapping briskly as he scrutinized his notes. But the relaxation could be deceptive: It could stem from resignation as much as confidence. And Karen's own confidence had begun to slip away. Their case was far too blurred for comfort, and Mr. Emory seemed to have the knack of coloring and recoloring simple facts with all sorts of curious implications.

Judge Schultz, as usual, was prompt. He settled himself, nodded the courtroom to its collective ease, and opened up his file. He took a minute or so to refresh his memory. He looked down at Mrs. Cimino, sitting quietly beside her attorney. The sight seemed to reassure him.

"I see both attorneys are here," said Judge Schultz. "So I think we might as well get started." He looked down at Philip. "Does the attorney for the petitioner have a closing argument for us?"

"I shall try to be brief, Your Honor," said Philip. He took a final look at his notes and rose. "Despite some of the complexities introduced in opposition, this is still a simple, straightforward case." He looked over at Mr. Emory and shook his head sadly at the spectacle of a distinguished attorney wasting his talents and the court's time on distracting trivia.

"Our petition asks for nothing more than a simple extension of the court's most recent ruling," continued Philip. "At that time, six months ago, this court found the petitioner fully competent, even though she was then undergoing treatment at St. Hild's Convalescent Hospital."

He looked over at Mrs. Cimino for a moment. She was sitting quietly in her seat, taking in the proceedings attentively. In her soft wool dress and very slightly bouffant hairdo, she seemed far distant from the gray, helpless picture he had just sketched.

"At that time the petitioner refrained from seeking the return of her assets to her personal control," he added. "Her primary goal was to concentrate on making the difficult transition from institu-

338

tional living to an independent mode of life. And it should be obvious to everyone here that she has successfully achieved that goal."

Philip paused, smiled approvingly at Mrs. Cimino, and let his eyes roam around the room, coming finally to rest on Judge Schultz. Lips slightly pursed, Judge Schultz was looking thoughtfully at Mrs. Cimino.

"The petitioner has been a resident of this city, a property owner here, and a business owner here," said Philip, ticking off each point on his fingers. "Although she is in Florida for her health, she continues to have strong ties here in Minneapolis, and the return of her assets to her control is well justified in terms of those ties."

He paused and looked over at Karen, smiling slightly, as though to draw her into the discussion.

"Of particular concern to us is the store that bears her name and the name of her family—Cimino Music. It is not a large business, but it has served the community for almost fifty years, and it has offered employment to members of this community. In times like these, we are certainly justified in seeking to maintain the continuity of a family-owned, family-operated business such as this."

Philip paused again and looked up at Judge Schultz, trying to see whether his key point would be accepted as such. Judge Schultz was impassive.

"We have submitted to the court a detailed plan describing how that continuity will be maintained," Philip gestured to a folder on his table. "The store will be under the direct supervision of the petitioner's granddaughter, subject to the guidance of the petitioner herself. Many family-owned businesses in this city offer ample precedent for this sort of arrangement."

"Your Honor will note that we make no allegations of misfeasance or malfeasance on the part of the trustee appointed to act for the petitioner. Any mistakes made were certainly honest mistakes and a natural result of difficulties inherent in taking over a small, specialized business. Nor would we suggest any error in the original decision establishing the trust. At that time, no one in the family was able to step forward and keep the store going."

Philip looked over at Mr. Emory, nodding kindly toward him as though to suggest that they were all participating in a friendly committee discussion.

"But circumstances change," continued Philip. "And the court wisely chose to recognize the petitioner's change for the better in declaring her competent six months ago. At the present time her health is even more improved, and a member of the family is now able to assist her with the store. I am quite sure that the court will recognize these new circumstances in reassessing the matter."

Philip paused again. He had made his basic case, and he wanted to make sure the court would ruminate upon it. He walked back to his table and took another quick look at his notes. Then he looked over at Mr. Emory, took a deep breath, and began to speak with a little more fervor.

"Minneapolis Southern Bank has elected to oppose this petition," he said. "And I'm sure it has not escaped the court's notice that it stands alone in this action, unsupported by any member of the petitioner's family. In so doing, it argues that the petitioner's best interests will be served by continuing the trust, even though the circumstances that justified its establishment have materially changed.

"Its basic assumption is that it is somehow better equipped to look after the petitioner's best interests than is the petitioner herself. And on the basis of this assumption, it seeks to decide where she will live, what she will live on, and how her business is to be run. For these questionable services, she is compelled to pay handsome fees."

One of the elderly backbenchers, a thin white-haired man in a brown jacket, snorted and poked one of his neighbors, a heavy man who had dozed off for a minute. But the other members of the chorus quickly quieted him with stern looks of reproof.

"Clearly no citizen of this country should be forced to endure this kind of coercive treatment," continued Philip, smiling back at his supporters. "Particularly when there is absolutely no question regarding the citizen's emotional stability or mental competence. Why then should the bank seek to retain its power over Mrs. Cimino?"

Again he looked over at Mrs. Cimino, tanned and fit, dressed with fashionable restraint, eyes alive with interest.

"If Mrs. Cimino were thirty-five years old, Mr. Emory would not be here this afternoon," said Philip, smiling up at Judge Schultz. "Nor would he be here if she were forty-five or fifty-five. It is only because the petitioner has spent seventy-seven years on this earth, nearly all of them in useful service to her community, that the bank sees fit to interpose itself between the petitioner and the assets that she has thriftily accumulated over the years.

"It is the petitioner's age which colors every bit of evidence Mr. Emory has put before us. If a younger person made a slip in judgment—even a costly one—we would let it pass. And if a younger person had spent the night at the home of an old and dear friend, we would point no finger of implicit scorn. And if a younger person were to seek the return of assets accumulated over a period of time, we would certainly admit the justice and good sense of such a claim."

It was time for another pause. Philip looked at his backbenchers: They were all quiet, attentive. He looked at Karen: She seemed pleased, optimistic. He looked at Mrs. Cimino: She was nodding, a slight scowl on her small face, as though the case should be decided forthwith and everybody sent home.

"No one denies that our capacities decline as we grow older," said Philip, directing his remarks to Judge Schultz primarily. "But this generalization must always defer to the nature of the particular individual. Most forty-five–year–old men, for example, are neither strong nor agile, compared to what they were when they were twenty-five. But *some* forty-five–year–old men are very strong and very agile, and it would certainly be an error in judgment to prevent them from playing professional football on the basis of their chronological age.

"So the chronological fact of age must properly defer to other, more compelling facts. Should Benjamin Franklin have been excluded from helping to draw up our Constitution on the grounds that he was eighty-one? Should Nadia Boulanger have been prevented from teaching composition on the grounds that she was eighty-eight? Should Golda Meir have been removed from office on the grounds that she had reached the magic age of seventy-five? Should we have taken the paintbrushes away from Anna Marie Moses on her one hundredth birthday?

"And these are not isolated examples." Philip again looked back toward his chorus of observers, as though about to call some of them up in support. "There are many men and women in this community whose lives testify to the proposition that chronological age offers no obstacle to useful service in this society."

Another pause. A long one. Intended to give Judge Schultz a

strong general principle with which to pry the trust free, levering it up from the solid base of changed circumstances already put forth.

"It is the notion of usefulness that is central to this case," said Philip, voice softer and directed primarily toward the bald-headed man frowning down at him. "In petitioning for the dissolution of the trust, Mrs. Cimino is in effect asserting her desire to continue contributing to the community and to the society at large. Her circumstances are such that she is now well able to make such a contribution, and the chronological fact of age offers no obstacle to her. In view of her present capacities and circumstances, I am confident that the court will grant her petition to have this trust dissolved."

The bald-headed man smiled thinly and sat back. Philip nodded slightly to Mr. Emory and returned to his seat. He pulled his papers and notes together into a neat pile and put them into his briefcase, as though to indicate that the matter had been effectively resolved.

Although his voice had risen a little toward the very end, he had tried to avoid using too many rhetorical flourishes, feeling that the most persuasive element in his case lay in the impression made by the conduct of his client, both under fire on the witness stand and as a quiet participant in the goings-on. After he sat down, he smiled at her once more.

And she at him.

Thursday, April 7, 2:20 P.M.

Mrs. Cimino sat back in her chair, letting herself go limp for a moment. During Philip's speech she had been intent, hearing aid turned up and eyes focused directly on Judge Schultz, as though to drill the argument into his mind. It had been a good argument: Mrs. Polanski would have liked the part about aged achievement, and Miss Schmidt would have liked that part about usefulness.

Certain that her case would prevail, she allowed herself to look around at the stage set in front of her. There was Judge Schultz up

342

above, and below him the court clerk, flanked by the court reporter. Over on her left, standing tall and mighty, was the bailiff, ready to execute commands and restore order, if needed. On her right, just beyond Philip, was Mr. Emory, rising to make his final remarks.

He looked tired; there was a slight stiffness to him, as though his feet ached. And there was a sad look on his freckled face. Mrs. Cimino smiled sympathetically at him: It was clear that Mr. Emory was quite conscious of the awkward position forced upon him by his employers.

"Your Honor," he began. "Let me start out by briefly reviewing the facts we have to work with." He bowed slightly in Mrs. Cimino's direction. "Just one year ago the eldest son of the petitioner asked that she be placed under the protection of this court. And at that time this court appointed Minneapolis Southern Bank as her trustee.

"That decision has demonstrably worked to the petitioner's advantage," he continued. "At the urging of her trustee, she was moved to a facility where she received first-rate care leading to her recovery. After her recovery, her trustee worked out an arrangement whereby she could move down to Florida and lead a comfortable, independent life."

Mr. Emory paused, as though to congratulate Judge Schultz for his vision, and Mrs. Cimino found herself nodding approvingly. Matters had worked out pretty well, all things considered, and it had certainly been a stroke of luck that had taken her from White Towers, with its husky ladies and Mantovani Strings, to St. Hild's.

"Today the petitioner comes before us and asks the court to set aside the fiduciary relationship which has worked so well for her." Mr. Emory shook his head as though hurt by the ingratitude of the action. "And I need hardly point out to the court that neither of her sons have indicated support of this petition. Nor have they participated in the plans she has drawn up."

Mrs. Cimino began to stir uneasily: The facts were accurate enough, but they were somehow incomplete. She had not thought much about George and Lisa, Harold and Gloria. And it was unthinkable that they should be ranged against her, tacitly shaking their heads along with Mr. Emory at her desire to set things right.

"This is not the time to speculate regarding the possibility of bitter family conflict in the future over the management of assets

343

now safely in trust," said Mr. Emory, looking blandly over at her. "But I'm sure the court's experience could provide us with many distressing examples of how well-intentioned actions have led to such conflict. Nor is this the time to speculate on the grim possibility of future ill health on the petitioner's part, though I'm sure the court sees the potential harm involved in her residence far away from this court's jurisdiction and from the community where her welfare has been a matter of sustained concern."

Mrs. Cimino reddened slightly. She put her sympathy for Mr. Emory aside: The man was twisting matters like a salesman of Florida real estate, except that he took the liberty of prophesying gloom and doom rather than increments of wholesome growth. She nudged Philip, trying to scowl him into objecting to what was going on. Philip smiled back and patted her hand.

"Instead of speculating, I propose to examine the petitioner's own speculative claim that both she and the music store will prosper as a result of her return to an active role in its management." Mr. Emory paused again and looked over at the two of them, shaking his head like a wise uncle trying to restrain a couple of giddy nephews. "Mr. Ryan has suggested that she, assisted by a young, inexperienced granddaughter, will be able to manage things more effectively than her trustee in the years to come.

"Mr. Ryan did not directly accuse the trustee—Minneapolis Southern Bank—of mismanagement. And wisely so. For he is well aware that the decisions of a trustee are subject to open scrutiny and review. As trustee, Minneapolis Southern Bank is manifestly accountable to the court, to the government officers who examine it, to its stockholders, to its customers, and to the continual ebb and flow of the marketplace. And he also knows that slight errors in judgment are far less important than the fact that any serious mistakes will inevitably come to light and be corrected."

Another pause. Another nudge, as Mrs. Cimino grew more irate at the way her barefoot farm boy in the Brooks Brothers suit was twisting things. Banks! Large faceless things that sat there like mushrooms in underground caves! Growing fat from the labors of honest men and women, taking their hard-earned money and riffling it through their fat white, sticky hands. And then covering everything up with a blanket of smooth words woven by high-paid lawyers. She scowled intently at Mr. Emory.

344

"Perhaps the store will prosper," smiled Mr. Emory, gesturing toward her in cheery good humor. "Perhaps not. We have no way of knowing. And the court will have no way of protecting the petitioner in the event that serious mistakes are made. The petitioner's granddaughter will not have to account to this court. Nor will other members of the petitioner's family. Nor will any artful and designing person who seeks to trick her. It is only her trustee who is accountable, just as it is the trust established by this court that provides her with the protection she needs."

Mrs. Cimino stopped scowling. Her brow began to furrow, and she looked up at Judge Schultz. Mr. Emory had brought the future into the room: a future populated with Mr. Desmonds, with Harolds and new schemes, a future filled with worries and responsibilities. Blandly suasive, his words coiled around her, bringing with them sudden doubt. She began to wonder why she had chosen to be greedy, seeking to alter a sound arrangement, when she was already content with what she had: sunshine, oranges, and music in the evenings.

"We have seen that the protection of this court has been of great benefit to the petitioner," continued Mr. Emory. "And we have also seen that the trustee has been flexible in responding to changes in the petitioner's circumstances and needs. And we have no reason to assume that this flexible protection will disappear in the future. So we must examine with great care the reasons advanced in support of removing that protection from her.

"Mr. Ryan has suggested that the chronological fact of the petitioner's age should not be a material consideration in the court's decision. And he has cited a number of persuasive examples in support of his suggestion that our senior citizens should be judged in terms of their present capabilities rather than in terms of their age category."

Mr. Emory nodded at Philip as though to suggest that the notion had intrinsic charm and merit. Then he shook his head—wise-unclelike again—and looked round the courtroom, taking the back-benchers into his warm arc of concern.

"Let's be fair," he smiled. "Let's be fair to the citizens of this society and to our public policy which rightly recognizes elderly citizens require reasonable protection. Are we to make Social Security dependent upon a means test? Or Medicare? Are we to reinstate crushing tax burdens upon elderly citizens who sell their homes? Are we to abandon all the progress we've made simply because Pablo Picasso and J. Paul Getty were able to take care of themselves?"

It was with distress that Mrs. Cimino noted stirrings of approval from the elderly backbenchers. She wanted to turn around and address them, pointing out a terrible flaw in Mr. Emory's notion of fairness. It was as though a strange creature had suddenly crept among them, artfully masked until the last moment. It was not a friendly creature, either to her or to them.

But she could not call it by name.

"And let's be honest," continued Mr. Emory, a knowing look in the gray-green eyes. "Mr. Ryan has made much of the petitioner's desire to be useful to the community. And he very clearly feels that the direct control of substantial assets is a necessary condition for this projected usefulness. Are we to infer that people without such control are useless, meaningless ciphers in our society? And are we to infer that people in ordinary walks of life do not contribute immensely—and crucially—to the functioning of our society? Can we honestly say that it is impossible for the petitioner to be useful and still remain under the protection of this court?

"What the petitioner is really seeking is increased power, increased responsibility, along with the increased worry and concern that are part of that responsibility. She is asking the court to put her in the same situation that contributed to her original breakdown last year.

"And what was that situation last year?" said Mr. Emory, staring meditatively at Mrs. Cimino. "It was desperate. That's what it was. The petitioner was helpless, her family was unable to assist her, and her physicians were unable to offer her anything more than custodial care."

Mrs. Cimino bowed her head, trying to blot out the white ghosts summoned up by Mr. Emory. She had almost forgotten about her worrying over money, over the store, over how to sort things into their proper envelopes. And she had almost forgotten her fearful accusations of poisoning, theft, and kidnapping: accusations directed against those who sought to help her. And she had tried to forget about Harold and George, painting a pleasant, understanding picture for herself.

It was not a true picture, even though she had been comfortable with it.

"Today, a year later, the petitioner comes before us." Mr. Emory moved over by Mrs. Cimino and gestured toward her. "She is tanned, fit, altogether charming in her demeanor, and obviously capable of looking after herself."

He smiled down at her, respect manifest, and looked challengingly around the courtroom as though prepared to debate any opposition.

"But a year from now, two years from now, five years from now." He paused and lowered his voice to almost a whisper. "Ten years from now. What will her condition be then? Can we take a chance? Should this court take such a chance?"

Another pause. Then three quick steps immediately back to the front of his table, followed by a quiet, direct address to Judge Schultz.

"The facts are clear." Mr. Emory shrugged slightly, as though to suggest that both closing speeches had been nothing more than conventional forensic exercises. "The petitioner has already suffered one breakdown requiring custodial care. In view of her age, the possibility of another breakdown cannot and should not be ignored by this court. In terms of its responsibility, the court is well justified in continuing its protection of her through the trust arrangement which has thus far worked very effectively in meeting her needs."

Mr. Emory sat down. He did not smile: either at Mrs. Cimino or at Judge Schultz. He stared straight ahead, focusing upon a small section of the wall about two feet to the left of the American flag. His freckled face was immobile, and so was his gangling rawboned frame. Even his right heel was quiet.

Everyone was quiet. But there were still sounds of breathing, of slight stirrings here and there. And underneath it all the soft hum of the ventilating system could be heard. Mrs. Cimino's left hand went up to brush a stray wisp of hair into place. It rested for a moment on the small ridged wheel positioned above her left ear.

She did not turn it off. But she turned it down a little.

Judge Schultz brooded over his quiet courtroom for a moment, much like a large black-robed owl surveying the terrain below. From his perch he was now expected to swoop down and seize justice up, no matter how blurred it might be among the myriad small facts set scurrying about during the hearing. He was not hungry for the task. Any more than he had been hungry for the rhubarb pie at lunch. But the pie had been part of the menu: He had taken it, and it was now rumbling inside him.

And a decision was part of the judicial process. Rumbling or not, he was expected to provide one. Dyspeptically he scowled at his avuncular chorus of backbenchers, as though to remind them they were in his courtroom only on sufferance. He looked down at his notes, trying to find a neat black springboard to send him soaring.

He remained earthbound, thoughtful. He had never been a brilliant man. And he was not a brilliant judge. He was earnest, conscientious. But he found little joy in the law and even less in being a judge.

His father had been a brakeman for the Great Northern, and he had started out after high school in a local awning factory. There he had sat, cross-legged, sewing foul, paraffin-impregnated tents for the Army until September of 1942. A desire for fresh air had led him to enlist in the Army Air Corps, where he had gone into a meteorological cadet program. He had finished up with a commission and a certain amount of confidence in his ability to deal with facts.

After the war he had drifted into college via the GI Bill and thence to a law degree. He had not been a clever student, but he had been thorough. And both the hours and company had proved to be much more stimulating than sewing tents had been. After passing the bar exam he had gone to work for the government in Washington, coming back a few years later to start both a practice and a family.

In 1964 his friends had urged him to stand for judge: He had done so, not really expecting to be elected. Once elected, he had found himself in the strange position of handing down orders for others to execute, much like the owner of the factory throwing canvas down on the floor to be trimmed, punched, and sewn. Even though the hours were pleasant, the pay good, and the prestige flattering, he had never been able to feel comfortable as a judge.

In his youth he had seen the courts hem the working man in with injunctions against strikes and subtle defenses of corporate private property, retreating only in the Jones and Laughlin Steel case when confronted with the threat of Roosevelt's court-packing plan. Now, in middle age, he saw the courts putting their power to use as a tool for forcing social change upon a recalcitrant polity. So he was nervous about extending judicial power beyond its traditional limits.

But it was his judicial abstractions that most troubled Judge Schultz. Originally Janus-faced, they had always balanced rights against responsibilities, encouraging all concerned to search for a delicate point of compromise. But now they seemed to stare at him more stonily, more fixedly, with only the aspect of rights showing forth. And that with shrill insistence that happiness be both pursued and guaranteed throughout the declining years of western civilization.

He was a good judge: Like most people who do their duty well, he took no great pleasure in the act.

But he managed a smile for Mrs. Cimino, sitting down below him, small and vulnerable.

"Mrs. Cimino, this court has listened to the evidence and argument advanced in support of your petition," he said. "And it is quite clear that you are a charming, capable lady."

He paused and looked over at Mr. Emory. Mr. Emory's gray-green eyes ceased focusing on the wall long enough to look back and exhibit mild interest.

"It has been suggested that your trustee is somehow responsible for your recovery and present state of health," continued Judge Schultz. "The court finds this reasoning specious, since such a responsibility would also hold in cases of ill health as well."

He shook his head and smiled thinly at Mr. Emory. Mr. Emory nodded, as though in firm agreement with the judge's shrewd powers of observation.

"It has also been suggested that the court should recognize your store as a family business," he said, looking over at Philip. "But the court notes that only one member of the family is involved in plans for the return of this business to your control."

After shaking his head at Philip, Judge Schultz looked directly at Mrs. Cimino, compelling her attention.

"The issue on which this court chooses to rule, then, will exclude consideration of how effectively this particular trust has served your interests. And we shall also put aside the question of how dissolution of this trust might contribute to the well-being of the store and its employees. As we see it, the issue centers upon the petitioner's capacity to act in her own best interests, lacking the protection of the trust established a year ago in her behalf."

He sat back for a moment and looked over at Mr. Emory again. Mr. Emory was sitting quietly, scratching his chin in a thoughtful manner.

"In terms of this issue, the possibility of another loss of capacity has been raised by counsel for the trustee," said Judge Schultz. "But we find this possibility far too speculative in view of the hazards that all of us face." Again he smiled thinly at Mr. Emory. "Dark predictions such as these have little place in a court of law."

He sighed and turned his attention once more to Philip.

"But we are troubled by counsel's suggestion that the age of the petitioner should be ignored in dealing with this matter," he said. "While we might grant that elderly people are no more prone to errors in judgment than the rest of our citizenry, we must still recognize that such errors can be unusually damaging. To lose a lifetime's savings at the age of forty is unfortunate; at the age of seventy it is disastrous!"

It was with greater firmness, almost with passion, that Judge Schultz looked down at Mrs. Cimino.

"At the present time, the petitioner's assets are under the protection of this court," he continued, "with the result that she and her estate are effectively insulated against the wiles of artful and designing persons. Last year the court was asked to take on this responsibility, and it intends to handle that task prudently.

"What we need, Mrs. Cimino, is a solution that will meet two objectives," he said, leaning forward and addressing her in a more intimate tone of voice. "First of all, we want to give you back control over your assets, making no restriction as to whether you use them wisely or foolishly. And this is basically what you are petitioning for, is it not?"

Cautiously, Mrs. Cimino looked over at Philip, who nodded at her to reply directly.

"Yes, Your Honor," she said in a low voice.

"And at the same time we want some protection for you," he said, smiling genuinely for the first time. "In terms of our responsibility, we want to be sure that a serious error in judgment or a serious misfortune will not have disastrous consequences for you. Would you grant that this is a reasonable concern on our part?"

Mrs. Cimino nodded, this time without turning to Philip for guidance.

"I note that your stock portfolio is valued at slightly over one hundred thousand dollars," he said, pulling a piece of paper over from the side. Together with your Social Security, the income from that portfolio should be adequate to provide for your basic needs.

"So I would like you to sit down with Mr. Ryan and place these particular assets in trust, allowing the trustee discretionary power to invade the principal in the event that your needs require this to be done."

He looked over at Mr. Emory once more before turning back to Mrs. Cimino.

"I see no reason why the trustee should not be of your own choosing, Mrs. Cimino, though I am going to require you to submit the document to me for my approval. Do you understand the nature of the solution I'm proposing?"

"I think so," said Mrs. Cimino, trying to invest her voice with sufficient volume and authority. "It would mean that I get the store back, along with the building and the savings accounts, as long as I put the rest of it in trust for a rainy day."

"Exactly!" said Judge Schutlz. "You pick out the umbrella for your rainy day and let me take a look at it."

He permitted himself a glance at the backbenchers to see if his homely figure of speech was appreciated. Of those still there, one was scowling at him. But another was nodding happily.

"And what do you think of our solution?" he said, peering down at her, his manner slightly deferential.

"It's not what I asked for, Your Honor," said Mrs. Cimino slowly. "But it seems to make good sense."

"I'm glad you agree," said Judge Schultz, beaming and trying his best to read enthusiastic approval into her neutral tone of voice. "I hereby order all assets returned to the petitioner forthwith with the exception of the stock portfolio. The portfolio I order the trustee to hold until such time as the petitioner submits a new trust arrangement to me for my approval. At that time I will order the present trust dissolved and the assets transferred into the petitioner's new trust."

With a rap of the gavel, the quiet courtroom was immediately transformed into a graceful legal quadrille: The parties to the Cimino matter withdrew, their places taken by another brace of attorneys. For Mrs. Cimino, Karen, Philip, and Mr. Emory, the drama was over, much like a daytime movie from which they were hurried out into the bright glare of afternoon sunlight.

But for Judge Schultz there was still another play to direct and frame a conclusion for. As he pushed the Cimino file aside and pulled the next one over, he again dwelt mournfully upon the dreary ambiguities of his office: an office where success lay in balancing matters so that all parties emerged feeling a little disappointed.

Litigation! The nation was sinking into it, prodded there by hosts of uncalloused graduates from heavily populated law schools. And all the while the land went untilled, the mills untended. A nation growling at itself while other hands crept in to build its automobiles, buy its farms, and do the work once done by earnest folk.

For solace Judge Schultz set his mind wandering back to the tent factory. There, working in a dimly lit loft, he had painstakingly punched out the grommet holes and ringed them round with twisted cord. A tedious job, and far from handsome pay at sixty cents an hour. But the tents had been made of solid stuff. And his mind had still been free to soar, to dream of noble things.

Best of all, he had been able to whistle. So he had filled the space around him with lively, well-shaped, rhythmic tunes. And what a shame it was that justice should be tuneless, forbidding that contentious beasts be soothed with cheerful, friendly swaths of melody winding through the room like silken threads, smilingly binding all therein as one fair fellowship of wholesome intercourse and joy.

"Are you sure you won't have something, Mother Cimino?" Lisa, vivid in a purple blouse and long plaid skirt, gestured invitingly toward the large silver tray on the coffee table. On it, massed like an irregularly size chorus from the Chekhov Club, were small bottles containing Courvoisier, Tia Maria, Curaçao, and other punctuation marks conventionally placed after dinner to signal the entry of serious discourse.

"No, my dear," smiled Mrs. Cimino. "The coffee will be enough for me." She sipped a little to show good faith. "It's the best I've had in a long time."

"We get it from a little shop over at the new mall," said Lisa airily, looking proudly round the room to encompass Harold, Gloria, and Karen in a challenging arc. "And it's worth a little extra just to stand there and let that rich, dark smell seep through you." She breathed in deeply, dramatically, so that her breasts strained forth to take the eyes of Harold and clasp them to her.

"It's nice you have the time," said Gloria, pale green eyes looking away from Lisa's pose to take in George, dressed in sober brown and sitting in a corner over by the Chickering piano.

"I don't know whether it's time or simply energy," laughed Lisa. She bent gracefully down to pour the liqueurs, after which she rose easily and similing, brought them around the room. "George says I have the stamina of a lumberjack."

"Wonderful!" said Harold, his shrewd blue eyes still intent upon her. "And how's old George do when it comes to keeping up with you?"

"Dandy!" said Lisa. In one quick motion she went over by George and sat down on the floor next to his chair, gazing up at him with a mixture of admiration and knowingness. "As long as he doesn't put on weight."

"He's certainly looking well," said Mrs. Cimino. She glanced around at all of them and smiled approvingly. "You're all looking well."

"It's packaging," said Harold, bushy eyebrows raised with slight amusement. "Packaging is what sells the product." He looked over at Karen, sitting on the couch beside her grandmother. "Isn't that what they're teaching now in those business courses?"

"I think it depends on the business," said Karen, smiling back at him and then taking refuge in her liqueur.

Mrs. Cimino gave her hand a reassuring pat. Karen was still shy around the other members of the family, as though her confidence suddenly evaporated in the familiar warmth of a setting where everyone still thought of her as a slow, chubby girl. During dinner Harold had tried to interrogate her on her plans for the music store, but she had avoided answering in any detail, with the result that Lisa and Gloria had dominated the conversation.

It had been a lovely dinner. The oak table had been beautifully set with the Haviland china, flanked by assorted silver pieces she and Frank had accumulated over the years. Sitting down, she had felt uneasy at first, much as though she had crept back from the grave to view her own things in an alien setting: the silver, the papier-mâché table, the Chickering, the other antiques. But the sight of her family gathered together once again had restored her spirits.

So she was grateful to Lisa for urging Harold and Gloria to drive up from Des Moines, celebrating her small victory in Judge Schultz's court. Of the grandchildren, only Karen had been able to come: Ann, Gretchen, and Patrick were still away at their various colleges, and Kevin was playing in a golf tournament at the country club, carefully justified as an action of good sense in terms of Harold's warehouse business.

Harold had been very enthusiastic about the warehouse, a long-awaited dream finally fleshed out with the help of a number of investors whom he had assembled from customers of the company. With Kevin as the titular head, he was now able to avoid any apparent conflict of interest between his role as an employee of a heavy equipment company and his role as owner of a warehouse in which equipment purchased through him might be stored.

Gloria had not chosen to comment on the matter.

"Is this the white knight?" said Harold, listening to the sound of an automobile pulling into the driveway.

"I think so," said Karen. She got up and went over to the door, opening it to ease Philip's entrance as much as possible.

Mrs. Cimino beamed with pleasure as Philip came in. Like Karen, he was shy. And he stood awkwardly in the hallway as Karen introduced him. But they made a nice picture: Karen, well figured and straight in a black cocktail dress, and Philip standing beside her in a light tan sports coat and dark brown slacks. With friendly words and quick apologies they went out the door, on their way to an evening of dancing and modest self-congratulation.

"Not bad," said Harold, always the first to voice a judgment. "Though it seems to me the old man was more of a dynamic sort."

"I think he's very attractive," said Lisa, giving a little artificial shiver that made her long dark hair ripple.

"He's a good lawyer," said Mrs. Cimino.

"He should be," said Gloria. "With his father to set him up in a going practice."

"What's wrong with that?" said Lisa.

"Nothing at all," said Gloria, pale green eyes looking over at Mrs. Cimino, as though to suggest that the voice coming at her from the other end of the room was nothing more than a minor irritation.

Mrs. Cimino stirred uncomfortably. Lisa and Gloria seemed by nature contentious, each one taking the other's measure with quick, prodding, cryptic remarks. During dinner Gloria, voice slightly hoarse and edged, had belittled regional re-creations of Neil Simon and *Bye, Bye, Birdie,* while Lisa had characterized country clubs as tasteless monuments to alcoholic boredom. Fortunately, Harold had been able to manage the conversation, so there had been no sustained conflict.

"Good," said Lisa. "I'm glad you approve of him."

"I didn't say I approved of him," said Gloria. She got up and poured herself another goblet of brandy.

"You don't approve of him?" said Lisa, dark brown eyes dancing with soft malice. "I'm sorry to hear you say that."

"I neither approve nor disapprove," said Gloria, short reddish curls shining in the light as though about to flame higher while she shook her head jerkily from side to side in emphasis.

"Good," said Lisa brightly. "I thought maybe you were worried over the fact that his father helped him to get started."

"I don't worry about anything," said Gloria, speech blurring just a little. "Not a thing."

"Good," said Lisa again, this time accompanying her approval with a long, slow, catlike stretch. "I'm a terrible worrier."

"They say it's not good to worry too much," said Mrs. Cimino, sensing that the conversation might best be shifted over to safe philosophical ground.

"That's easy to say," said Lisa. "Particularly for someone like Gloria, who's never really had anything to worry about."

"Everyone has something to worry about," said Gloria, bolting the last of her brandy down.

"But you just said that *you* didn't worry," said Harold, looking over at her with mild irritation.

"I was lying," said Gloria. "I worry about my children."

She looked over at Lisa. "If she had children of her own she'd understand."

"That's a little unfair," said George, uncrossing his long legs and leaning forward.

"No, it's not unfair," said Lisa quickly. "Gloria is absolutely right."

"She is?" said George, puzzlement creasing his long, somber face.

"Absolutely," said Lisa, nodding firmly. "A mother always has an obligation to her children."

"Is that right?" said Harold to Gloria.

"Right," said Gloria absently. Her pale green eyes focused on the Courvoisier bottle as though judging how many well-placed steps would take her to it.

"Absolutely right," said Lisa. "And the children always have an obligation to their mother." She smiled sweetly at Mrs. Cimino before turning her dark brown eyes back to where Harold and Gloria were sitting.

"Maybe we should be getting back to the hotel," said Mrs. Cimino, not without nervousness. The exchange was beginning to remind her of the way in which Mr. Stewart and Mr. Ayledotte had gone back and forth.

"We have plenty of time," said Harold, bushy eyebrows knit a little. "And it isn't every day I get a chance to talk with my sister-in-law."

"It's a very nice hotel," said Mrs. Cimino, trying to steer them into safer waters.

"It'll do," said Gloria. Her plan clearly in mind, she pushed herself up and took three steps over to the coffee table, pouring herself another brandy and making the return trip in good order.

"It's expensive," said Lisa. "But it's wonderful of you to come up." She sighed and looked up at George. "I wish we could have seen more of you this past year."

"I've been busy," said Harold. "We've all been busy."

"That's right," said Lisa. "Especially George." She took his strong brown hand and pressed it lovingly to her cheek. "After Mother Cimino's eye operation, it seemed I hardly saw him, what with the hospitals, doctors, social workers, and the rest of it."

"I was glad to do it," said George slowly. He looked over at his mother for a moment.

"And I'm glad you were able to do it," said Harold, not to be outdone in the general display of warmth.

"I'm glad, too," said Gloria hoarsely, looking down at what remained of her brandy.

"I guess everybody's glad except me," said Lisa, scowling over at Harold. "I'm sorry, sorry that *you* weren't able to do more."

"We did all we could," said Harold flatly.

"That's a matter of opinion, isn't it?" said Lisa.

"We did *all* we could," said Harold, more of an edge in his voice.

"All?" said Lisa. "With a big house, live-in help, and plenty of room?" She darted up and went over to the couch, standing beside Mrs. Cimino in a fiercely protective posture. "Room enough for a twenty-one–year–old man to loaf around in, but not room enough to have your own mother down for a visit!"

"That's all over and done with," said George, a fixed smile on his face.

"All done with," said Gloria. She gazed thoughtfully at her goblet, now completely empty.

"Apparently not," said Harold smoothly, more to his mother than to anyone else. "Lisa seems to think that Gloria and I should have stepped in and done more." He looked up at Lisa with apparent good humor. "Is that what you're trying to say?"

"Exactly!" said Lisa. She placed her right hand on Mrs. Cimino's shoulder as though to shield her from the unnatural creatures on the other side of the room.

"I don't deny mistakes were made," said Harold. He shook his head sadly. "But we're not the ones who made them."

"What mistakes?" said George, suddenly injured and truculent.

"The original petition was a serious error," said Harold.

"But you agreed to that!" said George. He got up and stared down at his brother in puzzled wonder.

"I had to agree," said Harold, sitting easily back. "From where I was, down there in Des Moines, it wouldn't have been right to second-guess you."

"That's right," said Gloria. "It wouldn't have been right." She stared blankly down at the knotted muscles in her brown legs, trying to think of a clearer phrasing for the matter.

"Wrong, wrong, wrong!" said Lisa. "George acted upon sound professional advice, and you know it."

"He acted hastily," said Harold.

"I did the best I could," said George. He looked appealingly over at his mother.

"We all did," said Harold. He smiled and stood up, pleased at having brought the conversation round to its original starting point.

"Everything has worked out for the best," said Mrs. Cimino, nodding cheerfully around the room: a room grown more tense now that Lisa, George, and Harold were on their feet. "Why can't we leave it at that?"

"Why not?" said Harold. There was coldness in his voice as he looked at Lisa and George. "Didn't you say something about wanting to go back to the hotel?"

"It's early yet," said Lisa. "And there's lots to talk about."

"Lots," said Gloria, looking meaningfully at the Courvoisier bottle again.

"If Gloria's tired, why don't you two go on ahead?" said Lisa. Her brown eyes looked over at her sister-in-law with obvious concern. "George and I will bring Mother Cimino over later on."

"There's no point in your making an hour-long drive," said Harold. "It doesn't make sense."

"We'll enjoy it," said George, arms folded, firmly set in his stance.

"Is that what you want?" said Harold to his mother.

"It's not a bad hotel," remarked Gloria absently. Now on her feet, she found her way to the hall and stood there.

"Are you coming with us or not?" said Harold, his manner grim, his square face set in the way his father's had always been in difficult moments.

"I don't know," said Mrs. Cimino, looking round the room and trying to smile. She wished Karen were still sitting beside her.

The evening was beginning to grow awkward, far past the point where humor or sentiment might salvage it. Fresh from one court appearance, she had no wish to convene another, weighing praise and blame in the delicate measure demanded of her. And in that contention small words, small actions would be read as charged with meaning, eloquent as whole passages to those who sought their validation from her.

"Maybe I should take a taxicab," she said. "That way I could stay a little longer and George wouldn't have the trouble."

"Why waste the money?" said Harold. "It's not as though it was out of our way."

"Twelve dollars!" said George. "It doesn't make any sense at all." He looked accusingly at his brother, as though Harold were somehow the cause of this curiously aberrant suggestion.

"Boys!" said Mrs. Cimino sharply. She rose and freed herself from Lisa's hovering protectiveness. "I have almost a hundred dollars in my purse, and I don't like being told what to do." Her resolution grew as she looked at her family: Harold and Gloria over by the door, George and Lisa at the other end of the room. "I am taking a cab and that's all there is to it!"

With this she marched over to Harold and Gloria, pulling them down to kiss her goodbye. Walking outside with them, she stood on the porch and waved as Harold helped Gloria into their Cadillac. After the big car started up and purred its way out to the street, she stood there a moment longer before going into the house.

When she came back to the living room, only George was there, sitting back in his chair and lighting up his briar pipe. From the kitchen, clattering sounds could be heard as Lisa busied herself with the dishes and silver. Mrs. Cimino shuddered inwardly at the thought of her silver being put to suffer the harshness of a dishwasher. But she resisted the urge to assist and instruct. Her first order of business was to phone for a cab, which she did.

After making her phone call in the den, she came back and sat down on the couch.

"I'm glad you have the Chickering," she said.

"We had it tuned last month," said George. "Would you like to try it?"

"No," said Mrs. Cimino. "I haven't played since I was at St. Hild's."

"That's too bad," said George. "It used to be fun when we gathered round and sang."

"Those were good times," said Mrs. Cimino. "Even in the little house before we moved to Elm Street."

"I liked that house," said George. He lit his pipe again and drew heavily in to get it going.

"I wish," said Mrs. Cimino. She paused, searching for a bright diamond to catch what light there was and focus matters for her, just as her lost ring had done. But the ring was gone, and so was the time for talking about it, asking awkward questions. Rechanneling her regret, she sighed. "I wish I had written you more when you were in the Army."

"But you wrote me lots of letters," said George, eyes puzzled, but easing back in his chair.

"Not enough," said Mrs. Cimino. "Marie Ochs wrote her boy every day." She nodded sadly at the thought.

"You wrote plenty," said George loyally. "And you sent me some cookies once." He puffed on his pipe a moment. "And besides, you were busy with the store."

"We were always busy," said Mrs. Cimino thoughtfully.

They sat there in silence a little longer. Then George got up and went in to see if Lisa needed help. Mrs. Cimino sat there by herself quietly, looking over at the Chickering, half tempted to get up and strike a few chords just to hear its full, rich, mellow sound again.

But the taxicab came, pulling into the driveway with great dispatch.

The parting was surprisingly easy. Hugs, kisses, promises to write, and admonitions to take special care in negotiating whatever twistings and turnings might lie ahead. Framed in the porch light's circle, George and Lisa waved her goodbye as the cab squealed out of the driveway and off toward her downtown hotel.

They were a good-looking couple.

Saturday, May 14, 2:30 P.M.

A slight breeze had come up, set in motion somewhere out in the Gulf of Mexico, like a whisper diminishing in volume as it floats over to the other side of the room. But there was enough movement to blunt the edge of the afternoon heat.

With delicate judgment the young woman decided to open her front door and let the moving air in through the screen, even though her drawn shades still held some of the morning's coolness trapped inside the small frame house. The breeze was warm, slightly moist, but it felt good against her face as she stood in the doorway.

With the natural interest of a neighbor the young woman watched a large enclosed truck pull up and stop directly across the street from her. Once at rest, the truck's cab disgorged two stocky men in gray overalls. One of them squinted at the address for a moment before motioning his companion to follow him up to the door of Mr. Feldman's house.

Even before they knocked she could hear the sound of barking from within.

"For a little dog that B-Flat sure has a big bark," she said, turning toward her husband, a large, beefy young man sprawled out on an old sofa in their living room. They had bought a flowered cover for the sofa from Sears, so the sofa would brighten the room a little. But it was still lumpy.

"Maybe the heat's bothering him," said the beefy young man. He took another pull from his can of beer.

"They're delivering something," said the young woman. She watched the two men in overalls come back to their truck and open up the back. "Something big."

"I'm glad *they're* doing it," said the beefy young man. He yawned, savoring the pleasure of his day off. "This is no day for heavy lifting."

The young woman watched the two men wrestle the large oblong padded object down from the truck and onto a dolly. After pausing for breath and repositioning, they trundled the object up the walk and through the doorway, good-humoredly enduring direction from a small gray-haired lady who had come out to hold the door open for them.

"I think it's a piano," said the young woman. She came back into the living room.

"I bet it's for her," said the beefy young man, still lying on the couch and gazing meditatively up at the ceiling.

"How come?"

"I dunno." The beefy young man looked over at his wife and smiled. "It just seems more ladylike."

"My aunt used to play the piano," said the young woman. "She was real good."

"The one in Lake Charles?"

"Shreveport," said the young woman. "She lived in Shreveport."

"That's a nice town," said the beefy young man.

"She played on Sundays at the Four Square Gospel Church," said the young woman. "And she was real good."

"At church, huh?" The beefy young man picked up his can of beer and took another pull. "Didn't they have an organ?"

"They sure did," said the young woman proudly. "They had an organ and they had a piano, too." She looked down at her watch. "A big one."

"That must have been some church."

"It was," said the young woman. "It was a real nice church."

The piano that Mrs. Cimino directed into the front bedroom was not a good church piano. A Yamaha, it lacked the size and percussive authority to compel attention and coerce a choir into staying on pitch. But it was ideal for the front bedroom: a gleaming walnut spinet, once unwrapped from its sugans and pads, that suddenly reshaped its surroundings, while leaving room for bookcase, chairs, worktable, and convertible sofa bed.

And it was a tactful instrument, provided with a middle pedal that materially softened the impact of hammers upon strings. So there was no danger of offending neighbors, once the scales and chords started to sing forth, even late at night. It had been expensive, shockingly so when compared with what the Chickering had cost years before, but Mrs. Cimino was pleased. It seemed right for her. And Barney had been able to get a discount from the salesman.

She checked the piano for scratches and signed for its delivery. After the men in overalls left, she opened the back door and let B-Flat in from his temporary exile. B-Flat importuned her, so she sat down on the sofa and let him present his just claim for strokings and rubbings. Like most spaniels he was a basically promiscuous creature, insatiably lusting for affection, even from a stranger's hand.

And she was still a stranger. Chumish and Fazola, the two Siamese cats, had not quite accepted her as an equal. Even though she wenched for them in kitchen matters, it was clear that their return to the bedroom would be a long time in coming. By winter, perhaps, when the rains came and the moisture crept upon them, they would be more gracious, less prone to turn their backs on her in dignified disdain.

But the cats were the only pocket of major resistance. Barney's daughter, across the bay in Tampa, had opened the door quickly, including her in the Sunday dinners and other family outings. And Barney's friends—most of them widowers—had been glad to stop by for a meal or for a late afternoon's swapping of old stories and new plans.

Even the neighbors were pleasant to her, much more than would have been the case on Elm Street, had that been Barney's home. For this was a neighborhood of small houses: bungalows with no more than two bedrooms, one bathroom, dining alcove. It was a neighborhood located just this side of transiency. A neighborhood filled with an odd mixture of old people hanging on and young people starting out. A neighborhood in which people spoke but rarely called one another by name.

Which was good.

She and Barney had discussed marriage. And they had discussed starting out together in a retirement community. The discussion had been initiated by Barney, who had worked out an entrance payment that would set them up in a one-bedroom apartment at Sea View. There, with a small monthly fee, they would be completely safe, completely sufficient, taking their meals in a well-appointed dining room. The proposal made sense, particularly in view of the fact that it would not be long before the state of Florida declared Barney a hazard to public highway safety.

And Sea View had been lovely: just south of Dunedin, with lounges, activity rooms, a breathtaking expanse of ocean stretching out from their balcony, and easy access to a private beach. There was a swimming pool, a big one, with countless deck chairs set around it. The elderly bodies in the deck chairs had been tanned, firm, glowing with wiry health, sometimes getting up to go over to the large, circular Jacuzzi to sway sensuously as the music of their anecdotal voices played around them. Almost Oriental, it was as though a thoughtful Old Man of the Mountain had built a walled earthly paradise into which the prosperous faithful were permitted to enter and disport themselves after years of wholesome, earnest work.

B-Flat turned over on his back, a clear signal that stomach scratching was now called for. Mrs. Cimino bent over and softly raked him up and down. There were no pets at Sea View. It was quiet there. And there was no gentle hum of traffic outside to cry the existence of a world where people, young and old, lived their lives and went about their business.

People like the young couple across the street: he a truck driver, she an X-ray technician at a local hospital. A young couple starting out in a small frame house just as she and Frank had done.

There were no young couples at Sea View, no children going noisily by on their way to school four blocks over. There the kindly range of human goings and gettings would be walled off, pleasantly but firmly, just as it had been at White Towers and St. Hild's. But it was still worth talking about.

Like marriage.

B-Flat turned back over. He jumped up. He headed for the door and stood there, tail wagging. Once again, Barney's old station wagon had made it safely into the driveway. Barney came in the kitchen door, packages in hand.

"It's here, said Mrs. Cimino. She got up and gestured expansively toward the front bedroom.

"Great!" said Barney. He put the packages down on the sofa and went over to the front bedroom doorway.

"Looks good, doesn't it?" said Mrs. Cimino. She went over by him.

"It looks tremendous!" said Barney. He went in, opened up the piano, and struck a few ornately voiced chords.

"It's no Steinway," said Mrs. Cimino. "But I'm no Liberace either." She gave one of her embarrassed little laughs.

"A Steinway!" said Barney. "A Steinway would blow down the whole neighborhood, and we'd have the cops zipping in here to bust us."

"We certainly wouldn't want that," said Mrs. Cimino, smiling slightly.

364

She had been told of Barney's last adventure with the police, three years ago. It had begun when he and Myron were driving home from a Bar Mitzvah job. Barney had been at the wheel, weaving a little. So a police car had pulled them over and taken the two of them down to the station, along with Barney's tenor saxophone.

They had opened up the case and looked at the saxophone, and they had looked at Barney suspiciously. Suspecting the instrument of being stolen, they had commanded him to assemble it. He had done this, slowly but adequately. Still disbelieving, they had asked him to play it as clear demonstration of his claimed ownership. He had done this, and to their mounting horror: His big fat sound reverberated throughout the building, bouncing back and forth from one cement wall to another, rousing the drunks in the tank to sodden cheers and stamping of feet; with the result that the watch commander himself came rushing out to quiet the disturbance.

The watch commander had not been amused. Nor had the officers. They had all scolded Barney roundly and sent him directly home.

"Is that the music?" said Mrs. Cimino, looking back at the two packages on the sofa.

"Sure is," said Barney. He went over and opened up one of the packages. In it were two books of standard tunes and a half dozen pieces of contemporary sheet music.

"That's enough to keep me busy," said Mrs. Cimino. It was with curiosity that she looked over at the other, larger package.

"I thought it might be ready," said Barney. "So I stopped by on my way home." He opened it up with something of a flourish. It was a white sign, nicely lettered, that spelled out "Esther Cimino—Piano Instruction—Reasonable Rates." In the upper left-hand corner was a treble clef, balancing the phone number down in the lower right-hand corner.

"That's a good sign," said Mrs. Cimino. She stepped back to get a better look.

"How about it?" said Barney, snapping his fingers as though to set a tempo. "Shall I put it in the window?"

"Now?" Mrs. Cimino quailed at the notion, even though it was something they had discussed for some time.

Like marriage.

"I don't think I'm ready yet," she continued. "Let me see how it works first."

Helplessly, as though urged by some strong inescapable contract, she went into the front bedroom and sat down at the Yamaha piano, taking care to engage the softening middle pedal. There she ran through a few scales, drifting from these into broken chords. It was almost fifteen minutes before she attempted a complete song. And this was a slow one, "Am I Blue?"

From the living room Barney had been listening quietly, a smile on his thin face. But with the completion of the chorus he opened up the closet and took out his clarinet case. And by the time Mrs. Cimino had slowly worked her way through "It Had to Be You," the clarinet was fitted together and ready to play.

He came into the room and sat down on the convertible sofa bed. Mrs. Cimino paused, striking an A for him to use in tuning up. They began to play the tune together, she gladly relinquishing the melody to him.